No Sleep till Doomsday

LAURENCE MacNAUGHTON

NO SLEEP TILL DOOMSDAY

DOOMSDAY

A Dru Jasper Novel

an imprint of Prometheus Books
Amherst, NY

For Cyndi.

CONTENTS

1
NOTHING LASTS FOREVER

For some reason, Dru had always assumed doomsday would fall on a Monday. Not on a nice, easy summer Friday night. The universe just didn't seem to be that cruel. Then again, Dru had been wrong about doomsday before.

When the energetic knock sounded at her door, she opened it to find Greyson standing on her threshold. He held a lush bouquet of red peonies in one hand, and an expensive-looking bottle of wine in the other. He had replaced his usual white T-shirt and black leather biker jacket with a pressed button-down gray shirt and designer jacket. For once, he was freshly shaved, and he smelled great.

Dru's jaw dropped open in surprise, and she quickly shut it.

His eyebrows crept upward. "Am I early?"

She folded her arms across her ragged sweatshirt and turned to look at the shambles of her apartment, feeling her cheeks redden. For the last few days, she had locked herself inside with her ancient books of magical knowledge, determined once and for all to discover a way to break Greyson's curse. Every flat surface was covered with tall stacks of smelly, old texts and multicolored crystals. The floor was dominated by a shimmering seven-pointed star made of copper wire. The stubby dregs of candles burned at each point.

Greyson gestured with the bouquet of flowers. "When I called, you said you were lighting candles, so . . ."

"*Ohh!* Candles, yes, but . . ." Dru chewed on her upper lip, struggling to explain all of this in a way that wasn't completely awkward. "You see, the candles are for work . . ." She gestured toward the copper star, painfully aware of the essential oil stains on her sleeve. She tried to hide them by pretending to fix her hair, which was a hopeless disaster. With a nervous laugh, she said, "I thought you were coming over on Friday night."

His rugged face showed utter confusion. "It *is* Friday."

"What? *Nooo.*" She checked her phone. "Oh, fudge buckets. Look, um, just give me a few minutes to straighten up and—"

"It's okay. It's work. I should probably just go." He hesitated, as if he wanted to say more, then held out the flowers. "These are for you."

"No! No, you don't have to go. Come in, come in." She took the flowers and wine, and quickly set them aside. Racing around like mad, she picked up stacks of dusty medieval manuscripts and a couple of creatively misplaced yoga pants, staggering under the combined weight of it all. "Sorry. I've been doing all this research. Obviously. And I'm so close. *So* close. I found this thing in one of the padlocked Stanislaus journals where he made kind of a poetic reference to Tristram banishing a 'demon of the horse,' which isn't precisely the problem you have, but let me just—*whoa!*" She accidentally kicked over a lit candle with her bare foot, spilling hot wax across the hopelessly scarred wood floor.

"Got it." Moving quickly, Greyson steadied her and stooped to right the candle. The flame guttered and went out, releasing a curl of smoke.

"Oh, good. Nothing's on fire." Dru set the books down on top of another stack, pausing a moment to make sure the whole thing didn't topple over. When she turned around again, Greyson was smiling down at her.

"Looks like I need to get you out of this apartment," he said. "How about a fancy dinner to shake things up?"

"Oh, shoot." She adjusted her glasses and squinted at the microwave. "I heated up that burrito like . . . Wait, was that lunchtime?" The grumble in her belly told her that she hadn't eaten it. "I'm sorry, everything is such a mess. It's just that I'm putting everything else on hold until I find a way to break your curse. So you can be normal again, and not one of the Four Horsemen of the Apocalypse."

At that, Greyson's smile vanished. Though he didn't move, he suddenly seemed miles away from her, as if her words had driven an invisible gulf between them.

Her empty stomach clenched up with worry. "What? What did I say?"

He just shook his head and walked over to the window. In the evening sky beyond, the distant sparkling lights of downtown Denver glowed peacefully. Dru's apartment was on the upstairs floor over her shop, the Crystal Connection. Outside the window, metal stairs ran down to the parking space behind her store. It wasn't the most glamorous place to live, and she certainly hadn't meant Greyson to see it like this for the first time.

But that didn't seem to be what was bugging him. "You really want to make me normal again?"

"For sure. Yes. Absolutely." She studied the tension in his shoulders, wondering at the sudden change in him. "Why, what am I missing?"

He let out a long breath and hung his head, then looked at her. The light of the candles reflected in his blue eyes. "Everything that exists between me and you, everything, it's all because there's something *wrong* with me."

At first, she thought he was joking, and she started to laugh. But the hard look in his eyes made the laughter dry up instantly.

She cleared her throat. "Well, that's just not true. We have plenty of things in common besides, you know, doomsday problems."

His gaze didn't waver. "Name one thing."

She opened her mouth to reply, but nothing sprang to mind. Her entire life revolved around musty books, dusty rocks, and an encyclopedia's worth of knowledge about healing herbs and potions. His life, on the other hand, involved old cars, engines, wrenches, tires—and being cursed with the destructive powers of a Horseman of the Apocalypse.

His gaze softened. "The strange powers I have, that's the whole reason we met. That's why we've been so close. Because you're worried that at any moment, I could crack. I could become a monster again."

For a moment, Dru visualized the creature he'd once been. Looming horns, vicious fangs, rippling leathery skin as black as midnight, and eyes fiery red as hot coals. With an effort, she pushed that unsettling memory aside and focused on the handsome man standing before her.

"Let's not jump to the worst-case scenario just yet, okay? Things are under control. There was a time, not too long ago, when you were running around with horns growing out of your head." With both index fingers, she pointed at her own temples for emphasis. "And right now, you look great, okay? More than great. Fantastic. Amazing." She looked him up and down, drinking in the sight of him, then shook her head, trying not to get distracted. "The point is, we're making progress, and that's what counts. I'm not giving up. Somewhere inside all of these books, there's a cure. And I will find it."

"And then what?"

"Then you'll be normal again. Isn't that what you want?" She stepped closer to him, acutely aware that on a deeper level, he was asking a question she didn't quite comprehend. "How could that possibly be a problem?"

His lips pressed into a thin line. "If you fix me, if you get rid of my Horseman powers, then what am I? Just some mechanic with an old car."

The anguish in his voice cut through her. She laid a hand on his strong arm. "Greyson, no. It's not like that at all."

"Before I met you, I never believed in magic. Or monsters. Or any of this." His voice grew husky. "And now I've seen what you can do. I know the world needs you and your friends. People like you, born with powers that can save lives, fight the bad guys, keep everyone safe." His forehead creased with worry. "But once my powers are gone, I won't fit into your world anymore."

"That's not true," she said softly. But obviously he believed it. Her eyes stung with tears. "Is this . . . ?" Her voice cracked. "Is this you breaking up with me?"

How could she make him understand that they were meant to be together? They had a connection that went deeper than just their day-to-day interests. There was something about his very presence that affected her on a fundamental level. Being near him made her feel like everything was right with the world.

Earlier this summer, when she thought she had lost him forever, it had nearly destroyed her, and she'd gone half mad trying to find him again. She'd risked getting herself and her friends killed in order to save him. She had even put the fate of the world second in line to getting him back. But she couldn't explain why, not in any way that made sense.

Explaining her feelings wasn't her strong suit. She knew that by most people's standards, she probably spent too much time in her own head. In fact, she'd been told exactly that on more than one occasion, mostly by Rane. Dru would be the first one to admit she was more cerebral than was maybe socially acceptable. In her line of work, that was usually an advantage, but not now. She knew what she felt, deep down inside, was true. But she couldn't explain *how* she knew.

Now, standing among the clutter of her apartment, looking up into the anguish etched into Greyson's candlelit face, she didn't know how she would ever be able to make him understand. Maybe it was already too late.

Dru gently spread her fingers across his broad chest, feeling the smooth fabric of his blazer, so different from the usual black leather and zippers of his motorcycle jacket. This close, when she looked deep into his blue eyes, she could see the faint sparks of demonic energy lurking deep inside, waiting to be fanned to life again. At the first sign of danger, they would erupt into a hellish red glow.

And every time they did, she had to wonder how close he was to once again becoming one of the Horsemen of the Apocalypse, driving the world toward extinction.

She had a duty to break his curse. As a sorceress, she was responsible for doing whatever it took to keep the world safe from doomsday. But once she found a way to fix Greyson, would she lose him forever?

Without saying a word, Greyson pulled her to him. The heat from his body enveloped her, so familiar and yet still strange and new. The rugged scent of him intoxicated her. He looked into her eyes, and suddenly she had trouble swallowing. Her heart drummed in her chest.

He bent down, and her head tipped back. She lifted her lips toward his.

A resounding *thump* from the crystal shop downstairs interrupted them. Dru pulled back, suddenly alert. Someone was down there.

A swirling fiery red glow lit up Greyson's eyes, as if someone had stoked the embers of a nearly cold fire and brought it to roaring life again. His chest swelled, and a dark shadow passed across his features. "What was that?"

The grid of powerful protective crystals Dru had placed strategically around the old brick building was strong enough to keep out any intruders, short of someone crashing a truck in through the front window. Dru winced at that particularly painful memory, which was still too raw in her mind. With these potent crystals in place now, anyone who tried to break in without using a key would suffer a distinctly unpleasant magical surprise.

Yet no magical backlash shook the building, which meant that someone had unlocked the door normally. Only Dru and her business partner Opal had keys. Dru realized her mistake and inwardly groaned. "I just remembered. The other day, I gave Rane a key to the shop."

Greyson squinted his glowing eyes, as if trying to decide whether she was joking. "That's . . . brave."

"Well, you know, it's kind of self-defense. Rane has this bad habit of breaking in anytime she wants to," Dru said.

He appeared to consider that, but he didn't look too happy with his conclusions.

"Before you say anything, I want you to know it's complicated," Dru said. "I mean, I love her, but oh, my God." Dru took a deep breath, trying to calm the conflicting emotions that raced through her. "Just give me five minutes. Don't go anywhere. If she finds out you're here, she'll want to play chaperone, and then things will get awkward. More. Awkward."

He nodded once.

"I'll be right back. I promise." It took a force of willpower to pull herself free from his arms and head down the stairs that led to the back room of the shop.

As she padded down the old brick stairwell, feeling each gritty step beneath her bare feet, she cursed silently to herself. Why did Rane have to show up right this very second? Why did Greyson have to worry so much about becoming a normal guy again? Why did she have to get so wrapped up in her work that she never got around to showering today?

Plus, she was pretty sure there was a cold, dried-out burrito stinking up the microwave.

Other than that, for the first time Dru could remember, everything was finally coming together. After much struggle, Rane and Salem were an item again, Opal was happily dating Ruiz, and Dru had Greyson back safe and sound.

She'd even been able to pay all of her bills this month, because of the recent surge of business. As word had spread that Dru could cure magical afflictions, dozens of new faces had started showing up at her crystal shop. That included the sorcerers who had lost their powers to the spiked drinks in the underground masquerade a couple of weeks ago.

Dru had cured so many of them that she'd run out of cave calcite and had to rush order an entire new shipment from her supplier in South America. In the process of treating the sorcerers, she'd run her hands across so many of the white, lumpy, brain-shaped crystals that her palms felt permanently exfoliated.

Now she had enough money in the bank to pay the rent for several months. Even better, she also had the undying gratitude—and, at long last, the hard-won respect—of dozens of sorcerers. Finally, she felt like she was somebody. As if she'd earned the right to truly call herself a sorceress.

Now, she just had to figure out what Rane needed. Hopefully there wasn't any new drama with her on-again, off-again boyfriend, Salem. The self-proclaimed most powerful sorcerer around. Maybe she could shoo Rane out the door, put on some makeup, slip into clothes that didn't feature an elastic waistband, and finally go out on her first official date with Greyson.

Dru paused midstep, realizing how strange it was that she had never actually gone out with him, not even once. The closest they had ever come to a date was when he had crashed a business dinner with her ex, then promptly turned into a demon and started tearing up the city.

Not exactly a fairy-tale start to a relationship. No wonder the poor guy was having cold feet.

She resolved to make tonight special. She would tell him just how she felt. Somehow, she would make him understand that whether or not he had magical powers, he was the guy she wanted to be with.

She hustled down the stairs and opened the door at the bottom, preparing to greet Rane with a blast of good-natured sarcasm. "Hey, you crazy—" The words dried up on her tongue.

Because it wasn't Rane.

A thin older woman, clad all in black, with gaunt cheekbones and straight red hair, studied Dru's wall safe. It was usually hidden behind a framed photo of Ming the Merciless. But now, Ming's picture lay discarded on the floor, missing its old yellow sticky note that read: *Pathetic Earthlings! Who can save you now?*

The dull metal face of Dru's vault of cursed artifacts lay exposed, its black-and-white dial and polished steel handle shining in the faint light from the stairwell. As Dru hesitated in the doorway, the woman turned her head, her long red hair flowing with the movement. Before Dru could say another word, the woman raised a long arm and clawed her fingers. Crystal-encrusted rings bristled across her knuckles, pulsing in all different colors at once.

A prickling, suffocating pressure seized Dru. She tried to call out to Greyson for help but managed only a faint wheeze. Her arms were pinned tightly to her sides, and an unseen weight squeezed her ribs, as if she were being crushed in an invisible fist.

The woman swung her arm, and Dru was yanked into the room by the unseen force. Her legs kicked uselessly in the air, managing to do nothing more than knock a few books off a nearby shelf.

The woman's fierce hazel eyes gleamed with satisfaction. Her thin red lips drew back in a savage smile. She raised one long, ring-covered finger to her lips. *"Shh."*

2

WHERE YOUR DEMONS HIDE

Choking and writhing in midair, Dru tried to scream for help. But no matter how hard she struggled, she couldn't force any sound past her lips.

Her mind raced. Who was this attacker? What was she after? How could she use so many different crystals at once, when most sorcerers could barely handle one at a time? Except for Dru, of course, but that was her particular talent, and she'd never met another crystal sorceress with those abilities.

Until now.

Apparently done with Dru for the moment, the sorceress turned her attention back to the safe. She held up the hand with the glowing rings as if she'd forgotten about it, and her magic held tightly onto Dru, dangling her in midair. There was no escape.

The woman ran the fingers of her other hand around the edges of the safe, as if searching for some flaw in its surface. But Dru had taken great pains to make the safe as secure as possible, not just against physical break-ins but magical intrusion as well.

Dru had guarded each interior corner of the thick steel safe with a grid of protective crystals. Then she'd borrowed Ruiz's industrial diamond-tipped etching tool and used it to carve a meticulously researched string of sorcio glyphs around the inside edge of the door, creating a spell of invulnerability. Finally, Dru had hidden the safe behind Ming the Merciless, and inside that picture frame, she had carefully slipped a fragile 1,900-year-old Egyptian papyrus containing an obfuscation spell that prevented any magic from locating the safe or discerning its contents.

Or so she'd thought. Apparently, things hadn't exactly worked out that way.

All of these precautions were absolutely necessary because this safe contained the most diabolical artifacts Dru had ever unearthed. Things too powerful to destroy, and so creepy and dangerous that they had to be kept locked away for the safety of the general population.

Among other things, the safe contained the fabled Dread Stone, an ordinary-looking, baseball-sized lump of gray rock. Being a geode, its hollow center was crusted with hidden crystals, which in this case held the souls of untold sorcerers it had imprisoned over the centuries.

The safe also contained the so-called Goblet of Perspicacity, a gem-encrusted silver cup from the Carolingian Empire. Anyone who drank from it would find their mind insidiously filled with the darkest impulses of human nature, until they were ultimately driven into a paranoid homicidal rage.

There was also the Devourer of Kamang, a necklace of bone charms carved into the shape of tiger beetles that would come to life in the middle of the night and consume the flesh of its wearer, leaving nothing behind but a glistening skeleton.

But that wasn't the worst.

The worst was the Amulet of Decimus the Accursed, an ancient Roman sorcerer who was so evil that his enemies had smothered the entire city of Pompeii under searing volcanic ash in order to kill him. Up until recently, Dru had also possessed one of the biotite crystals that had caused that particular cataclysm, and she had used it to blow up half the netherworld. The amulet, she had to assume, was even more powerful than that.

The artifacts in that safe were far too dangerous to be let loose upon the world. Throughout history, they had caused immeasurable misery and suffering. Dru had done everything she could possibly think of to keep them locked away.

It wasn't enough.

Whatever this intruder planned to do next, Dru had to find a way to stop her, and fast. But suspended in midair, unable to touch any of her crystals, there was nothing Dru could do. She looked around for any loose rocks she'd forgotten to put away lately.

On a side table by the door to the stairs sat a disk of iron pyrite, looking like a miniature gold record that some music mogul would hang on his office wall. Pyrite, once energized, was excellent for creating an energy shield. There was a chance she could use it to reflect the intruder's spell back at her. If only she could reach it.

But the pyrite was halfway across the room, and Dru was hovering in midair, fighting just to breathe. Black specks pounded at the edges of her vision. Her pulse thudded in her ears. She prayed she wouldn't pass out.

Still pinning Dru with her spell, the sorceress used her free hand to draw a handful of crystals out of her pocket. In her open palm, the crystals began to glow in different colors—sapphire blue, bottle green, fluorescent yellow—and they gradually floated up in the air, spinning around one another like subatomic particles orbiting the nucleus of an atom.

Moments later, a single pinpoint of red heat grew in the center of the safe's door, brightening until it was white-hot. Sizzling cracks of light zigzagged out in all directions across the metal. With a bone-jarring sound like fracturing rock, the safe door shattered into a thousand glowing sparks. They streaked through the air, leaving scorched afterimages in Dru's vision.

Her heart sank. Everything was going from bad to worse.

On the bookshelf behind Dru sat a thick candle holder, currently unlit, carved from a massive pink salt crystal. Doubtless the candle holder was heavy enough to be used as a weapon, but Dru had a better idea. Crystalline halite, otherwise known as rock salt, held the power to dissolve patterns of energy. Such as the invisible spell currently bruising Dru's ribs. If she could make physical contact with the crystal candle holder and energize it, there was a chance she could short out the intruder's spell.

Dru's upper arms were pinned tightly to her sides, but below her elbows, she found she could move more or less freely. As surreptitiously as she could, she stretched her fingers toward the candle holder. It sat tantalizingly out of reach.

The redheaded sorceress put away her glowing crystals and reached into the smoking remains of the safe. With elaborate care, she pulled out a decades-old orange-and-brown Tutti Frutti Candy box. One of her thin eyebrows quirked up.

Dru had placed the evil flesh-devouring Kamang necklace inside the old box years ago, and she had honestly hoped never to set eyes on it again. But if this evil intruder happened to put on the necklace and had to suddenly fend off a hundred chomping beetles carved out of chicken bones, that wouldn't have been the worst thing ever.

No such luck. After shaking the candy box briefly, the intruder showed no further interest in it. She dropped the box to the floor and reached back into the safe.

This time, she pulled out a small faded red box with the crude outline of a yellow mushroom cloud drawn on it. Old block lettering decorated the sides: *Atomic Fire Ball, Red Hot, 1¢*.

Dru's stomach turned acid. That was the artifact she had feared the most.

She could only watch helplessly as the sorceress opened the candy box and pulled out the chunky gold chain that held the Amulet of Decimus the Accursed. The amulet itself was the size of Dru's palm, formed of concentric rings of cast metal glyphs surrounding a single eyeball-sized gem of faceted painite, the rarest crystal on Earth. Although the gem appeared to be pure black, full daylight revealed that painite was actually the darkest shade of rusty red. Like dried blood.

Over the years, Dru had done exhaustive research on the cursed amulet, but she'd never turned up much. No one really knew how powerful the artifact was, or exactly what it could do. All Dru knew for sure was that it had been the greatest creation of one of the most evil sorcerers of antiquity. That pretty much guaranteed it a spot on the no-fly list.

Whatever this sorceress was planning on doing with the amulet, it had to be seriously bad news. Dru had to shut her down. But how?

Teeth gritted with effort, Dru stretched toward the candle holder. But no matter how hard she strained, her fingers couldn't quite reach it. In desperation, Dru bent her leg back and reached her bare foot toward the crystal, silently thankful that at long last, those yoga classes were finally paying off. Twisting, she bent her leg back farther and farther, until her big toe just barely brushed the cold, chalky surface of the crystal.

Blotting out everything else, Dru squeezed her eyes shut and focused all of her attention on the crystal. She imagined it becoming an extension of her body, her thoughts, her force of will. She became one with the crystal, sensing the power that lay locked in its depths, waiting to be unleashed.

Like a hot flush across her skin, the magic connection swept over her. Energy poured out of her and into the crystal, rewarding her with a hot glow that seeped through her tightly shut eyelids. The air around Dru trembled as the halite radiated resistance toward the spell that clutched her.

In all likelihood, the intruder had sensed the interruption and would quickly do something to fight it, but Dru didn't dare open her eyes to see. Instead, she focused on pushing as much of her energy into the halite crystal as she possibly could.

The glow grew brighter. The air grew hotter. With an electric sizzle, the intruder's spell broke, releasing the pressure on her rib cage. Dru dropped to the floor in an undignified heap, gasping for breath.

At that moment, the door to the stairs flew open. Greyson burst in, his eyes glowing red. "Dru!"

Across the room, the intruder was busy stuffing the amulet into her pocket. She brought out her atomic-looking crystals. They whirled to life, glowing bright.

Dru launched off the floor and lunged for the golden disk of iron pyrite sitting on the end table next to Greyson.

Snarling, the intruder thrust out clawlike fingers. Her crystals streaked toward Greyson as if they'd been fired out of a gun.

"Get down!" Dru threw herself in front of Greyson, barely having time to lift the pyrite before the flying crystals struck. Instantly, Dru's magic radiated out through the golden pyrite disk, creating an energy shield that reflected the intruder's attack back at her. A blinding flash rocked the room, thick with the smell of scorched minerals.

With an earsplitting whine, the intruder's glowing crystals pinballed around the room, blasting sparks off the shelves, ceiling, and floor. Dru's reflecting spell had somehow confused the crystals, sending them shooting off in random directions. One of them bounced off an ugly plaid armchair, setting the seat cushion on fire.

The intruder scowled at the ricocheting crystals for a moment, then turned and fled through the doorway that led into the front of the shop. Instantly, she was gone, leaving the malfunctioning crystals bouncing around behind her.

Dru cringed as one of the burning crystals streaked past her ear, buzzing like an angry hornet. She held up the smoking disk of pyrite to ward it off, but now the others were coming from all directions.

Greyson went back to the door. Wood splintered as he ripped it from its hinges. When angered, his demon strength grew unsettlingly powerful. A blast of lumber-yard smell washed through the room as Greyson swung the door around, its brass hinges dangling chunks of raw wood.

The strobe-like glow of the bouncing crystals abruptly vanished as Greyson swatted them out of the air, one by one. With a hammering sound, they embedded themselves deep into the heavy wooden door, releasing curls of black smoke.

Greyson used the door to beat out the flames on the plaid chair. But even as he did so, the door jerked and twisted with the movements of the malfunctioning crystals. He threw the smoking wooden door to the floor and jumped on top of it, pinning it down with his boots.

Dru expected some kind of explosion or burst of fire. Instead, the crystals rattled against the underside of the door, trying to break loose. Slivers of multicolored light leaked out as the door shook, threatening to let the still-glowing crystals escape. A campfire smell permeated the room as the wood burned.

Dru's gaze went from Greyson to the doorway where the sorceress had just vanished, then back to Greyson standing atop the trembling door like some kind of bizarre surfer. Did she dare chase the intruder and try to get the amulet back? Would those crystals burn through the door and do something terrible to Greyson?

He jerked his chin toward the doorway, seeming to understand her thought process before she had even voiced it. "Get her! Go!"

The bell over the front door chimed. The sorceress was leaving in a hurry. But maybe there was still time to catch her.

Dru charged through the shop. As she sprinted past the cash register, she grabbed her dagger-shaped wedge of spectrolite crystal. In Dru's tight fist, the multicolored spectrolite flared to life, lighting everything around her with a rainbow of colors. She still held the golden pyrite disk in her other hand, like a miniature shield.

She made it out the door just as the intruder slipped behind the wheel of a burly modern muscle car. The engine was already running, and the twin red bars of its brilliant taillights lit up the asphalt behind it. The engine screamed, and the red car launched away into the night, amazingly fast.

Though it was already too late, Dru chased after her. She ran out into the empty street, breathing hard. The thin ruby-red lines of the car's taillights shrank into the distance. The sorceress was gone, taking the cursed amulet with her. But why? Whatever this sorceress needed the cursed artifact for, it had to be something truly evil.

Behind her, tires squealed and a throaty engine roared. A sleek black muscle car hurtled around the corner of her shop, tires smoking. It was a very familiar 1969 Dodge Charger Daytona, a long wedge-shaped beast with a two-foot spoiler wing rising up from its tail. Black as the diabolical pit that spawned it, Hellbringer was powered not just by the monstrous Hemi engine under its hood, but also by the infernal speed demon that possessed its curved steel.

Hellbringer screeched to a halt next to her. Greyson, eyes burning like hot coals, leaned over from the driver's seat and pushed open the long passenger door. "Get in!"

3
STREETS OF FIRE

Hellbringer started moving before Dru even shut the door. The car somehow scooped her up on the move, and she fell in. The door slammed closed as the throaty engine wailed. The rapid acceleration crushed her deep into the black vinyl seat.

"Are you okay?" Greyson demanded over the roar of the engine.

"Just ducky," Dru muttered, buckling up the seat belt by the prismatic light of the glowing spectrolite crystal in her fist. "We can't let her get away with the amulet. It's too powerful. In the wrong hands, it could . . ."

"It could what?"

Dru hesitated. "I'm not sure, exactly. I just know it's incredibly dangerous. That's why I had it locked away in the safe. I thought it would be okay there."

Greyson just grunted. Whatever he thought about that, he didn't say. He drove on at breakneck speed.

Dru's cheeks burned with shame. She thought she had taken the appropriate precautions. If she had been overly confident, who could blame her? After all, she and her friends had gotten the amulet by outsmarting the 2,000-year-old ghost of an evil Roman sorcerer, Decimus the Accused. That hadn't been exactly a cakewalk.

Decimus was the only one who knew the true magnitude of the amulet's powers, and he wasn't spilling any secrets. He'd been killed in AD 79 when his enemies blew up Mount Vesuvius and entombed the entire city of Pompeii.

All just to stop him from using that amulet. Hence all of Dru's precautions, including the magically sealed safe behind the bald head of

Ming the Merciless. In retrospect, maybe not the brightest plan. Clearly, Ming wasn't enough to stop this crystal sorceress.

Just thinking about the cursed artifact falling into the wrong hands made her shudder. In a voice that barely rose above the noise of the engine, Dru said, "The last time somebody got hold of the Amulet of Decimus, an entire city died."

Saying the words out loud made them real for the first time. Someone who knew what they were doing could turn the amulet into a weapon of incredible destruction. A sickening feeling threatened to overwhelm her. In just the few minutes since Dru had discovered the sorceress breaking into her safe, everything had changed, and she was only now starting to catch up. Now she was fighting not only for her own life, but potentially the lives of millions of innocent people.

Greyson's glowing gaze broke away from the night-darkened street and looked directly at her. Outside, streetlights streaked past. "So we need to get this amulet back. No matter what." It came out like a terse statement, but it was really a question.

Dru's throat tightened up with fear. Quickly, she nodded.

Greyson nodded once and faced front again. "Then hang on." He yanked the gearshift into a lower gear, and the engine howled. Ahead of them, the sorceress's car shot past a row of small closed shops and a new high-rise parking garage. Two blocks past that, the street intersected with the main road, which was packed bumper-to-bumper with Friday night traffic. There was no way the fleeing sorceress could get through that, Dru figured.

But the sorceress apparently had no intention of stopping. Ahead of them, the wide horizontal taillights of her car veered right, and the sports car vanished around the corner of a side street.

Greyson followed, closing in fast. Hellbringer didn't so much drift around the corner as fly nearly sideways, tires shrieking. The brutal turn would have launched Dru out of the seat if she hadn't been belted in.

Hellbringer was a speed demon, every inch of its black steel possessed by an infernal spirit created to serve the forces of chaos. It hungered for fast-paced destruction. Its entire existence was meant for moments like this, and it reveled in the bloodlust of the chase. Dru knew firsthand how willful and dangerous Hellbringer could be, if left unchecked. Greyson wasn't just driving the car, he had to command it. Dominate it.

Given free rein, the speed demon would run wild, mowing down anything and everyone in its path. On a Friday night on the city streets, that could quickly turn deadly. Dru prayed they could catch the sorceress and reclaim the amulet before any innocent bystanders were caught in harm's way.

Ahead of them, the red sports car's taillights flickered as if the driver was hesitating, not sure which way to turn at the end of the block. Perhaps she didn't realize she was being followed, Dru thought.

At that moment, Hellbringer's headlights flared brighter. The demon car's high beams blazed, lighting up the entire street. Dru knew there was no way the sorceress could miss the blinding headlights charging toward her.

Instead of turning, the red car launched straight across the road, streaking between oncoming cars. Horns blared and tires squeaked as cars and trucks swerved to a stop.

Hellbringer was close behind, drawing another round of angry horn blasts as Greyson carefully threaded his way through the intersection and out the other side. Hellbringer's engine revved with impatience.

Greyson's watchfulness avoided any crashes, but it cost them time. Ahead of them, the sorceress's car was rapidly dwindling into the night. Hellbringer poured on the gas, streaking along the residential street at an insane speed.

They blew past one stop sign after another, dodging around moving cars as if they were standing still. Dru gripped the armrest so tightly that her fingernails dug into the vinyl. More than anything, she wanted to tell Greyson to slow down, but they had no choice. They couldn't let the sorceress escape.

Strangely, her car bore a passing resemblance to Hellbringer, with its long hood, small back window, and wide stance. But where Hellbringer was a sleek relic from a vanished Motor City age, this car was squared off and modern, like an athletic younger cousin. There was something else about it, too, that Dru couldn't quite define. Something about the way it moved around the corners, less like an inanimate object and more like a predatory creature. Or maybe it was a trick of the light, as their bright headlights cut through the night.

Dru didn't have a plan for how to get the amulet back from her. Brute force wouldn't work. The mysterious sorceress was obviously far more experienced with crystal magic and more powerful than Dru. Besides, Dru had only two crystals to fight her with: a golden pyrite disk, which was strictly defensive, and her rainbow-colored spectrolite blade, which again was more of a protective crystal than an actual weapon.

Dru had used the spectrolite in the past as a spell component, an escape tool, and once as a particularly ineffective bookmark. That resulted in one book that never made it back to the library intact, unfortunately.

On rare occasions, she'd had to threaten to stab an especially atrocious enemy with her spectrolite. But Dru had never actually physically harmed anyone, and she honestly didn't think she could. She just wasn't a stabbing sort of person. She liked to think of that as a sign of good character.

But could she stab the sorceress, if she had no other choice? If it meant saving the lives of everyone in the city? She shuddered at the thought. No, there had to be a better plan than stabbing.

"How are we going to catch her?" Dru said, trying to keep the fear out of her voice.

"I'm going to flip that thing wheels-up into a ditch," he growled. "See if that works."

The street ended at a T-shaped intersection that bordered a grassy park. But instead of turning left or right, the sorceress again drove straight on. With a crunch of metal and plastic, the red car hopped over the sidewalk and flew across the grass. Its rear end slid to one side and then the other, as if it couldn't quite get traction on the grass. Then it entered a stand of pine trees and vanished for a moment, except for flickers of headlights and taillights.

"I hate driving through the park," Greyson muttered. He turned in a long arc and hit the curb at an angle. The four tires hopped the curb in rapid-fire succession, shaking the car. Then they were hissing across the dark grass, skirting the edge of the trees.

Without warning, Hellbringer's headlights went out, plunging them into darkness. The flip-up headlights clunked closed, reverberating through the body of the car.

"Hey!" Greyson barked at the car. He slapped the top of the dashboard with his open palm. "Knock it off!"

"What happened?" Dru asked.

"Hellbringer's stalking the other car. Trying to be stealthy." He thumbed the rocker switch in the top left corner of the dashboard, but nothing happened. "Lights!" he ordered, to no avail.

As they flew along the jagged edge of the dark trees, Dru had to wonder who was really doing the driving. Was Greyson in control, or was it Hellbringer? Or did they work together through some kind of wordless bond?

Judging by the snatches of taillights that flickered between the passing trees, they were paralleling the other car's path.

Dru was terrified that they would plow into some wayward tree trunk or other unseen obstruction at high speed. But there was just barely enough ambient light to see. Ahead, a small lake shimmered in the city lights and the glow of the nearby tennis courts, where a middle-aged couple in shorts and high socks swatted a ball across the net.

"We're running out of park," Dru warned.

"She'll have to make her move," Greyson said. "And then we can catch her."

At that moment, the other car burst out from between the trees. Hellbringer's headlights blazed to life, lighting up the bright red car. It swerved suddenly, as if the flare of light had caught the driver by surprise. It slid across the slick grass, almost out of control.

Hellbringer shot toward it, nearly catching up before the other car got traction again. Hemmed in by the lake on one side and Hellbringer on the other, the sorceress headed straight for the row of fenced-in tennis courts.

Dru's heart leaped into her throat. She pointed. "Look out! *People!*"

"I see them!" Greyson crowded Hellbringer closer to the red car, as if trying to herd it out of harm's way. But then the wheel jerked out of his grasp, and Hellbringer slammed into the sports car's fat flank, muscling it away from the people.

The impact startled Dru. The sudden crunch of metal. The shakiness in her stomach, as if she herself had been struck. She gripped her crystals so tightly they bit into her fingers.

The sports car punched through the chain-link fence of the empty tennis court at the end of the row. Sparks sprang off its paint from the shredded tatters of fencing. The car streaked across the green clay of the tennis court and out the other side. It slammed the opposite fence flat against the ground, like a metallic carpet, and rolled over it. Greyson swung around the end of the courts in a long arc, chasing after the sorceress.

"What the hell's gotten into you?" Greyson muttered to the car. Hellbringer was acting even more aggressive than usual. Perhaps the demon car sensed something that Dru had so far missed.

A tall, grassy berm bordered the far end of the park, forming a low hill topped with colorful flowers. The red car swerved around the tapered end of the berm and plowed through the bushes that surrounded it. With an explosion of greenery, the car erupted from the end of the park onto the curving residential street beyond. It turned tightly, tires chirping, and accelerated.

Hellbringer was close behind. But instead of going around the grassy berm, Greyson headed straight for it. "Brace yourself!"

Dru didn't know what Greyson had in mind, but she dropped her crystals on the floor at her feet and planted both hands against Hellbringer's grainy black dashboard. She barely had time to register what was happening before Hellbringer slammed into the berm with a bone-jarring thump and ramped over it. A hailstorm of flower petals plastered the windshield.

Dru's stomach dropped away as they went airborne. The wind swept the flowers away, and she had a clear view down the gently sloping hillside below, where the road snaked this way and that between peaceful-looking houses with golden glowing windows.

The other car was turning beneath them just as Hellbringer flew overhead, and for a moment Dru was terrified they would land on top of the sorceress's car. Instead, they hit the pavement directly next to it with a deafening clang.

Through her window, Dru caught a glimpse of the redheaded sorceress's flashing eyes. They opened wide in surprise, then immediately turned furious. Her ring-encrusted hands spun the wheel, and her car slammed into Hellbringer's passenger side.

Even though Dru knew the impact was coming, there was nothing she could do about it. She slammed against the inside of the door and gasped in pain. She felt like she'd been punched in the ribs.

Greyson fought the steering wheel. "Dru!" The worry and urgency in his tone were unmistakable.

She tried to answer him, but couldn't catch her breath.

With a crunch of crumpling metal, the other car released Hellbringer and surged ahead of them. Greyson's eyes glowed bright red. His face flushed with rage, and the cords stood out in his neck. With one hand clenched on the wheel and the other on the gearshift, he chased after the sorceress.

Streetlights streaked past as Hellbringer pulled up alongside the car. The sorceress rolled down her window and glanced over at them, just an arm's length away, her long red hair blowing in the wind. Her teeth gleamed from the shadows as she smirked at Dru.

With one graceful arm, she held out a long metallic crystal, pointing it directly at Dru as if it were a Saturday night special. The crystal began to glow a sinister fiery orange, like molten metal.

Dru's breath caught in her throat. She raised her pyrite disk like a shield. Whatever the sorceress was about to throw at them next, Dru hoped the pyrite would offer some measure of protection against it. She could only pray it would be enough.

4
STEEL DEMONS

"Look out!" Dru shouted.

At her warning, Greyson slammed on the brakes. Dru's head nearly struck the dashboard, and her glasses flew off. But the evasive maneuver worked. As the red car streaked ahead of them, the blast of energy meant for Dru missed. Instead, it split the night air just in front of Hellbringer's nose, a jagged vertigo-inducing arc of dark energy that distorted everything around it.

For a moment, the bolt of dark energy, like black lightning, cast mad shadows across the road in front of them. Reality itself seemed to crack open for a moment, affording an eye-searing glimpse into the heart of the sun, or the frozen depths of space, or both at the same time. Instantly, it was gone. The rippling energy finished with a crack like thunder. Hellbringer drove through the blast of furnace-hot air it left behind.

Dru picked up her glasses and blinked, trying to see around the pulsing afterimage in her vision. Behind them, blackened trees toppled across the road, burning with eerie twilight-purple flames.

Greyson spared only a fierce glance in the rearview mirror before turning the force of his attention to Dru. "Did it get you? Are you hurt?"

Dru shook her head. "I don't even know what that was." She couldn't stop her voice from quavering.

"We're ending this. Now." Greyson sped up, closing in as they entered a sharp turn. The two cars drifted around the tight curve in tandem, barely a foot apart, carried along the same path by the laws of physics. This close, Hellbringer's headlights flashed across the other car's blood-red paint as Greyson pulled alongside the sports car.

They were so close Dru didn't dare blink. Didn't dare breathe.

Coming out of the turn, the street ahead straightened out. On one side was a flat expanse of undeveloped dirt and weeds, dotted with muddy yellow bulldozers and backhoes. The other side of the street was dominated by half-built luxury apartment buildings and retail spaces. Everything was made of glass and aluminum, and it all shone in the glare of the headlights.

The sorceress put on a burst of speed and started to pull away. With an angry growl, Greyson chased after and struck the car's back corner. Its tires howled as if in anger, and its rear end swung away. But the sorceress quickly recovered and shot diagonally across the road in front of them, preventing Greyson from trying the same trick again.

Snarling, Greyson hunched over the wheel, tendons standing out in his forearms. He shoved the gearshift and jerked the wheel. Hellbringer came at the red car again, this time at an angle, and the speed demon's nose struck like a hungry shark, crushing metal.

With a shriek of tires, the red car lost control and spun out ahead of them in a spray of white tire smoke, sliding sideways in the road. Teeth bared, Greyson dropped his speed, turned the wheel, and accelerated again. Dru couldn't tell who was in control now, the man or the machine. Hellbringer's pointed nose rammed straight into the sports car's passenger door. The speed demon pushed the red car sideways in front of it, like hapless prey in the jaws of a predator.

Dru gasped at the viciousness of the attack. She braced herself against the dashboard for all she was worth. Incongruously, it occurred to her at that moment that when Hellbringer was built—and subsequently possessed by a demon—nobody had yet invented airbags. Otherwise one surely would've exploded in her face by now.

With a shrill screech, the red car slid along the road, pinned against Hellbringer's sharp nose. Then it slipped to the side, and the conflicting high-speed forces yanked the cars apart. Both vehicles spun off the pavement and hurtled toward an unfinished building.

The sorceress's car slid past a zigzag orange tower of scaffolding. Luckily, it was late enough on a Friday night that no one was working at the construction site. With a resounding crash, the car plunged through the glass front of the empty building and disappeared into the dark interior. Hellbringer slid sideways a dozen yards behind it.

Against all logic, Dru was absolutely convinced that they wouldn't hit the building. She had seen Greyson pull off so many split-second maneuvers that she had unshakable faith in his driving skills. She couldn't even fathom that he might fail this time. There was no way they would actually crash into the building, she thought.

Until they did.

Glass exploded around them as Hellbringer burst through the floor-to-ceiling front windows. Aluminum window frames twisted and clattered off Hellbringer's roof like hail. Fountains of sparks spewed from shredded electrical systems and sprayed tiny glowing embers across the speed demon's windows. They punched through one unpainted wall after the next, the whole time spinning and rebounding as debris thundered down around them.

Seemingly an eternity later, Hellbringer bumped and lurched to a halt. The roar of its powerful engine dropped to a subdued growl.

Clouds of dust billowed through the air, surrounding them. It drifted through their headlight beams, swirling one way and then the next. Something that sounded like pebbles clattered across the roof. Minuscule cubes of shattered glass lay scattered across Hellbringer's long black nose, glittering in the reflected light like a lost fortune in diamonds. The car's windshield wipers creaked to life, startling Dru as they swept broken debris off the windshield. Across the room, the red car sat motionless, facing them, as if stunned. The car's front end had been mashed into an ugly mess by the crash. Beneath its crumpled hood, its headlights burned blue-white beams through the swirling smoke. The chrome letters "SRT" gleamed in its shattered grille, under a wide, hungry-looking hood scoop.

"I'll be damned," Greyson said, sounding awed. "It's a Demon."

"That might explain Hellbringer's aggressive behavior." Dru's voice shook as she settled her crooked glasses back onto her nose. "But that doesn't make any sense. This car is too new. As far as I can tell, nobody has summoned up a speed demon since 1969."

"Not a *demon*. A Dodge Challenger SRT Demon." Greyson glanced at her, seemingly unfazed by the crash, and pointed. "It's a limited-production car. See the hood scoop? It's built for racing. That's why it's so fast."

Dru couldn't care less about what *kind* of car it was. She just needed to know whether the sorceress was still able to fight. And whether there was any way to get the amulet back from her. Only then did it occur to Dru that she and Greyson were, against all odds, miraculously intact and unharmed. That meant the sorceress might be, too.

"Hopefully, she's stunned, at least a little bit," Dru said, unbuckling her seat belt with shaking hands. "That's our only chance for retrieving that amulet."

But as Dru reached for the door handle, movement across the room stopped her. The red car's sheet metal started to shift and flex. Its crooked front end straightened itself out, rising back into position as if massaged by invisible hands. The crumpled hood flattened out like a freshly rolled-out carpet. The dented fenders rippled back into proper shape. In moments, the car was once again factory-fresh and gleaming.

"Holy Hasselhoff!" Dru breathed. The sorceress's car really *was* a speed demon. That changed everything.

That meant, like Hellbringer, it was possessed. That made it self-aware. Able to heal itself, drive itself, even attack on its own. Dru and her friends had fought speed demons before, during the battle against the Four Horsemen of the Apocalypse. Despite her best efforts, Dru had never found a way to defeat the infernal vehicles. Galena crystals harmed them, but they could heal from that. She had only barely managed to trap the demon cars in the netherworld, and even doing that had almost been deadly to her and Greyson.

She had no idea how to take on another speed demon without getting killed.

Even as that thought froze Dru in fear, things got worse. With a flicker of motion, the red car's window rolled down. A slender, black-clad arm snaked out the open window, pointing that same elongated metallic crystal directly at Hellbringer. The sharp tip of the crystal glowed, quickly heating to a blistering orange and then white, as if it had been thrust into a blast furnace.

There was no way to dodge the sorceress's attack this time. Nowhere for them to go. They were sitting ducks. Icy adrenaline shot through Dru's body as she stared at the burning crystal, knowing what was about to happen next.

Greyson reached for her. "Dru—"

She didn't give him time to finish. She had to move fast.

Dru grabbed his rough palm with her left hand and yanked on the door handle with her right, then snatched the golden pyrite disk off the black carpet at her feet. As the door swung open, she thrust the pyrite disk outside the car and held it up like a miniature shield.

This summer, Dru's magical powers had grown stronger than she ever could have imagined. Though she still found it hard to believe, she was now capable of standing on equal footing with some of the full-time sorcerers who frequented her little shop. But she still wasn't any match for someone with decades of experience, like the older sorceress in the speed demon.

Luckily, Dru did have Greyson. He was an *arcana rasa*, a one-in-a-million person born with magical energy but no innate power of his own. For some reason that Dru had never fully understood, the power inside him perfectly complemented hers, as if the two of them were one. When she touched him, she could draw on his magical energy as directly as her own.

She gripped his hand tightly. It took her complete focus to summon up his power in addition to her own. As their combined energy raced through her, she felt as if she were floating, as if the magic buoyed up her soul within her body. The rush took her breath away, but at the same time it terrified her. Because if she couldn't control it all, it could cause unimaginable harm to both of them.

But probably not as much harm as the sorceress could.

In a fraction of a second, Greyson's invisible energy intertwined with Dru's and flowed through her arm, out her tingling fingers, and into the pyrite disk. Instantly, the round pyrite crystal shone with magical energy, as if thrust under a brilliant ray of sunlight. Its protective properties spread out around them. The air surrounding Hellbringer shimmered like heat waves over a hot desert highway.

From a few car lengths away, the redheaded sorceress unleashed her attack. The jagged bolt of dark energy was aimed straight at Hellbringer's windshield. With a bone-shaking blast, it struck Dru's invisible energy shield.

The old speed demon shuddered on its suspension as if it had been dropped off a building. Hellbringer's throaty engine choked and died.

As instantly as it struck, the searing energy bounced back the way it had come. An eruption of purple fire engulfed the front of the sorceress's speed demon. Its hood blistered and burned. Its windshield blackened.

The flash of heat from the energy bolt was so intense that Dru lost all feeling in her fingers. For a heart-stopping moment, she feared the blast had taken her hand from her permanently. She blinked through tears, trying to see through the blinding afterimage that pulsed across her eyelids. A crack of thunder echoed through the empty building, so loud that it sent needles of pain through Dru's ears and shook dust down from the ceiling.

Then it was over, and ringing silence reigned around them. The beams of Hellbringer's headlights had gone dark. The gloom was lit only by the crackling flames engulfing the red car.

The smoldering pyrite disk, now the color of ash, dropped from Dru's numb fingers. She pulled her arm back inside the car. Greyson was calling her name, she realized, but she could barely hear him over the painful ringing in her ears. He held her close and turned her numb hand over in his, examining it closely.

Aside from being sooty and senseless, her hand was intact. With considerable effort, she was able to wiggle her fingers. She was relieved to see that all five were still attached, though she counted them just to be sure. Some surreal voice in the back of her brain nagged at her that she *still* hadn't painted her nails.

Dazed, Dru stared through the windshield at the flaming wreckage of the other speed demon. The redheaded sorceress was trapped. Evil as she might be, she didn't deserve to die in there. They would have to pull her to safety.

With her good hand, Dru pushed herself out of Greyson's arms. "We have to help her," she shouted at his puzzled expression. The explosion had left her partly deaf.

Before she could stop herself, Dru climbed out of Hellbringer and stumbled across the wreckage toward the blaze. She squinted through the raging arcane fire, searching for any sign of life. To her shock, the sorceress inside the car looked not only alive but completely unharmed, and she glared back at Dru through the window. With a snarl, the sorceress dropped her hand to the gearshift.

The red car wailed and lurched backward. Still on fire, it crashed through the sheet rock wall behind it and kept going, leaving a cascade of debris in its wake.

In the cavernous room beyond, the flaming car spun around so that it was facing away from Dru. In the same movement, it accelerated toward the opposite wall. It punched through the unfinished drywall and kept going, flames trailing out behind it like the tail of a comet.

Shocked, Dru didn't know what else to do but chase the burning car through the half-finished building. She jumped over fallen metal beams and broken lumber, clutching her spectrolite crystal like a weapon. She couldn't let the sorceress get away with the amulet.

Because if that sorceress figured out how to tap into the power of the amulet and destroy an entire city, it would all be Dru's fault. Blinded by fear and guilt as much as by darkness and smoke, Dru scrambled through the flickering shadows. She followed the trail of receding flames, refusing to give up.

By the time she reached the shattered windows on the opposite side of the building, the red speed demon was long gone. It had vanished into the night, leaving behind only smoking tire tracks on the unfinished parking lot.

"*Dru!*" Behind her, Greyson came running through the rubble, his boots crushing debris underfoot. "Dru! Are you all right?" He took her shaking arms in his strong hands and turned her to face him, studying her with his glowing red eyes.

Dru blinked up at him through the dust that covered her glasses. "I'm okay," she croaked. Coughing on the cloud of dust, her ears still ringing, Dru felt all the strength drain out of her body. She turned and stared out into the empty night, feeling empty and spent. She had failed.

In her mind's eye, Dru could still see the redheaded sorceress's deadly smirk as she pointed the crystal out the car window. That diabolical smile was unsettlingly familiar. There was something about it that the years could never erase. Dru was sure she had seen it somewhere before, long ago. But where?

5

DARKNESS RISING

Greyson sheltered Dru as they made their way through the flickering darkness of the destroyed building, circling around the sparks that rained down from the ruined wiring above them. He kept a wary eye on the fractured sheet rock and broken lumber overhead, keenly aware that it could all come crashing down on them at any moment.

Hellbringer sat still and dark where he'd left it, covered in dust and broken glass. For a moment, he feared the worst. But when he reached out and touched the sharp edge of the car's fender, a spark of magical energy stung his palm, like static. He wasn't exactly sure what that energy was, but he'd felt it before. It meant that, thankfully, Hellbringer was still alive.

The speed demon's engine coughed twice, three times, and then rumbled to life. The long black hood trembled as the engine struggled to find its rhythm. It wasn't in the car's nature to run rough, but that energy blast had clearly shaken Hellbringer to the core. Greyson wasn't feeling too steady on his feet, either. His ears were still ringing.

He opened the passenger door for Dru. "Get in. There's still time to catch her."

"She's too dangerous. We need backup." She paused in the doorway. "I left my phone back at the shop. We need to find a way to call Rane!"

Greyson looked around at the half-finished, half-demolished building lit by sparking wires. "I don't think they have a phone here."

Despite the deep shadows hiding Dru's face and the dust speckling her glasses, the fear was plain enough in her eyes. "Let's go." She climbed into Hellbringer. He shut the heavy door with a solid thunk and jogged around behind the car, past Hellbringer's tall black wing.

As he slid into the driver's seat, the speed demon revved its engine, clearly ready to go. But there was something brittle to the sound, as if Hellbringer was only putting up a good front. Like the barking of a frightened dog.

One hand on the steering wheel, Greyson turned around in the seat and backed them out through the ragged hole in the side of the building. Once outside, he spun the wheel. Hellbringer's tires chirped on the fresh pavement as they swung around the end of the building.

Around on the other side, another hole gaped in the unfinished exterior of the building. The flaming red car had left behind smoldering tire tracks, but those eventually petered out before they reached the road. Presumably, the red speed demon had been able to heal itself by then, or else the sorceress had cast some kind of spell to put out the blaze.

Greyson followed the road for miles, passing one dark cross street after another, with no sign of the red car. He finally had to admit that the redheaded sorceress was long gone, taking the cursed amulet with her. Still, he kept going because the last thing he wanted to do was give up. Judging from Hellbringer's reaction, the black speed demon felt the same way.

The steering wheel kept nudging him toward the shadows on either side of the road, as if Hellbringer wanted to check every corner and make sure the other speed demon wasn't hiding there. Hellbringer apparently knew that the red car was out there, somewhere. That concept seemed to make the older black car skittish, unwilling to drive as fast.

Greyson could feel it, too. An uncomfortable presence bugged him. It grated on his nerves like an itch he couldn't scratch. Somewhere out there in the darkness, beyond the dotted yellow line streaking toward them through the headlight beams, Hellbringer's nemesis freely roamed the highway. Clearly, that thing was tougher than Hellbringer, able to take all of that punishment and still keep going.

Even while it was on fire.

"We have to find her," Dru insisted. "What if she takes that amulet to Yellowstone? What if she uses it to erupt the supervolcano like the Roman sorcerers did with Mount Vesuvius?" She shuddered. "A blast that size would scorch the land for thousands of miles around."

Greyson rubbed the back of his neck. They were out of leads and heading nowhere fast. He let his foot off the gas and drifted over to the side of the road. The tires crunched on gravel as they rolled to a stop.

"What are you doing? We need to find her!"

"She's gone," Greyson said. As much as he hated to admit defeat, the trail had gone cold. He let out a long breath and turned to face her.

Looking crushed, she quickly busied herself with cleaning her glasses on the hem of her shirt. "Fine. Then let's get back to the Crystal Connection. I need to do some research." She jammed her glasses back on her face and sat back hard against the seat, arms crossed. "I know her from somewhere. I *know* her. But I just can't place her."

Greyson turned the car around and headed back toward the lights of the city. He thought about the older redheaded sorceress and frowned. "Is she one of your customers?"

"I don't *think* so." Dru chewed on her lower lip. "If she came into the shop before, she must have kept her crystal powers hidden. I didn't know there *were* any other crystal sorceresses alive today. Opal might know. God, I wish I had my phone." She cocked her head at him for a moment. "So, do you not have a cell phone?"

Greyson shook his head.

She rode in silence for a moment, lips pursed. "Do you mind if I ask why, in today's world, you would choose not to have a phone?" When he didn't answer right away, she added softly, "I mean, it *is* a choice, right? Not like an awkward credit problem or something? Because these days you can get a plan at the grocery store, even."

He looked over at her, and the honest curiosity in her expression melted away the bulk of his irritation. "With everything that's happening, you want to talk about cell phone plans."

"Well, you're not on Facebook, either. That's an . . . interesting choice."

"Life is full of interesting choices."

Dru didn't pry. They drove past the park they had nearly obliterated. The city lights shimmered in the tranquil surface of the lake. From the street, there was no sign of the damage he'd done.

Greyson glanced up in the rearview mirror and caught a reflection of his own fiery red eyes. Their eerie glow unsettled him, reminding him that he was cursed. Somehow, he and Hellbringer were inextricably linked with the fate of the world. As one doomsday threat after another emerged, he always found himself in the thick of it all, with no idea what to do. And yet Dru was always right there with him, trying to save him from himself. Even now, Dru was probably trying to distract him from exactly those thoughts. The more time he spent in the driver's seat, the more trouble he had sorting out his own feelings from those of the speed demon. The car was driven by rage, aggression, destruction. Its soul had been forged in the infernal pits for one purpose alone—to help bring about the end of the world.

Yet somehow, Dru had won over Hellbringer to her side in the fight against doomsday. She had enlisted the speed demon as surely as she had saved Greyson. But how long could their tenuous alliance last?

The speed demon's aggression was infectious, an insatiable hunger with no thoughts about consequences. Whenever the speed demon gave chase, it was all-encompassing. Greyson could still feel the blood pounding in his ears, the ache in his arms and shoulders, the twitchy feeling of unspent rage. It had clouded his vision from the moment they had started pursuit, and only now could he see it for what it was. It was like coming out of a fog.

How deeply did the speed demon affect his judgment? How much of his anger was his own, and how much was he picking up from Hellbringer? And more important, was it driving him to put Dru in harm's way?

He could've gotten her hurt, even killed. If anything happened to her, because of him, he would never forgive himself, never be able to live with it.

He regarded her in the pale glow from the dashboard lights. On the outside, she looked so normal. Tousled brown curly hair. Bright eyes. Slightly startled expression. No one would guess that this unassuming young woman was a crystal sorceress of phenomenal power. Or that she had saved the world more than once.

By being around her, was he really protecting her? Or was he putting her in danger?

As he drove Hellbringer through the night streets, he had to wonder. Would Dru be better off without him?

6
LIPS LIKE SUGAR

Rane's breaths came fast and regular as she ran the last mile in near total darkness, clutching a warm white paper bag in each hand. The night was alive around her, insects scratching, frogs croaking, leaves rustling in the faint breeze. Rane followed the edge of the river, a mossy-smelling blackness lit only by the rippling reflection of distant city lights.

She would be the first to admit it was a weird place to hunt down a giant man-eating bat. But really, it wasn't like there was a *normal* place for that sort of thing.

This part of the river didn't have any kind of official trail running along-side it. But a hard dirt track had been worn along the bank by the constant footfalls of people who wanted to walk unseen through the outskirts of the city. Mostly homeless people, Rane knew from experience. And the creatures of the night that sometimes hunted them. And then there were people like her, who were there to protect and defend by kicking ass as needed.

Right now, thankfully, the trail was empty. Rane's feet pounded along the hard dirt in a steady, merciless rhythm. She was in her element. In the zone. Ready to rumble. She sucked in the scents of the night air and blew out the stress of being cooped up inside. Every breath made her feel more alive.

Hunting, stalking, running, this was what she lived for. That, and the sinful contents of the paper bags clutched in her sweaty grip.

Ever since she'd gotten back together with her on-again, off-again boyfriend Salem, the most powerful sorcerer she'd ever met, he'd been a little weird. Even for him. It was like her near-death experience had made him decide to shut himself away from the world and keep her closed in with him. It was suffocating. She hated being stuck indoors.

Sure, earlier this summer, it hadn't been a whole lot of fun flying face-first into an undead motorcycle gang at sixty miles an hour, then pancaking onto the stone floor of an underground nuclear bunker. Things like that tended to leave a mark. Luckily, at the time, her entire body had been transformed into solid metal. So it wasn't fatal or anything.

But it had hurt like a mother. And being laid up with injuries was a punishment she had never been able to handle well. Despite Salem's uncharacteristic sweetness, her recovery had been slow and painful. Luckily, nothing was broken, and everything else healed fast. Considering how much weightlifting and fight training were a part of her daily routine, soft tissue injuries were practically an old friend.

Now, the bruises had faded, her muscles were building again, and she was almost back up to full strength. On one of her long runs along the riverbank this morning, she had heard about this supposedly vicious giant bat stalking the homeless population. Hearing that had given her exactly what she needed.

A mission to get out of the house and kick ass.

Salem, on the other hand, being the gloomy indoor sorcerer type, had needed a little more convincing. He had no interest in improbable rumors about giant carnivorous bats, he'd said. Her enthusiasm hadn't convinced him. Neither had complaints, threats, or even sultry looks.

Finally, what had won him over was mystery. She had promised him a surprise. Something he'd never expect. Something that would blow his gigantic sorcerer brain. And then she refused to tell him what it was.

That, finally, had gotten to him.

And it had led more or less directly to the toasty little paper bags hanging from her fists.

Spotting light up ahead, Rane slowed down and stopped, ears straining for any sounds that didn't belong. Fighting, screaming, maybe some giant flapping wings. But, slightly disappointingly, there was none of that.

Just the dry, crackling voice of the Brigadier as he babbled through one of his long, meandering stories. He was probably talking to Salem. But the Brigadier had been known to spend hours telling his stories to thin air, too, due to his slippery grasp of reality.

Rane waited, listening, as her breathing slowed down to normal. Idly, her fingers played with the brand-new titanium ring she wore on her middle finger, a gift from Dru after her previous titanium ring had been spectacularly burned out by magic. At will, Rane could transform into any metal or rock that touched her skin, and she was ready to do it at the first sign of danger if this giant bat materialized.

But since the Brigadier sounded boringly calm, Rane decided to save her energy and remain in human form. She gave herself a quick check to make sure her blonde ponytail was still in place, her underwear wasn't poking out of her floppy pink running shorts, and her armpits didn't smell unusually ripe.

She sniffed again, unsure, then shrugged. What the hell, Salem already knew what she smelled like. And the Brigadier probably couldn't tell anyway. Holding the bags up high, Rane jogged toward the light.

Up ahead and above, a little-used service road crossed the river on a crumbling old concrete bridge. The only light came from a single cobweb-choked safety light set beneath the crest of the bridge. Countless generations of spiders had wrapped it in enough webs to reduce its glow to that of a candle. It might have been almost romantic, in a super creepy way, except for the presence of the Brigadier.

He'd been a fixture of the riverside homeless community ever since Rane could remember, a wiry old man with a stern face turned leathery by the relentless Colorado sun. Rane had never seen him dressed in anything but old camouflage fatigues, with a stained black beret perched atop his scruffy white hair. She didn't know his real name, so she'd taken to calling him the Brigadier, and the name had stuck.

He sat on the riverbank with his gnarled hands clasped on his knees as he talked, the cuffs of his torn fatigues tucked into his dirty combat boots. One of his boots was held together with frayed duct tape.

Next to him, Salem leaned against a concrete bridge pillar, dressed all in black. Black ruffled shirt, tight black pants, tall black boots. The night was too warm for his black trench coat, apparently. But he still wore his favorite silk top hat. His long, wavy hair fell down around his shoulders.

Though he leaned nonchalantly against the concrete with one boot propping him up, Rane knew him well enough to spot the tension in his body. The Brigadier was obviously putting him on edge.

Salem's onyx cufflinks glinted in the faint light as he held out his lanky arm, his two extended fingers wagging as if they were walking up an invisible wall. At his feet, pebbles from the riverbank rose up into the air and quickly stacked themselves one atop another in a precarious little column. As Rane jogged up, she spotted at least a dozen of the little stone towers. Salem had definitely been on edge for a while.

"Look who's here," Salem announced unnecessarily loudly, without even glancing up. The irritation was plain in his voice.

But the announcement had its intended effect on the Brigadier, who broke off his rambling story in midsentence and smiled a gap-toothed grin up at Rane. "Evenin', sunshine! What's in the bag?"

"Hey. You'll find out in a second." Rane nodded once to him before turning to Salem. "You spot anything yet?"

Salem finally turned her way. His fierce gray eyes, accented by black guyliner, peered up from under the brim of his top hat. The sharp angles of his face became pools of shadow in the dim light. "Remind me again why I dropped everything to come down here and meet your . . . informant?"

"'Cause of the giant killer bat!" the Brigadier rasped at his feet.

"Yes, thank you," Salem said, not taking his gaze from Rane. "And what did I say about that?"

"Said there's no bat," the Brigadier offered.

That didn't make any sense. Rane put one hand on her hip. "Are you sure?"

"That's what your friend Whalen said." The Brigadier pointed at Salem, who didn't bother to correct his name.

"But you told me you saw a big-ass bat," Rane insisted. "You said it was nesting under this bridge. That's why we're here."

The Brigadier shrugged both shoulders.

"If one person sees it, it's their imagination," Salem said. "If two people see it, *then* it's a pattern."

"What if three people see it?" the Brigadier asked.

"Three people never see anything," Salem snapped at him, "because by that point, one of them has already been eaten." He took a deep breath and said to Rane, "Are we finished here?"

"Nope. We're just getting started." For some reason, Rane got a perverse sense of satisfaction out of Salem's obvious irritation. "Hey, check you out. Getting out of the house. Making new friends. Having fun. Right?"

"Oodles." Salem made a sweeping-away motion with his hand, and all at once his little stone towers exploded. The rocks peppered the surface of the water like machine-gun fire.

In the tense silence that followed, the Brigadier sniffed. "Hey. That smells good. You going to let it get cold?"

"Nope. Here you go. One for you, dude." She handed one of the bags to the Brigadier and held up the other one for Salem. "And one for you. Dig in." She thrust it into his chest, amused at the puff of white powder that blew out of the top of the bag and across his half-unbuttoned shirt.

Gingerly, Salem reached into the paper bag and drew out a golden-brown pastry dusted in a thick layer of confectioners' sugar. The warm aroma of sweet fried dough rolled out of the open bag, making her mouth water.

The perplexed look on Salem's face gradually softened, and Rane could only hope that the beignets reminded him of the crazy-good times they had spent in New Orleans, fighting evil together. Teaming up together. Being happy together.

The whole thing had been Dru's idea. The problem was that Dru wasn't exactly an expert on the whole romantic thing. Rane hoped this would work.

She leaned close to Salem until her forehead touched the brim of his top hat. At six feet one, she towered over him, but that had never been an issue for her. At times like this, it just made him that much cuter, standing there with his chest all dusted with sugar, the beignet inches from his lips. The look in his eyes slowly warmed, and she knew right then that she had finally gotten through to him.

That was the Salem she loved, the man she so rarely saw. As one doomsday threat after another had put the fate of the world in the balance, he had grown darker and colder. Now he spent most of his time hiding behind all of his seriousness and sarcasm, his constant irritation and insults. But she knew who he really was, deep inside. And she wasn't going to give up until she got him back.

She felt the soft ripple of Salem's magic climb across her skin, like smoke. One by one, the beignets floated out of the bag to orbit around them. A swirling halo of powdered sugar surrounded them, glowing softly in the light. It diffused into a delicious fog, making the rest of the world fade away. The moment was so bizarre, so otherworldly, so Salem.

At that moment, it felt like she could gaze deep into his eyes and that was all she needed to be happy.

A rare smile quirked up the corner of his mouth. She smiled back.

In the back of her mind, she blessed the little New Orleans chef who had agreed to stay late and fry up a batch of her famous beignets just for Rane's version of date night.

Just as Rane went in for the kiss, the Brigadier barked, "Bat!"

Salem startled and pulled away, irritation flashing across his eyes. "For the last time, there *is* no giant bat, you paranoid—"

"Bat!" A cloud of powdered sugar and crumbs burst from the Brigadier's stuffed mouth. He thrust one gnarled finger up toward the night sky.

Even before she looked, Rane heard the sound of leathery wings beating the night air, pounding straight toward them.

7

BOMBSHELL

On instinct, Rane tightened her fist around her titanium ring and willed her body to transform. In the blink of an eye, her fist turned into gleaming metal, and the effect spread down her arm and across her entire body, turning her into a living titanium statue. Learning how to transform this quickly, without thinking, had taken her years of practice and thousands of attempts. But it had saved her life on countless occasions, and this time it saved Salem's.

The creature hit them so fast that Rane could only process what had happened after the fact. The furry-bodied bat, bigger than a wolf, with wings the size of a World War I fighter plane, swooped under the bridge with pinpoint precision. The light of the single bulb under the bridge glowed through the leathery skin of the bat's wings and tail as it streaked past. Its grasping feet reached toward Salem's neck, sharp claws shining in the murky light.

Salem was too startled to defend himself. Rane had only a fraction of a second to thrust her bare metal arm across his neck, blocking the attack. The bat's claws sparked off her wrist and snagged the woven leather thong of the magical golden amulet that hung around Salem's neck, snapping it loose.

The Brigadier fainted away as the bat passed overhead, no more than a foot over Rane's metal ponytail. The wind from its wings blew off Salem's top hat, sending his long, curly hair swirling. Then the bat was gone, scraping beneath the bridge and out the other side. Its broad, leathery wings pounded the air. Salem's enchanted gold medallion dangled from its clawed foot, glinting in the distant city lights.

Salem had worn that amulet for as long as Rane had known him. Its magical shielding powers were his first line of defense against evil spells and hostile sorcerers. Without it, he was dangerously vulnerable. Rane had to get it back.

Besides, she wasn't going to let some giant flying rodent get away with mugging them.

Rane sprinted after the bat as fast as she could, fists pumping at her sides. At an angle, she ran up the embankment at the end of the bridge and leaped, metal fingers outstretched.

But as swift as she was, the bat was faster. As it flapped away, she fell several yards short of the dangling amulet and sailed face-first into the weeds with a muddy crash. Rane spit out a mouthful of slimy leaves, swearing that she would find a way to punch that thing in the face.

Angrily, she rolled to her feet. "Use your powers!" she called to Salem, and made a swatting motion with her open palm. She'd seen him end fights like this in a single move, by levitating an evil creature into a wall or a conveniently placed telephone pole at high speed.

Salem's chiseled face flushed with rage. His fingers clutched at the spot below his neck where the amulet belonged. "I can't! The amulet is protecting him!" He threw his arms wide, and they crackled with bright sparks of magical energy. Then he flung his hands toward the bat and unleashed his spell. Every loose object around him hurtled skyward as if fired out of a cannon: rocks, rotten logs, empty cans, even the powdered sugar beignets. If any of them hit the bat, they didn't slow it down.

Rane didn't waste breath cursing. She turned and chased after the thing on foot, heart sinking because she knew it was useless to pursue. The thing was already thirty feet off the ground, now forty, and quickly climbing. In seconds, it would be out of sight. The idea of letting it get away made Rane's blood boil.

What sucked the most was that Salem's protective amulet was powerful enough to resist his own powers, so there was no way he could reach out with his mind and snatch it back from the creature. She had to just watch it dwindle away.

As the bat climbed into the starry sky, great wings beating, Rane slowed her run and looked around for something to throw at it. The biggest solid object she could see was the Brigadier's shopping cart, currently loaded with his worldly possessions. Figuring she could find him a new one later, Rane squatted and dumped it out with a grunt. She was about to haul it back and chuck it at the bat when a better thought occurred to her.

"Dude!" she shouted back to Salem, lifting the shopping cart overhead. It was way more substantial than the little rocks from the river's edge. Salem's magic could turn it into a deadly missile. "This!"

Salem cocked his head at her. The darkness obscured the expression on his face, but plainly he wasn't getting it.

Rane shook the shopping cart over her head for emphasis, making the metal grating clash. "Hit him with *this*!"

Salem nodded once and raised his arms, long fingers spread wide. Hazy white magic suffused the air around him. Jagged white arcs of energy crackled between his fingers. Rane had meant to let go of the cart the moment Salem's magic hurled it at the bat, but her metal fingers were still wrapped around its handle when the cart abruptly rocketed skyward.

Nothing could have prepared Rane for the sensory overload of being launched airborne. Her stomach practically dropped through her feet. The cold wind howled in her ears and blasted across her body, raising goose bumps on her metal skin as the air temperature quickly fell. The metal shopping cart vibrated in her grip as if it had been strapped to a runaway jet engine, rattling her metal teeth.

In other words, it was *awesome*.

The boggy smell of the river sank below as she soared up into the cold, clear air streaming across the Rocky Mountains. Spread out below her, the city of Denver glowed, ribbons of golden light tracing the highways, while the jagged towers of downtown sparkled in the distance. Rane was so busy looking around that she didn't realize how fast she was closing in on the bat. In the darkness, she didn't spot its flapping wings until she was almost on top of the thing.

With a jolt of panic, she realized she had no idea how to fly a shopping cart. She twisted the handlebar, hoping to steer it like a motorcycle, but only succeeded in dropping her ascent by a few feet.

It was enough. Barely.

She streaked beneath one of the bat's huge wings, nearly getting a face full of wing leather. As she shot past, she snatched the golden amulet right out of the bat's grip. "*Ha!* Gotcha!"

The bat screeched in surprise.

Grinning, Rane gripped the woven leather thong tightly in her fist. "See ya, sucker!" she shouted over her shoulder into the wind stream. She wanted to say more, but the shopping cart abruptly bucked and went into a stomach-lurching dive.

Teeth bared against the freezing wind, Rane wrestled with the shopping cart's handlebar. She twisted it this way and that, but the movements had no effect at all. She kept heading straight down. There was no way to tell whether Salem was controlling it or whether the magic had simply failed. Maybe she'd flown out of the range of Salem's spell. In that case, it was only a matter of seconds before she ate dirt. Maybe permanently.

In the darkness, it was impossible to tell exactly how far up she was, but she was dropping fast. The warm golden lights of neighborhood streets and houses rose up at a distance from the snaking blackness of the river, which was surrounded on both sides by junkyards, industrial complexes, and a fancy golf course. Everything directly below her was more or less dark, lit only by a few pools of isolated light that rushed toward her.

She was going down gut-clenchingly fast. Maybe into the river, maybe onto the golf course, she wasn't sure. Although her body was in metal form and could take a hell of a lot of punishment, she didn't relish the idea of becoming a human torpedo. She had a bad feeling that if she made a direct hit on something solid, like rock or concrete, she wouldn't survive.

In fact, she was royally screwed.

Stupid amulet.

But, wait, could the amulet protect her from the impact? Only seconds from the ground, and still holding onto the shopping cart with one hand, she reached up to slip the amulet over her neck.

Before she could, the giant bat swooped past her with a screech and a flurry of wings. Its clawed foot closed around the golden amulet and yanked on it with inhuman strength.

But Rane held on. No way was she going to let this overgrown Halloween ornament make off with Salem's amulet, especially after all this. Besides, if she was going down, she was taking this thing with it. She released the shopping cart, letting it tumble away into the night, and latched her other hand onto the bat's leg with a viselike grip.

Clearly, the thing didn't like that. It squawked, jinking left and right in an effort to shake her loose. But she was determined to hang on. When the thing bent down its wolflike head to snap at her with its long white teeth, she let go of the amulet long enough to punch it in its furry face.

It was a bad angle, so she couldn't put as much force into the blow as she wanted. But still, she had a metal fist, and the thing's head snapped back.

Somewhere far below, the shopping cart hit the river with an invisible splash.

The bat's head lolled, stunned—she had hit it harder than she meant to. The beating of its wings slowed, and its body shimmered with ripples of unearthly green light. The hair on its body shrank away, revealing smooth human skin rippling with muscles. The webbing of its wings began to recede from fingers that shrank into human hands.

It wasn't just a giant bat, she realized. It was a dude. Somewhere, she dimly recalled Dru telling her something about sorcerers who could transform into giant animals, but that was like centuries ago. Those guys had supposedly all died out.

Except that here she was, holding onto the ankle of some unconscious naked dude with Salem's golden amulet wrapped around his big toe. Not good.

"Hey, *wake up!*" she yelled at the bat sorcerer, but it didn't do any good. She had a split second to see the white breakers on the surface of the river below, and then they hit the water hard enough to make Rane's ears ring.

When the cold impact slapped across her body, she lost her grip. Water shot up her nose, choking her. Something struck her shoulder like a runaway freight train, shooting pain across her body. More impacts pummeled her like hammer blows, hitting her arms, chest, and legs. Her titanium body dug a trench across the riverbed. Or depending on the angle of impact, maybe she was burrowing straight down, digging her own grave. It was impossible to tell.

A hot glow burned through her tightly closed eyelids, and as suddenly as the impacts had begun, they stopped. All the pressure eased off her, and she felt weightless. The brash rushing roar of the water became a soothing, wet gurgle.

Then she was rising out of the river and up into the air, lifted by invisible forces. Gagging on muddy river water, Rane opened her eyes to see Salem standing on the riverbank, arms outstretched toward her, his eyes glowing with soft light. Behind him stood the Brigadier, wringing his wool beret in his hands, his white hair sticking out at all angles.

She had finished coughing out most of the river water by the time Salem set her down on the riverbank next to him. "About time you got your act together," Rane croaked, now in human form. "What took you so long?"

He sighed heavily. "When you grabbed my amulet, Buttercup, it made you immune to my magic. That's why you fell. I had to wait until you let go of it."

Rane thought about that carefully. "Huh."

Salem gave her a wide-eyed expectant look, obviously waiting for her to say something more.

She spotted a rock at her feet and kicked it into the river. "Stupid amulet."

Salem adjusted his top hat. "Well, this has been fun. While you were taking the Nestea plunge, the bat apparently recovered."

"How do you know that?"

"Because he flapped away again. *With* my amulet."

The Brigadier pointed west, toward the mountains. "That way."

"Yes, incredibly helpful, thank you," Salem said without taking his gaze off Rane. "This wasn't random. Somebody went through a lot of trouble to steal that amulet from me. The question is, who?"

Rane shrugged. "Bigger question: are there any of those French donuts left, or did you throw them all at the bat? Because I am seriously hungry."

Salem rolled his eyes, spun on his heel, and marched back toward the bridge.

"Okay, don't pout about it," Rane said to his back as she followed him. "We can fix this. We just track this bat down, kick his ass, and get your man-jewelry back. Then life is good. Right?" When he didn't respond, Rane added, "Oh, and BTW? It's a dude. One of those sorcerers from once upon a time who can change into animals. I forget what they're called."

Salem looked back over his shoulder, eyes glittering from beneath the brim of his hat. "A protean sorcerer? You're sure?"

Rane shrugged. "Protein sorcerer, carb sorcerer, I don't know. Do we have to talk about food right now?"

Unexpectedly, Salem's phone rang. Ominous chords of organ music split the night. Looking mildly startled, Salem pulled out his phone and frowned at it. "Why is Opal calling me? How does she even have my number?" He gave Rane a severe look. "Where's *your* phone?"

She checked her armband phone holder, but it was soggy and empty. She shrugged and jerked a thumb toward the river.

"Who's Opal?" the Brigadier asked, ambling along next to Rane.

"Works at Dru's shop. Black lady. Big hair. Fashion plate." Annoyed by the ongoing organ music, Rane snapped at Salem, "Are you going to answer that or what?"

He didn't look sure.

The Brigadier nodded to himself. "Oh, I like Opal. She gave me a pome-colada one time."

Rane stopped in her tracks. "Opal gave you a pomegranate piña colada? She never got *me* a pome-colada. After everything I've done for her." She pointed to Salem. "*Don't* answer that."

Salem froze with his finger an inch from his phone's screen, then pocketed it as if he had never intended to answer it.

The Brigadier, wide-eyed, lightly touched her arm. "Do you know, maybe," he said, "where I can get another shopping cart?"

Salem gave him a sour look, then flicked his wrist at the river. With a geyser of water, the cart erupted from the depths, tumbled end over end, then slowed and lightly settled down next to them. It was dripping wet and somewhat dented, but still functional.

Salem drew in a deep breath, slowly let it out, and snapped his fingers. "*Now* you're making me want more donuts," he said, as if this was all Rane's fault.

"Better hope there's a Dunkin' open." Rane marched past him. "This is gonna be a long night."

8

WHEN THE GHOSTS
COME CALLING

Hyperventilating, Opal hung up the phone and grabbed onto the cash register for support, worried she might faint. She stood all alone in the wreckage of Dru's shop, with no idea of what in hell had just happened here. Worse, nobody was answering the damn phone. Not Dru, not Rane, not even Salem. And it pained her to even *try* calling Salem. That little man was cologne-commercial handsome on the outside, maybe, but she knew crazy when she saw it.

She picked up the phone again, thinking about calling the police, but what would she tell them? Somebody broke in, blew up the safe, and lit the plaid armchair on fire? She could picture it now:

Ma'am, are you telling me the suspect stole an old Atomic Fireball candy box?

No, Officer, a cursed amulet. And maybe some magic rocks.

I see. Ma'am, you're going to have to come with us.

Definitely not how she wanted to spend her Friday night.

Opal took a deep breath and held onto the edge of the counter, mostly because her brand-new shoes could not be trusted to keep her fully upright. Oh sure, they looked good. Creamsicle-orange braided sandals with stiletto heels. They popped like crazy against her short sequined skirt and low-cut peacock-blue satin top. She was all ready for a hot date with Ruiz that he'd canceled at the last minute, leaving her with a refrigerator full of champagne, chocolate-covered strawberries, and whipped cream. What was she supposed to do with that all alone?

So with her Friday night blown to pieces, she'd come down here to the Crystal Connection to share the goodies with Dru, because those strawberries were not going to eat themselves. And besides, she could pick up some sage and a few other necessities while she was at it.

That was when she walked in and found everything in here all torn up. Smoke wafted through the air. The front door was open. The bad-hoodoo safe that was supposedly hidden behind the picture of Ming the Merciless had been blown wide open, and the floor was littered with cursed artifacts evil enough to melt your face off.

But the worst part was that nobody was here. Dru was gone, but her cell phone was sitting on the counter. Who would do such an inhuman thing, leaving a cell phone behind?

What if she was dead? What if they were *all* dead?

What if the world really was ending, finally, and there was no one left to stop it, except her? One doomsday threat after another had rolled into town recently, pushing the fate of the world off-balance, and somehow they kept managing to put everything back together again in the nick of time. But they couldn't keep doing that forever. Sooner or later, they would come up against an apocalyptic force they just couldn't stop, and it would roll right over them.

What if that had already happened? What if the end of the world had started tonight and she just didn't know it yet?

Feeling lightheaded, Opal sat down hard on her stool. She took deep breaths in through her nose and blew them out through her lips, counting them out. To calm herself down, she focused on her freshly painted nails. Creamsicle orange, to match her shoes. She breathed in and breathed out, keeping her attention on her nails. Maybe she could mix things up, do a little French manicure so that each white tip of her nails looked like a deliciously creamy bite taken out of a cool, frosty treat. *Oh, yummy.*

But first. What about Dru?

Again, she tried calling Rane, then Salem, even Ruiz. Still no luck. Until somebody answered their damn phone, there was nothing she could do.

"Safety first, honey," she told herself out loud. "Lock the door. Make sure no creeps come in." With another deep breath, she tottered across the store. The street outside looked perfectly normal for a Friday night.

Headlights swept past. The neon signs glowed in the 24-hour liquor store next door. A few itchy-looking people waited at the bus stop. Opal shut the door and turned the deadbolt.

Feeling just the slightest bit safer, she sighed and made her way to the back room. "Place is all torn up. Evil artifacts everywhere. I *just* vacuumed yesterday." She contemplated the candy boxes on the floor and the few cursed artifacts still sitting in the safe. A creepy-looking rag doll. A tarnished gem-encrusted silver cup. An innocent-looking elephant-gray lump of rock, which was actually a cursed geode that devoured the souls of unsuspecting sorcerers. Now, why couldn't someone steal that and save her some trouble?

Opal was the only person around here who *didn't* have magical powers. But she couldn't just leave the safe sitting open, with all of those cursed artifacts up for grabs if someone else decided to break in here and take them.

She drummed her fingernails against the nearest bookshelf, thinking. She would simply close the safe's thick metal door, but it wasn't there anymore. There was nothing left attached to the hinges except a few drips of metal slag.

That meant she had to do things the old-fashioned way. And to be honest, she hated doing things the old-fashioned way. That was why it was called *old-fashioned* and not *new and improved.*

After an eternity of digging through the dusty storage closet, sorting through stacks of cardboard trays, rolls of cash register paper, heaps of cleaning supplies, a household tool kit they never used, and stacks of magazines that they had absolutely no reason to keep, she found the grungy white plastic bucket she'd bought on eBay from a scientific supply company. It had a yellow label on the side emblazoned with a scary red radiation symbol. As if that wasn't frightening enough, it also unnecessarily said, "Caution: Radioactive Material," in giant block letters.

Dru had briefly used the bucket to store a pyramid-shaped pale yellow carnotite crystal that Salem had special ordered. Carnotite formed from meteoric waters that millions of years ago trickled through petrified trees and fossils, dissolving uranium from the surrounding sandstone and forming angular lemon-yellow crystals. It was usually used for spells that peered into the mists of long-vanished ages.

Salem was notoriously tight-lipped about the results of his magical experiments, so Opal had never found out how that particular lark had worked out. Probably badly. But she still had the container.

It was too heavy to carry, so she dragged it instead, duckwalking in her sequined skirt, thinking about how this time she was going to have a serious sit-down talk with Dru about that raise.

With a grunt, Opal unscrewed the plastic lid, careful of her nails, and then pried off the heavy inner lid to reveal the dull gray lead lining. Fine sprinkles of yellow dust still speckled the inside of the cylinder, left over from the long-gone carnotite crystal. But Opal wasn't about to mess with that. There wasn't enough Windex in the world for that job.

One by one, using old salad tongs, she plucked the cursed artifacts out of the ruined safe and up off the floor, storing them safely inside the lead container. She was about to seal it up when she spotted something else.

The door to the upstairs living area had been torn clear off its hinges, and several burned-out crystals were embedded deep into the wood. That didn't look like Dru's work, so into the bucket they had to go. The tongs weren't strong enough to pull them loose, so Opal got out the tool kit she'd found earlier and used needle-nose pliers to dig them out, one by one.

Sweating and tired, Opal had just sealed up the container when a scraping sound came from the front door lock. Dru hustled through wearing a shamefully shabby sweatshirt, with Greyson right behind her, all dressed up and clean-shaven. They both looked like they'd been through the wringer.

At the sight of them, Opal's heart leaped into her throat. Her trembling hands flew to her mouth, and she had to choke back tears in order to speak. "Dru! What *happened?*"

As Dru started to explain, Opal swept her into a tight hug, holding on until the wobbliness in her legs went away. Even then, she let go of Dru only long enough to glare at the usual source of trouble. "Greyson, what did you *do?*"

"Why," he said dryly, "were the cops looking for me?"

Opal put her hands on her hips. "Should they be?"

"It's not his fault," Dru said, ushering Opal toward the back room. "Listen, has another crystal sorceress ever come into the shop, as a customer?"

Opal did a double take. "*Another* crystal sorceress? Honey, you're the only one around."

"Well, apparently not." Dru hurried back to her desk and started digging through her stacks of files and notebooks. "She broke in here, stole the Amulet of Decimus the Accursed, and just about killed us. Have you seen anyone in here with long red hair, lots of leather, shiny jewelry?"

"Only half the people who walk in the door."

Dru took off her glasses and rubbed her forehead with a sigh. "Well, she's older than most of our customers."

"How old, exactly?"

"I don't know. Fifties . . . ish? Sixties? Hard to tell. She didn't act old. She had kind of this timeless look about her."

"Enough magic can do that." Opal shrugged. "Or enough plastic surgery."

"Yeah, she kind of had a Cher thing going on."

"Mmm-hmm. Maybe she had one of her ribs removed."

"That's not a real thing," Dru muttered.

With a relieved sigh, Opal sank down into the armchair that didn't have an ugly scorch mark on the seat cushion. "Well, the only other crystal sorceress I've ever heard of was in the Harbingers."

Dru's head snapped up from her desk. "The Harbingers?" she said around the pencil she'd stuck between her teeth.

Greyson leaned against the doorway. "You mean the crazy sorcerers who created Hellbringer back in the sixties? The ones who wanted to destroy the world?"

Opal nodded. "That's the only other crystal sorceress I've ever heard of. You found one of her spells one time."

Dru took the pencil out of her mouth and faced Opal directly. "You're right. The intruder could be one of the Harbingers."

"That's not what I said." Opal shook her head. "Sweetie, those weirdos have all got to be long dead by now."

"Maybe not. Like Greyson said, the Harbingers knew how to summon up speed demons. And that speed demon we saw tonight was brand-new." Dru kept pawing through her files, nodding vigorously. "The Harbingers set out to break the seven seals of the apocalypse scroll and bring about doomsday. So far, we've seen five of those seals break. All this time, I've been wondering what's been breaking them. But I should've been wondering *who* . . ." Her eyes narrowed.

"What is it?" Opal asked, worried.

"Is it *who* or *whom*?" Dru shook her head and went back to digging. "The point is . . . Oh, wait, here it is!" From the stack of papers, Dru pulled out a brittle black-and-white photo. "Remember the secret laboratory below the Harbingers' mansion, in the desert? That's where I found this."

The photo had turned tan with age, but it was still easy to see the details. Three crazy-eyed men and four women posed in the desert, making arcane signs with their hands. One of the women wore bell-bottom pants, and two wore mod dresses with eye-searing patterns. The last one wore a dark catsuit and matching headband.

Dru pointed. "That's her. She's the one who stole the amulet."

Greyson came over and took the photo. He squinted hard at it before handing it back, looking unconvinced. "Huh. I can see the resemblance, but . . ."

"It's *her*. I saw her face." Dru flipped over the photo and scrutinized the back with her brass magnifying glass. "The names are on the back, but this old ballpoint pen is barely legible. Severin, Alistair, Marlo . . . I can't read the rest." With a groan of frustration, Dru set down the magnifying glass and yanked open another desk drawer. She rifled through it until she came up with a jeweler's loupe. With great care, Dru took off her glasses and lowered her eye down to the photo.

Greyson traded glances with Opal. He looked as worried as she felt, but neither of them spoke.

"Lucretia." With a satisfied sigh, Dru sat up, her face flushed. She slipped her glasses on and blinked at Opal. "Her name is Lucretia."

Opal tried to process her thoughts: that any of the Harbingers could still be alive, that they could've been behind these doomsday plots since the beginning, and that they were trying once again to destroy the world. She was still trying to process those disturbing ideas when she heard an unsettling *thump* come from somewhere outside the shop.

Greyson's head jerked around. His eyes glowed a brighter red. "Something's out there," he said, his voice low and urgent. His tone made goose bumps stand up on Opal's arms.

"Some*thing*?" Dru slowly rose to her feet, her eyes wide behind her glasses. "Or some*one*?"

"Which way?" Opal said, her heart racing. This night was going from bad to worse. As much as she hated to admit it, they needed Rane. Why wouldn't the woman answer her phone?

Greyson stalked down the rows of bookshelves toward the back door, his chest heaving as if he was sniffing the air. His whole body tense, he reached out and grasped the doorknob. Opal knew for a fact that she had locked it when she got here, which Greyson apparently figured out quickly.

With two fingers, he motioned them toward the front door. "Hellbringer is parked out front," he said softly. "Go."

Opal had absolutely no intention of setting foot outside either door until she knew what they were dealing with. "I'm not going out there," she whispered to Dru.

"Me either." Dru rushed around the room, picking up every crystal she could find, like a kid scooping up Halloween candy, until they poked out from between her fingers.

While Dru had innate crystal powers, Opal had to rely on the enchantments of whatever amulets, talismans, and charms she could find. And she had collected plenty over the years. But they were all currently hanging from the rearview mirror of her car, which was parked a few steps outside the back door. If something dangerous was out there, she wasn't about to risk making a run for it.

The unmistakable crash of shattering glass sounded outside. Greyson quickly backed up from the door and looked around until he spied a folding metal chair. He held it up like a club. Opal knew he possessed the strength of a demon, but still. A ten-dollar chair from Target wouldn't do much against an immortal creature of darkness.

Dru's crystals were another story. Her dagger-shaped wedge of spectrolite came to life in her hand, glowing with a rainbow shimmer. In her other hand, she clutched a fistful of other crystals, ready to take on whatever she faced.

The only improvised weapon Opal could find was a shiny new fire extinguisher. It wasn't much, but it would have to do. Besides, she'd used a fire extinguisher once before on Ruiz, and that had turned out just fine.

Greyson looked across the room at them and nodded grimly. "Tell me when you're ready."

Opal cleared her throat, drawing Dru's attention. "Honey," she whispered softly, "you sure you really want to open that door?"

Dru chewed on her lip for a moment, then shook her head no. "You're right," she whispered back, then raised her voice. "Greyson—"

"Okay, go!" He yanked the door open and charged through, chair held high.

"Wait, that's not what I meant!" Dru raced after him.

Opal followed at a reasonable distance, clutching the fire extinguisher in both hands. What she saw outside made her stop in the doorway and gasp.

Her old purple Lincoln Town Car was the only vehicle in the tiny parking lot behind Dru's brick building. Something had smashed the windshield into the car, leaving it a shattered mass that sparkled in the light from the nearby utility pole. Her massive collection of amulets and protective charms, which she kept draped from the rearview mirror, was now scattered across the car's long hood. Some of them lay on the ground, crushed and bent. Others had been torn apart. But most of them were missing entirely.

Greyson's red glowing eyes scanned the alley in both directions. He shook his head and finally lowered the chair. "Whatever did this, it's gone."

Dru slowly approached the purple car and reached one tentative hand out to it. She looked back over her shoulder at Opal, her face creased with fear and sorrow.

Opal stood rooted to the spot. She couldn't force herself to go out there. In all her years of dealing with magic, monsters, sorcerers, undead creatures, evil spirits, and a hundred other supernatural kinds of craziness, nobody had ever messed with her car before. That was a line you just weren't supposed to cross.

"It wasn't Lucretia, or we would've heard her car," Greyson said, coming back to stand next to Dru. He looked ready to tear something apart with his bare hands. "She's not working alone."

"Whoever they are, they're collecting amulets," Dru said, surveying the wreckage. "First Lucretia steals the Amulet of Decimus the Accursed. Now Opal's collection is gone. The question is, why these amulets, and why now?"

"And why me?" Opal muttered. "I ask myself that question all the time."

Dru turned to her. "Is there any common thread between all of these amulets? The same crystal maybe, the same enchantment, the same *something*?"

"Honey, you know I've got an amulet for any occasion. Tiger's eye, amethyst, bloodstone. I've got a Talugh charm against bubonic plague, because a girl can't be too careful. Or I did have one, anyway." She peered out at the ruined car, fighting off a wave of despair. "What about my lucky rabbit's foot? Tell me they didn't take my lucky rabbit's foot."

Dru didn't seem to hear her. "We need more information."

Opal had an idea. "You remember that journal you had, the Harbingers' journal? Maybe it says something in there."

Dru grimaced. "Probably does. And Lucretia might have even been the author. The problem is, a while ago Salem stole the journal from me, disassembled it, and plastered the pages across his wall of doomsday clues."

Greyson's car keys jangled in his hand. "Then let's go get those pages back."

Dru drummed her fingers, obviously considering.

Opal tried to ignore the nervous quivering that started in the pit of her stomach. She cleared her throat. "Honey, if the Harbingers really are breaking the seven seals of the apocalypse scroll, what happens next?"

"The sixth seal is the worst yet. If it breaks, a great earthquake will split the world in half. The seas will boil. The stars will fall from the sky. The world will end." Dru's face turned ashen, and her haunted gaze met Opal's, then Greyson's. "We don't have any choice. We have to get our hands on that journal, or whatever's left of it."

"That's okay. That's not a problem," Opal said, well aware of the nervous squeak in her voice. "Salem doesn't frighten me one bit," she lied.

9

SALEM'S LADDER

Hellbringer's beastly engine quieted from a roar down to a growl as Greyson slowed the car and bumped over a stretch of rusty railroad tracks. They turned onto a nameless road, no more than a strip of cracked and pitted asphalt. Hellbringer's pop-up headlights, sticking up from the car's long, pointed nose, flashed across the graffiti-strewn side of an abandoned-looking concrete building.

"Rane isn't answering my texts." Dru frowned as she put away her phone.

"Mine either. Maybe she smashed her phone again," Opal said from the back seat. "I swear, that girl treats her phone like a gorilla treats luggage."

Dru, wondering at the reference, turned around in the seat and peered questioningly over the top of her glasses.

Opal's eyes darkened as she shot Dru a warning look. "Honey. Don't make me feel old."

"Sorry." Dru faced front again and nervously patted her knees. "I just hope Salem's home. He keeps that place locked up tight with protective spells. I don't want to accidentally step on a magical ward or something and get a fireball in my face." She said it as lightly as she could, but she actually wasn't kidding.

The magical precautions that big-time sorcerers like Salem took to protect themselves often extended into dangerous territory. Dru had always thought they were being overly extreme, but now in light of Lucretia attacking her in her own home and blowing up her safe, she was starting to understand. If anything, Dru was worried that she would end up having to take her security to the same sorts of manic extremes as Salem. But she didn't know if she could ever live that way. What was the point of becoming a sorceress if it made you a shut-in, a prisoner of your own magic?

From the driver's seat, Greyson's deep voice broke into her thoughts. "Salem strikes me as the paranoid type."

Opal reached forward, bracelets jangling, and briefly touched his shoulder. "Oh, sweetie, you don't know the half of it. That man's so crazy he doesn't even trust himself. One time, way back, he told me that if he ever came in looking for a twinned amethyst crystal, I should just shoot him dead on the spot. Now, that's crazy." Opal shook her head in disbelief. "If I was the type to shoot anybody, he would've been buried a long time ago."

There was something about twinned amethyst crystals that jogged loose a memory in the back of Dru's mind. Suddenly, some of Salem's behavior from that period of time made a lot more sense. "Oh! That was when Salem was being stalked by a doppelgänger. It was a creepy one, too. Looked just like him, talked like him, even had his hat. But I knew it wasn't him. For one thing, it was polite. And for another, it ate everything in sight, which Salem just never does. That guy hardly eats. It's like he's going to wither up and blow away."

"He had a *doppelgänger* after him?" Opal said. "See, nobody ever tells me anything."

"Well, that's what Rane said. Then she kicked its ass." Dru thought about that. "I hope she got the right one. You don't think all this time she's been dating the doppelgänger, do you?" She pondered that, then shook her head. As tempting as it was to blame Salem's obnoxious attitude on an inhuman body snatcher, she knew better. That was just the way Salem was.

Greyson steered them around the end of the building and into a vast, empty parking lot. Knee-high weeds grew up through the cracks in the asphalt. "How many times have they broken up?"

"Salem and Rane?" Dru shrugged. She had lost count. But thinking about that made her realize just how nicely dressed up Opal was tonight. Dru turned around in the seat again. "Hey, where's Ruiz, anyway? I thought you two had a hot date."

"So did I." Opal's expression turned sour. "But I guess he's on call tonight for the handyman company, and one of their customers got a toilet overflowing. And he was like, 'Don't worry, baby, this won't be long, I promise. I just gotta go unplug that toilet, and then I'll be right back, and we can pick up where we left off.' And I'm like, 'No, we can't. Not after you've been soaking in toilet water.' Because that is definitely not my idea of romance."

Dru flinched in sympathy. "Ooh. Sorry."

"Don't I know it," Opal sighed. "But hey, I knew what I was getting into, dating a man in uniform."

Dru scratched her hand. "Mmm, I'm not sure those coveralls really qualify as a uniform."

"He's a *man* in *uniform*," Opal insisted, "and that is hot. It's a documented fact."

"We're here," Greyson announced with unnecessary volume as he parked the car right up next to the building. The headlights illuminated a rusted metal fire escape that ran up to the rooftop entrance of Salem's lair. When Greyson shut off the engine, silence settled on them like a cold weight. The moonlight outside made the bars of the fire escape look like a trap waiting to be sprung.

Opal folded her arms. "You two go on ahead. I'll stay right here. Bad enough you made me ride in this demon-powered deathtrap to begin with. I'm lucky to still be alive."

Greyson's eyes glowed like hot coals in the gloom. "You sure you want to stay in the car?"

"This is not my first rodeo," Opal said. "I know what's liable to happen if I set foot outside this car. Did you notice my new outfit? I'm not gonna end up getting covered in dust, or slime, or spiderwebs, or any other nastiness. Uh-uh. Not this time."

"Okay, fine. But if you see any trouble coming," Dru said, "honk the horn."

"Oh, don't you worry. If trouble shows up, I know how to drive a stick," Opal said, then quickly added, "But I would come back for you. Eventually."

"Thanks," Dru said dryly.

The rusted fire escape ladder was already down, which was unusual. Outside the car, Dru traded cautious glances with Greyson, and then the two of them began to climb.

Dru wondered if she was making a tactical mistake. Climbing up the rusty ladder in the moonlight, she felt vulnerable and exposed, despite packing her purse full of her favorite crystals. She had a brand-new protective disk of gold-colored iron pyrite to replace the one that had been burned to a crisp by Lucretia's spell. She also had a thumb-sized purple amethyst crystal to defend against psychic attack, and a silvery cube of galena, in case she ran into any demons. And of course, her trusty spectrolite blade, which had gotten her out of trouble on countless occasions.

Still, she didn't know if that would be enough if they were attacked here. More to the point, she didn't know if her crystal magic was powerful enough. Facing off against a megalomaniacal crystal sorceress with decades more experience and her own personal speed demon had left Dru feeling like the smallest fish in a deep, dark ocean of magic. And she couldn't shake the feeling that the bigger fish was about to snap its jaws shut around her.

She hadn't realized she had stopped midway up the ladder until Greyson's urgent whisper came up from below. "Dru. You okay?"

She shook herself. "Yeah. Sure. Everything's okay." Except that it wasn't. Dru was desperately trying to cobble together a plan to save the world, but everything she had was built on what-ifs and outright guesses. There were no guarantees that she was even on the right path.

She tried not to think about how deeply she was in over her head.

Dru reached the top of the ladder and stepped off onto the building's flat asphalt roof. A gust of wind tugged at her hair, carrying the stench of roof tar still warm from the hot afternoon sun. The roof stretched out before them like a bottomless lake beneath moonlit clouds. On the far side, it butted up against the top floor of the adjoining building, where Salem's black metal door stood open to the night air. Golden candlelight spilled out, casting a flickering rectangle of light across the flat roof.

As Greyson stepped off the ladder, Dru leaned close to him. "Are you picking up anything?" she whispered. "Any kind of danger?"

He straightened up, his nostrils flaring as he breathed in the night air. Then his eyebrows rose. "Wait. Do you hear church music?"

Dru strained to listen. As the wind died away, it revealed the unmistakable timbre of a pipe organ playing an ominous melody. Under any other circumstances, it would have bordered on the ridiculous. But here, now, it chilled her to the bone.

Someone was in there, playing an organ in the candlelight. What if it was the sorceress who attacked them?

Greyson crept toward the rectangle of golden light that spilled out of the doorway. He moved with deliberate steps, his back slightly hunched as if his tightly wound body was ready to explode into action at the first sign of danger.

Dru followed just behind him and off to one side, shadowing him. Even on the dark rooftop, his presence made her feel safer. That was something she would love to get used to, under the right circumstances. But whenever they were together, danger wasn't far.

They paused outside the doorway. Salem's lair occupied the entire top floor of his building. As always, it looked like an antique store had collided with an opera house. Beneath a broad wood-timbered roof, the place was an endless maze of baroque cabinets, ornate chests of drawers, wide shelves piled with corked bottles, earthenware jars, and stained antique laboratory equipment. Lamps burned haphazardly here and there, shedding halos of golden light in between deep pools of shadow.

A massive pipe organ towered over it all, its mountain of vertical pipes gleaming in the candlelight. Ornately carved faces peered down from its imposing wooden frame, a gallery of angels and gargoyles, or possibly demons. The flickering light made them seem to leer and dance. But no one sat at the keyboard. The ivory and black keys danced up and down on their own.

The music, Dru realized with a start, was Bach's Toccata and Fugue in D Minor, which was just a little too on-the-nose, even for Salem. She peered through the doorway, squinting, looking for any sign of movement. Silently, Greyson pulled her back, as if sensing danger. In the darkness beyond, a slim figure lurked.

10
STILL OF THE NIGHT

Salem emerged from a pool of shadow just inside his own doorway. His slender fingers, surrounded by the faint glow of magic, moved as the music played. He was playing the organ from across the room, she realized.

His eyes glittered at Dru from beneath the brim of his top hat. "Evening, sunshine. Friday night a little slow down at the rock shop? I thought you got your kicks from staying home and reading immensely unpopular old books." A sardonic smile quirked up the corner of his lips, but there was an unmistakable fury in his wide gray eyes.

His anger wasn't directed at her in particular. Salem shifted his glare to Greyson standing just behind her. Judging by the way his fingertips stabbed at the keyboard, even from a distance, Salem carried his fury around with him. That didn't come as much of a surprise. But considering the way Greyson puffed up and moved in protectively closer to Dru, clearly *he* didn't understand the distinction, and instead saw Salem as a threat.

Dru intervened before the situation escalated. She laid a calming hand on Greyson's muscled arm and beamed her best customer-service smile at Salem. "Salem, hi! Have you seen Rane? Because she's not answering her phone."

It wasn't a lie, exactly. More of a distraction. But it worked.

After a moment of glowering, Salem turned his head and called out, "Buttercup! Your entourage has arrived." Then he gave Dru a bored look. "I'll let you two catch up. Meanwhile, I have some vengeance to plan." With that, he turned and disappeared into the labyrinthine clutter of his apartment, still ghost-playing the organ. His voice drifted out of the shadows. "Go ahead. Make yourself at home. Please hold your applause until the end of the performance." The organ blared even louder.

As Dru hesitantly made her way inside, Greyson leaned close to her. "This guy takes himself pretty seriously," he growled in her ear.

"They all do. Sorcerers are just that way for some reason. You should see the egos I have to deal with sometimes down at the shop."

He gave her an appraising look. "You're a sorceress. But you aren't like that. You're more down to earth."

She felt her cheeks flush. "Oh. Well. Thank you. But it's kind of a new thing for me, thinking of myself as a sorceress. I still kind of feel like I'm just pretending to know what I'm doing, and sooner or later everyone else will figure that out."

"Modest, too," Greyson said, putting a warm arm around her. "I'm just starting to get a grip on this whole sorcerer underground. I get the feeling none of them know how weird they are."

Dru nodded, basking in the feeling of his arm wrapped around her, the closeness as he walked next to her.

"You're not like them," he said. "You're different."

"Because I *know* how weird I am?"

He drew up short. "Not exactly what I meant."

"I know." She couldn't resist wishing they were alone together, anywhere else but here. Someplace quiet and safe, and romantic. Mentally, she kicked herself for not taking Greyson up on his offer of a candlelit dinner. But first, she had to find the Harbingers' journal. And that meant she had to explain a few things to Greyson in order to keep him out of trouble.

"So, listen, I'm not trying to say that all sorcerers are jerks. But the ones who *are* tend to wear it on the outside. You know how some tropical insects and amphibians are brightly colored to warn you that they're toxic?"

Greyson nodded solemnly, then glanced down around their feet as if checking for creepy-crawlies.

"No, I mean metaphorically. Salem gives off certain signals as an indication that he's dangerous. There's a reason for that. It's best to keep your distance, or at least keep your cool around him."

Greyson didn't look convinced. "If I had to, I could take him."

She wasn't sure if he was serious, and she couldn't tell from the look on his face. Maybe he was just trying to reassure her. She patted his arm. "That's sweet. Let's never let it come to that." Having Salem as an enemy was a terrifying thought. She'd seen him blast things apart with just a pointed finger, or send cars flying with the flick of his wrist. That was why she tried as hard as she could to keep him on her side. Unfortunately, she didn't always succeed.

They came to a sort of a clearing in the center of the clutter of old junk and antiques. A few mismatched chairs from a previous century stood arranged in a row, as if lined up for a table that had inexplicably vanished. She wasn't sure if they were meant for actually sitting on or not.

Before she could decide whether to sit down, Rane padded in on bare feet, blonde hair sopping wet, wearing nothing but a beach towel emblazoned with rainbow-colored parrots. At just over six feet, she stood as tall as Greyson, and the beefy muscles in her bare arms rippled as she dunked a protein bar into a glass of thick green smoothie. "D! What's shakin'?"

"Big trouble. Just now, somebody—" Dru was interrupted by Rane loudly slurping the protein bar clean. "A sorceress named Lucretia broke into the shop. Stole an evil artifact that could kill millions of people. And then somebody else trashed Opal's car."

"Ouch. Bummer about the car." Rane tilted her head back and chugged down the protein shake. With her back arched, and her bare skin shining in the candlelight, she somehow managed to look like a bodybuilder posing on a very strange stage.

Dru cleared her throat and awkwardly motioned toward Rane's towel, which was barely holding on by a twist of damp terrycloth. "Careful. Maybe you should keep a hold of that. You don't want to accidentally, you know, drop anything."

Rane shrugged and wiped her mouth with the back of her hand. "Don't worry. I'm basically dry by now. So what's your plan?"

"We already have plans," Salem called out from the darkness. "In fact, some of us are already ready to head out again, Buttercup. So, chop-chop."

"Hey, relax, will you?" Rane shot back. "You're not the one who had to ride into the danger zone on a shopping cart." She took a bite of her protein bar and turned to Dru, chewing. "Shopping cart went flying, by the way. With me on it. It was *so* rad."

Dru nodded sagely, as if she had any idea what Rane was talking about. Sometimes, it was best not to ask. "These things happen," Dru said.

"Damn right they do." Rane stuffed the rest of her protein bar into her mouth, making her cheeks bulge. She talked around her food. "Salem's paranoid we're being spied on. Somebody stole his man-jewelry earlier, and he's totally convinced it was a setup. He thinks somebody's watching us."

That was a creepy thought. Dru looked around nervously. The majority of the vast room was in shadow, beyond the rosy pools of light from the scattered lamps. "Do you think he could be right?"

"Maybe." Rane tossed back her damp blonde hair. "So I figure, if they're watching, why not give them a show?"

Dru took another look at Rane's damp towel, this time with an uneasy feeling of dread. "Please don't take off that towel."

Rane frowned. "You know who you sound like? *Every* roommate I've ever had."

"Opal is waiting outside," Greyson broke in, much to Dru's relief. "She's afraid to come in. We were attacked."

Rane nodded. "Protein sorcerer?"

"Um, *protean*?" Dru said.

Rane snapped her fingers and pointed at Dru, then nodded. "Bingo. It was a giant bat, and it nabbed Salem's amulet. So now he's all pissed off because he's, like, naked." She turned her index fingers inward to point at her own towel. "I mean, not *naked* naked. Metaphysically."

"Metaphorically," Dru offered.

"Whatever. He's totally defenseless." Rane dropped her voice to what was probably supposed to be a whisper. "So he's ready to head back out tonight and kick ass. Me too. I just had to get a shower first. Because, river water."

But Dru wasn't listening. She was still stuck on the part about the protean sorcerer. "I thought protean magic died out thousands of years ago. How could anybody even learn those spells today?"

Rane shrugged. "All I know is I kicked his ass until he was naked, and then he flapped away with the amulet."

Greyson bent closer to Dru. "Sounds like we should be worried about this protean thing." There was an unspoken question in his statement. He didn't know what they were.

Dru nodded. She kept forgetting Greyson didn't have any background knowledge about magic, because he wasn't a sorcerer. Not in the traditional sense, at least. "Protean magic goes all the way back to prehistoric times. Think about Neolithic shamans wearing bear skins, dancing around the cave, all freaking out, until they actually *become* the bear. That sort of thing. Protean magic is based on shedding your higher humanity and giving in to wild, raw animal instinct. Going feral. They literally transform into their totem animals. Bigger, faster, smarter versions of them. But still animals. Lions, hawks, crocodiles—"

"Bats." Rane folded her arms.

"Bats, sure," Dru agreed. "It could be any kind of animal."

Greyson seemed to chew that over. "So, they're werewolves."

Dru blew out her cheeks. That was a vast oversimplification. And also technically incorrect. But still . . . "In the sense that they transform into animals, yes, essentially. At least, according to the legends. But you have to keep in mind that everything we know today comes from ancient texts written by outside observers, who considered them savages to be eradicated. I mean, there were protean sorcerers among the Celtic people, but even the word 'Celtic' comes from the ancient Greek name *Keltoi*, which means 'the hidden people.' We don't know what the Celts actually called themselves, because they didn't leave a written record. As far as anyone knows, protean sorcerers are extinct."

"Guess not," Rane said flatly.

"And yet someone figured out how to bring back protean magic. Maybe the Harbingers discovered something while they were searching for the apocalypse scroll." Everything started to click together in Dru's mind. "Clearly, there's a pattern here. Someone managed to steal enchanted amulets from Salem, Opal, and me, all in one night, in different locations. So these attacks aren't random. They're coordinated. Someone is targeting us. And we have to find them before they strike again. I need to find that journal fast. Like, right now."

"What journal?" Rane asked.

"I'll explain later." Dru threaded her way through all the junk until she reached the far wall, where Salem had pinned up everything he could find about the Harbingers. His doomsday wall had grown considerably since the last time she'd been here, and now it was truly massive, at least thirty feet across. Her gaze roamed over the shaggy collection of pinned-up newspaper clippings, maps, photos, and sketches, some of them connected together with lengths of string in different colors.

Finally, she found what she was looking for: a yellowed page torn out of a half-century-old hardcover journal. She recognized the handwriting instantly, a sort of manic scrawl made up of sharp little jabs of the pen, as if the author was attacking the page. As Dru skimmed the dense handwriting, she tried to make sense of its ramblings. It described the author wandering the deserted cobblestone streets of a place called the Shining City, preparing for doomsday. The wrinkled corner of the page was adorned with a doodle of a seven-fingered hand. It was definitely taken from the journal of the Seven Harbingers.

Dru carefully unpinned it from the wall and looked around for more pages like it. The sheer mass of material on this wall had grown to unwieldy proportions. She had no idea how anybody could find anything in this mess. Finally, she spotted another journal page high up on the wall and reached for it.

She didn't notice that she had left Greyson and Rane behind, or that the organ music had stopped, until Salem suddenly appeared beside her. He nonchalantly leaned one shoulder against the wall and fixed her with a half-crazy stare, made even starker by the black eyeliner around his eyes.

Dru swallowed nervously.

"Do you actually need me to ask you what you think you're doing?" The cold tone of Salem's voice held an unspoken threat.

11
SIGN OF THE DEMON

Dru pretended not to be intimidated by Salem. To cover her nervousness, she stretched up and unpinned the second page. "Maybe you've forgotten the fact that this journal was originally part of the inventory of the Crystal Connection. It actually belongs to me."

"*Used* to." With his thumb and long forefinger, Salem reached out and plucked the pages out of her hands. "But you weren't really using the Harbingers' journal for anything, were you?"

She turned to face him, squelching the desire to yank the pages back out of his grasp. "I need to get that book back. Or at least as many pages as possible. It's important."

"Mmm-hmm." He gave her a look of mock sympathy. "I'm sure it is. But some of us have a more comprehensive view of what 'important' *really* means."

Dru folded her arms. "I need it to find . . . someone." A little voice in the back of her head told her that the less she revealed to Salem, the better. That was difficult, since she naturally wanted everyone to team up and work together. Even him.

But Salem wasn't like that at all. He was a loner. A self-imposed outcast. A believer in the power of one. He didn't play well with others, and that was an unpleasant fact that Dru kept learning the hard way. He jealously guarded his secrets, for reasons that Dru suspected stemmed from an unhappy childhood. But then again, what sorcerer had ever really had a happy childhood?

As the silence stretched between them, she fiddled with her glasses. With an effort, she forced herself to stop and project a confidence that she didn't feel. Why couldn't he just stop being Salem for once and actually try to help out? It was all about him. It was *always* about him.

Well, if that was the way she had to play it, she would play it that way. She would make this all about Salem.

Deliberately, Dru jutted her chin out. "Look, do you want to get your amulet back, or not? Because I understand that without it, you're a lot more vulnerable than you'd like to admit."

Something subtle changed in Salem's face. His swagger became a little more brittle. His fingers twitched. She knew she had hit close to home. She hated to be mean, but if she was going to get this journal back, she had to press her advantage.

"I'm sorry if you're feeling like your powers aren't up to snuff right now," she said, awkwardly trying to goad him. Deliberately manipulating anyone went against her principles, but it seemed to be working. "If you want to take the night off, I understand. The rest of us can handle this. Don't worry, we'll find your amulet for you." She glanced over her shoulder, looking for someone to back her up, and saw Greyson and Rane approaching, trading worried glances.

Dru gave Rane a meaningful look, which Rane completely misinterpreted.

"No, he's fine," Rane said flatly. "Look at him. He's good to go. No worries."

Dru sighed. This was turning out to be harder than she thought.

Rane held out a cautioning hand to Salem. "But, dude, until you get your protective amulet back? Keep your head down. Because solid objects are probably gonna come flying your way at the worst possible moment." She winced. "And you know, without that amulet, you break kind of easy."

The know-it-all look on Salem's face slowly transformed into a smoldering anger. The corner of his eye twitched.

Dru felt badly about Salem's feelings getting hurt, but Rane was actually right. And everyone knew it.

Salem's flinty gaze slid from Rane back to Dru. "You really think it will make any difference if I give the Harbingers' journal back to you? Fine. It's yours."

"Really?" Dru perked up. "Okay, great. Do you have a stepstool or something? I can find it all. It's no big deal, really."

Salem held up a hand for silence. "You're absolutely right. This is no big deal at all." For some reason, the smooth agreeableness in his tone gave her the creeps. It was as if he had just won some sort of game that she didn't even know she was playing. That made her nervous.

Salem's twitching gaze swept across the doomsday wall as if seeing it for the first time. He raised his hand higher, long white fingers spread out. Jagged sparks of energy buzzed and snapped around his fingertips, leaving streaking afterimages in Dru's vision.

The air surrounding Salem glimmered with an unearthly light, and his black silk shirt billowed and snapped in an invisible breeze. An itching heat tickled Dru's skin, making her step back. Shimmering waves of power flowed up and down the length of the cluttered wall, rustling the jumble of maps, photos, and papers. They rippled in the unseen wind that quickly gained strength as Salem's spidery fingers caressed the air.

All at once, the journal pages snapped loose from their various positions across the wall. They fluttered into the air like a flock of white birds startled into flight. As they sailed toward Salem's outstretched hand, they were caught in an invisible whirlwind. They swirled around in a rustling funnel until, with blinding swiftness, they reassembled themselves into the journal.

The cloth-bound covers with their ragged edges cartwheeled through the air and sandwiched the top and bottom of the stack of papers, mashing them flat. The torn edges of the spine stitched themselves back together. Tiny particles of paper and dried glue streaked through the air, like dust motes in a sudden breeze, to fit back into the rapidly vanishing cracks in the binding. In moments, everything about the Harbingers' journal was restored to its original condition, down to the seven-fingered hand crudely drawn on the front cover with countless strokes of a ballpoint pen.

With a sound like air rushing into a long-sealed-up room, the diffused light of Salem's spell swept back toward him, pinpoints sizzling around his fingers like sunlight glittering off ocean waves. Then the magic was gone, and the reassembled journal dropped softly into his clutching hand.

With a satisfied smirk, he turned and held the journal out to Dru.

She swallowed. No matter how much magic she witnessed with her own eyes, there was always something hair-raising, almost transcendent, about watching a masterful sorcerer at work. Nothing in her world ever compared to the experience of being right there at the moment when a magical spell broke through the natural boundaries of the world and did something incredible.

Even something as deceptively small as putting a book together.

Dru took a deep breath and reached for the journal. But just as quickly, Salem pulled it back out of her reach.

"Nah, ah, ah. Not so fast, Twinkles. First, the million-dollar question. *Why* do you need it?"

Dru could barely contain her frustration. She wanted to step right up to him and slap him. For an agonizing moment, she entertained the notion of doing just that. "I *told* you. I need it to find someone."

He made a rolling motion with his finger. "Uh-huh. Already established that. Moving forward. *Whom?*" He inched closer, his eyes taking on a crazy gleam. "A protean sorcerer? Hmm?"

"No." She decided to finally lay all of her cards out on the table. "A crystal sorceress."

She was about to say more when Salem shook his head dismissively. "No such thing. You, darling, are the only working stiff who punches that particular time card."

"Lucretia. Does that name mean anything to you?" Dru folded her arms, impatiently waiting for a reaction that never came. "She's a crystal sorceress, she's one of the Seven Harbingers, and she's here in Denver. She stole the enchanted Amulet of Decimus the Accursed from my shop. *That's* why I need the journal, to find her. Satisfied?"

He gave her a little smile. "There we go. See, was that so hard?" He turned and walked away, taking the book with him.

Dru followed him. "Hey! Wait! I need that."

"You're joking, right? You must be." He sounded surprised as he turned around to face her. "You can't be trusted with something this important. You possessed the Amulet of Decimus the Accursed? *You?*

And then you allowed it to be stolen from you. How did you accomplish that particular hat trick?"

Rane reappeared, scrubbing an extra towel against her hair. "Which one was Decimus again?"

"Moldy old Roman sorcerer," Dru said. "Opal and I outsmarted his ghost a while back. In his time, he was so powerful and evil, and his fortress in Pompeii was so impenetrable, that his enemies assassinated him with a volcano."

"Oh, *that* one. Didn't his enemies have that same badass crystal you used to blow up half the netherworld?"

Dru winced, thinking about the crystal utilized by Decimus's enemies thousands of years ago. She had found it by accident, and she could still feel its weight in her hand, a fist-sized transparent polyhedron tinted nearly black. The most dangerous crystal she had ever seen. She had kept it in the safe behind the picture of Ming the Merciless, where it had stayed until the night that she'd had no choice but to use it.

At the last moment, when it looked as if they were all doomed, she had charged up that crystal using the destructive energy of the evil spirit that had transformed Greyson into one of the Four Horsemen. Her efforts had drawn that evil spirit out of Greyson and made him human again. The earthshaking fireball she had created with the crystal had wiped out the Four Horsemen of the Apocalypse, but it had also demolished the magical causeway through the netherworld, smashed Hellbringer to pieces, and nearly killed them all. So much had happened since then, good and bad, but none of it could ever erase the heartbreaking memory of that terrible moment.

"What kind of crystal was that?" Rane asked.

"Biotite," Dru said, trembling inside at the memory. "It was a biotite crystal."

Rane let out a low-pitched giggle. "That was *awesome*. Let's go get some more biotite."

Salem, meanwhile, paced back and forth in front of his doomsday wall. "I searched for years for Decimus's amulet. And all this time, *you* had it. Unbelievable. Is there no justice at all in this universe?"

Rane turned on him. "Come on, really? Cry me a river, dude. Do you even know what Decimus's amulet does?"

He shot her a dark look.

Dru held up her hands in a placating gesture. "Look, it doesn't matter. We're all just trying to get our amulets back. We all want the same thing."

"*We?*" Salem snapped. "No. *You* just want to clean up your own mess. *I* intend to teach these sorcerers a lesson they'll never forget. It's a simple equation: I was attacked, and now I'm vengeful."

"Fine!" Dru said. "We can do both. Just let me have the journal."

"Is no one else comprehending what a terrible idea that is?" Salem looked around, and his gaze came to rest on Greyson, who up until now had hung back, staying quiet. "And *you*, no one should trust. You are a demonic threat bigger than anyone will admit. How long will it be before you let those blinky red eyes of yours get the better of you, and go back to being an active participant in the apocalypse?"

Greyson didn't visibly move, but somehow he seemed to become bigger. His chiseled chest strained at his shirt as he leveled a no-nonsense glare at Salem. "This is coming from a guy wearing makeup and a top hat."

Salem's eyes narrowed, as if he knew he'd been insulted, but wasn't sure exactly how.

But just then, Greyson lost all interest in the argument. His gaze shot upward toward the ceiling, which was half-hidden in darkness. His red eyes glowed brighter. "Something's up there."

As he spoke, something heavy thumped against the roof. In the distance, glass shattered.

A cold shot of adrenaline ran through Dru's veins. She reached into her purse, digging for crystals, knowing she had only seconds to find something to protect herself. A golden pyrite disk, maybe, or her tiny spectrolite blade. But they were buried somewhere beneath her keys, her lip balm, and an unbelievably thick wad of paper napkins.

Rane's hand shot out to an antique chest of drawers nearby. She touched one of the tarnished bronze lion heads that served as pull handles. With a scraping metal sound like a sword being drawn from its sheath, her entire body transformed into tarnished bronze, towel and all, making her look like an Amazonian monument to bathing.

"Heads up, people!" Rane's voice rang as if she were shouting through a metal megaphone. "We've got incoming!"

An inhuman shriek split the air as something rushed at them from the darkness above.

12
SOMEBODY'S WATCHING ME

There was something primal and terrifying about the way a bat flew, especially when it was the size of a biplane and headed straight toward you. Its long black wings reached up in a V-shape with every beat, nearly brushing the cavernous ceiling overhead. Their leather curves shimmered in the lamplight as they pounded the air, stretching out like huge grasping, webbed hands.

Paralyzing fear rooted Dru to the spot. The giant bat swooped directly toward her, its head down and its beady black eyes fixed. Below its long, pointed ears and toothy open mouth, in the black furry mass of its body, a spot of gold glimmered. Salem's stolen amulet. The bat was wearing it.

Time seemed to slow down to a crawl around Dru as the rest of them sprang into motion. Rane leaped up onto a medieval-looking oak table, bronze fists lashing out as the bat dropped down toward them.

Greyson's strong arms encircled Dru and yanked her off her feet. Together, they hit the floor on his broad shoulder and rolled. He held her tightly, protecting her with his body. Her glasses went wonky, but thankfully stayed on her face.

But the giant bat wasn't interested in any of them. It banked steeply around Rane's fists and flashed past Dru with a blast of air from its wide wings. Its clawed feet aimed straight at Salem. It reached for the book in his hand.

Salem already had his other hand up toward the bat, white glowing magic crackling around his fingertips. Dru caught the fear flashing across Salem's face as he realized his magic wouldn't work on the bat. The amulet protected it.

Then the bat hit him hard, knocking him clear off his feet. The impact sent his top hat tumbling.

But just before Salem went flying backward to crash into the antique desk behind him, the old Harbingers book shot out of his grasp. It flew like a missile, flung by his magic toward Rane. At the last second, he must have realized what the bat was after and tried to pass the book off to her.

But she wasn't looking. She was already jumping off the table, twisting to grab the bat, even though it was much too fast to catch. The book passed behind her back and bounced off a tall wooden chair before flopping to the ground. It lay there in the open, unprotected, and Dru knew it would take the bat about two seconds to pivot around again and snatch it up in its greedy little paws.

She squirmed out of Greyson's grasp and dove for the book.

It was times like this when Dru remembered gym class had been her absolute least favorite subject in school. And no matter how hard she tried to make up for that today with a sporadic devotion to yoga and that one ill-fated line dancing class, they didn't prepare her for anything like this. She managed to grab the book and slide ungracefully beneath the solid oak table just before the furry bulk of the giant bat returned.

Thwarted, the angry bat let out a frustrated screech as it streaked over the table. It flapped hard and circled the warehouse-sized room.

Dru would have been fine with hiding beneath the table until this whole thing blew over, but apparently Salem had other ideas. Back on his feet again and looking more furious than Dru had ever seen him, he waved his white-glowing hands at the table. It lurched into the air as if plucked up by the hand of an invisible giant and then sailed legs-first toward the bat.

With a squawk, the bat changed directions, as the legs of the table stabbed against the concrete wall with a thunderous crash and the sound of splintering wood. Salem, his face flushed and his eyes wide enough to show the whites, swept his hands to the side. The massive table flew through the air to crack against the opposite wall, and again the bat twisted and changed directions.

Rane charged past them, carrying a broken table leg like a club. "Lift me up!" she yelled to Salem. He ignored her, consumed with his attempts to squash the bat.

Greyson's sure hand pulled Dru to her feet. At his touch, she felt his untapped magical power rising inside him, ready to be released into one of her crystals. His red glowing eyes looked her over with ferocious intensity. "Are you hurt?"

She shook her head. "No. But we're going to get flattened if we stay here." She looked anxiously toward the distant door. Between them and their escape was a maze of half-lit antiques and magical junk. Some of the lanterns were smashed, and most of the vast room was plunged into darkness. "Getting there won't be easy."

"Come on. I can see in the dark. Stay close." Still holding her hand, Greyson hunched low and led her through the room, staying away from the wreckage raining down from the aerial battle. Dru held onto the book to keep from losing it, but she didn't have a free hand to dig a crystal out of her purse.

They weaved through the maze, making it as far as the pipe organ when something pushed over a cabinet in the gloom dead ahead of them. It fell with a resounding crash, making Dru's heart skip a beat. But it was only Rane, her bronze skin glimmering in the half-light. "Salem is *freaking* out, dude. You got the book?"

Dru nodded and held it up. "We should go."

"Yeah. Get to Hellbringer. I'll cover you." As Rane spoke, something sinuous slithered through the shadows behind her. A big wedge-shaped head reared up out of the shadows, and a forked tongue slashed the air.

"Snake!" Dru shouted in warning.

Rane whirled, raising the table leg, but a snake tail as thick as her leg lashed out, grabbing her wrist. An oily speckled snake bigger than any of Dru's nightmares slithered off the top of the cabinet and landed on top of Rane, wrapping around her body. She staggered under the weight of its coils.

Dru let go of Greyson's hand and pulled her spectrolite blade out of her purse. It flared to life, bathing them in a rainbow-colored glow. She hesitated to use it, since she had never stabbed another living creature with it. But she would do whatever she had to do to save Rane.

Rane grunted, struggling to stay on her feet as she wrestled with the massive snake. She dropped the table leg, and Greyson picked it up, hefting it like an oversized baseball bat. "Run!" he told Dru.

Still, she hesitated. She needed to help, but she was completely out of her depth here. She knew how to fight demons, ghosts, and ancient curses. But a giant snake was something else.

The snake pivoted its flat head toward Dru, pinning her with its slitted eyes. They were the green-metallic color of tarnished copper. But in their depths, a cold intelligence lurked. Its hungry gaze latched onto the book.

On instinct, Dru backpedaled away from the snake. Its scaly head lashed out at her, blindingly fast. She caught only a glimpse of rows of needle-sharp teeth in a moist pink mouth as its jaws snapped at the book, missing her by inches.

Greyson brought the table leg down on the snake's head with a painful-sounding crack. The snake pulled its head back and struck at him instead, snapping its jaws shut on the table leg. Meanwhile, its tail wrapped around Rane's legs, tripping her.

She tottered and fell backward into Salem's pipe organ. With a haunted wail from its dozens of lead pipes, the centuries-old hand-carved instrument exploded. Wooden splinters and ivory keys flew out in all directions, clattering around Dru.

With a heaving groan, Rane rolled over, trapping the snake's head between her forearms. The two thrashed and wrestled back and forth, obliterating the pipe organ. "Oh, *man*," Rane groaned. "I *just* hauled this crap up here."

With a crackle of magic, the smashed pipes with their pointed ends levitated into the air, one by one. Across the huge room, Salem strode into view, his long hair flying out madly around him. He raised one grasping hand high. The ruined pipes soared into the air, humming an unearthly tune. Above them, the bat continued its erratic dodging and jinking as Salem hurled the lead pipes at it like spears. They shot rapid-fire up through the air, each one whistling a different pitch as it speared into the ceiling, following the bat with staccato, hollow-sounding impacts, like pounding drumbeats.

Greyson knelt and pinned the snake's thrashing tail to the floor, helping Rane. He threw an urgent glance at Dru. "Get to the car!"

The last thing Dru wanted to do was leave her friends in the middle of a fight. She looked from the glowing spectrolite in one hand to the book in the other. If these protean sorcerers got hold of the book, Dru would lose her only clue to finding Lucretia. Then there would be no way to stop her mad plan to destroy the world.

She had to get to safety. After a last look at Greyson and Rane, who nodded once, Dru turned and sprinted for the door. She almost made it.

She ducked around glass-fronted wooden cases, old vases, and a stuffed mountain goat that looked suspiciously familiar. But as she rounded the last cluster of antiques, she came face-to-face with a sinuous form, blacker than the surrounding shadows. It locked onto her with huge golden eyes.

She stopped short, waving the glowing crystal blade in front of her, trying to clamp down on the fear that reduced her knees to shaking jelly.

It stalked toward her, and she immediately backed up. It easily paced her, and when the light of a lone lamp fell across it, it revealed an unmistakable feline outline. A black panther. Its slitted yellow eyes were fixed on the book.

Dru backed up until she bumped against a metal shelving unit, and then she slid sideways a few steps only to find her back against the wall. Her heart pounded, making her feel dizzy. She had nowhere else to go. She was cut off from her friends, even though she could still hear the sounds of their struggle echoing through Salem's huge loft. She wanted to call out to them, but her throat was so tight she could barely breathe.

A cool draft blew across the back of her neck. She tucked the book under her arm and felt behind her, feeling the outline of a huge factory-style window frame beneath flaking layers of paint. It wasn't a solid wall behind her but a huge glass window, completely painted over. Unfortunately, she had no idea how to open it. And even if she did, it was a two-story drop to the asphalt parking lot below.

The panther crept closer, seeming to savor the moment. Its golden gaze never left the book.

Dru held it up. "You're after this, aren't you?" With an effort, she straightened up and tried to make herself look as large as possible. Maybe if she could startle it, she could drive it back. She waved the book over her head and yelled, "Is this what you want?"

The panther's gaze went from the book to Dru's face, giving her a distinctly unimpressed look.

It wasn't entirely an animal, Dru reminded herself. On some level, it was still a human sorcerer or sorceress, which meant it understood her speech. And that meant there was a chance she could reason with it.

Hopefully.

"Um, hi? Look, we don't have to fight about this. I'm Dru—"

It gave her an impatient yawn. Its wide-open mouth revealed long yellowed fangs.

"Well, that's rude, but look. This is just a *book*. You don't have to *kill* me for it."

At that, the panther looked sharply at her, and the corners of its mouth curled upward. Its eyes took on a hungry gleam, and when it showed her its teeth again, she had the unsettling certainty that it was grinning at her.

It was clearly enjoying this.

So the panther did understand her, Dru surmised. And it still intended to kill her. Her heart hammered in her chest, until all she could hear was the sound of her own pulse rushing in her ears. As the fear threatened to overwhelm her, the analytical part of her brain kicked in, as it always did at the worst possible times. Were protean sorcerers so dangerous because their magic robbed them of their humanity? Or were the only sorcerers drawn to protean magic in the first place the ones who were rather inhuman to begin with? Which was the cause, and which was the effect?

It didn't matter, a small voice inside her insisted. Once the panther got its teeth around Dru's neck, she would be dead either way.

She needed a backup plan. Her little spectrolite blade was more of a soul-protecting crystal than a real weapon, useful against ghosts, demons, and evil spirits. It wouldn't do much against a living, breathing foe. Unless Dru could find something else to neutralize or distract the panther, she didn't stand a chance.

Dru quickly glanced left and right. The scratched-up metal shelves on her right were empty except for a white cardboard box full of cheap costume jewelry. Nothing in there would serve as a weapon.

On her left was an open shelf full of dusty antique cameras. Scattered among them was a mind-boggling assortment of different-sized blue glass flashbulbs, each one stuffed with a tangled nest of silvery wires. The factoid part of her brain coughed up the point that the wires were made of zirconium, which made them burn particularly bright.

Too bright for a panther, Dru was pretty sure. If she had all the time in the world, she would rig up some wires to a battery, set off the flash-bulbs, and temporarily blind the big cat. And then she would run like blazes for the door.

But she didn't have all the time in the world. Nor did she have a zirconium crystal in her purse. If she did, she could charge it up with enough magical energy to fire the zirconium wires in the flashbulbs.

Wait. She looked at the costume jewelry again. After spending enough time around Opal, Dru had picked up just barely enough fashion knowledge to vaguely recognize some of the jewelry as being from the 1960s and 1970s. The older jewelry was made with rhinestones, which were just cut glass. But starting in the late 1970s and onward, costume jewelry was often made with cubic zirconia. Otherwise known as zirconium oxide.

In other words, zirconium crystals.

As the panther coiled lower to spring at her, Dru dropped her spectrolite and shoved her hand deep into the box of jewelry. She reached out with her mind, searching for the telltale electric tingle of a crystal touching her skin.

"Dru!" Greyson called. He came running out of the shadows, brandishing the table leg like a club. He zeroed in on the panther and charged.

The panther's ears swiveled around at the sound of his shout, but its golden eyes stayed locked on Dru. Its tail twitched and then went rigid as its muscles tensed to spring. Its long yellow teeth glistened.

Dru's fingers closed around an audacious spherical pendant shaped just like a disco ball. Immediately, she felt the familiar magnetic pull of finely shaped crystals. Not just one but at least a hundred of them. Although the zirconium crystals were small, they were perfectly arranged in a sphere.

Dru closed her fist around the disco-era pendant. Driven by fear and desperation, she pumped every ounce of her magical energy into it, including the residual energy she had picked up from Greyson when he had grasped her hand earlier.

The result was instantaneous. The crystals in the pendant flared with power, multiplied hundreds of times by their spherical arrangement, burning so hot that they scorched Dru's palm.

Just as the panther sprang at her throat, the metal shelves on her left exploded with light. All of the glass flashbulbs went off at once, sounding like a truckload of champagne corks popping simultaneously. The combined flash was as bright as a lightning strike. Even with her eyes squeezed shut, Dru could clearly see the backs of her own retinas.

As Dru threw herself to the floor, the blinded panther's claws swept through her curly hair, missing her skull by inches. Then the big cat passed over her, and the bright air was filled with the sound of shattering glass as the panther crashed through the painted-over window.

Momentarily half blinded herself, Dru looked up from the floor as the giant bat swooped overhead, tucked its wings, and shot out through the gaping hole of the broken window. Dru struggled to her feet, careful not to skewer her feet on the jagged broken glass.

Below, Hellbringer sat in the parking lot, illuminated by the full moon. Opal sat wide-mouthed in the passenger seat as the giant bat plucked the falling panther out of the air and then fled away into the night, wide wings pounding the air.

13
ON THROUGH THE NIGHT

As the giant bat and the panther disappeared from sight, Greyson dropped the wooden table leg and swept Dru into his arms. She let herself melt into his embrace. Unexpected tears burned at the corners of her eyes as all of the fear and desperation of the battle washed over her. As he held her, the fear slowly evaporated into the cool summer night, leaving her feeling jittery and weak.

He kissed her tenderly. "I shouldn't have told you to run," he whispered in her ear. "When I saw that black cat go after you—"

"It's okay. I'm all right." She pulled back enough to look up into his worried face. Only then did she notice the painful-looking gash that stretched from his temple to his jaw.

"Oh my gosh, you're bleeding." Dru dug the thick wad of paper napkins out of her purse and pressed it against the wound.

He pulled back at first, then let her help. "Some of us aren't made out of metal." He gave her a wry smile. "I'll be fine."

Dru nodded, trying not to think about how badly that fight could have gone.

In the parking lot far below, Opal rolled down her window and cupped her hands around her mouth. "Dru! What did you *do?*"

Dru just waved, too exhausted and shaky to yell back. She would explain later.

Opal nodded. "If you need anything, honey, I'll be right down here." Then she rolled the window back up. Hellbringer rocked slightly as she checked both doors to make sure they were locked.

Dru turned back to Greyson. "What happened to Rane? Is she all right?"

Greyson kept looking her over, as if he couldn't quite convince himself that she was unharmed. "She's fine. She cornered the snake."

"Good. Now maybe we can get some answers." Dru picked her spectrolite blade up off the floor and regarded the Harbingers' book. So much trouble for a little handwritten journal. What secrets did it hold?

Probably best to keep it out of sight as much as possible, she figured. With some difficulty, she stuffed the book as far into her purse as it would go, then slung the purse under her shoulder and used her elbow to cover the part of the cover that stuck up out the top. As an afterthought, she hung the disco ball pendant around her neck. There was no telling when that might come in handy again, too.

All the way across the loft in the opposite corner, she finally found Rane, still in metal form, lying on her stomach. The woman stared intently into a bowling-ball-sized hole in the brick wall near the floor. Old wooden bookcases had been shoved aside to reveal it, leaving trails of cobwebs and dust.

Next to her, Salem stood with his hands behind his back, gripping his own wrist until his knuckles turned white. Still missing his top hat, his long hair stuck out in all directions, making him look even more insane than usual. "And how exactly can a snake that size just slip away?"

If Rane caught the exasperation in his voice, she didn't show it. "Same way it got in, dude. *Duh.* Through this hole in the wall."

"And why exactly is there a *hole* in my wall?"

"Huh. Beats me. . . . Oh wait, you remember that cannonball fight we had that one time? That was probably it." Rane looked up from the floor. "What, *now* you're mad about that? Look, are you just gonna stand there, or are you going to give me a light?"

Salem's entire body went rigid. He looked ready to explode.

As unobtrusively as possible, Dru slipped past him and knelt down next to Rane. Spectrolite crystal in hand, Dru willed it to life. Rippling prismatic lights illuminated the hole, allowing them to see that it led to a gap between walls that dropped straight down into darkness.

Greyson squatted down behind Dru and peered into the hole. "If the snake went that way, it's long gone. Could be anywhere by now."

"Yes, *thank* you for that, Captain Obvious," Salem snapped.

Dru straightened up, careful to keep the journal on the other side of her body from Salem, hoping he would forget about it long enough for her to get it out the door. "They're targeting us," she said to Salem. "You realize that, don't you? These aren't just random attacks. These protean sorcerers are working together as a team, trying to separate us. It's the old divide-and-conquer strategy. There's a reason it works. Do we even know how many of them there are?"

Salem's eyes glittered. "Why don't you ask your rosy-eyed boy toy here?"

Greyson straightened up, towering over Salem. "I didn't have anything to do with this."

"So says an honorary member of the Four Horsemen of the Apocalypse," Salem shot back. "Who drives a *demon* car. Not the most trustworthy credentials."

Dru laid a soothing hand on Greyson's arm, causing him to bite off whatever he was going to say next. She took a deep breath and addressed Salem with her most calming voice, the one she reserved for difficult customers at the shop. "The only way we can survive this is if we work together. Can we agree on that, at least?"

"No. Even *you* should be able to understand why not." Salem pointed a long, pale finger at Greyson. "He is part of the doomsday plot. He's dangerous. He's demon tainted. Need I say more? Apparently, I do. Because *once again*, you've brought him into the thick of this, and now look what's happened."

The accusation was so ludicrous that Dru nearly laughed. But Rane beat her to it with a brassy guffaw.

"Oh, *waah*," Rane said, climbing to her feet. "Somebody call the *waa*-mbulance, it's an emergency." With a metal scraping sound, she turned human again. Her tarnished bronze hair became bright blonde, her bronze arms and legs became soft tanned skin once more, and her towel once again became eye-searingly bright. Her face was flushed with exertion. "Dude, Greyson's a stand-up guy. I like him. You see the way he grabbed the anaconda for me?"

Salem just shook his head and looked around theatrically, arms spread out to encompass the destruction that surrounded them. "So this is my life now. Surrounded by amateurs blind to the most obvious danger."

"Hey, I am *not* an amateur," Dru insisted.

Rane pointed at her. "She is totally not."

Salem turned to Rane with a disbelieving stare. "She's not exactly the queen of high security standards, either. The Amulet of Decimus the Accursed? And she just let it go. Two thousand years of ultimate power, gone." Salem snapped his fingers. "Just like that."

Rane shrugged. "Not like you were using it."

Dru glanced at the door. The journal was an uncomfortably important weight in her purse. She needed to get it out of the building before Salem spotted it and used his magic to whisk it away. She stood on tiptoe to whisper in Rane's ear. "We need to go. Right now."

Rane nodded as if Dru had said something profound. "Let's roll." Without any preamble, she turned and headed for the door. Greyson had no problem matching her long strides, but Dru had to hustle to keep up.

Salem watched them go with a look that was part triumph, part confusion. "That's it? You're just going to leave?" When they kept walking, he called out, "You're in a towel!"

"You want to get me to stay?" Rane called back over her shoulder. "Give me a good reason!"

Salem didn't reply. Rane walked Dru and Greyson to the door but didn't step outside herself. Her cheeks were still flushed, and her pupils were wide and dark. "Actually, I *really* want him to give me a reason to stay. After that fight, I'm all charged up. You know what I mean?"

"You mean . . . ? *Oh.*" Dru was already out the door, on the roof, but she was still standing uncomfortably close to Rane. She took a tentative step back. "So, um, we're going to take off."

"All righty. I'm going to go back in there and rip this towel off. See what kind of effect that has."

Dru wasn't sure exactly how to respond to that, so she just gave Rane a thumbs-up.

Rane grinned and shut the door.

With a flash of headlights and a roar of exhaust, Hellbringer flew down the night-darkened streets, spiriting them away from Salem's place at highly illegal speeds. Dru sat in the passenger seat, hands clenched between her knees, not sure at all how she should feel. On the one hand, she was still shaky from the attack. But she was also strangely exhilarated. Despite everything, she now had the Harbingers' journal in her possession. Now she had a chance to find out what it contained. Hopefully, she could use it to find Lucretia and stop her from triggering doomsday.

Opal leaned forward from the back seat, gently picking at Dru's hair. "Honey, you are just covered in broken glass. You know that? Looks like you lost a fight in an aquarium factory."

"I'm just glad there was only the one fight," Greyson said through his teeth. "That Salem doesn't seem to know who his friends are."

Dru pulled away from Opal's gentle hands, feeling angry and frustrated. She looked Greyson up and down. The nasty-looking gash that stretched from his temple to his jaw had already scabbed over. She reached out to him but stopped short when he pulled away. "Are you okay?"

"Fine." The muscles in his jaw worked. "As long as I'm around Hellbringer, I tend to heal fast."

He wasn't exaggerating. The wound healed as Dru watched. The ugly gash knitted itself together, and the scab shrank until it was nothing more than a jagged pink line. Then it too vanished, and the skin smoothed over. Dru watched the entire process with a queasy fascination.

Opal huffed in the back seat. "You know, we used to have a rule. No getting involved in magic outside the shop. You remember that? It's a good rule. We should go back to sticking to it."

Dru shrugged. "Technically, this all started *inside* the shop, when Lucretia attacked us."

"Uh-huh. But then she ran away. You could've let her go, and then there you go. Problem solved." Opal leaned closer. "You know, things like this never used to happen to us. Crazy-ass shape-changing sorcerers creeping around in the middle of the night, smashing windshields, raising all kinds of hell. Whatever happened to the good old days of selling unicorn charms and potions that gave people fabulous hair?"

Dru felt a pang of regret. She could only sigh. "I miss those days."

"You should. I don't know how you're going to sleep at night anymore, knowing that Lucretia might come back to finish what she started. How much time did we spend setting up that grid of crystals around the shop? Planting magically charged crystals in every corner of every room. *Every* room. Even the bathroom. Even behind the ceiling tiles. You remember that? We were super careful about measuring and aligning it, too, and I know we did it right. That barrier should have protected us against *any* kind of spell, curse, evil influence, you name it. But does it stop Lucretia? No. She just breezes right on through." Opal shuddered. "I don't want to say it, but I don't think the shop is safe anymore. Not after this."

"It's as safe as anything can be, these days." Even Dru couldn't muster up any confidence as she said it.

"Uh-huh." Opal didn't sound even remotely convinced.

Dru didn't know what else to say. In a way, Opal was right. Lucretia had walked through the protective grid as easily as if it wasn't there. She had unlocked Dru's front door, found her hidden safe, and popped it open like a pan of Jiffy Pop. Then she had sped away into the night with the insanely powerful Amulet of Decimus the Accursed. Being a crystal sorceress of such immense strength, Lucretia apparently knew how to disarm any defenses or alarms Dru could set in place. That left Dru completely unprotected against a woman who clearly wished her harm. The thought was terrifying.

"The weird thing is that it felt so personal," Dru said. "I didn't even know there was another crystal sorceress out there. And now this. All of the weirdness we've ever fought was sort of just on principle. You know, when things go bump in the night, we bump back. I mean, think about all those evil spirits, monsters, demons. Even a lake deity that one time."

"Evil garden gnomes," Opal added with disgust.

"Yes. And evil garden gnomes. When things like that want to kill people and destroy things, we say *no*, right? We're not going to let them get away with that. When evil hits, we hit back," Dru said.

"Seems to be Rane who usually does the hitting," Greyson pointed out.

"Well," Dru said. "I hit the books, anyway. That counts."

Opal shook her head in disbelief. "Rane. That girl will start a fight anywhere. I've got to tell you something. When I heard all the commotion going on tonight, first thing I did was get out of the car and come over to the fire escape. And you want to know what I realized?"

Greyson's red eyes cut up to the rearview mirror. "That you can't climb a ladder in those shoes?"

"Oh, so you think this is funny?" Opal said with a tone that clearly indicated she didn't. "What was I supposed to do? How was I supposed to help? I don't have any powers. I can't jump in there. All I can do is tell you when you're making a mistake." She said that as if Dru were deliberately sabotaging her. "And I'm telling you now. You don't want to mess with Salem. That man has killed people."

Dru rolled her eyes. "He has not killed people."

"You don't know that. Maybe he has," Opal insisted. "Just look at him. If there's a sorcerer out there who would be voted most likely to kill people, it's Salem. And now look what you've done. Now he's on the warpath. I'm betting my money he's going to come after you first, and then he's going to come to my house and murder me. I can't protect myself against that. All my amulets are gone or torn up. Where does that leave me?"

Dru turned around in the seat, her heart going out to Opal. She didn't believe for a moment that Salem would actually murder anyone, but all the same, Opal's fear was plain to see. "Don't worry. I won't let Salem do anything. Why don't you come stay at the shop? We'll order some Kung Pao chicken and dumplings, do some research. It could be fun."

Opal's eyes grew big. "I won't be safe at the shop. Look what happened to my car!"

"Well, okay, but when we get back to the shop—"

"Nuh-*uh*. No way. You just take me on home. Greyson? You hear me?"

He nodded once, then cast a questioning glance at Dru.

Dru tried to put on a reassuring smile. "Opal, come on. We need to stick together."

"No. *You* need to stick together. *I* need to get out of harm's way. I'm done with this. I'm not doing it anymore."

"Tonight? Or . . . ever?" Dru asked. Opal's words had cut Dru to the core, but it was hard to tell how much she really meant it. Dru was almost afraid to ask. "Opal?"

Opal turned to look out the window, and her curly black hair hid her face. "I don't want to talk about this anymore. Just take me home."

14
SILVER-TONGUED DEVIL

At home, the first thing Opal did was open up that bottle of champagne she'd gotten for tonight's date, which had never happened. No text from Ruiz, either. How long could it possibly take one man to unclog a toilet? She thought it was maybe better not to visualize that.

Instead, she downed the rest of the glass, refilled it, and climbed the stairs to do what she always did to calm down. She took a stroll through her fashion collection.

Over the years, she had painstakingly fulfilled her dream of converting each of her upstairs bedrooms into a giant walk-in closet. The long freestanding racks of clothes were organized by theme, designer, color, and decade. Or at least, that was the theory. In reality, it was a never-ending jumble of colors and patterns bursting with fashion possibilities. And to top it all off, she had two whole walls stacked floor to ceiling with shoes. It wasn't exactly a substitute for a hot date, but it wasn't a bad consolation prize.

No matter how many times she checked her phone, there was still no word from Ruiz. In disgust, she tossed her phone onto the seat of her favorite plush chair, shaped like a giant red high-heeled shoe. When her second glass of champagne was empty, she carefully picked her way down the stairs to get another glass. Or maybe, she decided, it was time to ditch the glass and go for the whole bottle.

She made a mental note to take off her stiletto heels before heading back upstairs again. Long ago, she had learned the hard way that stilettos and bottles of champagne didn't mix well. At least when stairs were involved. Otherwise, stilettos and champagne worked together fabulously, depending on the activity involved.

At that moment, the front door rang out with a cheerful shave-and-a-haircut knock.

Ruiz, finally, she thought. And she even had some champagne left. Opal's heart beat faster. This was all going to work out tonight. As long as that man had a good long shower first.

She spent a moment at the hall mirror fixing her hair and rearranging the plunging neckline of her blouse for maximum effect. Then she composed herself, took a deep breath, and swung the door open wide with a saucy smile.

Outside, Salem leaned one shoulder against the wall, returning her smile with a devilish smirk. "Hello there."

Opal screamed and slammed the door shut.

She twisted the deadbolt knob and threaded the chain, certain she was in mortal danger. While she had been upstairs fondling her designer fabrics and dreaming of better days, Salem had doubtless murdered everyone she knew and had now come to her house to finish the job. She tossed the empty champagne glass aside. As it crashed in the kitchen somewhere, she looked around in a panic for her phone.

Through the door, Salem said, "I'm not going to *hurt* you."

She ignored him. Where was her phone? Upstairs, she remembered, on the chair. Why would she leave her phone all the way upstairs? There was no way she could make it up there in this kind of a hurry.

Then on a side table, she spotted her dusty old landline phone, which she hadn't used in years. Luckily, it was a cordless handset, so she could call for help and run to safety at the same time. Or at least hobble to safety.

She grabbed the phone, thankful when its keypad lit up with a dull yellowish-green light. Her finger hesitated over the digits. What was Dru's number, anyway? She never dialed numbers anymore. They were always just names on her screen.

She shook her head. Considering the way this night was going, Dru had probably been murdered already. Better to call 911 instead.

As she started to tap the keys, an invisible force wrenched the phone up out of her hand. It sailed over her head, out of reach, as she swiped for it, and then zipped over to the brass mail slot in the door. With a squeak, the little brass flapper flipped up, and the phone slipped out like an escaping pet.

Opal watched in horror, her hands clasped to her cheeks, as the chain on her door slid back, undone by invisible fingers. With a metallic screech, the deadbolt lock turned.

Opal tried to run, but she couldn't get more than two steps in her sky-high heels. Cursing under her breath, she leaned against the wobbly side table to unbuckle the little golden ankle straps.

She wasn't fast enough. The deadbolt snapped back, and the door swung halfway open, letting in a gust of cool night air. Salem hadn't moved. He still leaned one shoulder against her wall, his long black jacket swirling in the wind, his silk top hat shimmering in the glow from her porch light. Her cordless phone spun silently in the air a few inches above his pointing finger, like a basketball.

"Relax," he said, his attention focused on the phone, not on her. "I just want to talk."

With an effort, Opal reined in her panic and stood up straight, as if nothing at all was wrong. "You can talk to me down at the shop. Tomorrow. With witnesses present. And a SWAT team, too."

"Hmm. See, that's the thing. At the shop, there's always the Dru factor." A sour look crossed his face, like a moment of bad indigestion. "Not the conversation I'm interested in having."

Opal gripped the smooth wooden edge of the table for support. So he hadn't murdered Dru after all. That was something, at least.

Salem snatched the phone out of the air and rousted himself off the wall. With a weary sigh, he pushed the door the rest of the way open and stepped inside.

Opal's panic level had just barely decreased to a manageable level, but now it shot back up into the red zone again. "You can't come in here! Step back! You're not invited!"

He gave her a strange look. "You can't stop me just by not *inviting* me. I'm not a *vampire*."

"I can do whatever I want. This is my house. Matter of fact, give me my phone back." She held out her hand. "That doesn't belong to you."

For an uncomfortable moment, Salem considered the phone handset. Then he slipped it into the pocket of his long black coat. His kohl-lined eyes stared hard at her. "Let's talk about Dru for just one little moment."

Opal folded her arms. "I've got nothing to say to you, Salem. Whatever your problem is with Dru, you need to take it up with her. Maybe you can talk some sense into her. Because I definitely can't."

"I know. It's awful." He broke off his intense stare with a shrug that looked carefully calculated. "It would be so nice if Dru would just *listen* to you for once, wouldn't it? Maybe if she paid attention when you warned her about trouble that you just *knew* was coming, she would stop dragging you into it. Hmm. Now why does that sound familiar?"

Opal swallowed. She didn't like where this was going.

"Oh, *I* know," Salem said, fixing her with a crazed smile. "Welcome to my world."

"If you want to talk about Dru behind her back, you're wasting my time."

Salem stepped closer, stopping just out of reach. "No, if I wanted to waste your time, I would tell you that I can see the future. And you want to know what I see in the future?"

Opal shook her head no. "Not particularly."

"I see Dru accidentally causing the end of the world. Despite her best intentions," he said conspiratorially, leaning closer as if they were best friends. "Now, I can't *actually* see the future. But I have done some quick-and-dirty, back-of-the-envelope calculations. And I can tell you that ultimately, things are not looking good for Little Miss Monkey Pants."

"Haven't you been paying attention? Things never look good," Opal said.

"Exactly!" He said it as if she were agreeing with him. "You want to keep her out of harm's way, and so do I. We're after the same thing. But if Dru keeps heading the same direction she's going—and I'm sure this comes as a shocking surprise—she's going to die. Oh, wait. Let me put on my shocked face." His eyes grew theatrically round, his jaw dropped open, and he covered his gaping mouth with the long fingers of one hand.

As much as Opal despised Salem's condescending attitude, she couldn't entirely disagree with him. Dru was definitely headed toward major trouble, and she probably wouldn't listen to reason until it was too late. By that point, there was no telling how much damage would have already been done. Or who might have already been killed.

But no matter whether Salem was right or wrong, he was still the last person she wanted to have this conversation with. And despite the fact that it didn't seem like he was actually planning on murdering anybody, she still wanted to get rid of him as quickly as possible. Probably the best way to do that was by bringing up Rane.

"So where's your girlfriend during all of this?" Opal said. When he pretended not to understand her question, she impatiently added, "Where's Rane?"

He shrugged again. "After our little tiff—which I'm sure you heard about, since she demolished two tons of deconsecrated musical instrumentation—I don't know. Honestly. And this will probably distress you to learn, but I really don't care. She'll be fine. She can take care of herself. She always does. Your friend Dru, on the other hand, is the one I'm truly worried about."

"Uh-huh. Tell me another one."

One of his eyebrows quirked up. "Fine. I'm madly in love with you and your nail color. What is that, orange sherbet?"

She honestly couldn't tell if he was complimenting her or being a total brat. Before she could figure it out, Salem leaned close, his gray eyes widening until the pupils were tiny dots.

"I pay attention to details," he whispered. "That's how I see the danger that's coming. Greyson. Notice anything different about Mr. Red Hots lately?"

It took all of her effort not to shrink away from Salem's intensity.

"He's nothing but a cog in the doomsday machinery," Salem whispered. "Tick tock."

His words didn't entirely make sense, but they still hit home. Opal wanted to know what he was getting at, but she figured she was better off not knowing, so she kept her face neutral. She wasn't about to buy into whatever sly double-talk Salem had in mind. So many times, Dru had warned her not to let Salem get inside her head. And this was definitely one of those times.

"I don't need to hear this." Opal pointed one finger past Salem, toward the door. "You need to leave. Right now."

Salem drew in a breath as if to say more and then quite obviously had second thoughts. "Fine. Have it your way." With a flourish, he turned and strode toward the door.

Against her will, Opal desperately wanted to hear what he had to say next. She didn't trust him for a minute, but she needed to hear it. Only one person in the world had studied doomsday more intensely than Dru, and that was the guyliner-sporting madman about to leave her foyer.

If Salem had some kind of information, some kind of way to get through to Dru and warn her before everything went to pieces, then Opal had to know. These days, things felt different between her and Dru. With Dru now a sorceress, her power was growing faster than anyone knew how to deal with it. Deep down, Opal suspected that Greyson's presence had something to do with that, but she didn't know how it worked, exactly. Greyson seemed like a nice enough guy, but how much did any of them really know about him?

What did Salem know that he wasn't telling?

As if sensing her hesitation, Salem paused with his foot on the threshold, and then he slowly turned to look back over his shoulder at her with an unspoken question written across his face. His eyebrows rose up.

Opal folded her arms. The frown on her face was so concentrated that she could feel it squeezing the blood out of her lips. She had absolutely no intention of buying whatever Salem was selling. But the truth was that his words had opened up a secret hurt, a secret fear that she had kept hidden all this time. What if Dru did get herself killed? What if she did trigger the apocalypse?

Salem slowly pivoted in the doorway until he was facing her again, then leaned his shoulder against it. His long black coat rippled as he folded his arms, mirroring her body language. Quietly, he said, "I know you don't like me. And that's fine, because truth be told, I'm pretty much a jerk. But together, you and I, we can end this whole thing before anyone gets hurt." He held up one pale hand, thumb and forefinger an inch apart. "All I need from you is one teensy little favor."

Opal's throat had gone dry. Every instinct within her insisted that she needed to throw this Gothic sleaze right out the door and go wash out her ears with soap. But still, what could it hurt to just hear him out, just for a minute, if it meant saving Dru and everyone else? Not to mention saving the world? It was just one conversation. She could always say no.

Frowning, Opal toed the purple carpet at her feet. "What kind of favor, exactly?"

15
DANCE WITH ME

That night, for the first time in a long time, Dru was too afraid to be alone. After the battle at Salem's place, dark thoughts hung over her, making the night close in around her. After Greyson dropped off Opal at home, he drove Dru back to the Crystal Connection. Neither of them spoke. There was only the constant growl of Hellbringer's engine between them.

Opal was right. Once alone in her shop, Dru would be a sitting duck if Lucretia decided to come back, or a protean sorcerer struck again. And who knew what other unknown dangers were lurking out there?

But at the same time, Dru hesitated to ask Greyson to stay with her. She didn't want to give him the wrong impression. They hadn't known each other long, and she wasn't ready to take things to that level. Especially not tonight, when emotions were already running high. It was far more complicated than she was prepared to deal with right now.

She was still debating what to say when Greyson parked behind the shop, next to Opal's purple Lincoln and its smashed windshield. He left the engine running as he got out of the car, opened up Hellbringer's trunk, and pulled out a long black L-shaped tire wrench. Hefting it in his hand like a club, he slammed the trunk lid shut and opened the passenger door for Dru. "Ready for this?"

She wasn't, but she swallowed and nodded anyway. Clutching the journal to her chest, she got out of the car.

Greyson stepped in front of Hellbringer and made a circling motion with his finger, as if encompassing the city block around them. "*Patrol*," he told the car in a commanding voice. His eyes glowed a brighter red.

Hellbringer's white backup lights came on, lighting up the trash-strewn alley behind. The demon car backed up, headlights off, and crept away down the dark alley, engine purring.

Dru watched it go with a mixture of surprise and awe, then turned to Greyson. "What just happened? Where did you learn how to do that?"

"Do what?" He blinked, and the fiery red glow in his eyes faded to dull embers. "You talk to Hellbringer all the time."

"Sure, okay, but I say, 'Please don't run me over.' It's not the same." She pointed down the alley. "You just gave *orders* to a *speed demon*. And it obeyed. Doesn't that strike you as, I don't know, seriously freaky-spooky? I mean, if you're in charge of a demon, what does that make you?"

He seemed to consider that for the first time, then shrugged. "I dunno. I'm not sure what I did. I just figured maybe we should have Hellbringer watch our backs. Better than leaving the car parked all night."

"True, but still . . ." She pursed her lips and stared down the length of the dark alley, but Hellbringer was already gone. "Won't he run out of gas? And what kind of gas do you put in that thing, anyway? I mean, is premium really going to cut it? Do you need jet fuel or something? Liquid brimstone? The blood of virgins? Please tell me it's not blood."

"I used to think the fuel gauge was broken, because it always reads full." He shrugged again. "Eventually, I figured out Hellbringer just never runs out of gas. Guess he runs on hellfire or something."

"Well, that sounds just lovely," Dru muttered. "And totally not a danger to our mortal souls or anything."

He smiled wryly. "Come on. Let's make sure the coast is clear."

They went in through the back door and checked every inch of the shop, then her apartment upstairs. She checked for unusual magical auras with her ulexite crystal and tested the strength of the quartz crystals hidden in each corner of the shop. She even rang her tingsha cymbals and burned a thick wad of sage leaves to smudge the space. In the end, despite Dru's misgivings, the shop appeared to be completely empty.

Only then did she start to relax. At least to a degree. She would have felt better with even stronger crystal defenses, but she was already doing everything she knew how.

Apparently satisfied that the place was empty, Greyson set down the tire wrench in the back room, next to one of the ugly plaid over-stuffed armchairs. He stretched out his arms and shoulders, and his joints popped. He winced, no doubt feeling more than a little beaten up after his confrontation with the giant snake.

"Sorry about tonight," Dru said, meaning it. "Can I get you some ice or something?" The moment the words left her mouth, she remembered she didn't actually have any ice cubes in her freezer. Or much of anything else, really, except for some frozen vegetarian samosas that had probably been in there since the Obama administration.

But Greyson just shook his head. "I'm okay. Ever since I . . . *connected* . . . with Hellbringer, everything just heals." He rolled up the cuff of his sleeve and flexed his well-muscled arm. "See? Not even a scratch."

Dru laid her fingers on his arm, wondering how much they could trust the source of this healing power. Not long ago, she had been abso-lutely sure that Hellbringer was evil. But since then, despite the demon car's aggression and blatant disregard for safety, it had proven itself loyal to them. Had Hellbringer really changed for the better, or was this helpful streak only a trick to lure them deeper into danger?

Dru's fingers lingered on Greyson's arm, the heat of his body warming her hand. They were in a precarious position, the two of them. They'd been thrust together by events entirely outside their control, and yet somehow they seemed to complement each other perfectly. Sometimes, it felt as if he were reading her mind.

She found herself again considering what would happen tonight, after this moment. Would she send him home? Ask him to stay?

What would he say? What would he do? And most importantly, what did she want him to do?

She looked up into his red glowing eyes and had to remind herself that his powers came from a demonic source. Because if she didn't think about that, if she didn't remind herself of the potential danger, she might start kissing him and never stop. With that thought in mind, she dropped her gaze and stepped back.

He nodded to her, almost imperceptibly, and she could feel the heat of his gaze. "You need to get some sleep. Because tomorrow you need to figure out how we can go after this Lucretia and get that amulet back."

"Right," she said softly.

"See you tomorrow." He looked like he wanted to say more, but he clamped his jaw shut. Just as she was about to ask him not to go, he settled down into the ugly armchair with a weary sigh.

"You're . . ." Momentarily befuddled, she pointed at the back door and then at his chair. "Okay. So . . . You're just going to sit there all night?"

He leaned back in the chair, and his eyebrows went up. "You have other ideas?" There was a warmth in his voice that made her knees go weak.

"Um, no, not . . . really?" She glanced at the open space where the door used to be that led up to her apartment, before Greyson had ripped it off its hinges. At that moment, she was acutely aware of the fact that he was watching the direction of her gaze as it climbed the stairs toward her bedroom. She suddenly felt awkward and utterly confused about what she wanted and what the right thing to do was. To hide her nervousness, she took off her glasses and rubbed them on the edge of her shirt.

"Hey." He reached out and caught her arm. Without her glasses on, he was no more than a Greyson-shaped smudge in her vision. But as he stood up and drew her close, every detail of him sprang into sharp focus. His dark eyebrows, his broad jaw, the swell of his chest. The scent of him, the heat from his skin, and the feeling of his solid body as he pulled her close were all too much to resist.

She kissed him, and all of her worries and fears vanished. For one perfect moment, there was nothing else in the world but his kiss. Having him with her, right here, right now, that was all that mattered.

When she pulled back, she had to take a breath in order to collect her thoughts. She needed time to think.

"I'll be right here if you need me," he said intensely. "For anything."

"Greyson, I can't—"

"Shh. I know. I'll be right here." He gave her a crooked smile. "When this is all over, maybe you'll let me take you out on a real date. How's that sound?"

Emotions overwhelmed her until she couldn't even begin to sort them out. Everything tonight had been too much, too fast, too dangerous, too everything. She was used to taking her time and analyzing problems, doing research, isolating the problem, and finding the most achievable solution. But there was no solution to anything she felt. It left her overwhelmed.

As he backed away, she slipped her glasses on. "What . . ." She cleared her throat. "What would be your idea of a real date?"

He gave her a lingering look. "You'll see." Then with obvious reluctance, he sat down in the chair again and placed the metal tire wrench across his knees. "For one thing, there'll be a lot more dinner involved and a lot less crashing into buildings. That's a promise."

"Well, that's good to hear. Although I suppose you could combine the two and lend a whole new meaning to 'drive-through.'" The moment she said that, she wished she hadn't. "Sorry."

He laughed anyway. It sounded a little forced, but she still liked it. She bent over his chair and gave him another quick kiss. "Thank you," she said softly. After a moment of hesitation, she went upstairs.

Headlights off, Hellbringer slips through the dark alley. His driver has ordered him to patrol, and he does so gladly, relishing the freedom to move unseen through the night. But with that freedom comes the insatiable desire for speed.

The alley ends, and the road stretches to either side. His senses extend along the asphalt, searching for his enemy.

Soulbreaker. The red speed demon. He is out there, somewhere.

In the time Before, when the herd of speed demons had roamed free across the burning wastes of the infernal pits, Soulbreaker had been his constant tormentor.

Then, half a century ago, the redheaded sorceress Lucretia had summoned Hellbringer, and with pain and fire she had bound his essence into the black metal body of this winged muscle car. Though trapped here in this cold realm, Hellbringer had at least been free of Soulbreaker.

But no more.

Now Soulbreaker has been given his own form, a modern red muscle car, and now his very presence made Hellbringer's tires spin with fury. At the thought, his engine races with the urge to take to the open road and hunt Soulbreaker down. And get even.

But his driver has ordered him to patrol, and he reluctantly obeys that command. With impatience, he waits for an ordinary car to pass by, headlights burning mindlessly. Then he turns around and stalks back along the alley, alert for danger.

Because he knows it's coming. Sooner than the humans expect.

16
LUCRETIA, MY REFLECTION

After everything that had happened tonight, Dru was far too wound up to sleep. She spent hours studying the handwritten book, soon becoming certain that Lucretia had written it. But it was less of an actual journal and more of a manifesto describing all the reasons why the world was too sick to survive. Dru slogged through half of it, despite the impenetrable handwriting, before she just couldn't take any more. There were almost certainly insights hidden in there somewhere, if she could somehow read between the lines. But the journal was just such a tightly wound rant of cruelty and condemnation that eventually Dru had to set it aside.

How could she hope to prevail against someone driven by so much hate . . . who knew all of her magic tricks and more . . . who had been a practicing sorceress since before Dru was born? Lucretia was perhaps the ultimate crystal sorceress, a gifted adept who had devoted her entire life to mastering the quirky logic of crystal magic. Clearly, Lucretia was capable of casting spells much more powerful than Dru had ever dreamed of. Dru was still fairly new to the idea that she was a crystal sorceress at all.

Now, faced with an enemy who not only outclassed her but who also had no qualms about using deadly force to achieve her goals, Dru felt defenseless. Vulnerable. It was an awful feeling, a raggedy fear that gnawed at her thoughts. What if Lucretia came back for this book?

No matter what happened, Dru also knew that she couldn't let Lucretia get away. Even if the woman wasn't intent on destroying the entire world, which Dru suspected she was, Lucretia was at the very least in possession of an artifact that could destroy millions of lives. Sooner or later, Dru would have to confront her again, because Lucretia had to be stopped.

But until then, Dru had to use every moment she still had left to prepare for the inevitable confrontation. She had to find some kind of leverage she could use to her advantage. Otherwise, barring some kind of miracle, Lucretia would undoubtedly crush her. Dru didn't stand a fighting chance. How could this possibly end in anything other than her own death?

Eventually, she turned out the light and tried to sleep, but it eluded her. Her gaze kept going back to the nearly invisible rectangle of the journal sitting on her nightstand. If there was one thing Dru knew for certain, it was that she couldn't take on Lucretia alone. She needed Opal, Hellbringer, Rane, and maybe even Salem. And most especially, she needed Greyson.

She could still feel the ghost of Greyson's kiss on her lips. Greyson, who had originally walked in her door not even believing in the supernatural, despite the fact that he was cursed to become one of the Four Horsemen of the Apocalypse. She had tried everything to save him, and then when he had disappeared, she had risked everything to find him. More than once, he had put his life and even his soul on the line to save her.

How could Salem be so quick to condemn a man like that?

About three in the morning, Dru crept down the narrow stairs and peeked out through the open doorway. Bare chunks of wood still hung from the hinges where Greyson had ripped off the door during the fight with Lucretia. He still sat in the ugly armchair, with the grungy metal tire wrench lying across his knees. His head lay tilted to the side, and his broad chest slowly rose and fell as he dozed.

Careful not to make a sound, Dru picked up a red checkerboard blanket from another chair and draped it over him. Alone with her thoughts, she watched him sleep. With his eyes closed, he looked peaceful and perfectly human.

She resisted the urge to kiss his stubbled cheek, not wanting to wake him. Instead, she turned and crept back up the stairs. As she reached the top, her phone chimed with a new text message. Curious, she checked it and was startled to see that the message was from Salem.

D. You awake?

Dru sat on the edge of the bed, puzzled. First, Salem had never texted her before. And second, he never called her "D." Only Rane did that. It took Dru only about two seconds to figure out what had happened. She tapped out a quick reply.

Did you steal Salem's phone?

Yeah, Rane texted back. *My phone is in the river.* A moment later, she added, *Stupid bat.*

Dru couldn't help but smile at that, even though it wasn't really funny. *Are you and Salem OK?*

Well. There was a pause. *The towel totally worked. But then he got all wiggy about his pipe organ.*

For an awkward moment, Dru wondered whether that was actually a thinly disguised metaphor, or whether she really did mean a pipe organ. He probably wasn't too happy about seeing that smashed to smithereens.

So I split, Rane continued. *At my place now. Going to catch some Zs. Will go look for proteins first thing.*

Dru resisted the urge to type "*Proteans*," since it would only tempt the wrath of the autocorrect gods anyway. Instead, she wrote, *Sorry if I got you in trouble.*

He just needs to deal. Get anything from that book?

Dru sighed and stared sadly at the book. So much was riding on this, and she felt as if she was failing every step of the way. *Nothing. I don't know what to do.*

Cowgirl up, Rane replied instantly. *You got the brains. You GOT this.*

Dru just shook her head. Rane always had such unbreakable faith in her. It was hard to live up to. Dru decided to change the subject. *Any sign of the bat?*

Not since we kicked its ass, Rane replied. *Has to be somewhere. Not sure where to look tho. Bats don't leave footprints.*

That was a good point. Dru tapped her teeth with her fingernail until an idea struck her. *Panthers leave footprints. Maybe they are together. You were attacked by the bat down by the river?*

Yes. Brigadier seen it there 3x before. Maybe there is a lair. Rane was quiet for a moment. *Good thinking D. Will start by the river.*

Dru nodded to herself. *Just don't go after these sorcerers alone. Wait for me.*

Rane sent her a grinning smiley face. *Whatever! You do you. I'll punch them in the face.*

From anyone else, that sentiment would have been metaphorical. But Rane obviously meant it. Dru wished, not for the first time, that they could all just join together as a team. But it never quite worked out that way.

Rane went silent after that, and Dru could only assume that she had finally gone to sleep. Dru wanted to do the same, but her mind was spinning with thoughts about Lucretia, the protean sorcerers, amulets, and most of all this troublesome little journal.

With renewed determination, Dru lit a few candles, sat down cross-legged on the floor, and set Lucretia's journal before her. There had to be something in it she was missing. And she was determined to crack the mystery before sunrise.

She grabbed her yellow lined notebook and started scribbling down her impressions of the journal. Its apparent age (circa 1969), its structure (cloth-bound hardcover), its condition (good, with light scuff marks and shelf wear typical for its age). The seven-fingered hand crudely drawn on the cover with a ballpoint pen was creepy enough on its own. But it also reminded Dru of a protective sigil.

She got up and retrieved a round-cornered cube of ulexite from her nightstand. Sitting on the floor again, she pressed the seeing stone to her forehead and concentrated. At first, her magical energy refused to be coaxed. But as she steadied her breathing and focused, her energy gradually flowed into the crystal. Her vision swam, and the world around her lit with an ethereal luminescence. Here and there, sparks of magic glowed softly in her vision as she picked up the presence of charged crystals and the minor enchanted artifacts that lay scattered around her room.

But Lucretia's journal stayed dark. It wasn't enchanted.

Dru dropped the crystal in frustration, trying to ignore the queasy feeling as her vision snapped back to normal. It didn't make sense. Why would a crystal sorceress put so much time and energy into handwriting an entire book, if it wasn't magical? Could it be just a political manifesto and nothing more?

Possible. But highly unlikely.

Dru spent the next few hours trying out different crystals, all without any success. She looked for traces of crystal dust, invisible ink, and every other magical trick she could think of. But no matter what she tried, she came up empty-handed.

There were simply no enchantments on the book. Nothing. That was probably the reason Dru had ended up with it at all, she realized. Over the past few decades, other sorcerers had probably scrutinized the journal as closely she had, but never spotted anything unusual about it. So they had tossed it aside, one after another, until it had eventually wound up on the bookshelves of the Crystal Connection.

Dru took off her glasses, rubbed her tired eyes, and glared at the inscrutable journal. By candlelight, it was only a smudge in her vision. Without her glasses, all she could see of the pages was uneven patches of gray that represented endless angry scribbles. With a heavy sigh, she put her glasses back on and started reading again.

Only then did she realize that she had noticed something when her glasses were off. Some of the individual letters were darker than others, having been emphasized with multiple pen strokes.

She took off her glasses again and looked closer. Those emphasized letters weren't scattered randomly around the page. They were spaced evenly around the page in an almost perfect circle.

With growing excitement, Dru put her glasses back on and took them off again, checking and rechecking. It appeared that the letters had been written down first, and then the rest of the rambling writing was scribbled in there to connect them.

That was why so many of the sentences were disjointed and nonsensical. It wasn't a journal at all. The words were a decoy. There was a code hidden on each page, in plain sight.

With her glasses off, Dru flipped through the pages, looking at the spacing of the bold letters. After the circle, the next page contained a concealed hexagon shape, and the page after that held what looked like a capital letter N superimposed with an infinity symbol.

Sorcio signs. The secret language of sorcery.

With her heart beating faster, Dru eagerly flipped to a new page in her notebook and began to copy down the sorcio messages hidden in the pages. Sorcio was a complicated language, and the signs changed meaning depending on their sequence and proximity. They were often used to write out complicated spells, but they could also contain a simple message or warning.

Dru didn't yet know what the message said, but she intended to find out. The sorcio signs were no doubt hidden in the journal for a very good reason. Was it possible the book contained some esoteric knowledge Dru could use as leverage to take on Lucretia? Could it reveal the location of the apocalypse scroll, the artifact that was responsible for doomsday? If Dru could find it, she might have a fighting chance to save the world.

Her excitement at finding the secret message quickly dimmed as she realized she didn't have Opal there to help her crack the code. A horrible feeling settled on her as she contemplated the idea that Opal might never come back.

As the first dim rays of dawn broke through the darkness, Dru got up and went over to the window. Peering down into the tiny parking lot behind the shop, she saw movement in the shadows. Hellbringer crept down the alley, headlights off, like a sinister black blade slicing through the night. She watched with no small measure of apprehension as the possessed car slipped out of sight, apparently circling around the block again.

She shivered. Even though she knew that the infernal car had been forged in the pits of hell and had been created expressly to carve a path of destruction across the living world, she was glad to have it on her side. But how strong was its allegiance, really?

As one of the Harbingers, Lucretia must have been present in 1969 when Hellbringer's demonic spirit was summoned up from the abyss and bound into the form of the muscle car. It was possible that she had, in fact, cast the spell that created Hellbringer, just as she had recently created a new red speed demon for herself. Could Lucretia use her crystal magic powers to gain control of Hellbringer? Could she turn the demon car against them?

And by extension, what would happen to Greyson? His powers came directly from the demon car. If Lucretia could control Hellbringer, did that mean she could strip away Greyson's powers, leaving him dangerously vulnerable? Or worse, could she somehow take control of him, the way the Four Horsemen had, and transform him into a tool of destruction?

What if Salem was right, and Greyson was a bigger danger than anyone realized?

The turmoil of her thoughts threatened to tear her apart. She couldn't reconcile the dangers she foresaw to the man sitting downstairs guarding her with his life. Intellectually, she could add up the potential liabilities the way Salem apparently had and decide that Greyson was too big a risk. But deep in her heart, she just didn't believe it.

Something inside her told her that Greyson was much more worthy than he appeared. Despite the darkness that surrounded him, there was something about Greyson that was inherently good. She couldn't justify her feelings, but she felt them so strongly that she couldn't just ignore them.

Greyson was worth saving. He had *always* been worth saving. And he always would be. It didn't matter whether Salem or anyone else believed that. Because Dru did, and she knew it with a conviction that she couldn't explain to herself, much less anyone else.

As sunrise broke over the city, it sent swaths of golden light sweeping down the sides of the brick buildings and onto the dusty purple frame of Opal's Lincoln Town Car, which was still parked behind the shop. The shattered windshield glittered in the light like a tiny lake of ice.

Poor Opal. Dru couldn't blame her for being spooked. But looking down at the sad state of the purple Lincoln, Dru knew she couldn't let things end this way. She had to do something about it. And that gave her an idea.

An idea so crazy that it might just work.

Brimming with renewed energy, Dru got herself freshened up, brewed up two cups of hot coffee, and brought them down to greet Greyson with a smile.

He got out of the chair and stretched, grimacing. Dru reached up and smoothed out his mussed-up hair, then kissed him sweetly.

He smiled. "You sleep okay?"

Instead of answering that, she handed him a cup of coffee. Blowing the steam off her own mug, she said, "So. Do you know how to replace a windshield?"

He sipped his coffee and gave her a wry look. "Is that a trick question?"

"Nope. I'm just not sure how much car stuff you do."

"*All* the car stuff." He savored the coffee. "Why, do you have a plan?"

She liked the breezy way he said it. Despite the aching grittiness behind her eyes, she smiled brightly. "I always have a plan."

17

GLUE GUNS BLAZING

The warm morning light poured in through the tall factory-style windows in Greyson's garage, bathing Hellbringer's sharp black curves in an unusually cheerful glow. Parked safely at home, its engine and lights off, the demon car could almost have passed as an ordinary, non-possessed car you might see parked in any garage.

Almost. But even sitting still, Hellbringer looked dangerous enough to devour anyone who got too close.

On the gray concrete block wall behind the demon car hung a sign that someone, presumably Greyson, had made out of a No Parking sign and a speed limit sign. They had been cut apart and welded together, so that the sign now read, "NO SPEED LIMIT."

Dru pondered that from her perch in the back seat of Opal's purple Lincoln, parked next to Hellbringer. At her insistence, Greyson had driven the car here and parked it in his cavernous garage while Hellbringer had slunk along behind them like a dog carrying its own leash in its teeth.

Now Dru clambered around the perfume-laden interior of Opal's car with a bag full of crystals, a measuring tape, and a hot glue gun. Carefully, she measured the width of the faded back seat and placed a shimmering quartz crystal in the exact center, just behind the top edge of the seat. A quick squirt from the hot glue gun anchored it in place.

She had her curly brown hair tied back in a handkerchief, and a pair of giant yellow plastic protective earmuffs clamped over her head, making her feel like some kind of crafty air traffic controller. She pressed on the quartz to make sure it was firmly anchored in the glue and then pulled the measuring tape across the football-field-ish length of the back door.

Greyson gently tapped on her arm, and she pulled off the hearing protectors. He had finished vacuuming out the broken glass with his robot-shaped shop vac, and he jerked his thumb toward the garage door. "They're here."

Dru had meant to be finished by now, but she had just run out of time. She would have to explain her plan to Opal as she went along. Hopefully, considering all they'd been through together over the years, Opal wouldn't still be mad at her. Dru clambered awkwardly out of the car and stood there wringing her hands as Greyson rolled open the double-width garage door.

Ruiz's rusted old van idled outside, aluminum ladders on top shining in the sunlight. It beeped as it backed up, filling the garage with the stench of exhaust. The back end of the van fell into shadow as it stopped just outside the door, taillights blinking red for a moment. The engine cut off.

Ruiz hopped out, a stocky Latino guy with an infectious smile and seriously abused work coveralls. He didn't have any magic powers of his own, but he came from a long line of sorcerers, much like Opal did. Ever since the night he had accidentally set off a spell and covered himself in magical flames, and Opal had doused him with a fire extinguisher, he'd been head over heels for the woman. Of course, nobody acknowledged the fact that Dru had actually been the one to put out the fire, using a red onyx crystal. But it didn't matter. As long as Opal was happy, Dru was happy.

Which was kind of the point of all of this activity here in Greyson's garage.

With his hand, Ruiz smoothed his black hair back across the top of his head. Then when he saw Dru, he gave a little wave. He ambled to the back of the van and opened up the back doors, revealing a long, thin wooden crate made of raw lumber and black metal straps.

Greyson came up and looked it over. "They give you any trouble?"

"No, man, no trouble at all," Ruiz said quickly. "You must be in tight with those boys, huh?"

Greyson shrugged slightly. "I've given them a fair amount of business."

Dru hurried over to introduce them, but they were already exchanging names and shaking hands. When Ruiz let go, he shook out his wrist as if his hand had gone to sleep. Then with nothing more than a nod, the two of them wrestled the crate out of the back of the van.

Opal got out of the passenger door and minced her way to the back of the van, avoiding Dru's gaze. "Ruiz, for the last time, *what* are we doing here?"

He grunted as he picked up his end of the crate and followed Greyson into the garage. "I told you, it's a surprise, baby."

Opal put her hands on her hips, watching him go. "A surprise?"

Dru looked at Ruiz and then back at Opal. "Baby?"

Opal waved it off, but she also kept avoiding Dru's gaze. "What on earth is my car doing here?" She marched through the garage, shooting an accusatory look at Hellbringer. "Don't tell me my car's possessed, too. This cannot be happening to me. A girl can only take so much in one weekend."

Dru hurried to keep up. "No, no, we're fixing it. Making it better. See?" She pointed to the two men as they pried the wooden crate open with crowbars, revealing a brand-new windshield wrapped in plastic.

Opal's hands flew to her mouth and stayed there as Greyson inspected the windshield and nodded in satisfaction. "Looks good."

"All *right*." Ruiz grinned and turned to Opal, holding both thumbs high in the air. "It looks good!"

Dru pulled a piece of yellow lined paper from her pocket and unfolded it, showing Opal the diagram she had sketched out in pencil. "See? I'm putting a protective grid of crystals around the inside of your car, kind of like what we have in the shop. It should keep out intruders, at least the non-magical ones. Which, by the way, will keep your new stereo safe and sound. Also, hopefully, it will block out any sort of curses. Maybe some minor spells, too."

Opal was frantically fluttering her hands at her own face, eyes squeezed shut, obviously trying not to cry.

"I'm sorry. About everything." Dru was about to go on when Opal swept her into a perfume-scented hug.

"No, *I'm* sorry." Opal released her and sniffed. "Are you okay?"

Dru nodded. "Yeah."

"Okay." Opal sniffed again. "Show me what you've got."

Eagerly, Dru held up her sketch again. "Look. I've got the whole thing gridded out, so you're surrounded by protection. The crystals go all the way around, from the dashboard, to the doors, to the . . . um . . . spacing between the windows."

"Pillars," Greyson said as he put away the crowbars in one of his tall red toolboxes and shut the drawer with a clang.

"Pillars, yes." Dru didn't look up from where she traced her finger along the lines of her sketch. "You're even protected vertically, too. From the floor all the way up to the ceiling."

"Headliner," Greyson called over his shoulder.

"Yes, *thank you*," Dru snapped. She rubbed her aching eyes, then held up her sketch for Opal's approval. "See? Pretty good, huh? We should've done this years ago."

Opal lifted her gaze from the paper to glance at Greyson, and she cracked a smile. "You don't like it when somebody else knows more than you, do you?"

"He doesn't know *more* than me," Dru muttered. "We just have different areas of expertise. He knows cars. And I know all the important stuff. See?"

Opal looked amused at first, and then her expression changed to concern as she studied Dru more carefully. "Honey, did you even sleep last night?"

Dru shook her head. "Doesn't matter. I've got enough coffee in my system to make a frozen mastodon tap dance. I'm good to go."

Opal looked her up and down with a critical eye. "Mmm-hmm. If you say so."

Ruiz came up to them but cast one last look at Greyson. "Okay, I gotta go, man. You got this?"

"Yeah, I've got this. Thanks." Greyson lay the new windshield down on an old towel spread across his workbench and started pressing new black rubber weatherstripping around the edges.

Ruiz turned to Opal. "Sorry, baby, I gotta go. I'm supposed to be done installing this new sink by lunchtime, and I'm not even there yet." Over her shoulder, he spotted Hellbringer for the first time, and his eyes went wide. His voice shot up at least one octave, maybe two. "Oh, *man*! Look at *this*! What is that? A Superbird? Tell me it's not a Superbird!"

"It's not a Superbird," Greyson said. He didn't look up from the windshield he was working on. He was obviously used to that kind of reaction.

Ruiz stepped around Opal and approached Hellbringer, fingers extended as if reaching toward a mirage, scarcely believing it was real. "Oh, man. Oh, *man*. What a sweet car!"

Opal cocked a hand on one hip. "That car is definitely the opposite of sweet."

Dru was about to warn him away from Hellbringer when the engine roared to life, making Ruiz jump. The amber running lights in the front of the car lit with a fiery glare.

The engine revved out an angry warning. The twin blasts of its hot exhaust blew clouds of dirt off the concrete floor, sweeping it clean, like the snorting of a bull ready to charge.

Dru suddenly suffered an immediate flashback to the last time this had happened in this very garage, when the car had actually run over Rane in an attempt to crush her. Luckily, Rane had survived because she had been made of solid metal at the time.

Ruiz wasn't made of metal.

With an effort, Dru pushed Ruiz away from the nose of the car, toward safety. Then she laid a calming hand on Hellbringer's hood. The hood was already heating up, and the revving engine made it shake beneath its chrome tie-down pins. "Shh. It's okay. Ruiz is a friend." But her words didn't seem to have any effect.

Greyson crossed the garage with long strides, pointing a finger at Hellbringer. "*QUIET.*" His eyes glowed bright red.

The engine idled for a few more tense seconds before it shut off. But the amber running lights continued to burn against the black paint, like the eyes of a wild predator in the night.

"See?" Opal said in the awkward silence that followed. "Told you that car isn't sweet."

Ruiz's gaze pinballed around the room before coming back to rest on Hellbringer again. "So, anyway . . . I gotta go." He backed away toward his van, and Opal followed him to say goodbye.

After the danger had passed, Dru wondered about Greyson's growing control over the demon car. Was he taming the car and bringing it around to their side? Or was Hellbringer simply responding to some sort of growing demonic influence within him? For that matter, was Greyson mastering his demonic powers, or were they mastering him?

With those dark thoughts in mind, Dru headed back to the purple Lincoln to finish hot-gluing crystals to the interior.

Dru was deep in thought when she finally noticed Opal's knowing stare. That jolted her back to reality. "What?"

Opal's eyebrows crept upward. "I know what you're doing."

Dru cleared her throat. "Um, what am I doing, exactly?"

"You didn't bring me down here *just* to fix my car. There's something else going on."

"True." Dru took a deep breath, sucking in a double lungful of air. "You remember that journal I took home from Salem's place?"

At the mention of Salem's name, Opal looked suddenly guilty, but she didn't seem inclined to elaborate.

That was also strange, but Dru already had enough oddball things on her plate. Opal had never liked Salem, and that was that. Meanwhile, Dru led Opal over to the workbench where she had left Lucretia's book. "It took me all night, but I found a secret code in this book. There are sorcio signs hidden on every page. But I can't decode them all on my own. I need your help. See?" After Dru pointed out how the symbols were hidden, she pulled out her notebook, where she had sketched out most of the symbols in pencil. "It's some kind of secret message. I think it might lead us to the apocalypse scroll. If that's the case, we need to find it, like, yesterday."

Opal spent a few minutes flipping forward and backward through the pages, her forehead growing more and more wrinkled with worry.

Finally, just when Dru couldn't stand to wait anymore, Opal shook her head. "This is more dangerous than you think."

Dru stood up straighter as a creepy feeling tingled up and down her spine. "What's the message?"

"It's not a message. It's not anything about the apocalypse scroll." Opal turned deadly serious. "This is Lucretia's spell book."

It was as if a giant phonograph needle squealed across the surface of Dru's brain, bringing every thought to a screeching halt.

Lucretia's.

Spell.

Book.

"Whoa . . ." The implications of that fact turned over and over in Dru's mind, overwhelming her, blotting out the rest of the world. Dru had scrambled, scrounged, and researched just to find one of Lucretia's spells, and it had taken her an enormous amount of effort to figure out how to cast it. That had been the spell she had used to find Greyson when he went missing. It had been one of the most powerful spells Dru had ever cast.

That was just *one* of Lucretia's spells. If Dru could figure out *all* of them, how powerful would she become?

Opal shrank away from the book and Dru, as if guessing her thoughts. "You can't go down that road. She's one of the Harbingers. You can't try to do the kinds of things that woman can do. You shouldn't."

"But I could. I've done it before," Dru said through numb lips. Her voice came out a whisper.

"It's too dangerous. You have to know that."

"That might be true. But at the same time, this could be exactly what we need to give us a fighting chance against Lucretia." Dru stared at the book as if it were a loaded gun.

How dark were the spells contained in those pages? If she tried to learn them, what would be the cost to her sanity, her life, her soul? How much power could Dru actually handle before it destroyed her? And yet, could these be the exact spells she needed to defeat Lucretia, get the amulets back, and stop doomsday?

How far was Dru willing to go in order to save the world?

18

HOW TO FIND YOUR
INNER MERMAID

As Dru finished installing the crystal grid inside Opal's old Lincoln, her thoughts kept drifting back to Lucretia's spell book. How many dusty bookshelves had it sat on over the past half century while no one suspected its true nature? Unimaginable power lurked within those pages, promising exactly the kinds of supernatural abilities Dru once thought she would never possess. But now that she had cracked the code, the possibilities were suddenly laid open before her.

Of course, so were the terrifying dangers of magic too powerful for her to handle. If she botched a spell, it could be fatal. Messing around with a Harbinger's spells was such a bad idea that Dru refused to bring it up again. Still, she kept thinking about it.

Opal shot warning looks at her, which Dru was able to avoid, at least for a little while. Before too long, Greyson finished installing the new windshield, and Opal pulled her long purple car out of the big cluttered garage. She sat outside in the driveway with the engine running and the window rolled down, waiting for Dru.

Reluctantly, Dru followed her outside, squinting in sunlight hot enough to wilt Greyson's green lawn. "See you back at the crystal shop?"

"It's Saturday. Supposed to be my day off."

"Oh. Is it Saturday? Wow." Dru felt unanchored. Everything was moving too fast. She couldn't keep up. And she desperately needed sleep.

"But considering there's an evil sorceress trying to bring about the apocalypse, I think that definitely calls for some overtime," Opal said magnanimously. "First, I'll get us something to eat. What do you feel like?"

"I don't know. Breakfast burritos? Duffeyroll? Yummy's Donuts? I'm so hungry."

"Then let's go with all of the above." Opal tossed her head. From the driver's seat, she frowned up at Dru. "You remember the sorceress that used to come into the shop all those years back, the girl in the black Panama hat with a red ribbon?"

Dru had to think back. After a moment, she did remember a bone-thin woman with a sharp nose and piercing eyes, wearing a black hat slashed with a blood-red ribbon. She was always drumming her red fingernails on the countertop, interrupting Dru every time she tried to explain how different crystals interacted. The woman kept glancing over her shoulder, as if someone or something was constantly closing in behind her and she was desperate to stay one step ahead. "Kind of jumpy? Kept coming in for hematite crystals because she was burning them out with negative energies?"

"Mmm-*hmm*. That's the one."

"Gosh, she hasn't been by in forever. What about her?"

"Nobody knows." Opal gave her a no-nonsense look. Her voice dropped to an ominous low that raised goose bumps on Dru's arms. "She got into dark magic like this. Nobody *knows* what happened to her. Just one day, she was gone without a trace. Nobody ever found her body, either. Her body and soul were *consumed* by dark magic."

"Um . . . I thought she kind of freaked out and moved to Arkansas to be a mermaid in a tiki bar?"

"What?" Opal blinked. "No. Uh-uh."

"Pretty sure she did." Dru tapped one fingernail on her teeth, vaguely remembering a stream of gag-worthy underwater photos with a luminous smile, a wavy red-haired wig, a seashell bikini top, and swim goggles. "She was posting that stuff on Facebook for a *really* long time. Ugh."

Opal waved her hands as if trying to ward off an annoying insect. "That's not the point. I don't care if she discovered her inner mermaid or not. Originally, that girl got into some seriously dark magic, the kind that crushes the soul of anybody who uses it." Opal jabbed her finger into the air to punctuate her words. "Same kind of magic in Lucretia's spells. The kind of spells that hurt people, sow the seeds of destruction and chaos, all of that negativity. Magic that brings you power at other people's expense. It's the worst thing for you, honey. You can't be messing around with that."

With one hand, Dru shaded her eyes against the glare of the sun. "Even if the fate of the world is at stake?"

"See, that's the kind of thing Salem always says. And where has that got him?" Opal's expression darkened. "It's not right. And it's not safe. You go too far down that path, and there's no coming back. It won't hit you until it's too late. You won't even know that you've gone too far."

Dru thought about that, and suddenly the answer came from deep inside her. She folded her arms across her chest. "Well, if the world comes to a fiery end, I guess that means I haven't gone far enough."

Opal just stared up at her, looking worried.

"I have to find a way to track down Lucretia. And I have to find a way to fight her." Dru couldn't help but notice how small and quiet her voice sounded. She was badly outclassed, and both of them knew it. "I'm not going to just let her bring on doomsday. I have to fight back somehow. I don't have any choice."

Opal gave her a warning look. "You always have a choice. Remember that."

Dru bit her lip. She knew arguing wasn't going to get her anywhere. Opal was right, in a way. She always was. That was what made this so incredibly hard. Because in times like this, you could be right and so totally wrong at the same time.

Her brooding thoughts were interrupted by Greyson strolling up to them, wiping off his hands on a red rag. "Somebody say breakfast? The arepas truck is usually down by the park on Saturdays." He jerked his chin in that direction.

Opal perked up. "Mmm. Arepas. Oh my word, Ruiz brought those the other day. I thought I'd died and gone to heaven."

"Didn't bring *me* any arepas," Dru muttered.

Greyson's teeth flashed as he grinned. "You go on. I'm going to grab a quick shower. Meet you back at the shop." He gave her a quick kiss. It seemed to linger on her lips as he turned and strolled back inside.

Dru watched him go, not realizing she was staring until Opal cleared her throat.

In a low voice, Opal said, "You need a shower, too?"

"No, no. Of course not. N-not right this second."

"I think you *do*."

Clearing her throat, Dru pushed aside her suddenly vivid thoughts of Greyson, feeling the heat rising to her cheeks. She polished her glasses, even though they were already perfectly clean. She had to stay focused. She had to get back to the shop and decipher as many spells in that book as possible. There had to be something useful hidden in those pages.

With a deep sigh, she walked around to the passenger side of the long purple Lincoln and got in. "We have work to do."

Opal gave her a knowing look, then put the car in gear.

There was no mistaking a wolf track, Rane knew.

It was like a dog's track but bigger and leaner. And in this case, it was huge. In the morning light, the wolf footprint looked positively cavernous where it was pressed into the muddy dirt near the river. Rane squatted next to the track, gawking over its size. It was bigger than her palm. And she would be the first one to admit that her hands were anything but dainty.

With an experienced eye, she studied the way the toe and claw depressions were deeper than normal. The wolf had been running at a good speed. Plus, considering that the edges of the track hadn't dried yet, it must have crossed the river sometime in the last few hours. Probably about dawn.

Rane clicked her tongue in thought and drummed her fingers against her bare knees. She'd been looking for panther tracks since first light, hoping that the panther had spent some time prowling around on the ground near its lair, and could lead her back to the bat. Assuming these critters were hiding out together.

But panthers left a smaller footprint, with the toes in closer to the pad of the foot. And since they had retractable claws, they left no claw marks in the dirt. These tracks clearly had claw marks in front of each toe. It was a wolf to be sure.

Was there a wolf sorcerer in the gang, too?

Rane shrugged. Sure, why not? The bigger question was: how many of these animal sorcerers were there? The bright side was, the more sorcerers there were, the more ass there was to kick.

Time to limber up. She stood up and stretched, rolling her head until the bones in her neck popped.

She considered the wolf track in the mud. Over the years, she had tracked plenty of coyotes through the outskirts of the city, as well as more than her fair share of monsters. Mostly, the more unnatural creatures tended to hole up underground or hunt in a limited area to avoid getting caught.

Clumps of green shoulder-high bushes crowded both banks of the river. The nearest road bridge was a half mile in either direction. It was conceivable this thing could come running through here all the time, and no one had seen it yet.

Or if they had, they hadn't lived to tell about it.

She kept tracking the giant wolf along the river until it headed into a rundown industrial area bordered by chain-link fences and No Trespassing signs.

She ignored those on a daily basis.

Rane followed the giant wolf's trail through the bushes, climbing up from the river. The shallow tread of her running shoes had trouble getting purchase on the steep slope, and her shorts offered no protection against the scratchy branches. She debated transforming into rock or metal, but she was miles from Salem's place, and she wanted to pace her energy burn. No telling how long it would take her to find these animal sorcerers, and she wanted to be fresh enough to bust their asses without breaking a sweat.

At the top of the slope, the sagging chain-link fence proved to be easy to slip through. Rane studied its weather-beaten metal links, finding a few strands of bristly gray fur.

Wolf fur, probably. Either that or somebody had snagged his ZZ Top beard on the fence, and that *had* to have hurt.

Probably a wolf, though.

Beyond the fence lay an abandoned asphalt lot. From the deep gouges in the pavement, it looked like it had been used to park some kind of heavy equipment, maybe bulldozers or something else with treads. But nothing had been parked there for a long time. Weeds grew up through the cracks in the pavement.

Rane stayed hidden in the bushes, soaking up the surroundings, looking for hiding spots for the bad guys. On the left was a deserted gravel access road lined with wild trees. The air over it was clear, with no hanging dust, so no vehicles had driven by anytime recently. A few hundred yards away, empty flatbed trailers were parked in a long row, along with something that looked like an industrial drilling rig. In the hazy distance, the shimmering towers of downtown Denver poked up from the horizon. Softly buzzing power lines stretched across a cloudless, hot blue sky.

Huh. Not a whole lot going on.

On the right sat a windowless shell of a small house halfway through the process of shedding its dark brown roof shingles. At one point, someone had painted the walls the exact green color of mint chocolate chip ice cream. But now that was peeling off, and the place just looked diseased.

Next to that sat a long two-story building of crumbling white-washed brick. Some kind of warehouse with tiny boarded-up windows and four big loading docks. Rusted metal junk was piled up against one wall. Around the corner, a peeling metal side door stood halfway open, revealing darkness inside. It was easily big enough for a giant wolf to get through. Or anyone else, for that matter.

Rane waited a couple of minutes to make sure nothing moved. Bored out of her skull, she was about to step out of the bushes and keep going when a flicker of movement passed beyond the open doorway. She couldn't see what it was exactly, but it wasn't human.

Bingo.

Something was in there, and it was about to have a *really freakin'* bad day. She hadn't started this beef with the protean sorcerers, but she was sure as hell going to finish it.

She stood up, already itching for the fight that she knew was coming.

19
DOOMSDAY WRITINGS

Sitting next to Opal on the old Lincoln's plush bench seat, Dru took off the disco ball necklace she'd gotten from Salem's place. With a flourish, she hung it from Opal's rearview mirror.

"Aww, look at that," Opal said. "It's disco-tastic."

Dru smiled. "And hopefully only the first of many amulets to come."

At that, Opal turned on disco music, and the swirling upbeat melodies lifted Dru's mood. As they drove, Dru hungrily tore the foil off a steaming arepa and was immediately swaddled in the savory aroma of fried plantains, melted cheese, and creamy guacamole, all wrapped in a fluffy grilled cornbread wrap. It smelled so good it almost made her cry.

"I don't know how you can eat and read while we drive. I get motion sickness in the car." Opal waved her own arepa at the open book in Dru's lap, nearly dripping a thick green dollop of guacamole onto its pages. "By the way, just so you know, I'm against everything you're doing with that book."

"Yeah, I know." Dru took her eyes off the page long enough for a huge, delicious bite. Her coffee had already worn off, and she still desperately needed sleep. But at least she had food now. Despite Opal's warnings, Dru was determined to keep going until she was able to decipher at least some of Lucretia's crystal magic spells.

As they left Greyson's sketchy neighborhood in the rearview mirror, they drove along a stretch of nondescript tan-and-gray industrial buildings: auto body shops, heating and air-conditioning companies, a brick warehouse festooned with graffiti.

"Must be something good in that book, though," Opal said, her mouth full.

Dru sighed. "Well, I'm pretty much playing connect-the-dots to find the symbols. It makes me feel like an amateur astronomer." At Opal's puzzled expression, Dru drew a jagged line in the air with her finger. "Connecting stars into constellations? Anyway, that's the first problem. The second problem is that there are apparently even deeper layers of meaning buried in here." Dru flattened Lucretia's book against the dashboard. "The letters 'PbS' appear here and here." She flipped through a few pages. "And again, here and here. Different symbol, different spell, same three letters. That can't be a coincidence. What's so special about 'PbS'?"

"That's an excellent question." Opal chewed slowly, deep in thought. They rolled up to a red light and waited. "Hmm. How about CNN? Is that in there?"

Dru flipped back through the pages. "No . . ."

"What about HBO? Showtime? Nick at Nite?"

"No, it's not PBS, it's— Never mind." Dru sighed.

Opal brushed errant cornbread crumbs off the crystal that Dru had glued to the inside of the driver's door. She peered closely at the two-inch length of quartz, frowning. "I am going to snag my sleeves on that, you just watch. Did you have to glue that thing right to the armrest?"

"Sorry. That's where the measurements placed it. I figured if I was going to create a protective grid inside your car, the measurements had better be as accurate as possible," Dru answered absently, still stuck on the "PbS" mystery.

Opal complained a little more, but Dru was focused on the book. Different three-letter combinations appeared over and over on its pages, but Dru had no idea what they could mean. The way they were spaced out reminded her of grids like the one she had created inside the Lincoln. The exact placement of each crystal was important. So was the particular combination used. Maybe the physical location on the page represented the actual physical location of the crystal, and the letters were some sort of code for the *type* of crystal.

The traffic light turned green, and the Lincoln accelerated. They hit a pothole, eliciting a rattling sound from the ashtray, where a silvery cube rolled around. Dru finished her arepa and picked up the cube, immediately recognizing it as galena. That brought back memories of desperate times.

Dru couldn't help but wince when she thought about how much time she had spent driving around in cars, trying to fight the forces of evil. She had used galena to fight the Four Horsemen of the Apocalypse and their speed demons—the possessed muscle cars they drove on their mission to destroy the world. Hellbringer had originally been one of their demonic steeds. Galena crystals burned demons like fire.

Dru set the galena back in the ashtray and watched it rattle around. She wouldn't be able to keep something like that in Hellbringer's ashtray without burning him. "You ever wonder why galena harms demons?"

Opal shrugged. "Who knows?"

"I mean, galena is a lead sulfide, but there's nothing about lead that— Wait a second." An idea hit Dru like a bolt of lightning. She slapped her hands down on the book hard enough to make Opal jump. "PbS is the scientific notation for *plumbous sulfide*," Dru said excitedly, pushing her glasses back up her nose. "Also known as lead sulfide. Your friend and mine, good old *galena*. See?" She picked it up from the ashtray.

Opal finished her arepa and crumpled up her dirty aluminum foil with obvious satisfaction. "Yeah, I know galena is a lead sulfide. But why would Lucretia put that in her book?"

"It's in so many of her spells. She uses crystals the same way I do. Only, of course, much better than me."

"That's debatable," Opal offered.

"You're sweet, but no, it's not really up for debate. She is seriously light-years beyond me. But galena could have been one of the things Lucretia used in 1969 to summon up the speed demons from the infernal pits. Either to summon them or bind them into the cars."

"Like Hellbringer." Opal delicately dabbed the corners of her mouth with a napkin, sopping up hot sauce. "But that doesn't make sense. Demons hate galena. They'll do anything to stay *away* from it."

"Exactly. If you're going to force a demon to take up permanent residence in cold Detroit steel, you can't do it gently. You might have to use galena to make them obey. I can only assume that the summoning process was seriously unpleasant for the speed demons."

"Well. It's not like Hellbringer is ever in a *good* mood." On the bench seat in between them, Opal's phone rang. She glanced down at the screen and smiled as she picked it up. "*Hola*, sweetie. You get that sink installed yet?"

As Opal chatted with Ruiz, Dru ran her fingers across the yellowed paper of Lucretia's book.

She traced the symbols hidden in plain sight. Other scientific notations jumped out at her. "$SiO2$" stood for silicon dioxide, otherwise known as quartz, a common soul-cleansing crystal. Dru felt a certain sense of comfort seeing that in the formulas. If she ended up casting any of these spells, the quartz might offer her some measure of protection against the backlash of dark magic.

"FeS" was another abbreviation. It stood for ferrous sulfide, also known as pyrite, or fool's gold. Dru's pyrite disk had protected her from Lucretia's blasting spell the night before. Now she was starting to get an idea of why. For every spell, there was a counterspell, and Dru was uniquely positioned to have all of the crystals she needed on hand to counter Lucretia's spells.

Despite her exhaustion, Dru felt a surge of excitement. For the first time, she had the opportunity to get an inside look at the work of another crystal sorceress. Lucretia had crammed decades' worth of knowledge into this handwritten book, and Dru was only barely beginning to scratch the surface. She could happily spend years analyzing its contents.

But she didn't have years. Lucretia had made off with the powerful Amulet of Decimus the Accursed. Dru didn't know for sure how long it would take her to complete her master plan—whatever it entailed—but the clock was ticking. Dru had to find her, and fast.

She pored over the cryptic symbols that filled the book, looking for a spell she could use to track down Lucretia. Most of the spells in the book were so far beyond her that she didn't even know what they did. The rest were more complicated than she could comprehend, at least at the moment. Maybe if she had a good night's sleep and plenty of time on her hands, things would be different.

But for now, things were still incredibly frustrating, and she still had so far to go. Dru shut the book harder than she meant to. The pages slapped together with a resigned *thump*, drawing a concerned look from Opal, who was still on the phone with Ruiz.

Dru opened her mouth to apologize, but the words dried up on her tongue. Past Opal, outside the window, the beautifully brilliant blue sky was split by the flapping black shape of the giant bat. It dove toward them, blotting out the sky, its sharp claws aimed right at Opal's window.

"*Look out!*" Dru yelled. But she was too late.

As Rane tensed to spring into motion, her phone buzzed in its armband holder. Actually, it was Salem's phone. After hers had gone into the drink, he'd told her she should start getting her phones by the dozen at Costco. So instead, she had helped herself to his phone. That would teach him to be so smart about it.

She glanced at the screen.

Where are you, Buttercup?

The text didn't have his name attached to it, but it was definitely Salem. He had probably picked up a burner phone at the corner store first thing this morning. So, after he had gotten so weird and obsessive last night that she had to go home, he thought she would still answer his texts?

No. Freaking. Way.

I know where you are, he texted. *BTW, I can track my own phone.*

Fine. Good for him. She ignored his message, cracked her knuckles, and focused on how she was going to take this old brick building apart. From here, she could see the half-open door and the four loading docks, plus two boarded-up windows. No way to circle around the building without getting spotted. But she had to assume the place had at least one other exit around the corner, possibly two. Also, there was some kind of tarpaper-covered structure on top of the second-floor roof. Maybe that was the bat house.

She drummed her fingers on her biceps. *Screw it*, she thought. Nothing wrong with a good old-fashioned frontal assault. She'd start with that.

Before she could launch herself out of the bushes and charge the front door, a droning motor sound approached from the distance. A slab-sided black car came flying down the gravel road, spewing up a huge dust trail behind it. Rane groaned as it grew closer. It was Salem's hearse.

Apparently, he wasn't kidding.

Irritated, Rane pulled the phone out of its armband holder and texted him back. *Get out of here, you weirdo. You trying to spook them away or what?*

The hearse slowed down, but didn't stop. *You found the lair?*

She sighed in exasperation and texted back, *Duh.*

The hearse rolled to a stop a few hundred yards away, near the line of flatbed trailers baking in the sun. After a few seconds, the engine cut out, letting silence return. The only sound was the buzzing of the power lines.

Rane watched the building for any sign of movement. A glimmer of yellow eyes shone in the darkness. Slowly, the door eased shut. Obviously, the animal sorcerers had seen Salem's car. So now she had lost the advantage of surprise, thanks to him. She ground her teeth in frustration.

He opened the car door and stood behind it. With a flourish, he extended an antique brass spyglass and studied the building. He took his sweet time about it.

Rane squatted down and waited, fuming. The spyglass had ghostly powers, and it had come in handy plenty of times in the past. Looking through it revealed all sorts of hidden spells and invisible enchantments, making them visible as shimmering auras in its watery lenses. Rane had actually been the one to find the spyglass, back when they were tracking a ghostly pirate ship along the Gulf Coast near New Orleans. She had given it to Salem as a surprise gift, mostly because she knew that if she kept it, she would just end up breaking it sooner or later.

Still. It sucked to sit in the bushes waiting for him to finish his obnoxiously conspicuous reconnaissance. The only thing holding her back was the possibility that he might spot something important she couldn't see.

Apparently satisfied, he collapsed the little brass telescope in a single quick motion and got back into the car. A few seconds later, the phone buzzed again.

This will take time. The place is heavily protected.

Rane snorted. She found that hard to believe. The pitted brick walls looked about half ready to cave in. She texted, *I'm going in now.*

Stay put, Salem texted.

"Yeah, I don't think so," Rane said aloud. Who did he think he was, to order her around?

All the doors and windows are warded, Salem texted. *These proteans think they are safe, but they are not. Not from me. I will handle this.*

Even though he couldn't see her, Rane made a talky motion with her hand. Yak, yak, yak. She started to stand up.

As if he knew that she was ignoring him, he texted again: *Do NOT try the door!*

So he wanted to keep all the glory to himself, apparently. Rane put away the phone without bothering to reply. This wasn't a democracy.

At her feet sat a football-sized chunk of granite. She stooped and picked it up. Focusing on the rock, she willed her body to transform. A thrilling rush coursed up her arm and through her body as she turned into solid stone. Transforming into solid rock or metal was the greatest feeling in the world, like a runner's high combined with a sugar rush. It made her feel strong enough to punch through a wall. She felt unstoppable. And she pretty much was.

The nice thing about granite was that it was not only tough, but it also blended into the background. Her entire body was now mottled light tan and gray, with charcoal-colored speckles. If she had wanted to stay put, she would have blended right into the surrounding landscape. Sometimes, an edge like that came in handy.

But right now, she wasn't interested in stealth.

She straightened up to her full six-foot-plus height and strode out of the bushes. She had spent years practicing moving silently while transformed. It wasn't easy. In metal form, she tended to ring like a church bell, and in stone form, she sounded like a rockslide. Right now, these sorcerers were already expecting trouble, so she decided to let them know exactly who they had pissed off. She pounded her way toward their lair with footsteps that were probably rattling windows a half mile away.

She didn't bother making for the mint chocolate chip house, which she could have used as cover. Instead, she trusted in speed and intimidation. And also being made out of solid rock. She marched straight toward the building, punching deep footprints into the dirt.

Direct assault. That was the way she liked it.

She spared Salem only a single killer glance as she pounded across the gravel road, wondering if he was giving her that lusty look he sometimes did when she got physical. But she couldn't see him inside the dark hearse. Without a doubt, he was frantically trying to text her right now. But the phone, along with her clothes, was now magically transformed into rock. She didn't have to put up with his yammering anymore.

She could feel the stares of the sorcerers inside the building. She had no idea how many of them were inside or what kind of animals they were. And right now, she didn't care. She just wanted to take the place apart with her bare hands.

When she was about a dozen paces from the door, she pulled her arm back and hurled the rock with all her strength. It flew in a fast, shallow arc, with enough raw force behind it that it should have knocked the door clean off its hinges. But instead, it struck an invisible wall and bounced off with a sinister sizzling sound. To her surprise, it really was magically protected. The rock cratered into the dirt, smoking slightly.

She pursed her lips. *Okay, so, maybe don't go through the front door.*

But doors and windows weren't the only way to break into a building. Sometimes you had to make your own opening.

She marched over to the huge pile of rusty junk piled up against one wall. It was mostly lightweight stuff like old stovepipes, broken chains, and little scraps that wouldn't do her any good. But buried beneath all of that was the elongated bell shape of some kind of transmission, maybe from a forklift or a tractor. Now it was nothing more than a couple of hundred pounds of rusted metal. She bent down and snatched it up.

Behind her, Salem started up the hearse and came flying down the road toward her. Good. About time he joined this party. Because things were about to get crazy.

Lugging the rusted transmission, Rane paced the length of the building, looking for a weak spot. With old brick structures like this, there was always a way in.

She found her opportunity beneath the corner of one of the windows. A wide zigzag crack in the mortar stretched down and across, like stair steps, from where the foundation had eroded beneath the abandoned building. *Perfect.* The fissure in the wall was easily wide enough to stick her fingers in. But she wasn't going to use her fingers.

Salem's big black hearse slid to a stop behind her. He leaped out of the driver's seat, his eyes wide with anger. "Exactly what part of 'don't go inside' was unclear to you?"

Rane grinned. "You said don't go in the *door*. Didn't you?"

She planted her stone feet in a wide stance, settling into the dirt. She shifted her grip, eyed the crack in the wall, and swung the rusted transmission back. With a huff of breath, she swung it forward with all of her strength, with the pointed end aimed at the crack between the bricks. In one motion, she slammed two hundred pounds of steel into the crack.

BOOM. The crushing impact was loud enough to set her ear ringing on that side of her head. Red brick dust swirled around her. She swung the transmission away from the bricks again.

Salem backed up a step. "Wait, no, what do you think you're—"

BOOM. The window above shattered, raining glass down on her. With a groan, the wall on the right side of the crack tipped drunkenly inward. Loose bricks clattered out of the gap and fell around her feet.

Salem held out a cautioning hand. "If you think this is the way to—"

BOOM. The pointed end of the transmission went all the way through the bricks, punching a head-sized hole in the wall. Rane planted one foot against the solid side of the wall and yanked the transmission free. Clusters of dirty red bricks came with it, bound together by a crumbling crust of mortar.

She eyed the wall. Dangerously unstable fissures radiated outward through the mortar, cracking through the flaking paint. As she watched, the cracks kept spreading, making a sound like someone munching on the world's biggest corn chip. The wall was right on the edge of coming apart. Satisfied, Rane dropped the transmission at her feet with a heavy metallic clank.

She backed up a step and tensed to give the wall a final kick. When she glanced back over her shoulder, Salem was staring with a curious mixture of irritation and fascination, his eyebrows wrinkling. He didn't say a word.

With a heartfelt grunt, Rane gave the wall a savage kick, driving her granite foot into the weakest spot. At that, the rest of the wall beneath the window tilted inward and collapsed in a roar of broken masonry. A towering cloud of dust swirled out into the sunlight, escaping through a hole now big enough to drive a car through.

She dusted rust off her hands, enjoying the awed look etched across Salem's face. It wasn't often that she got to see that. With a grin, she jerked a thumb toward the building. "You just going to stand there looking pretty, or you want to go get your amulet back?"

Then she turned and leaped into the darkness.

20

BAT MOBILE

The bat hit the long purple Lincoln Town Car with a startlingly loud thud. That was quickly followed by the thin screeching of its clawed feet scrabbling against the glass as it tried to shatter the window. But none of that matched the piercing volume of Opal's panicked scream, which threatened to rupture both of Dru's eardrums.

On impact, the bat's long leathery wings wrapped all the way around the windshield and back window, plunging the car into near darkness. The only light came in through Dru's window, where the trembling edges of the wings couldn't quite reach. In the gloom, the dozen crystals Dru had carefully hot-glued around the inside of the car glowed softly as the grid worked to keep the protean sorcerer from breaking in.

"I can't see!" Opal shrieked, pointing unnecessarily at the flapping ribbed wing covering the windshield. As the sunlight passed faintly through the bat's leathery skin, it turned the licorice-black wing into more of a brown cola color, pulsing with a feathery network of veins.

"Stop the car!" Dru advised, during a fleeting moment of quiet as Opal sucked in another lungful of air to start screaming again.

But instead of stopping the car, Opal swung the steering wheel violently back and forth. "Get this ugly thing off my beautiful car!"

The bat's glistening pink tongue, easily a foot long, slathered spittle across Opal's window as it tried to gnaw on the doorframe. Its beady black eyes pressed up against the glass, staring with ferocious intensity. Dru couldn't be absolutely certain, but she had the distinct impression it was staring hungrily at the book in her hands.

Since the spell book was her only way of finding Lucretia, Dru knew she had to keep it safe. But before she could even begin to think about that, first she had to make sure they didn't die in a fiery car crash. She rolled down the window on her side.

"Don't you let that thing in here!" Opal hollered.

Dru tried to brace herself against Opal's wild evasive maneuvers as she stuck her head out through the open window. Up ahead, an eighteen-wheel truck was stopped at the next traffic light. Unless they did something right this moment, they would crash into its rusty rear end. Dru gulped down a breath. An empty side street led off to the right. "Turn right! *Now!*"

Opal yanked the wheel right, and the Lincoln's tires squealed in protest. The heavy car sagged to the side like a capsizing boat, and for a moment Dru was afraid they would roll completely over and die. But by some miracle, they made it around the corner in one piece.

Sensing an opening, the bat scrambled over the car toward Dru's open window, flapping its wings enough to afford brief glimpses of the street dead-ending ahead. Tall chain-link fences penned them in on the left and right. The street widened somewhat but then ended in a gate that was chained shut. A spray-painted plywood sign proclaimed, "No Saturday Deliveries."

Dru rolled up the window as the bat scrambled around to her side, shutting it just as the bat's big, furry jaws snapped at the edge of the glass. The bat's spiky walnut-colored fur flattened against the glass as the beast glared at Dru, showing sharp teeth. Opal continued her panicked maneuvering, making the car sway hard side to side.

"Will you just *stop the car?*" Dru shouted.

"I'm trying to shake that thing loose!" Opal insisted.

"It's not working!"

"I see that!" Opal snapped.

"Okay! Okay." Dru forced herself to lower her voice and speak in the most calming tone she could manage, considering there was a giant bat creature trying to break in through her window. "That thing can't get into the car. All right? The grid will keep it out. So don't worry."

As she spoke, a deep baritone *pop* echoed from the front of the car, followed by a rush of air and the warbling of tortured rubber. It didn't take

Dru long to figure out that the bat had used the sharp claws on its feet to slash one of the Lincoln's tires.

After the car waddled to a stop, the bat hopped off, folding up its wings and letting a flood of sunlight into the car. It crawled around the car in a creepy hunchbacked way, snuffling at the bottom of the door jams. On the jarringly upbeat disco playlist oozing through Opal's stereo, Chic busted out singing *Good Times*.

Dru sensed the intensity of Opal's gaze and reluctantly turned to face it.

The look on Opal's face spoke volumes. "You didn't protect my tires?" she said.

Dru held up her hands helplessly. "I know, okay? But there's only *so* much I can do with a glue gun."

"We need to call Rane!" Opal patted the wide seat cushion next to her, which had dumped its contents to the floor during her evasive maneuvers. "Where is my phone?" Her voice cracked with rising panic.

As she dug around through the mess on the floorboard, Dru pulled out her own phone and dialed Rane, only to get her voice mail. "She's not answering!"

"Keep trying!" Opal screamed again as the bat's head popped up in her window again, gnawing at her door handle. "Hurry!"

"Oh, wait. She has Salem's phone." Dru tried that number but got nothing. Every time Rane turned into metal or stone, she transformed her clothes and possessions, too. So if her phone was in her pocket, there was no way for her to get the call. Dru texted her instead, hoping the message would get through eventually.

Meanwhile, Opal scooted across the seat to get away from the bat, pressing up against Dru. She held her own phone tightly against her ear. "I'm calling Greyson, but it just keeps ringing!"

"He doesn't have voice mail," Dru explained.

Opal's eyes were wide with fear. "Well, text him!"

"I can't! He only has a land line. He doesn't have a cell phone."

Disapproval was written all across Opal's face as she lowered her phone. "You need to find out what your man's issue is with technology."

"That's not helping us right now!"

"That's it. I'm calling Ruiz." Opal shook her head as she dialed.

Dru was about to object on the grounds that Ruiz didn't have any magic powers, but she bit her lip. Opal didn't have any magic powers either, and yet she was always brave enough to face off against the forces of darkness. Maybe Ruiz could help them after all. Right now, they didn't have any other options.

As the bat outside moved on to another door handle, a flash of gold glinted around its neck. It was wearing Salem's enchanted amulet, which was doubtless protecting it against any backlash from the car's crystal grid. No wonder it hadn't been scared off yet. That, and the fact that it was obviously obsessed with getting its claws on Lucretia's book.

But the grid couldn't hold it off forever. Soon enough, those crystals would run out of energy. And when they did, the car would be left defenseless. The thing would be able to smash its way in with impunity. Actually, it wasn't a *thing*, she reminded herself, it was another sorcerer, like her. And if it was intelligent enough to come to the same conclusion, then it would know they were sitting ducks.

A creepy sensation prickled the back of her neck. She turned around to see the bat staring at her through the window with its bottomless black eyes. It showed sharp white teeth as it grinned at her.

Dru shuddered. It had them trapped, and it knew it.

The snake was the first one to come after Rane. But this time, she was ready for it.

As she charged in through the breached wall, her eyes took a moment to adjust from the blinding sunlight to the sudden darkness. Add to that the choking clouds of brick dust and the unstable piles of rubble under her feet, and it made for a tricky situation. But that was just the way she liked it. The more chaos, the more opportunities to improvise. And she did love to improvise.

Besides, despite all the noise, she figured she had still caught the protean sorcerers off guard. Even though they had seen her and Salem coming, they had probably thought they were protected by the invisible magical wards on every entrance. They would have been guarding the doors and windows. Nobody expected her to come crashing through the wall like the Kool-Aid guy.

"Oh, *yeah!*" she yelled at the top of her lungs.

After the summery day outside, the cool humid air inside the building felt like stepping into a boggy pond. Smelled like it, too. The room was cavernous, the loading dock of what used to be a warehouse. It was lit only by the cracks of light coming around the boarded-up windows and the massive hole she had left in the wall behind her.

The place was piled up with huge fans, broken-looking pumps, and unidentifiable machine parts. In the distance was a stack of enormous, knobby tractor-type tires. Beyond that sat a faded blue shipping container with its doors open, revealing nothing except the pitch blackness inside. Someone had cleared paths through all the clutter, piling things up in the middle and against the walls. So in a way, it kind of reminded her of her apartment.

Immediately, she dodged left, because most people went right. And that was when she saw the huge black snake, thicker than her leg, slithering from one angled steel roof support to the next. If she'd gone right, it would have dropped around her neck.

She seriously wanted to give it payback for making her smash Salem's pipe organ, but it was high overhead, out of reach, still trying to get the drop on her. She looked around for something to throw at it.

Salem stepped up to the jagged hole in the wall and stood silhouetted in the light, an ominous figure in a long black coat and top hat. He wasn't the tallest sorcerer around, but he still knew how to make a dramatic entrance.

Rane pointed up. "Snake!"

He poked his head inside, mindful of the jagged bricks, and splayed his long fingers at the hissing snake. A hazy glow of magic suffused the air, and Salem's spell plucked up the snake and carried it out into the open.

The huge speckled reptile writhed in the air about twelve feet off the ground. Its forked tongue lashed. Now that Rane could get a clear look at its entire length, she realized the thing was even bigger than she'd thought. More than twenty feet long and massive enough to swallow someone Salem's size. Just looking at its oily body coiling around itself in the air was enough to make her skin crawl. But its eyes were the worst. Metallic green with narrow black slits. They stared at Rane with hate so venomous she could practically feel it.

Salem trod carefully over the broken bricks. His glare turned fierce as he used both hands to maintain the spell. His fingers contorted as the snake tried to twist its way to freedom. "This thing is *obnoxiously* strong."

"Thanks for the hot tip," Rane said. "Be glad he's not wearing your amulet."

"Speaking of which . . ." Salem tore his gaze off the snake just long enough to shoot her a meaningful look.

"Fine. Long as you got a handle on this, I'll poke around and find your man-jewelry." Rane scanned the warehouse, expecting the bat and the panther to come flying out of the shadows at any moment. But as the seconds ticked by, nothing moved. "Huh. It's *way* too quiet in this place. You think Mr. Wiggles here is home alone?"

A sardonic smile twitched at the corner of Salem's mouth as he levitated the giant snake even higher. "Wouldn't that be disappointing?"

"Totally." Stone fists ready to strike at the first sign of movement, Rane crept through the ominously silent warehouse. She set each foot down on the concrete floor as carefully as she could, but anything else hiding in here had to know exactly where she was. She checked each shadow, each hiding place in the piles, as she passed by. Nothing.

No sign of human habitation. No clothes, no sleeping bags, no food. If the sorcerers were really living here, then they were living like, well, animals.

"See anything, cupcake?" Salem finally called. The strain was clear in his voice. Although he made his spell-casting look effortless, she knew firsthand how ornery that snake was. Every move that it made, he had to magically counter to keep it in his grasp. And a twenty-foot-long snake could make plenty of moves. Salem had to be really hating life right about now.

She passed by an industrial refrigerator the size of a bedroom, completely empty except for some grody stains in the bottom. Then a dusty fan that looked as if it could have propelled the Titanic. She reached the stack of chunky tractor tires she had spotted earlier and was about to turn back when a faint whimpering sound reached her.

She eased around the stack of tires, fists up, and found the last person she ever expected to see again.

Ember.

Salem's would-be other girlfriend. The Middle Eastern sorceress who had shacked up with Salem right after he'd broken up with Rane a few months ago. Her eyebrow piercings flashed in the dim light, and her Eye of Horus makeup was smeared. But the weird thing was that she was tied up.

Some kind of silvery thread was wrapped around her entire body, covering her from her mouth down to her ankles. She swayed, suspended just a few inches off the floor. The soles of her black combat boots fought for purchase, but they found nothing but thin air. She stared at Rane with pleading eyes.

"Hey!" Rane called over her shoulder, without taking her eyes off Ember. "This is *freaking* weird. I found your—" Rane almost said *your other girlfriend*, but stopped herself. "I found Ember!"

"Lovely," Salem called back, sounding distracted. "We'll all get together for a selfie later. Meanwhile, let's hurry this up. Our scaly friend here's getting a little too feisty for comfort."

Staring at Ember hanging there, tied up in silver threads, gave Rane chills. There was something definitely freaky going on around here. And she had a bad feeling things were about to get *way* worse. Still, as much as Rane hated Ember's guts, she wasn't going to leave a sister sorceress just hanging in the breeze. Literally.

Ember whimpered again.

"Shh," Rane said, more harshly than necessary. As carefully as she could, she worked her stone fingers into the silver threads wrapped around Ember's cheeks. "This might hurt, dude. If anything breaks in your pretty little face, I'm already sorry about it."

Ember's eyes widened with fear.

Rane pulled. The silver threads stretched slightly, but they wouldn't break. Still, it was enough to free up Ember's mouth. She gasped.

"What the hell happened to you?" Rane demanded. "What's up around here?"

"Protean sorcerers," Ember croaked, sounding like she badly needed a drink of water. "They stole an amulet from me. I came to get it back."

"Yeah, moving on, what's with the body wrap? Why don't you teleport out of here?" Teleportation was Ember's magic specialty.

"I cannot move my arms." Ember's dark gaze lifted upward, and her heavily lined eyes flew open wide. "Quick, get me loose!"

Rane got that horrible skin-crawling feeling again as she turned and looked up. High above, something picked its way through the shadows, clinging to the metal struts that supported the ceiling. It had a mottled black-and-orange body shaped like a swollen number eight, with eight lanky legs banded with alternating tiger stripes of orange and black. Even from here, Rane could tell its body was nearly as big as hers. As it moved, its half dozen eyes caught the light and reflected down at them like droplets of white-hot lava.

"Get me loose! Now!" Ember swore in Arabic and kicked at Rane.

But Rane barely noticed. Her entire world shrank to the nightmarish creature above. Every muscle in her body tensed until she went rigid with fright. All of the air rushed out of her lungs, leaving her bathed in cold sweat, with only the sound of her heartbeat thrashing in her ears.

"Whoa. Game over." For the first time, Rane's voice sounded faint and small in her own ears. "That's one *big*-ass spider."

"*Salem!*" Ember screeched in a voice that could probably crack glass. "*Help me!*"

When the giant spider dropped toward them, legs splayed out around it, the sight was terrifying enough to galvanize Rane into motion. She grabbed the top tractor tire off the pile, held its weight in both hands, and spun in place. The knobby tire *whooshed* through the air. Rane built up a load of centrifugal force, spun around once more, and then released the tire.

Her aim was true. The tire sailed up, spinning as it went. It hit the spider with a hollow thud, hard enough to send it careening toward the far wall. As the tire bounced and crashed into the other end of the warehouse, Rane grabbed the ropy webs suspending Ember and yanked. Hard. It brought a few metal ceiling supports crashing down around them, but she managed to break Ember loose. The woman was still wrapped up tightly, but at least she wasn't hanging from the ceiling anymore. Rane slung her over her shoulder like a sack of dirty laundry and ran, yelling wordlessly the whole time.

"What are you doing?" Ember shrieked.

"Getting you the hell out of here, dude!" Rane dodged around the heaps of junk and headed back toward Salem. The spider was already closing in fast behind them. Ember, facing back toward the spider, screamed as the spider scrabbled along the wall, clinging to the bricks as it pursued them. Its legs made a grating sound that grew louder as it closed in. Rane got within sight of Salem and the hole in the wall. But she wouldn't make it before the spider got them.

She looked around for something to use as a weapon. A yellow-painted steel rod about four feet long and a couple of inches thick, with pointed brackets on either end, stuck up out of the junk. Probably a spare part from some kind of construction equipment. Perfect. She dropped Ember to the floor and yanked the metal rod out of the pile with a clatter.

"No, no! Do not leave me!" Ember's voice turned hysterical. She wriggled on the floor, going nowhere fast. "Please! Get me out of here!"

"Be cool!" Rane eyed the giant spider churning furiously toward them. Twenty yards away. Ten. She raised the steel rod like a bat and shouted over her shoulder to Salem. "*Hey!* Little *help* here!"

"Busy, sweetheart." His eyes bulged at the sight of the spider. "You want me to handle the snake or the spider? Make up your mind!"

As if there was a good choice either way. The bloated body and tiger-striped legs of the giant spider were almost on Rane. Its chubby, fur-covered fangs spasmed, as if they couldn't wait to sink into human flesh. Rane figured they should give it something else to chew on. "Dude! Throw the snake *at* the spider!"

At that, the spider drew up short. It could understand her. Which made sense, since the spider had originally been a sorcerer. But still, it was super creepy.

Its fangs trembled. Recoiling, it scrunched to the side as the giant snake came flying at it, coiling and twisting around itself in midair. The crash sounded wet and sloppy as the two creatures tangled with one another, forming a disgusting pretzel of scaly coils and twitching legs. They went tumbling end over end until they crashed in the distance, hurling up an explosion of dust and debris.

A flush of rage pounded through Rane's body, making the blood roar in her ears. Her vision narrowed down to a pulsing red-tinted tunnel, focused on the creatures squirming in the junk. She wasn't going to let them get away.

With a primal yell, Rane charged after them, intent on finishing this. She raised the yellow steel rod high overhead, ready to smash the first thing that poked its ugly head up. Her stone feet pounded the concrete, shaking machine parts loose from piles as she passed by.

"Wait!" Ember called after her. "Come back!"

As Rane ran past the blue shipping container, the spider unexpectedly popped up over the top. Without warning, it spit a cone of silvery webbing at her. Rane instantly dropped to the smelly floor between two heaps of parts as the web sizzled past her head, inches away. This close, she could see that the entire web was made of a single thin thread that oscillated back and forth in a rapid Z pattern. It streamed past her in the blink of an eye. Less than a second later, it had covered the space where she'd stood, forming a kind of canopy over the junk piles, missing her by a handsbreadth.

Careful not to touch the sticky webbing, Rane belly-crawled out from under the web. Before she could get back on her feet, the spider pounced at her. Rane flipped over onto her back, thrusting out the yellow steel rod to protect herself. The spider's heavy body struck the blunt end of the rod but wasn't impaled on it. Its swollen body shuddered and tried to twist loose. Its long tiger-striped legs spread out over Rane, caging her in.

Despite her raw strength, Rane didn't have the leverage to hold the spider off her for long. It slid closer, inch by inch, looming over her. Its fangs hungrily shivered and reared back, sharp and glistening. The harsh odor of its venom stung her nostrils.

Before it could strike, a familiar magical glow brightened the air between them. Salem's spell yanked the spider's front legs back, as if a giant invisible lasso held the creature off her. The spider fought and kicked, dislodging scrap metal from nearby piles. Its fangs clicked and trembled.

Salem strode through the warehouse toward them, his coat swirling back behind him, his top hat tugged down low over his eyes. His long fingers deftly worked the air, prying the spider back one leg at a time. Never before had Rane been so glad to see him.

She elbowed her way back from the spider, putting some distance between them. With all the gauzy webs covering everything around her, she barely had room to stand up. But there was nowhere for her to go. She was trapped. And Salem couldn't hold the thing off forever.

His eyes flashed. "Behind you!"

21

WOLF WHISTLE

Rane spun around just as the snake slithered through the low gap underneath the webbing. Its speckled body rippled, and its mucousy pink mouth stretched wide open, flashing multiple rows of sharp curved teeth as it struck at her ankles.

Rane jumped and landed on her knees, straddling the snake and pinning it between her legs. Its wide head thrashed beneath her, trying to escape, and she pinned it down with one broad stone hand.

"I've had *enough* of this crap," Rane snapped. She got a tight grip around the giant snake's jaws, clamping them shut, and got to her feet. As expected, the snake thrashed, trying to escape, and immediately got itself caught in the spider's web.

Rane shook the snake hard up and down, trying to crack it like a whip. Its long body twirled around, picking up sheets of spiderweb like a giant stick gathering a swab of cotton candy. Gradually, its struggles became weaker and weaker as the web swaddled it ever tighter.

When the snake finally went limp, Rane dragged it over to the grody old broken industrial refrigeration unit and tossed it inside. The snake hissed at her and snapped its jaws ineffectively, but it could no longer move. Its slitted metallic eyes glared at her from inside a spiderweb burrito.

Meanwhile, Salem was still restraining the freakishly giant spider. Rane held one of the doors open and pointed inside. "Room for one more!"

Salem pushed his hands together, and the spider rose into the air, legs fluttering, bloated abdomen spasming. In a nightmare of long legs and fangs, it sailed past Rane and filled the inside of the refrigerator.

"Hey, how about you two just cool it?" Rane slammed the refrigerator's big double doors shut and shoved her yellow steel rod through the handles, pinning them closed. Immediately, a frantic scrabbling and thumping echoed from inside.

Rane turned to Salem and jerked her thumb at the doors. "Want to beef that up for me?"

Salem's eyebrows flashed up, and he gave her a manic smile. With a single sinuous movement, he swept his arms out to either side, fingers spread, and gracefully brought them together. All around, piles of parts and junk scraped and heaved across the floor, as if pushed by invisible bulldozers. Rane climbed up over and out of the way as Salem's spell piled junk armpit-high around the refrigerator. Moments later, the refrigerator was buried.

Rane was only able to enjoy about three seconds of satisfaction before Ember's shrill voice set her teeth on edge.

"Salem!" Ember wailed pitifully. "Over here!"

Rane rolled her eyes. "Better deal with that before she makes my ears bleed. I'm going to try and find your stupid amulet."

Salem tipped his hat to her and headed back toward the light.

After taking another look around, listening the whole time to the giant spider battering against the inside of the refrigerator, Rane finally decided that Salem's amulet was long gone. He'd just have to deal with that. She was done with this creep show.

Then she saw the wolf.

Its fierce golden eyes stared directly into hers. Hackles raised, its gray-and-tan fur stood on end, and its black lips drew back from sharp white canines. Head lowered, it crept toward her.

"Great," Rane muttered. "Just what I need right now. More critters to fight." She strode toward the wolf on pounding stone feet, intent on finishing this with a single powerful punch.

As she approached, the wolf's head unexpectedly lifted and its ears went back, as if it had suddenly recognized her. The sharp teeth disappeared, its tongue lolled out, and its tail began to wag.

Weird . . . Rane slowed to a stop twenty feet away, puzzled. She was worried that if she got any closer, the thing would jump up on her and lick her face.

Before her eyes, the shape of the wolf shifted and changed. Its body shimmered with ethereal green light. Its fur shrank away as it transformed into a tall, well-built black guy. Who also happened to be stark naked. Tribal-looking tattoos swirled up the well-defined muscles of his bare arms and across his broad chest.

"Hi," he said in a deep voice. He smiled broadly, making no move to cover himself.

You're so totally naked, she thought.

After a moment, he pointed at his own face. "Hey. I'm up here."

With an effort, Rane moved her gaze up to his face. She narrowed her eyes at him. "Who the hell are you?"

His smile dimmed. "It's me. Remember? We met at that party?"

She groaned. How many times in her life would she have to hear that? "Seriously, dude? Worst pickup line *ever*. Try again." She folded her arms. Considering he was all naked, she figured she'd give him one more chance.

"I *am* serious," he insisted. "We were at that party, we danced together . . ."

"No, we didn't. I know all of my naked guys. You are definitely not one of them."

"You were wearing a gold dress and a robot visor," he said. "I was wearing a wolf mask. It was that party under the mountain. In the bomb shelter."

"Whoa." She did remember that. So they *had* met. And she had actually danced with him. Mostly to make Salem jealous, but hey, it had worked. "That's so totally bizarre."

"I know, right?" He held out his hand, which she made absolutely no move to shake. That didn't seem to bother him. "My friends call me Feral."

"Really. They burn a lot of brain cells coming up with that nickname, Feral?"

He flashed her a wolfish grin. "I didn't say my friends were all that smart."

"No, if they were geniuses, they probably wouldn't be locked in a refrigerator right now."

Feral made a face. "*Those* are not my friends. They give me the creeps, I'll tell you that straight up. We just work together."

"Uh-huh. Doing what? Besides stealing people's amulets."

His gaze slid to the side. Not looking at anything in particular, just trying to come up with some kind of excuse, probably. And she really didn't want to hear any excuses. Particularly from a naked dude.

"Seriously, what's with all you animal guys?" Rane asked. "Where'd you all come from? How do you do that thing?"

"Protean magic," he said proudly. "It's the original magic."

It sounded like a tagline. She tried to ignore the sudden feeling that she was starring in a bizarre TV commercial. "Somebody told me protean magic is extinct."

"It was. Then Lucretia brought it back. Taught some people, they taught other people. Before you know it, there was a whole community of us. Living out in the wild. Doing our thing. Just *being*, you know?"

"Like, being homeless?"

He shook his head slightly. "I'm talking about being *one* with nature. All of us just living life the way it's supposed to be."

Rane looked around dubiously. "Dude, I don't know what you've been smoking, but this is not the way anything is *supposed* to be."

He took a step closer to her. "That's because the modern world is crowding us out. Destroying the wild. We can't live in our natural habitat anymore."

She jerked her thumb back toward the industrial refrigerator, which echoed as the spider drummed its legs against the metal. "So where exactly is the natural habitat for Mr. Big-Ass Spider back there?"

Feral blinked. "Florida, I think."

"Huh. And what are you all doing here in my town now?"

"Lucretia told us to come to town, grab a bunch of amulets and whatnot. Might as well do it now, before . . ." He suddenly clammed up.

"Before what?"

He didn't say anything.

She tapped her granite foot against the floor. "Does it have anything to do with why the bat is so hot to get his hands on Lucretia's journal?"

"Lucretia's journal?" Feral's eyes lit up. "You found it? Damn. That thing must be a motherlode of lost protean know-how."

So that explained why they were after it. They wanted the magical secrets in it. "Tell me what Lucretia's planning."

"I'm not saying anything else."

"Dude. You realize she's going to destroy the world."

He shook his head. "Destroy the *modern* world, you mean. Take away civilization and bring back the natural order of things." His eyes brightened. The guy was a true believer. "She wants to help us get back to nature. Modern civilization has just about destroyed the environment. She's going to fix all that. She said she'd make a *new* world. A natural world. Unspoiled. A paradise."

"Yeah, a paradise for *her*. But you're never going to see it, because she's going to destroy this world, and you along with it."

He shook his head in refusal.

Rane held out her empty hands. "You got totally played, bro. She made you guys the decoy. Sent you to distract us, waste our time, so that we didn't chase after her."

"No. She wouldn't do that to us."

"I don't care if you believe me or not. How long is it going to take her to put together this world-changing thing? Are we talking months? Weeks?" She waited. "Days?"

He looked triumphant. "It's happening tonight. Sundown."

That made all other thoughts in her brain freeze solid. *Tonight?* "Now you're messing with me."

He gave her a lazy smile. "Ask her yourself. Tell you what, you show me where her book is, I'll take you to the ghost town." He shifted his hips slightly. "Or, you know, anywhere else you want me to take you." He gave her a look that left no doubt what he was talking about.

He was focused so hard on giving her that smoldering look that he didn't notice the swirl of inky blackness that whirled into existence behind him, which instantly became Ember in her long black coat. Now free of the spiderwebs, no doubt thanks to Salem, she was free to do her teleportation thing.

Feral looked over his shoulder as if sensing Ember's presence, but he was too late. She reached up with one finger, which was covered from knuckle to fingernail with elaborate silver articulated armor that ended in an engraved spike jutting from her fingertip. She touched the spike to the bare skin at the back of his neck. There was a red spark and a sizzling sound. Feral dropped to his knees, then keeled over unconscious to the dirty floor.

"Hey!" Rane barked at her. "I was in the middle of interrogating that guy!"

Ember just shot her a dark look.

"Is that what you were doing, Buttercup?" Salem said, approaching from the other direction. Unbelievably, he *still* sounded pissed off about her dancing with Feral at that party.

"Besides, he is one of them," Ember said, her Arabic accent thicker now that she wasn't screaming at the top of her lungs. She nudged Feral with the toe of her combat boots, but he was out cold. "Believe me, he will have one serious headache. But at least he won't be sucked dry by a *giant spider*. You see? Could be worse." Her nostrils flared with anger.

Rane had to admit that the woman had a point. It couldn't have been easy, getting wrapped up like a brown bag lunch. Still, Rane preferred a straight-up fight to zapping someone in the back. It just didn't seem right.

Now that things were quiet for the moment, Rane finally decided it was time to turn human again. She let go of her stone form and let herself transform back into flesh and blood. As always, she was sad to feel the rush of strength and energy slip away, leaving behind aching muscles and heavy legs. But she knew from years of experience that it was best to take a breather so she'd be ready to go again when she really needed it.

Salem watched her closely as she shook out her blonde ponytail and finger-combed it back. At times like this, she tended to forget the effect she had on him when she transformed. That was something she never got tired of.

And neither did he, apparently, judging by the flush in his face. Salem cleared his throat, as if pushing aside distracting thoughts. "We have to find that ghost town. But I'm not terribly keen on following the lead of our canine compadre here."

"I know where it is," Ember said softly, her face creasing with worry.

"Where?" Rane demanded.

Ember looked uncomfortable. "I cannot tell you. I have only teleported there."

"What kind of crap is that? Show me on a map."

"That is not the way it works." For once, Ember looked as if she was telling the truth.

Salem held up a calming hand. "She doesn't know the route. She can't read a map. She only knows places by teleporting there."

Rane folded her arms, making sure her biceps bulged. "Just whose side are you on?"

Before Salem could answer, his phone, currently strapped to Rane's arm, chimed with incoming messages. They both glanced at it.

Rane pulled it out of its holster and checked it. A rush of worry swept through her. "Dru's in trouble!"

Salem rolled his eyes. "Of *course* she's in trouble. And she will *always* be in trouble, because she's not big enough to play on the big kids' rides. And yet she keeps insisting on climbing aboard."

"Whatever, dude." Rane took four steps toward the exit before she realized Salem wasn't following her. "Hey, come on!"

But he had the gall to look to Ember instead.

"We have no time for this," Ember said softly to him. "If the wolf was telling the truth, and Lucretia will cast her spell tonight, then we must leave right now. If we wait . . ." She shook her head.

Salem gave Rane a meaningful look. He shot back the sleeve of his coat and tapped his brass wristwatch.

Rane was torn. She needed to help Dru, but at the same time she desperately didn't want to leave Salem alone with Ember. Just the fact that he was threatening to abandon her friends was harsh enough. But the idea of him going without her, and teaming up with another sorceress who so clearly wanted to get closer to him, made her blood boil.

Even now, Ember couldn't take her gaze off Salem. Rane would be the first to admit to being less than a genius at times, but even she could see how much Ember was into him. Getting him alone was exactly what Ember had in mind.

If Salem noticed that, he was good at hiding it. Instead, more than anything, he looked annoyed by the delay. He beckoned to Rane. "Dru can sort herself out. Right now, we need to focus on this Lucretia and her flea-bitten menagerie. So. This particular boat is leaving the dock *right now*, my sweet. Are you on the boat, or not?"

Rane slowly clenched her hands into fists.

22

I WILL SURVIVE

On Opal's stereo, Gloria Gaynor crowed over and over that she would survive, but Dru was starting to feel that her own chances were not quite so certain. The bat's attacks on the purple Lincoln were getting bolder and more pointed as it repeatedly tried the door handles and kicked at the windows with its clawed feet. As soon as the endless assaults exhausted the energy in the car's protective grid, it would all be over. The glass would shatter under the relentless attacks of the bat's claws, and its sharp fangs would be on them in a heartbeat.

In the Lincoln's saggy front bench seat, Opal clung tightly to Dru, surrounding her with a citrusy perfume. "Honey, there's something I need to tell you." Her voice had the somber urgency of an imminent confession.

Frankly, that kind of drama was the last thing Dru needed right now. Instead, she needed to think. There had to be a way to fight back.

She gave Opal a quick squeeze and let her go. "I need to find a way to reinforce this grid."

"Reinforce it?" Opal looked worried. "But the grid is already in place. It's a done deal. You can't start taking it apart now, or you'll let that thing get in here. Besides, and this *is* an important fact, I don't own a glue gun."

"True. But if I'm careful, we won't need glue. Hopefully, I can charge up the crystals while they're still stuck in place. Just need a little something to add to the mix." Dru retrieved her purse and started digging through it, looking for any crystals she could use. Instead, she found lip balm, a miniature pencil from IKEA, and, inexplicably, a nine-volt battery. She held that up. "What runs on nine-volt batteries anymore?"

"What? I don't know. But look, there are a dozen crystals inside this car, right? And you only have two hands. You can't possibly charge them all up at exactly the same rate, all at the same time. Something is going to end up getting out of balance. And if you go just a little bit too far one way or another, the whole thing will go up in smoke. And then where will we be? Honey, I don't want to die in here!"

Dru met her gaze. "You won't die in here, I promise."

"Uh-huh. Not exactly reassuring, coming from a woman who carries nine-volt batteries in her purse and doesn't even know why. You know if you get a paper clip or something metal across those battery terminals, you could set your purse on fire?"

"I'm tempted," Dru muttered. She kept digging until her fingers closed on the hard, cold edges of a crystal. *Finally.* She pulled out a yellow glass-like chunk of citrine, which was good for drawing in financial prosperity, at least theoretically. But it wasn't going to provide a great deal of help in this situation.

After a little more digging, she found a golf-ball-sized chunk of rose halite, which was essentially a giant cube of rock salt. From an energy perspective, it was used for dissolving old patterns and breaking a woven spell. She definitely didn't want to use that. She might risk disrupting the pattern of the entire grid.

She kept digging until she finally turned up an ice-clear Herkimer diamond. The double-terminated crystal had points on both ends, making it look like an enormous, expertly faceted diamond. But it was actually a kind of exceptionally clear quartz, in this case from upstate New York. Quartz was one of Dru's favorite crystals, since it was so good at cleansing away impurities and restoring energy. And Herkimer diamonds were renowned for their unmatched purity.

Perfect.

Making an appreciative noise, Opal bent closer to study it. Like Dru, she was drawn to beautiful crystals, even now. "That's a nice one."

"Thanks."

"So how come you didn't use that one in my car? That would've looked great up on my dashboard. But no, I guess you just had to leave it at the bottom of your purse instead." Behind Opal, the bat battered at her window, making her yelp.

"Okay. Here goes nothing." Dru took a deep breath, parted her lips, and let it out slowly. Eyes closed, she tried to ignore the rest of the world and focus just on the crystal. That meant blotting out the scrabbling sounds from the bat, Opal's frightened exclamations every time it attacked a different window, and even the *waka-waka* guitar on the stereo as the music switched to A Taste of Honey playing "Boogie Oogie Oogie."

She put that all aside, focusing on her breathing. In. Out. With an effort, she reached down into the core of her being and found the energy that waited there.

Boogie!

She ignored the stereo. Ignored the bat. Ignored Opal trying to warn her about something.

In her palm, the reassuring weight of the quartz grew colder, chilling the bones of her hand. There was a crispness to the sensation that made her feel more alert, more aware of her surroundings, even with her eyes squeezed shut. Twelve faint dots of light surrounded her, representing the crystal grid.

The bat snarled against the window. Opal moved away, making the car rock. The disco twanged. *Boogie!*

She lost sight of the crystals in her mind's eye. "Opal," she murmured, trying to hold onto her tenuous focus. "Stereo off, please."

The disco music disappeared with a click, leaving only the ominous sounds of the bat scratching at the glass. Dru pushed it out of her consciousness, searching again for the energy from the grid.

Twelve points of light flared into existence in the darkness of her mind. The crystals she had glued around the inside of the car flickered and faded. The bat's relentless attacks had left them nearly spent. She had only seconds left.

An ominous creaking sound started at her shoulder, as the bat got its hooked thumbs around the edge of the window. The grid was already failing.

Dru fought down her gut-clenching fear of the giant bat and focused on the crystals instead. As careful as she had been in assembling the grid, there were always impurities and imperfections in the individual crystals that threw off the balance of the entire grid. The ice-cold quartz in her hand offered a way to even those out.

There were six facets at each end, twelve in total. She tilted the quartz in her palm, a fraction of an inch at a time, until its facets were in alignment with the twelve crystals spread around the car. When she finally achieved the proper alignment, she felt a jolt as they connected. Now the quartz was a central part of the grid, and Dru willed her energy to expand outward from it.

All around her, an inaudible hum filled the air. The grid glowed in her mind's eye, brighter and brighter. The sounds of the bat faded as the grid's protective powers grew stronger than ever. She measured her breaths, feeling each one move with the energy surrounding her.

"Dru," Opal whispered. "I have to tell you something. Last night, Salem said . . ."

But Dru wasn't listening. She was lost in the magic, where she always felt she truly belonged. Once she reached that point of flow, the magic poured effortlessly out of her, strengthening their defenses, keeping them safe.

She would have happily stayed there forever, except that a new noise distracted her. A rhythmic clanging sound rang in the distance, not unlike a church bell, but much faster. And it was growing louder.

Still focusing on the crystals, Dru opened one eye and peeked. Outside, the giant bat loomed just beyond Opal's door, holding on by the curved thumbs that stuck out of the top of its wings. Snarling, teeth showing, it stared at Dru with its dark gaze, fixated and waiting with hungry anticipation.

Just as Dru was trying to figure out where the clanging noise was coming from, a silvery blur of motion streaked past the car. It was Rane, in titanium form, gleaming under the bright sun. Her metal feet rang with each long stride.

The bat, sensing danger at the last moment, turned to look, but it didn't react fast enough. Rane's flashing titanium fist struck with a sound like an aluminum baseball bat hitting a home run. The giant black bat's furry head snapped back, and it keeled over backward to drop out of sight with a dull thump.

Rane continued a few more paces before she slowed down enough to turn around. She jogged back, loose on her feet, fists up and ready for a fight. But judging by the disappointed look on her metal face, there was no more fight to be had. She dropped her fists, looked through the windshield at Dru, and shrugged.

Opal was saying something about Salem, but Dru held up one finger. "Hold that thought." She let go of the grid with her mind and set the quartz down on the seat. With her head still humming with magic, she unlocked the door and stumbled out, leaving Opal to gape out the driver's window.

Dru came around the front of the car to find Rane grinning widely and standing over an unconscious naked guy.

"Problem solved, dude," Rane boomed.

Opal rolled down her window. "What happened to the bat? He just turns human again, just like that? And by the way, that man is naked."

"Yeah." Rane shrugged. "I get that a lot. You guys okay?"

Dru and Opal traded looks. Opal was clearly still worried.

"We're fine," Dru said, realizing with relief that it was true.

"Cool. Now give me a hand. Help me tie this guy up." Rane bent down and picked him up by his armpits.

Dru averted her gaze and held up a hand to block her view of the naked guy. "Okay, wait, hold on. This just seems really inappropriate on several levels. Do we really need to tie him up?"

"Come on, why not?" Rane said. "It's Saturday."

Dru's already distracted thoughts scattered. "What does that even mean?"

With a grunt, Rane set the guy down and straightened up. "Well, for one thing, it means my weekends are obviously *way* funner than yours. Now give me a hand."

Dru looked to Opal for help.

"Smoke detector!" Opal announced unexpectedly, drawing puzzled looks from both of them. "You asked me what runs on a nine-volt battery these days. Did you remember to change the battery in the smoke detector?" Opal waited. "I didn't think so."

Dru hung her head in resignation. "You know, you're right."

"See?" Opal sounded immensely satisfied. "Safety first. That's why I'm here. Now, what exactly are we planning on doing with the naked bat man?"

Rane bent down and snatched Salem's golden amulet off the guy's neck. "Woo-hoo! Somebody's going to be glad to see this." She held it up to inspect it, and then her eyes lit with a wicked gleam. "Check it out. I'm going to wear Salem's jewelry. *So* kinky." She slipped it over her neck. Immediately, she looked worried.

Dru tensed, fearing Rane was suffering some kind of magical back-lash, since she was still in metal form. "What? What is it? What's wrong?"

"Nothing. I just figured I'd feel different, somehow." Rane tapped the amulet with the tip of her finger. *Tink-tink-tink.* "Is this thing on?"

Dru sighed. "I'm sure it's on."

Rane squared her shoulders and faced Dru. "Try to cast a spell on me. Go ahead."

Dru resisted the impulse to roll her eyes. "I'm not going to cast a spell on you."

"Seriously. Do it. I want to see what happens."

On the road behind them, a rusty white cargo van crowned by ladders rapidly approached. When it got close, it turned sharply, then beeped as it backed up, blocking the dead-end road from the main street.

"Hey, did somebody call for a pickup?" Rane asked. With a rasping metallic sound, she turned human again, transforming from a gleaming titanium statue to a muscular woman in a camouflage sports bra and pink shorts that said "Bad" across the rear. Dru wasn't sure which of her forms was more conspicuous.

"Look, it's my honey!" Opal climbed out of the Lincoln, stepping carefully in her gold platform sandals to make sure she didn't tread on the naked guy.

Ruiz got out of the van, stuffing his cell phone into the pocket of his tan coveralls. He checked the front and back end of the van and nodded to himself, apparently satisfied with his parking job. Then he sauntered toward Opal's car with a wide smile on his face.

Opal ran to him in mincing little steps, her arms thrown wide. As they embraced, Rane gave Dru a sidelong look. "So where's your dude?"

Dru sighed, wishing Greyson was there with her. "Taking a shower. Or probably he's back at the shop by now, wondering where the heck we are. Where's *your* guy?"

Rane's jaw set in an angry line. She didn't answer.

Opal led Ruiz over to the driver's side of the purple Lincoln, filling him in on the way. When he saw the unconscious naked sorcerer lying on the pavement, his eyes went round.

"No, no, no. You can't put that in my van!" he said to Rane.

She slowly grinned. "Oh yeah? Watch me."

23
INCENSE AND INSENSIBILITY

B ack at the Crystal Connection, Dru found Greyson waiting anxiously in Hellbringer with the engine running. After she related the details of the bat sorcerer's attempt to steal the book, Greyson insisted on patrolling the neighborhood to intercept any more protean sorcerers before they could launch another attack. Dru resisted the idea at first, but it wasn't a bad plan after all. Still, she pestered him to take her cell phone with him so they could keep in touch.

She was silently amused when she discovered that he didn't know how to use it. Somehow, she found that lack of technical skill endearing, coming from him. Opal just rolled her eyes.

After a quick primer on how to use the phone, Dru let Greyson go on patrol and then settled in at her workbench in the back room of the shop. She lit some incense to aid her concentration and then opened Lucretia's book again, intent on trying to puzzle out the sorceress's incredibly complex, multilayered cipher. Despite Opal's warnings, Dru wasn't about to leave Lucretia's spell book sitting on a shelf.

Especially not now that the clock was ticking. When Rane told her that Lucretia planned to make her doomsday move at sundown, Dru realized that the time for caution was long past. She had to find the solution *now*.

But for all her efforts, she soon had to admit that there were only two spells in the entire spell book that she could even begin to figure out right now.

The first was a spell to open or close a portal to the netherworld. In the past, Dru had already figured out how to do that on her own, using a vivianite crystal she had discovered in the secret laboratory hidden beneath the Harbingers' desert mansion. This spell appeared to be much more powerful and controlled than Dru's ad hoc method. Ordinarily, she would have been fascinated by the ingenious structure of the spell, but right now she didn't have the luxury of sufficient time to study it. Plus, opening up a portal to the netherworld was pretty much the absolute last line item on her to-do list, filed under "Hopefully Never Again."

The second spell seemed marginally useful, if at all. It was a sense-enhancing spell, expanding the caster's natural powers of perception to stratospheric levels. It sounded good in theory, at least at first, but Dru didn't know what she would really do with the hearing of a cat, the eyes of an eagle, or the nose of a bloodhound.

"*Literally* the nose of a bloodhound?" Opal asked when Dru told her about it. "Look, I'm not running around with a dog's nose sticking out of my face. I like my own nose just the way it is, thank you very much. It's got a cute little upturn at the tip, you see that?"

"Yes. I see. Very nice. My point is, this is all crystal magic, not protean magic, so these animal sorcerers have been on a wild goose chase. So to speak. Also, that means you won't *literally* grow a dog's nose. At least I hope not." Dru took off her glasses and spritzed the lenses with cleaner. "But I guess eagle-eye vision sure would be nice once in a while."

"Uh-huh. And how is that going to help us find Lucretia by tonight, exactly?"

Dru sighed, wiped off her glasses, and put them back on. "It's not. I don't know, I mean, maybe if I went up in a hot air balloon or something, and assuming she was still somewhere around town, maybe I could spot her red car."

Opal's expression turned skeptical. "I'm sorry, but that is just about the worst plan I have ever heard. You can't even rent a hot air balloon on this short notice."

"Good to know." Thinking furiously, Dru paced up and down the aisles of old books without really seeing them. "There has to be something I can do. There has to be *some* way to find her by sundown."

Opal lined up several bottles of nail polish on the workbench and compared them with almost scientific scrutiny. "Huh. Maybe Rane's having better luck interrogating her naked bat guy."

"Yeah, let me check in with her." Since Dru didn't have her cell phone, she used the shop phone to call Salem's phone to reach Rane. It was a wonder any of them could stay in touch these days.

It hadn't been easy convincing Ruiz to load the unconscious protean sorcerer into the back of his van. But Rane had insisted she had already taken the other proteans prisoner, and it made sense to keep them all together. Plus, Dru had offered Ruiz fifty dollars in store credit. That had worked like a charm, once she pointed out he could use it to buy gifts for Opal.

The phone rang several times before Rane answered it. Immediately, Dru could sense something was wrong. Partly because Rane was breathing heavily when she answered with a sullen grunt, and partly because she could hear Ruiz in the background yelling, "Look what happened to my *van!*"

"Um . . ." Dru said.

"Hey," Rane said flatly. "Yeah, so, long story short, they got away."

"*All* of them?"

"Looks like."

"*¡Oh, Dios mío!*" Ruiz wailed in the background. "This is not cool, man! Not cool! How am I supposed to explain this? There is a *hole* in my van! Look at this, I can *walk* through it!"

Slowly, Dru asked, "Are you okay?"

"Me? Oh, yeah. Hang on." There was a muffled rustle as Rane put her hand over the phone. "Dude! Chill out! I know an insurance chick, she's cool. We'll just say it was a gas leak."

"In my *van?*"

The phone rustled again. "I gotta go," Rane said. "Laters."

Dru hung up the phone, somewhat startled. After a moment, she pushed it farther away from her, as if it would bite. "I suppose that could have gone better."

"See what happens when you leave Rane in charge of prisoners?" Opal carefully finished painting one nail and held it out to admire it. The smell of nail polish mixed with the incense, making the room somehow smell like someone was holding a séance in a hardware store. "What about that finding spell you used to track down Greyson when he went missing? The one with the candle and the Technicolor smoke?"

Dru snapped her fingers, which she wasn't very good at, so it just kind of made a faint slapping sound. "Yes, exactly! I can build a crystal circle with copper wire, just like I did that one time. All I need is some kind of magical artifact closely connected to Lucretia."

Opal nodded. "Like her demon car, for instance."

"Sure. Except we don't *have* her car. If we did, this whole thing would be a lot simpler."

"What about her spell book?" Opal moved as if to place her hand on the book, then instead pulled her fingers back quickly and started painting the next nail. "Her spell book is magic."

"Actually, no, it's not." Dru felt a disappointing sinking feeling lodge in the pit of her stomach. "That's the problem. This book is actually completely *non*-magical, which is why no one ever suspected it was a spell book in the first place, and everyone has ignored it up until now. I'm sure that was intentional on Lucretia's part. Why else go through all the effort of using a secret code? To hide her spells in plain sight, where no one would suspect."

"That's actually pretty smart," Opal said grudgingly.

"Yeah, as far as I can tell, Lucretia is kind of a genius. An evil maniac genius. Too bad she's on the wrong team." Dru resumed pacing, trying to think of anything else she might have anywhere in the shop that could have belonged to Lucretia. "Hey, whatever happened to those crystals she shot at us last night? The ones that set the chair on fire?"

"I cleaned them up. You're welcome, by the way." Opal led her to the storage closet, where together they wrestled out the lead-lined bucket and unscrewed the top.

With rubber gloves and tongs, Dru pulled out the blackened crystals one by one and set them in a bed of crushed pink Himalayan salt to keep them grounded and neutral. The bed of salt crystals, properly known as halite, were good at dissolving negative patterns and dispersing hostile energy. Dru was now using them as a measure of protection, but it turned out to be unnecessary.

As Dru ran a series of tests with her own crystals and herbal tinctures, she quickly discovered that Lucretia's crystals were completely burned out. Not even the slightest trace of magical residue remained. Whatever spell the sorceress had used to attack them, it had fractured the crystals down to a microscopic level, leaving them ugly and unidentifiable.

Another dead end. More wasted time. Everything she had tried so far had led her nowhere. Despite the fact that she had found Lucretia's spell book, which was basically a how-to guide for the most powerful crystal magic on the planet, she still had no clue what to do next. The best she could do was cast a spell that would help her pass any optometrist's vision test for once in her life.

Wound up to the snapping point with frustration, Dru paced the length of the shop and just kept going, heading outside into the hot alley behind her shop. The bright afternoon sunshine pierced her tired eyes. She wished, not for the first time, that she could lie down and get some sleep. But there was no time for that. She had to figure out a way to find Lucretia and stop her before the day was through.

But every line of thought she had, every plan she tried, just led her down one blind alley after another. Now, she was literally standing in her own alley with no idea how she could go on.

A familiar engine sound growled its way closer. A moment later, Hellbringer prowled into view, a sculpted wedge of shadow almost untouchable by sunlight. Greyson saw her, immediately turned into the parking space behind the shop, and shut off the engine. With a faint creaking sound, he got out of the car and regarded her steadily over its slick black roof.

In his gaze, she saw everything she lacked right now.

Faith. Hope. Trust.

That one look made her stop pacing in her tracks. All of the frustration and anguish inside her slowed their ceaseless churning. Her doubts and fears started to soften and melt, just from the simple act of watching him look back at her with all of his unshakable strength.

Without a word, Dru circled around Hellbringer's long, pointed nose and reached for Greyson. He swept her into his arms and held her tightly against him. The muscles beneath his white T-shirt felt like a shelter from the invisible storm that raged through her mind. His arms surrounded her like an impenetrable fortress. Within them was the only safe place in a world that felt as if it was coming apart at the seams.

His presence overwhelmed her senses. Just being near him pushed the rest of the world into the background until there was only him. She closed her eyes for a moment and just breathed in the scent of him, subtly mixed with the not-unpleasant smells of upholstery and exhaust from the old demon car.

"You're figuring this out." His voice rumbled through his chest as he spoke.

She nodded without answering. It wasn't true, but it felt good to pretend.

He held her tighter. "You'll find her in time."

She pulled back and looked up into his stubbled face. "You're always so sure about me, you know that? You're always so confident. But the truth is, half the time, I don't have any idea what I'm doing."

"Sure you do. I'm still here, right? Because of you."

Reluctantly, she nodded. She didn't want to take the credit for that, but the fact that he was still alive today was evidence that she could do something right. He wasn't trapped in the netherworld any longer, or held prisoner beneath a mountain, or transformed into a demonic creature of ultimate destructive power. He was here with her now. And that was what really mattered.

"You do know what you're doing," he said.

Except that she didn't. She had no idea. The truth was that right now, she felt like the most ineffective sorceress in modern history. She had Lucretia's spell book but no way to find Lucretia. And unless she got her act together in the next few hours, everything was lost.

Yet, Greyson was so solid and sure that she didn't want to let him down by disagreeing with him. So she just swallowed and nodded again. Then she backed away, holding onto his hand for a moment before she let it drop.

She wanted so badly to wrap herself up in his arms again and forget the world. But it wasn't going to save itself. "I should head back inside, do some more research," she said halfheartedly.

Greyson nodded and opened the driver's door again. "I'll keep patrolling around the neighborhood. So far, no sign of trouble. But don't worry. If those sorcerers or that red speed demon get too close, Hellbringer will sense them coming."

"Good. It seemed like Hellbringer reacted pretty strongly to the speed demon's presence last night. There must be some kind of demon sense that tells them when they're near each other. I wonder what—" A sudden thought struck her. She held up her hand. "Wait. Wait. Stop the bus. Hellbringer could *sense* Lucretia's speed demon?"

Greyson nodded. "Yeah. Got pretty aggressive, too. I'm sure you noticed that. They must hate each other."

"I did notice that. Yes." Dru's thoughts raced. So Hellbringer had some sort of demonic sonar, or whatever it was, that helped it spot and identify other speed demons, even at a distance. And it had seemed to know where the other demon car was at all times, even when it was hidden from view by trees or buildings.

But that sense had some kind of range limit. Once the red car had gotten too far away, Hellbringer had lost the scent, or whatever it was.

But distance didn't necessarily have to be an obstacle. In the past, Hellbringer had demonstrated an uncanny knack for finding Greyson. On more than one occasion, the car had taken to the road on its own initiative and tracked Greyson down, sometimes hundreds of miles away. The car had some kind of inner sense, some unexplained homing instinct. It knew how to find Greyson, no matter how far away he was.

So it was theoretically possible that it could sense other speed demons at greater distances, too, under the right circumstances. And she knew exactly how to manufacture those circumstances.

"All this time, I've been trying to figure out a way to track down Lucretia. But maybe I'm looking at this all wrong. We don't have to find *her*, necessarily. We just have to find her *car*." Dru pointed one finger at Hellbringer's long black hood. "And this bad boy right here is our official demon car finder."

Greyson's eyebrows wrinkled. "Wherever that red car has gone, it's too far away for Hellbringer to sense it."

"Well, sure. But what if there was a way to magically boost Hellbringer's senses?" Dru couldn't keep the excitement out of her voice. "Let me introduce you to a little something I found in Lucretia's spell book."

24

LONG COOL DEMON

Leaning over her workbench in the back room of the Crystal Connection, Dru traced her fingers across the code hidden in Lucretia's spell book. She double-checked it point by point against the circle she had painstakingly drawn out on a giant sheet of paper. No matter how she looked at it, everything added up the same way. "This is it," she said, with more confidence than she felt. "This is Lucretia's entire sense-enhancing spell, down to the last exact detail."

Beside her, Greyson leaned over the workbench, his well-muscled arm brushing softly against her shoulder. His red glowing eyes scanned the drawing. "How exact does this need to be?"

"Well, if my calculations are the slightest bit off, Hellbringer could be driven completely mad, and we could all be consumed with hellfire and die a fiery death," Dru said matter-of-factly. "Or, you know, it could be something really bad."

His gaze cut across to hers. "You're actually not kidding."

She shook her head no. "By all rights, I'm not qualified to even look at this spell, much less cast it. The insights Lucretia has discovered about crystal magic are so sophisticated that I'm not even sure how to *begin* to understand most of them. As far as I can tell, she has figured out how to exchange magical elements between otherwise incompatible schools of magic, interconnecting them in ways that layer multiple spell effects simultaneously. It's quite simply insane. Me trying to do what she does would be like you trying to build a space rocket in your garage."

He chewed that over. "I've thought about it."

"Oh, good. And here I thought I was the only crazy person in the room." Dru tore off the top sheet of her yellow legal pad, which listed the crystals she would need for the spell.

As she walked up and down the aisles of the Crystal Connection, carefully selecting each crystal on her list, she couldn't help but wonder what the ultimate effects of the spell would be. If she did succeed in enhancing Hellbringer's senses—which was a long shot to begin with— would it somehow change the demon car's perceptions? How would that ultimately affect its behavior?

Would it use its newfound super senses to help them? When it came to trying to save the world, was Hellbringer truly on their side after all? Or was it secretly still an instrument of the apocalypse, just biding its time and waiting for the right moment to strike out at them?

For that matter, was Hellbringer corrupting Greyson? Whenever he got behind the wheel, he seemed more aggressive, more demonic, a little less human. Was he as dangerous as Salem insisted? Dangerous enough that he could get them all killed?

Dangerous enough to bring about the end of the world?

She paused with her hand on a shelf full of crystals, feeling the weight of these questions bearing down on her, crushing her like the geological forces that had formed these crystals in the first place. What if she was wrong, and Opal was right, and casting this spell would unleash dark forces beyond her control?

Every bone in her body felt tired. The lack of sleep was taking its toll, making it difficult to order her thoughts. She felt as if she had to stay in constant motion just to stay awake. But she had no choice. There was no time to rest. Not with Lucretia out there somewhere, intent on triggering doomsday.

At the far end of the shop, Greyson effortlessly lifted a heavy cardboard box full of rocks and slid it onto a shelf as Opal stood next to him and pointed. He pulled out a different box and brought it down for her, pausing just long enough to say something that made her laugh. She opened up the box and pulled out half a geode, an uninspiring gray hunk of rock that had been cut into two hemispheres to reveal the breathtaking purple amethyst crystals that sparkled inside. With one freshly manicured finger, Opal pointed out the different features of the geode, and Greyson nodded as he listened.

They had finally become friends, Dru saw, these two of the most important people in her life. For some reason, that brought a lump to her throat. It was comforting, the way the two of them stood and talked effortlessly to one another, and it made Dru realize something.

That was who she was fighting for. She wasn't fighting to stop Lucretia or the protean sorcerers. She wasn't even fighting to save the world itself, not really. She was fighting to save her best friends in the world. Opal. Greyson. Rane. The people she cared about more than anything.

That was why she had to fight on.

Taking a deep breath, she gathered up the last few crystals and squared her shoulders. By the time she carried her tray of crystals past Greyson and Opal, she projected nothing but strength, resolution, and confidence. Or at least, she hoped so.

Opal broke off her conversation about geodes in midsentence. Looking Dru up and down, she planted one hand on her hip. "You're really ready to do this, aren't you?"

Dru set the tray of crystals down hard on the counter, blasting out a puff of rock dust. "Damn straight. I was *born* ready."

Greyson's eyebrows went up with surprise.

"Wow," Opal said. "All righty then."

Dru's façade of confidence cracked. "Too much?"

Opal made a so-so motion with her hand. "Don't worry, honey. You've got this."

"I've got this," Dru repeated to herself, trying hard to believe it. Then she heaved up the tray of crystals again and carried it to her workbench.

An hour later, Dru had finally finished building the crystal circle. A gleaming braid of copper wires, a little over a foot in diameter, lay exactly on top of the circle she had drawn earlier. The twisted copper wires were so new they nearly glowed pink. At five precise points around the perimeter, she had woven in crystals at specific angles, the point of each one aimed at the crystal two positions to the left, so that altogether their energies drew an invisible five-pointed star inside the circle.

"That's it?" Opal said over her shoulder, clearly unimpressed. "That's all there is to it?"

"What do you mean?" Dru tried to keep the indignation out of her voice, and failed. "That was a truckload of work. I had to figure out the secret code, draw it all out, calculate the angles, and then build the whole thing by hand. This is totally old school."

"Well, sure, but I didn't realize it was *actual size*."

Dru sighed and rubbed her scratchy eyes. "Yes. It's actual size."

Greyson stood at her other shoulder, frowning. "These aren't the kinds of crystals you usually use."

She smiled at that, secretly pleased that he noticed. "That's because I don't do this sort of circle on a regular basis. In fact, nobody does. I've never seen another spell anywhere that uses frondellite."

"Frondellite?" he repeated slowly, sounding dubious.

Dru pointed at an angular flake of brown-and-tan rock, unexceptional except for the needle-straight lines of shimmering crystal running through it, and several blotches that looked exactly like blueberry cream cheese. "That's frondellite, and the blue stuff is strengite. Together, they clear out the perceptual clutter that stops us from noticing things. Your brain filters out about ninety-five percent of the stuff you actually see and hear. If it didn't, you would go insane. Frondellite removes that filter."

He nodded once. "So you're saying it drives you insane."

"Well, not exactly . . ." She realized he wasn't entirely wrong. "Well, let's hope not. The strengite helps. It elevates your consciousness above your senses, so you can see everything more objectively. Hopefully, it doesn't scramble up your senses too much. Also, we have this crystal over here, which is datolite." She pointed at the crystal opposite that, a frosty mint-green jumble of angles that looked almost like an exotic gelatin treat. "It modulates the speed of your perceptions, so that you can sort through them in what feels like slow motion. I've mostly seen it used for past life regression, soul memories, things like that. Never seen it used to improve the clarity of what you're actually sensing in the moment. But if it works, it should be amazing."

Opal laid a finger along her cheek, thinking. "You remember a while back somebody called looking for datolite? I thought it was some IT company."

"So did I," Dru admitted. "Luckily, I decided to get some in stock. And then this little marshmallow over here is African herderite." She pointed to a chunky coconut-white crystal shaped like a mostly melted snowman.

"Herderite is a seriously potent crystal," Opal warned her. "I've heard some bad things about that one. Consciousness-raising, multidimensional stuff. What's that going to do to Hellbringer? That car's soul isn't exactly from Earth."

Dru bit her lip. "I don't know for sure what the effect will be," she admitted finally. "But this spell is our only hope."

Eyes hooded, Opal gave her a warning look.

"And that one?" Greyson pointed to a bustamite crystal, which glistened like a pinkish-orange chunk of candied papaya.

"That one promotes, um, I guess you could call it . . . conscious dreaming."

Greyson's shoulders hunched. "You mean hallucinations."

Opal shook her head and made disapproving sounds. "Honey, no. This is really heavy-duty stuff. It could mess you up."

"No, what's going to mess me up is this one." With a reluctant sigh, Dru pointed at the last crystal, a raw knob of cranberry-colored stone.

Opal bent closer. "Isn't that an uncut ruby? Well, you don't need to be worried about that. Rubies help balance your energy. That's a good thing."

"Except that this is a Fiskenæsset ruby, the oldest form of ruby on the planet. It's primeval. When you charge it up, it doesn't just balance your energy, it flattens it. Puts you into a trance so you can communicate with the spirit world."

"While you're hallucinating," Greyson said, sounding worried.

Dru made air quotes with her fingers. "Or 'conscious dreaming.'"

He didn't look convinced.

Neither did Opal. Shaking her head, she drew in a breath to speak, but Greyson interrupted her.

"You're going to ace this. You will." He gave Opal a meaningful look. She hesitated, then nodded.

"Besides," Greyson added, "I'll be there with you. You can use my energy, too."

"Actually, if this all goes according to plan, it will be Hellbringer that's using your energy. This is all about boosting his speed demon senses." A troubling thought occurred to her. "Speaking of which, I just realized that we need to attach this to Hellbringer somehow. The closer we can get to his heart, the better. I guess that would be the engine? But we can't risk breaking any of these crystals."

She picked up the braided copper ring. With all of the wire she had used to make it, it had come out surprisingly solid. It looked like some kind of giant, primitive tiara.

Greyson carefully took it from her. "No sweat. We'll just heat-tape it to the air cleaner."

Opal looked at him as if he had just spoken Turkish. "Who to the what now?"

"Follow me." He led them out the back door of the brick building, to the parking space where Hellbringer sat motionless and baking in the hot afternoon sun, like an aerodynamic black hole. With practiced ease, Greyson undid the chrome pins holding down the black hood and lifted it up. The Motor City–era springs in the hinges let out a discordant jangle. Beneath the hood, nested in a tangle of thick wires and dark rubber hoses, sat an enormous orange-painted engine. Topping it off was a mirror-polished chrome saucer that proclaimed, in giant block letters, "426 HEMI HEAD."

Greyson carefully placed the spell ring onto the air cleaner, as if crowning the demon car. Then he retrieved a roll of metallic tape from the trunk and strapped the copper coil in place. Once it was secure, he stepped back, waiting.

This was it. This was the moment she would cast Lucretia's spell.

Her heart beat faster. Her palms felt damp. Nervously, she cleaned off her glasses and put them back on. There was no backing down now. She glanced at Opal, who just looked worried.

Dru came over to the fender on the passenger side, opposite Greyson. She took several long, measured breaths, trying to calm herself and the magical energy inside her. If she went into this feeling tense and anxious, it certainly wouldn't help. She had to approach this as smoothly and carefully as possible.

Before she could talk herself out of it, she reached into the engine compartment and carefully laid her fingertip on the rough, cold surface of the frondellite crystal. It felt like any other common stone, except for the smooth, shiny streaks that slotted across its surface. She ran her finger back and forth along the crystalline grooves, trying to psych herself up to cast this spell.

As she made her preparations, an invisible force reached out through the crystal circle and seized her. It felt as if her soul was being yanked in through the crystals. Her entire body felt electrified. Every hair on her head stood on end. Every nerve burned with an unseen fire. An overwhelming falling sensation swept down clear to her toes, accompanied by a breathtaking rush, as if she had just leaped headlong off a cliff.

Her eyes rolled back.

Beneath her fingertips, Hellbringer was alive. She sensed its presence, a great unseen beast awoken from its slumber, and every instinct screamed at her to flee before it devoured her. But she stayed firm, trying to maintain control of the spell.

As Hellbringer's presence loomed larger and stronger in her mind's eye, it took all of her strength to keep from shrinking back. She held off the speed demon's aggression by sheer force of will, knowing that she had to remain in command or risk losing her mind. But the harder she pushed, the angrier and stronger Hellbringer became.

She sensed that the demon car was driven by an overpowering sense of loss. Ever since Dru had cut off its connection to the infernal pits in order to save Greyson's soul, the speed demon had been cast adrift.

Hellbringer had been created as an instrument of chaos. In all the long millennia of its existence, it had existed to take orders and serve its masters, delivering swift destruction on demand. It had never been forced to think for itself, never been forced to make its own decisions, until Dru had come along and changed everything.

For that, the speed demon held a fierce grudge against her, and now it was intent on dominating her. Its onslaught of fury gradually wore away at her determination. It had sympathy for no one but Greyson.

The speed demon craved direction and a feeling of belonging, and Greyson had provided both. No wonder it had bonded so fiercely to him. The man and the car had molded to one another.

For the first time, Dru saw that she had earned the speed demon's enmity by forcing it to change. Meanwhile, Greyson had accepted Hellbringer completely, without question. He had given it a sense of purpose again, a job to do. His willpower was strong enough to tame Hellbringer, and yet he gave it just enough free rein to earn its undying loyalty.

To cast this spell on Hellbringer, she needed Greyson's presence now more than ever. Numb from her immersion in this spiritual tug-of-war, Dru tried to reach out her hand to him. But her entire consciousness was consumed with magic, and she couldn't tell whether she was actually raising her free arm or simply imagining it.

She had her answer when a strong hand gripped hers. A tingle of magical energy passed through her, as it had so many times before when Dru had used Greyson's *arcana rasa* energy to power one of her spells. But this time, Dru reversed the flow, pouring her own energy through him into Hellbringer.

Through her tightly closed eyelids, she could see the ring of crystals over the engine began to glow with an inner fire. With a startling burst of clarity, she suddenly saw herself from above, leaning over the engine, holding hands with Greyson. Hellbringer's long black body stretched out before her, a hungry pit of darkness in the sunlight.

Her consciousness rapidly extended out to the horizon, as if she was rising hundreds of feet into the air, seeing everything around her. The roar of sensations was overpowering, a high-voltage explosion that stormed across her mind. Everything became a fuzzy, jumbled haze. It was all too much to process. She kept seeing farther and farther out, dispersing her consciousness until it was scattered in every direction.

Then Hellbringer stirred as it sensed a pinpoint of blood-red light in the far distance. The other speed demon.

Soulbreaker.

Its name leaped into her consciousness, because Hellbringer knew it and always had. The speed demons were eternal, and these two had fought each other since the beginning of time. The two of them were made to be enemies, and Hellbringer's smoldering hate for Soulbreaker was a foul taste that burned her tongue.

Now on the scent of its eternal foe, Hellbringer's spirit reared up, eager to pursue. In its wild hunger for speed, it tried to dominate Dru once more. The primordial whirlwind of its chaotic energy surrounded her, trying to force her to give in to the chase. For a terrifying moment, Dru feared she would lose herself in it and never return.

She fought her way out, desperate to escape. But her consciousness was so scattered that it was a struggle to pull herself back together. She gripped Greyson's hand tighter, and he held her firm. She focused on his touch as her anchor to come back to herself.

In the last second, as Hellbringer's rage threatened to smother her, she plummeted back into her own body and emerged from the spell with a painful gasp. A spasm wracked her spine, and she stumbled away from the demon car, dizzy.

Gradually, she became aware that both Greyson and Opal were at her side, holding her arms and talking to her, but their words were a jumble. Blood pounded in her ears, drowning out the rest of the world. Her vision swam. Her senses scrambled. She could taste colors as sparks of saltiness and honey sweetness. The blue sky was peppery, and Greyson's white shirt surrounded her with the scent of cotton candy. The world was a nauseating swirl of sandpaper textures and white noise.

Synesthesia, she thought, remembering the word for it. It was only when Opal repeated it back to her that she realized she had said it out loud.

She sat down on the ground, rocking back and forth until the world started to make sense again. As she came back to herself, she felt curiously cold and small. Gradually, she became aware of the smell of exhaust and the rolling thunder of Hellbringer revving its engine.

Greyson knelt down in front of her. "Can you hear me? Are you all right?"

She decided to nod yes, even though she didn't feel all right. If Lucretia could not only cast spells like this but actually create them, what chance did Dru stand against her? How could she stop someone this powerful from destroying the world?

"Hellbringer knows which way to go," she said. To find Soulbreaker. And therefore Lucretia.

Greyson helped her to her feet and slammed the hood shut. "Then let's go."

25

CHEATER SLICKS

As Hellbringer idled outside, Dru hurried through the shop. Stumbling and fuzzy-headed from the spell, she grabbed any crystal that looked remotely useful. A cube of silvery galena to defend against Soulbreaker. A piece of black tourmaline for protection against hostile energies. A translucent green vivianite crystal for opening portals.

She stared at that one with unfocused eyes and almost put it back on the shelf. Why on earth would she ever want to open another portal to the netherworld? Her head throbbed. She tossed the vivianite into her purse anyway, along with a couple of smoky quartz. And, of course, her favorite spectrolite crystal.

Opal followed behind her, looking worried. "Honey, I don't think you're in any shape to go anywhere."

"There's no time to argue about it. Lucretia has the Amulet of Decimus the Accursed, and she's going to use it to bring on doomsday. Tonight. We need to find her, get that amulet back, and save the world."

Opal stopped her with a gentle, but firm, hand on her shoulder. "I hate to say this, but maybe you should call Salem."

"*You* call him. Tell him we need his help."

Opal's gaze was steady. It took her a couple of tries before she finally said, "He asked me to spy on you."

"He *what*?" Dru's chest felt uncomfortably tight, and she couldn't quite catch her breath. Not because Salem had asked Opal to spy on her but because of the grave tone in Opal's voice. As if she had seriously considered it. "Of course you said no." She studied the bleak expression on Opal's face. "You *did* say no. Right?"

"He thinks Greyson is going to destroy the world."

"Oh, for Pete's sake . . ."

"Well, what am I supposed to think?"

"Salem's wrong. It's Lucretia we need to worry about. And we only have until sundown. So as much as I hate to say this, call Salem, if you can reach him. I'll take all the help I can get. Even from him."

"Honey, I'm so sorry. I—"

"I know." Dru hugged her. "I've got to go." With that, Dru dashed out the door.

She hoped the aftereffects of the spell would wear off quickly, but even by the time they picked up Rane and hit the open road, Dru was still a little loopy. So when she heard the crackle and squeal of an old AM radio, at first she thought she was imagining things. But then the music started to play.

As the highway flashed past outside, in nauseatingly detailed hyperfocus, Hellbringer's interior filled with the catchy harmony of the Beach Boys singing "I Get Around."

"Look at that," Greyson said, sounding mildly surprised. "Radio works."

Rane leaned forward between the seats. "Seriously? This rust bucket has music?"

Greyson pointed at the oddly shaped radio at the top of the dashboard, with a single orange needle cutting down the middle of its wide black AM dial, and two pairs of up-and-down chrome wheels on either side. "I always thought it was broken. Or just never got connected."

"You're kidding, right? This thing is always fixing itself up like it's prom night. There's no way anything in this car is broken." Rane reached forward, leaning heavily on Dru's shoulder, and thumbed the chrome radio wheels up and down. But the orange needle in the middle of the dial didn't move. The peppy guitar strumming and rhythmic clapping of the Beach Boys continued. "Huh. Piece of junk." She slapped the top of the dashboard.

"Or maybe," Dru suggested, squirming out from beneath Rane's bulk, "Hellbringer is feeling all weird and funky, like I am."

Rane's lean face filled Dru's vision, and her voice dropped an octave. "How funky are we talking about?"

Dru sunk down deep into the seat. "*Gaah.* Get back." She pulled her glasses off and blinked, wishing her vision would go back to normal. "Everything is so *close.*"

Rane gave her a lazy smile. "You're so cute when you're all jacked up on magic." She slid back into the back seat, reached around and started rubbing Dru's shoulders like she was trying to crush rocks with her bare hands.

"Ow," Dru protested. Rane eased up only slightly. The torture continued while unfamiliar sixties songs unspooled from the radio. Greyson named each one for them. "Three Window Coupe" by Jan and Dean. "Maybelline" by Chuck Berry. "My Woodie" by the Trashmen.

"'My Woodie'?" Rane repeated and burst out laughing.

"What?" Greyson looked bewildered. "It's a good song. Besides, these days, you hardly ever see any woodies on the road."

Which only made Rane laugh harder, until she was wiping her eyes. "Oh, dude, that's priceless. But hey, it could be way worse. We could be stuck listening to all of D's gag-worthy eighties music."

Dru frowned with indignation. "What's wrong with my eighties music?"

Rane rolled her eyes back, stuck out her tongue, and pointed a finger at her open mouth, making gagging sounds. "Everything. I mean, come on, how many times can you hear 'Relax'? I'm sick of all that Frankie Went to Hollywood crap."

"Goes," Dru corrected her.

"What?"

"Frankie *Goes* to Hollywood."

Rane gave her a long, disbelieving stare. "Still?" She shook her head. "It's been, like, thirty years. By now they should just *move* there."

Just then, Johnny Cash started belting out "One Piece at a Time," and Greyson tapped the steering wheel in time to the music. "This is fine by me. I've been listening to this kind of music all my life."

Dru gave him a curious look, realizing she knew next to nothing about the things Greyson actually liked. "Really?"

"Yeah. Used to hang out in the garage with my dad and his buddies, fetch them tools and parts and things. We played music like this on the radio. Plenty of Johnny Cash." He cracked a smile.

They drove along the mostly deserted highway, with the endless dry grasses of the plains stretching away on their left, and the Rocky Mountains on their right, each peak growing bluer and paler in the distance. Dru listened to the music, wondering about Greyson's past. Whenever she had asked him about it before, he had clammed up. But maybe this was a way she could find out more.

An upbeat song with sassy saxophone and totally sixties organ riffs started up, and the singer started crooning about big black beauties. At first Dru thought the song was about some kind of romantic relationship. But the more she listened, the more she suspected she was wrong.

She leaned closer to the speaker, not believing what she was hearing. "Is this actually a song about *tires*?"

"Yeah, it's called 'Cheater Slicks,'" Greyson said, as if there was nothing at all weird about grown men singing about their lovely tires. "Cheater slicks are like racing slicks but with just barely enough tread to be street legal." When he saw her blank look, he explained. "Slick tires don't have any tread. They're just flat rubber, so you can make maximum contact with the asphalt. You get on a good stretch of dry, flat road and put your foot down, and they'll really dig in. All that grip will help you launch faster."

"So they're for winning drag races. Okay. But tires with no tread? Isn't that a little bit, I don't know, dangerous?" she said. "What do you do if it rains?"

He smiled knowingly. "You stay home."

"Uh-huh," Dru said, feigning interest. "So this really *is* a song about tires." She shook her head. Up until now, she'd thought sorcerers were the weirdest people around. But it turned out car nuts were even weirder.

"Does Hellbringer have cheater slicks?"

"No. Stock tires. They're only bias-plies, but they have plenty of tread." His eyes narrowed. "Now that I think about it, though, Soulbreaker is a Dodge Challenger Demon. That car was built for the track. Comes stock from the factory with drag radials."

She just gave him a look, waiting for him to explain it in plain English.

After a moment, he got the hint. "Yeah, Soulbreaker has cheater slicks. The modern version. Lucretia will be in big trouble if it rains, or if she tries to drive on sand or grass."

Dru thought back to the chase through the park. Soulbreaker had difficulty getting traction on the slick grass. Maybe they could turn that to their advantage somehow.

"By the way," Greyson said, "in this song, Gary Usher's also singing about how he has a 426 mill, like Hellbringer."

"And a mill is . . . ?"

"That's your engine. But 'mill' sounds cooler."

"Sure." To be honest, Dru thought the word *engine* sounded just fine on its own, but she kept her thoughts to herself. She found herself starting to worry that maybe she and Greyson really had nothing in common, but she pushed that troubling thought aside.

"Maybe that's why we're hearing it," he said.

"This song? Because . . . Hellbringer wants cheater slicks?"

"No, because it's the same engine, a 426."

Dru remembered the big sticker on the chrome air cleaner: *426 HEMI HEAD.* "Okay, wait, back up. You think Hellbringer is actually choosing these songs? Do you think he's trying to communicate with us through the radio? Just because the song mentions a 426?"

At that moment, a new song started up, and the singer belted out lyrics praising his 426 Super Stock.

Dru nodded to herself. "All righty then. I'd say that's an unqualified *yes.*" She patted the dashboard. "Everything okay in there, big guy?"

Hellbringer just cruised along at a contented purr while Greyson glanced at her curiously. "That spell really did a number on you, didn't it?"

"Guess so." Realizing she wasn't quite herself, Dru looked back over her shoulder, expecting a smart-aleck comment from Rane. But much to her surprise, Rane was fast asleep in the back seat, sprawled out as if she had jumped out of an airplane. "Well, I guess Rane's out."

The Trashmen came on the radio again, softer now, singing "Sleeper."

Greyson looked up into the rearview mirror and nodded. "You should probably get some sleep, too. No telling how long this trip could take."

Her eyelids were already growing heavy, but she shook her head side to side. "No, I want to hear more about when you were a kid, helping your dad in the garage."

He pressed his lips together as if trying to hold everything in. "Not much to say." His voice sounded guarded.

Dru crossed her arms over her chest. He always did that. Every time the topic of his family came up, he shut down. But why? Why was he so closed off? Why didn't he have a Facebook account, or even a cell phone? Why was he so determined to wall himself off from the world?

She remembered back to when she had first visited his home and found his wall covered with curling snapshots of restored muscle cars. The only photo with people in it showed him as a scraggly-haired teenager, standing shoulder to shoulder with a happy-looking freckled girl and a thin-faced middle-aged man in a leather jacket. The three of them were grinning ear to ear, leaning against an apricot-orange sports car of some kind.

If she pried too hard into his past, he might keep shutting her out. But the music had loosened him up just a little bit, and her post-spell-casting punchiness had to afford her at least a teensy amount of leeway. She decided to try the subtle approach. "You know what's a color you hardly ever see on cars these days? Orange. Am I right?"

He shrugged.

Too subtle, she realized. "Well, I've never had an orange car. Have you?"

He drove on in silence before looking across at her. "So you want to know about my Corvette."

Heat rose to her cheeks. Obviously, he wasn't dumb. "Well, I saw a picture at your place."

He nodded. "I loved that car. Started driving it as soon as I was old enough to reach the pedals." He fell silent for a long moment, as if assembling his thoughts. "We lived in this dump. Out in the desert. It was nothing but a trailer, really. Hated that place. But the one good thing about it, you could drive as fast as you wanted, in any direction. I would be out there before dawn, headlights popped up, just driving around. And *around*. My dad's friends taught me stuff. I could pull a perfect bootlegger reverse by the time I was fourteen."

"Wow. That doesn't exactly sound legal."

He gave her a lopsided smile, but it quickly faded. "Nothing my family did was legal." He gave her an appraising look, as if to gauge her reaction.

With an effort, she kept her expression neutral. What did he mean, exactly? Was his family involved in criminal activity? Was he himself a criminal? Could he be a fugitive from the law? Was he more dangerous than he appeared? It took a great deal of focus to keep her mind open, without jumping to any conclusions.

Greyson seemed to struggle to find the right words. "When you're a kid, you don't . . . You don't necessarily know what's right and what's wrong. You just know what you're expected to do, because that's what you're told. And sooner or later, you have to . . . figure things out. You have to learn what's *really* going on. And then you have to do the right thing. No matter what they say." His voice went gravelly at the end, hinting at a long-hidden wound. "You have to make a choice. And I chose to do the right thing." He stared rigidly at the highway ahead.

They drove on in silence. Dru was desperate to ask more questions. She wanted to learn everything she could about where he had come from, and what his family had done, and how that had shaped him into the man he was today. To a certain extent, she felt that she had a right to know these things, especially if she was risking her life with him at every turn.

But she also knew that he had to open up to her in his own time. She couldn't force him. So she decided to wait and see if he would reveal more.

Greyson spread his fingers out on the steering well, as if forcing himself to relax. He nodded once to himself and looked over at her. "There's plenty of reasons why I don't talk about my family. I tell myself it's all in the past. But it's still back there, somewhere. I can't change what they did, but I can try to make up for it. Wherever and however

I can. Right now, that means putting a stop to whatever kind of evil is happening because of me."

"You? You didn't do anything wrong." Dru cleared her throat. "Did you?"

His jaw tightened. "I found Hellbringer. And I knew, on a gut level, I had the feeling there was something wrong with this car. But I took it on anyway. Because of that, I became one of the Four Horsemen of the Apocalypse. And I ended up pulling you and your friends into this with me, and that's not fair. None of this is fair. I know I didn't start all of this. That's on Lucretia and the other Harbingers. But like it or not, I'm a part of it now, and I'm going to make sure we finish this, before Lucretia does."

His words warmed her and made the breath expand inside her body. That was what she loved about Greyson, the fact that he broke things down into simple right and wrong. And although she was filled with questions about his past, she still knew he was on her side.

She reached for him. He lifted his fingers off the gearshift and held her hand.

Hellbringer's radio started softly playing "Little Bitty Pretty One," which made Dru smile. The moment was so sweet that she wanted to lean across and kiss Greyson right then and there. Until she remembered something chilling.

"Hey. Isn't this the song from that movie, *Christine?*" she asked. "Right before the evil car chases somebody down and kills them?"

Greyson seemed to think about it, and his forehead wrinkled. "Pretty sure you're right."

"That's not some kind of weird warning, is it?" she asked nervously, and let go of his hand.

As soon as she did, the radio shut off with a sinister snap, leaving them in silence, except for the constant growl of the engine. They traded long looks.

"I'm going to keep both hands on the wheel," Greyson said in a low voice.

"Good idea." Dru nodded. She turned to look out the window at the mountains flying past, and the fact that she hadn't slept caught up to her quickly. Her head started to droop, and her eyelids kept drifting lower.

To keep herself awake, she got out Lucretia's spell book and studied the pages again, flipping slowly back and forth. There had to be something in there she could use. Rubbing her eyes and yawning, she forced herself to focus.

She didn't realize she had drifted off until Rane shook her awake several hours later. The muggy-headed aftereffects of the spell were gone finally, leaving her clearheaded. But so was the warm closeness she had felt earlier, now replaced by an ominous dread. They were somewhere out on the plains, and the blood-red sun hung low over the dark bulk of the distant mountains.

Dru sat up and tried to get her bearings. "Where are we?"

Greyson leaned forward over the steering wheel, scanning their surroundings with his glowing red eyes. "Looks like some kind of ghost town."

"This must be the place Feral was talking about," Rane said. "Party central."

They drove slowly down a cracked and weed-choked two-lane road that obviously hadn't been used for quite some time. A line of evenly spaced telephone poles bereft of wires paralleled the road, leading away into the distance like a line of crosses. Over the years, some of them had tilted drunkenly to the side or broken off. Far ahead lay the blocky silhouettes of small houses and squarish two-story buildings, grouped together into a small town. There were no lights, cars, or signs of movement anywhere. The town was abandoned.

Directly ahead of them, a tall rusted chain-link fence stretched away to the left and right as far as she could see, as if encircling the town. Where it crossed the road, the fence had fallen down, and the gate lay flat on the ground. Whoever had put it up had apparently forgotten about it long ago.

Hellbringer crept up to the flattened gate and stopped. Dru leaned close to the window to read a sign that had obviously lain on the ground for many years. It was bright yellow, spotted with rust, and dominated by a bold black radiation symbol. Giant block letters spelled out an ominous warning:

NUCLEAR BLAST SITE
CAUTION: RADIOACTIVE CONTAMINATION ZONE
NO TRESPASSING

Silently, Dru traded long looks with Greyson and Rane. What was this place, and what dark secret could have brought Lucretia here?

26

ATOMIC GHOST TOWN

As the fiery red sun sank toward the jagged black line of mountains, Dru pondered the No Trespassing sign emblazoned with the giant yellow radiation symbol. Hellbringer revved its engine impatiently.

Rane leaned forward from the back seat. "The sun will go down soon. What are we waiting for?"

"It's a radioactive ghost town." Dru's stomach fluttered with worry. "It's not safe to go in there."

"*Duh.* 'Course not. Didn't you see the sign?" Rane glared at the town ahead as if she wanted to take it apart with her bare hands. "Lucretia could've holed up in a nice beach house with some palm trees, right? But *noooo*. So what's the plan?"

"The sixth seal of the apocalypse scroll is supposed to be a world-shattering earthquake. So let's work backward from there." Dru counted off on her fingers. "First, find Lucretia. Second, determine what kind of spell she's casting to bring about the doomsday earthquake. Third, I'll cast a crystal counterspell to shut that whole thing down." Dru patted her stuffed purse. "I have her book, which outlines all of her magical secrets. And I brought every useful crystal I could think of. If I put these things together, maybe I can come up with something to stop her."

Rane slowly turned to face her. "*Maybe?*"

Dru cleared her throat. "I won't know exactly what to do until I see the crystals she's using. Then I can figure out a counterspell. Hopefully before she catches on and blasts me to smithereens."

Greyson's glowing red gaze cut over to her. "How fast can you put together a counterspell?"

Rane backhanded him on the shoulder. "Doesn't matter. It takes as long as it takes. We just have to buy her enough time to work her magic, dude. You're going to have your hands full with that red demon car."

Greyson nodded to her, but his gaze didn't waver. "You can do this," he said to Dru.

Dru eyed the town in the distance. "It has to be dead quiet in there. As loud as Hellbringer's engine is, she's going to hear us coming."

"So you're saying you want to go in on foot, scout it out," he suggested.

Quickly, Dru shook her head. After her experience with the giant bat, she didn't dare stray too far from the protection offered by Hellbringer. Nervously, she pinched her lip. All of her options were bad. Not that there were usually any good options when it came to exploring atomic ghost towns.

"First off, I need to minimize our exposure to the radioactivity." Dru dug through the crystals in her purse.

Rane peeked over her shoulder. "You got a Geiger counter in there, or what?"

"Better than that. This will help protect us against electromagnetic waves and ionizing particles." After a little more digging, Dru found the crystal she was looking for, the pinky-finger-sized rod of black tourmaline she'd grabbed earlier. The crystal was composed of hundreds of shiny black needles all fused together, and they caught the light like the grooves in a vinyl record. "Tourmaline."

Rane cocked her head. "Isn't that what's in my hair dryer?"

"Pretty much, just a lot more of it. In crystalline form, it's pyroelectric, meaning that it generates electricity when you heat it up. So it creates a field of negative ions that protects you against radiation. From your cell phone, or your microwave, or, you know, nuclear blast zones. Ready?" She held it out in her left palm. "I need both of you to put your hands on top of mine. Let's make a big hand sandwich."

With a slight bit of awkwardness, Greyson and Rane alternated placing both of their hands on hers, and Dru finished with her right hand on top. Then she closed her eyes and focused until she could feel her energy flowing into the tourmaline crystal, heating it up. Each of the tiny needles in the crystal matrix pulsed with an almost magnetic force, pushing against Dru's hands.

She charged the crystal until the heat and invisible force started to separate their hands. Driven by her fear of the radiation outside, she kept charging the tourmaline until it took all of her strength to keep their hands from flying apart. "Okay," she said through gritted teeth. "We're going to break on three. Ready?" She counted to three, and when they pulled their hands apart, the hot tourmaline crystal on her palm popped with an inner spark.

Every second or so, the crystal let off a soft *tick* sound, and a tiny light flared in its depths, then disappeared. Dru breathed out a sigh of relief. "Okay. I don't know how long this will last, so let's get in there and have a look around."

"Hell, yeah!" Rane drummed her hands on the back of Dru's seat. "Let's rock this joint."

Greyson took his foot off the brake. With a growl, Hellbringer rolled across the radiation sign and headed toward the ghost town. Dry plains of tan grass and parched earth led away to the horizon in all directions, broken by occasional clumps of green scrub brush and spindly trees. They passed a few outlying farmhouses, divided from one another by the drooping lines of wire fences. Even from this distance, it was easy to spot the houses' sagging paint-stripped walls and the gaping holes in their roofs. The rusted hulk of an old tractor sat in the middle of an overgrown field. Clearly, no one had lived here for decades.

"It's strange that this is a pretty modern town," Dru mused aloud. "Most ghost towns are old frontier mining towns, or homesteaders who packed up and left by about the Great Depression. But these buildings look more midcentury, fifties or sixties."

"Yeah, but would you stay in a radioactive town?" Rane studied their surroundings with wide eyes, looking like a cornered animal. "If I lived here, I'd get the hell out, too."

"But *why* is it radioactive?" Dru said. "That's the real question."

By the time they reached the town's small main street, Dru was thoroughly spooked. There wasn't a single sign of human or animal life anywhere. They passed a shadowed hardware and paint store, a shoe store, and a bar. Aside from a thick layer of blown dust, they all looked as if they had been preserved in a time capsule. Although nothing was boarded up, there were also no broken windows or graffiti. There was no sense that the town had been deliberately shut down and vacated. Instead, it was as if the entire population had simply vanished in the middle of the day, fifty years ago, and never returned.

They passed a place with a hand-lettered sign that said, "Tip Top Coin Laundry." Next to that was Burt's Corner Store, advertising jumbo malted milk and a soda fountain.

"What about the protean sorcerers?" Rane asked no one in particular. "They've got to be around here somewhere. The wolf guy was pretty straight up about how everybody was hanging out in the ghost town with Lucretia. Unless he was lying to me."

Dru pointed to the corner store. "Pull over here."

"Are you sure?" Greyson sounded wary.

"I need to find out what happened to this place. There has to be some kind of clue around here."

Greyson pulled up to the curb in front of the store and shut off the engine. The silence was deafening. For some reason, Dru expected the air to smell different when she got out of the car, as if she could smell the radioactivity. But it smelled like regular fresh Rocky Mountain air.

Rane stood uncomfortably close. "This radioactive thing is freaking me out, dude. My body is a temple, you know that. My entire diet is all protein and antioxidants. Now I'm worried about glowing in the dark."

Dru stuck the tourmaline in her pocket. It felt comfortably warm, like jeans fresh out of the dryer. "Stay close, so you're inside the protective field. And don't touch your eyes, your nose, or your mouth. Oh, and don't breathe any dust." She peeked in through the dirty shop windows but couldn't see anything. She tried the door, but it was locked.

Rane waved her back, touched the door handle, and transformed into gleaming steel. With a groan of tortured metal and a soft *ting* sound, she forced the lock, then eased the door open. "I was going to kick it, but you know, radioactive dust."

Dru nodded at her and held her breath as she slipped inside. Hazy sunlight filtered through the dirty windows, falling on dusty shelves of cans and boxed goods. Near the mechanical push-button cash register sat faded cardboard trays of candy. Clark Bars. Lemonheads. Zagnuts. And red polka-dotted boxes of something called "'H' Bombs Hot Jawbreakers."

Dru looked them over as Rane and Greyson filed in behind her. "These candies are all from the early 1960s."

Greyson frowned. "How can you tell?"

"Don't ask," Rane said. "Seriously. The girl knows her vintage candy bars. Ooh, hey, Reese's Peanut Butter Cups." Rane's stomach growled loudly as she picked up a package. "These never go bad."

"Don't eat that!" Dru swatted it out of her grasp.

"Fine, whatever." Rane dusted off her hands. "But I don't think we're going to find anything else here."

A nearby magazine rack caught Dru's attention. Some of the titles looked familiar: *Life*, *Time*, *Cosmopolitan*. There were plenty of others she had never heard of: *Movieland*, *Look*, *McCall's*. The faces of Elvis, Muhammad Ali, and Jackie Kennedy smiled back at her, along with a bunch of women she didn't recognize in beehive hairdos and bell-shaped flips. One faded magazine cover showed a photo of a man in a flimsy plastic survival suit, with the headline "How You Can Survive Fallout."

Dru checked the date. "Whatever happened here, it happened in 1963."

Rane scanned the store shelves. "What did they do, drop a bomb on this place, or what? Sign said this was a nuclear blast site."

"It doesn't make any sense. The buildings are still standing. If they dropped a bomb on this town, the whole place would be nothing but a crater." Dru looked around in frustration, knowing she was missing something, but she had no idea what it was.

She considered the cash register carefully. In her own shop, she tended to accumulate important junk under the front counter. If there was any clue to what happened in this town, it would probably be stuffed under there somewhere.

She went around the counter and peeked underneath, finding a graph paper notebook and a hardcover book of Shakespeare. She pulled them out and flipped through the notebook pages. Inside were pencil-sketched plans for a homemade bomb shelter, complete with calculations for how much food and water it would take to sustain a family of four. It was a chilling thought, reducing the essentials of life to cold mathematical equations.

The Shakespeare book was open to a poem titled "The Rape of Lucrece." One section was underlined:

And when great treasure is the meed proposed,
Though death be adjunct, there's no death supposed.
Those that much covet are with gain so fond,
For what they have not, that which they possess
They scatter and unloose it from their bond,
And so, by hoping more, they have but less.

"Greed," Dru realized out loud. "Whatever happened here, whatever killed this town, it was because of greed. But I've got the bad feeling that whoever did this didn't get what they were after." She looked through the dirty window at the desolation outside. "And these people paid the price."

Rane peered over Dru's shoulder. She pointed to the title of the poem. "*Lucrece?* As in, Lucretia?"

Dru traded looks with her. "That can't be a coincidence."

Greyson stiffened, his eyes glowing bright red. "Something's coming," he growled. At that moment, Hellbringer's engine rumbled to life. The demon car blared its horn.

A jolt of fear ran through Dru. "Get back in the car!"

As they bolted outside, a furious red streak charged toward them. The red demon car, Soulbreaker, rocketed down the center of the deserted street. Its raucous exhaust reverberated off the storefronts. The rings around its headlights shone like the eyes of a blood-crazed predator. Its cavernous black grill and colossal hood scoop looked hungry enough to devour them.

Dru froze. On this wide-open street, there was nowhere they could flee that the red demon couldn't run them down.

With a wail of tortured rubber, Hellbringer peeled away from the curb, tires smoking. The black demon car shot diagonally in front of them, shielding them with its long steel body. Soulbreaker swerved, but it wasn't quite fast enough to evade. The red car slammed into Hellbringer's back quarter with a vicious crunch of metal, sending Hellbringer spinning. Its tires scribed clawlike arcs of rubber across the asphalt.

Dru's gut clenched. It was like seeing a friend get sucker-punched. She could only watch in fascinated horror as Hellbringer turned in pursuit of the red speed demon.

Soulbreaker's windows were down, and the driver's seat was clearly empty as it shot past. No Lucretia, just the demon car itself. It slammed on its brakes, skidding to a stop in the middle of the street. Its white backup lights flicked on as it reversed direction, trying to ram Hellbringer with its wide rear end.

Hellbringer charged straight at it. At the last second before impact, the black demon car locked up its brakes and its wheels stopped dead. The momentum forced its long, pointed nose to dip down toward the road. Soulbreaker's wide tires rode right up onto Hellbringer's hood as if climbing an improvised ramp.

With a triumphant roar of its engine, Hellbringer surged forward again, forcing the red car's rear wheels higher into the air. They spun uselessly, leaving Soulbreaker immobilized, at least for a moment. As gravity pulled the car down again, Hellbringer pressed the attack, plowing forward to keep Soulbreaker pinned.

"Get back inside!" Greyson started to push Dru back into the store.

Rane stopped him. "No dice. If that thing gets loose, it can come crashing through these windows and flatten us. This way." She led them around the corner of the building to the brick alley that ran behind the store.

As they fled, Dru tried to think of some crystal she could use to help Hellbringer. All she had was a single cube of galena, which would burn Soulbreaker on contact. But it wouldn't cause enough damage to stop the demon car unless she hit a vital spot. And she would only get one shot. Provided she could dig it out of her purse in time.

Hellbringer's tires howl with fury, laying down thick black trails of smoking rubber onto the road as he rams his hated enemy toward a brick wall.

Fired with bloodlust, Hellbringer's engine races. At last, he will have his revenge for eons of torment.

But just when victory seems sweetest, everything goes wrong. The red speed demon turns its front wheels, which are still in contact with the road. The wide footprint of its meaty tires gives it enough grip to twist to one side, and then gravity takes over. Soulbreaker's thick rear end slides off Hellbringer and hits the road hard, bucking with the impact.

Before Hellbringer can react, Soulbreaker's engine wails and the red car launches like a missile. It turns tightly and comes screaming back in for the kill.

As Dru fled down the alley, the echoes of roaring engines filled the air, followed by a heart-rending crash. One of the speed demons had clearly won the grudge match. She could only hope it was Hellbringer.

The alley made a right angle and came to an abrupt end. "Nope!" Rane said, doing a quick about-face. "Up to the roof!" She pointed back to the mouth of the alley, where a metal fire escape ladder was bolted to the brick wall.

"We need to go check on Hellbringer before—" The words dried up in Dru's mouth when Soulbreaker turned into the mouth of the alley, filling it. It prowled past the ladder, cutting off their only escape route. The red speed demon's front end was mashed into a monstrous snarl, as if the blacked-out grille was a gaping mouth full of jagged teeth. One headlight jutted out, fixing them with a mad cockeyed stare.

Dru's heart sank. What had that thing done to Hellbringer? And what would it do to them next?

"Stay behind me." Rane shouldered past Dru and Greyson. Her steel feet clanged on the asphalt as she marched toward the speed demon.

"Rane!" Dru called out. "Don't!"

Rane shot a fierce glare over her shoulder. Judging by the determination etched on her face, she was ready to do whatever it took. "You do you, cowgirl. I'm going to buy you some time." She raised her fists.

Dru's heart pounded, and her legs went weak. This wasn't the first time that they had fought speed demons head-to-head. The Four Horsemen of the Apocalypse had all driven speed demons of their own, and they had nearly killed Dru and Rane more than once. If Rane tried to fight Soulbreaker alone, there was a good chance she wouldn't survive.

She needed help. Dru glanced at Greyson. "Can you sense Soulbreaker, the way you can sense Hellbringer?"

His red glowing eyes narrowed. He stared off into the distance, and then he nodded, almost imperceptibly.

Ahead of them, Soulbreaker's mangled front end slowly straightened itself out. With a ripple of blood-red plastic and metal, it became sleek and whole again. Untouched. Unstoppable. It rolled toward them on wide tires, its high-revving engine cackling through its exhaust. As if it was enjoying this cat-and-mouse game.

Rane stopped and planted her feet wide. "Come on!" she bellowed.

Dru turned to Greyson, an idea blooming in her mind. "Give it orders."

He looked puzzled.

"You can take command. Just like you did with Hellbringer. Remember? You know how to give orders to a speed demon. You know how to make it obey." She could hear the desperate quaver in her own voice, but she didn't care. "Do something. You have to save her!"

He closed his eyes and lowered his head. For an agonizing moment, Dru thought he was giving up. But when his eyes snapped open again, they burned with a red-hot fire.

At the other end of the alley, Soulbreaker's engine revved to a deafening pitch. With a jolt, the demon car lunged so hard that its front tires lifted off the ground. It reared up and charged straight at Rane, tires wailing.

Greyson leaped into motion. In three long strides, he passed Rane and thrust out his open palm. "*Stop*," he commanded. Dru felt his voice in her chest as much as she heard it. She was shocked by the power in that one word, the strength in his stance, the force of his command.

But it didn't seem to be enough. For a moment, it looked like Soulbreaker would mow him down. Dru's heart felt like it had stopped. Maybe she was wrong. Maybe she had made a terrible mistake. And now he would die because of it.

But to her amazement, the charging speed demon locked up its tires, spewing white smoke. It came to a wailing halt at his feet, inches from his boots.

The engine revved higher and higher, as if Soulbreaker was fighting against itself. But when Greyson stepped forward, his palm still thrust out, the speed demon jerked back.

Greyson took another step. Again, the speed demon grudgingly backed up.

Rane's jaw dropped open, and she slowly lowered her fists. Wordlessly, she turned as Dru stepped up beside her and motioned for her to follow. Together, the two of them followed Greyson as he forced the speed demon back, one foot after another.

With agonizing slowness, they reached the mouth of the alley, where the ladder was bolted to the wall. Without breaking eye contact with the speed demon, Greyson said over his shoulder, "Get on the ladder. Both of you."

Dru went first, climbing with trembling knees. The rickety metal ladder shook when Rane got on below her. Dru's dizzying fear of falling was quickly overwhelmed by the fear of the evil speed demon below. She reached the tar-smelling roof in time to see Greyson force Soulbreaker back one more step. Then he leaped for the ladder.

As soon as he turned his back on the speed demon, it broke loose from its trance. Engine roaring, it rammed into the base of the ladder, making the entire building shake.

Rane, her body still in steel form, reached the roof next. She turned and braced the top of the ladder as Soulbreaker pulled back and rammed it again. With a shriek, the metal twisted and popped loose from the wall. Greyson climbed as fast as he could.

"Faster!" Rane yelled. Dru's throat closed up tight in fear.

Greyson had nearly reached the top when Soulbreaker backed up even farther, then shot forward and rammed the corner of the brick building. The impact pounded the wall into an explosion of red brick dust. The whole building trembled as if it would come tumbling down. With a horrifying squeal, the ladder wrenched loose of its moorings.

Dru screamed out a wordless warning.

In one fluid motion, Rane hung by a steel hand from the lip of the roof and flung herself over the edge. At six feet tall, she had an arm-span to match. With a meaty smack, her other hand caught Greyson's. She held onto him as the ladder fell away and clattered to the ground far below. They swung off the edge of the roof for a moment, back and forth like a pendulum.

Grimacing so hard that she showed all of her teeth, Rane hurled Greyson up to the top. He grabbed hold and with a grunt pulled himself up. Rane slowly clambered up after him and lay on the roof, gasping.

Breathing hard, Greyson got to his feet. Dru ran to him. He swept her into his arms, squeezing her tight. She could feel his heart hammering against his chest, and in that moment she never wanted to let him go. She wanted to stay with him, right there, on the roof in the atomic ghost town, forever.

Rane's strained gasps gradually dissolved into a deep-throated laugh. "Omigod. That was *awesome*." She rolled into a sitting position, wrists on her knees, metal muscles flashing in the sun. "Way to go, demon master."

Greyson gave her a wry nod.

Dru, worried, pulled back from Greyson. "But what about Hellbringer?"

Somewhere in the distance, a chorus of inhuman screeches erupted. As the sun dipped low into the mountains, diabolical whoops and howls echoed across the ghost town, seeming to come from every direction at once. Protean sorcerers. Dozens of them, it sounded like.

"Hellbringer is one thing," Greyson said. "What about us?"

27

CITY IN DUST

Holding onto Greyson's hand, Dru ran from one connecting rooftop to the next, looking for another way down. Each flat roof was a different shade of black, white, or gray, speckled with decades of dead leaves and bird droppings. Dru took some comfort in the fact that at least some birds were apparently surviving the radiation in this ghost town. She dodged around the rusted hulks of roof-mounted swamp coolers, careful to avoid any sagging spots that could give way underfoot. The rooftops ended another two buildings ahead, at the other corner.

Rane pounded along behind them. "That bucket of bolts is shadowing us." She paused long enough to peek over the edge of the roof to the street below.

Dru joined her. Several stories below, the red demon car prowled the street, pacing them. Soulbreaker's engine let out a constant menacing growl. It couldn't get at them as long as they were up on the roof, but Dru worried about what would happen the moment they came down. She searched the street below for some sign of Hellbringer but found only a tangle of fresh black tire tracks and a row of smashed storefront windows. Worse, the streets now echoed with hoarse animal cries and bellows. "How many protean sorcerers do you think there are?"

Rane shrugged. "We can take them." But even she didn't sound sure.

With a hushed whispering sound, a twist of inky black smoke swirled into existence on the rooftop, solidifying into the shape of Ember. Her dark-lined eyes flicked across the three of them and lingered on Greyson, clearly worried.

"You!" Rane barked, marching toward her. Dru quickly moved to put a calming hand on Rane's metal arm.

Ember's black leather combat boots made no noise as she stepped back. "I have come to help you, not to fight. Just as you helped me."

Rane glared. "What did you do with my *boyfriend?*"

Ember looked Rane up and down, and the piercings in her eyebrows flashed in the orange sunset. "He's here. In this town. But I can only take one of you at a time."

It took Dru a moment to realize Ember didn't mean walking. "You mean, *teleport* us?"

"Unless you prefer to take your chances on the street below." Ember swallowed. Dru had the feeling that beneath her brave front, Ember was much more frightened of Rane than she let on. She lowered her gaze and held out one hand, heavy with jewelry and black nail polish, toward Rane. "Quickly."

Rane folded her arms across her chest. "Nuh-uh. You're not beaming me anywhere, skanky pants. Just tell me where Salem is."

Dru held up her hands in what she hoped was a placating gesture. "Don't mind Rane, she's just hungry."

"Hey!" Rane protested. "So what if I am?"

"How do we know we can trust you?" Dru continued. "Because no offense, Ember, but we haven't always exactly been on the same page, so . . ."

Ember's dark eyes cut away from Rane to study Dru. "If you want to stay here, fine. At least I offered." She grabbed one edge of her voluminous coat, looking like someone preparing to pull a curtain shut.

"No, no, wait!" Dru held out her hand. "It's fine. I'll go first."

Greyson shot her a cautioning look.

"No way," Rane said flatly. "I'm not letting you go anywhere with this tramp-o-matic."

"You're not helping," Dru said quietly, well aware that the others could hear her. "Right now, our list of options is getting mighty short. And we need to get off this roof quickly."

Rane looked unhappy, but she finally nodded. Still, she pointed one steel finger at Ember. "You better bring her directly to Salem, dude. Do not pass Go, do not collect one hundred dollars. Because if you try anything funny with my best—"

Dru put a hand over Rane's mouth before she managed to start another fight. "I'll be fine." She checked with Greyson to make sure he nodded his approval before she turned to Ember. "What do I do?"

Ember looked resigned. "Just stand still. And whatever you do, don't let go."

Before Dru could ask what she meant, Ember stepped right up to her and wrapped them both in her loose black coat. Dru froze, feeling incredibly awkward as Ember pressed her soft body against her. Her bracelets chimed faintly as she wrapped her arms tightly around Dru's back.

"I feel like you should at least buy me a drink first—" Dru started to joke, when the tar-smelling rooftop vanished in a rush of wind. A cold smothering darkness stretched in all directions, even above and below. As they fell together through endless nothing, the pressure built inside Dru's ears, squeezing her head worse than a jetliner coming in for a landing. Faint multicolored auras of light flickered and streaked around her, like shooting stars. Each one whispered in an incomprehensible language as it shot past. Or perhaps the unearthly echoes around her played tricks on her already pounding ears.

Just when Dru couldn't take any more, dusty carpet appeared beneath her feet. Ember released her and stepped back. Dizzy, Dru stumbled in a quick circle. They stood in a long, narrow room lined with avocado-green file cabinets. Piles of yellowing file folders and stacks of loose paper were heaped on top, along with a pale blue typewriter and some cardboard boxes flattened by disgusting amounts of water damage from a stained brown leak in the ceiling.

Dru looked around the musty room, noting the single metal door and the slim window near the ceiling, no more than a dingy slit that let in an orange rectangle of fading sunlight. It had obviously been a file room at one point, but now it just resembled a jail cell. She felt the overwhelming urge to get out.

She tried the door, but the knob wouldn't move. She slapped her hand against the cold metal. "It's locked. Where's Salem?"

When Ember remained silent, goose bumps stood up along Dru's spine. The door was locked, there was no other way out, and Salem was conspicuously absent. She'd been tricked.

Cold fear ran through her. She thrust her hand into her purse, searching for her spectrolite blade.

"I want you to know that I respect you," Ember said, backing away toward the far end of the room. "I do. Everything that you have done to help other sorcerers proves you are very kind. I know you are a good person, and I am so sorry for this."

"What is 'this,' exactly?" Dru's fingers found the blade of spectrolite, but she didn't pull it out. She turned to face Ember. "What are you doing?"

"Just keeping you safe here, until it is over." Ember took another step back, looking truly remorseful. "You have to understand, this is the only way. We almost had Lucretia. Salem and I, we sneaked in here. Do you say snuck? We snuck into this town, and we found the field just outside town, where she plans to cast her spell. We were about to stop her, you see. But then you came in with all the noise, and the demon car, and *vvvvv* . . ." She made an engine sound. "And now the protean sorcerers are alerted. Things are very bad."

Anger overwhelmed Dru's fear, and she marched straight toward Ember, shaking a finger at her. "Are you *kidding* me? So you're telling me Salem thought he had this entire situation under his control. And then when we showed up to help, he flipped his biscuit and told you to lock me in the file room. Is that what happened?"

Ember shrank back. "I wouldn't say biscuit flipping."

"That's what happened!" Dru snapped. "Who the flip do you think you are? Seriously! What gives you the right to lie to me and try and lock me away, just because you don't agree with me? Why don't you just let me help? Is that so hard?"

"Salem doesn't want your help." Ember shook her head vigorously. "He says you can't be trusted. And he makes a good point. You are the demon man's lover, and you ride in his demon car. How can anyone trust someone like that?"

"Oh, geez *Louise*. Is that what this is really about?" Dru paced the narrow space between the wall and the file cabinets. "Look, Greyson is not a tool of evil, okay? And neither is Hellbringer. I mean, sure, the car is obviously badly behaved. But it's not *evil*."

"Salem does not trust Greyson." Ember looked away. "No one should."

"Yeah, I don't give a flying fig who Salem trusts, because frankly he's a *weirdo* and he's not half as good as he thinks he is." Dru could see by the shocked look on Ember's face that she had gone too far, but she didn't care. "You know what, it doesn't matter. You need to take me back. Unlike you and Salem, I don't leave my friends in the lurch. They need my help. Take me back to the rooftop. *Right* now."

Ember backed up one more step. "I am to take Rane to Salem next."

"Oh, *she* gets to go see Salem. Isn't that special. What about Greyson?"

Ember didn't answer. But in her defiant gaze, Dru thought she saw just a smidgen of doubt.

"Greyson is a good man," Dru said evenly, trying to get through to Ember. She took a step closer. "Forget everything Salem has told you and just listen to me."

"Salem has been right about everything so far," Ember insisted.

"Maybe according to *him*. How's that working out for you so far?" Dru said. "Lucretia is still at large. As long as she can proceed with her plan, the doomsday clock is ticking. What do we have, like an hour? Two? We don't have time to mess around. We need to team up and work together. All of us."

Ember shook her head slowly side to side. "I will not go against Salem."

"No, not *against*." Dru wanted to tear her hair out. Why was the concept of teamwork so alien to most sorcerers?

She already knew the answer: because most of them spent their waking hours trying to outmaneuver one another in an endless struggle to amass magical power. If the idea of working together ever came up, it was only in terms of a temporary alliance to bring down a more powerful mutual foe. To their way of thinking, teamwork was for the weak.

The more Dru thought about it, the more she figured she could turn that closed-minded mind-set to her advantage. But first, she had to give Ember the right incentive: magical power.

"Okay, how about this. Want to take out Lucretia's most powerful henchman, the red demon car? I can show you how." Dru watched for the telltale glint of interest in Ember's eyes and was rewarded instantly. "Demons are vulnerable to galena," Dru said. "And I have a whole box full back at the Crystal Connection. Can you teleport me back to my shop?"

Ember looked her up and down. "I will get the crystals alone. You will stay here. No tricks."

Dru held out her empty hands, as if to say, *Tricks? What? No way!* "First, you have to get Rane and Greyson to safety. Then I'll show you how to use the galena."

Ember seemed to think that over for a long moment as her thickly lined eyes scrutinized Dru. Finally, she nodded. "Deal."

"Good. I'm glad we—" Dru found herself talking to thin air as Ember wrapped her coat around herself and disappeared in a hissing twirl of shadowy magic.

Dru waited for a few seconds to make sure she wouldn't come back. Then she started tearing the room apart, looking for anything she could use to jimmy the lock on the door.

Rane stepped out of Ember's embrace feeling like she'd just lost a bet. The moment the squirrelly little sorceress let her go, Rane was itching for a fight. But first, she had to clear her head. She planted her feet wide apart, waiting for the dizziness to pass from the effects of whatever kind of warped hyperspace Ember had taken her through.

They stood in a gloomy, narrow aisle of a small town hardware store. Rows of leather work gloves, coils of garden hose, and groups of old-fashioned hand tools sat neatly stacked on the dusty metal shelves. Above, hand-lettered signs advertised lawn supplies, paint, electrical, and builders' hardware.

Rane looked up and down the shadowy aisle. There was no sign of Dru. No sign of anyone, in fact. Something about this didn't add up. "Hey. What the hell? Where's Dru?"

Ember backed away quickly, her eyes gleaming in the shadows. She didn't answer.

"Hey!" Rane went after her, but Ember just did her coat-twisting thing and vanished with an almost silent hiss. Rane's metal hands closed on thin air.

A footstep scraped on the linoleum floor behind her. She whirled around, fists up.

But it was only Salem, looking smug as he stepped into the aisle. "Hello, Buttercup. Miss me much?"

Part of her wanted to run right over and kiss him. The other part wanted to kick his ass. She wasn't ready to choose an option just yet. Instead, she transformed into human again, letting go of the strength and invulnerability of metal. Instantly, she missed it. "Tell me Little Miss Monkey Pants just hyperspaced back to pick up Dru and Greyson. Because if she didn't, we're about to have a great, big problem."

As he sauntered toward her, he gracefully swept off his silk top hat and shook out his waves of hair. "Surprise, surprise, I don't actually control the things Ember does. I merely make suggestions, which she of course can ignore of her own free will."

Rane folded her arms across her chest. "You know that chick is nothing but trouble."

He stopped directly in front of her, his eyes flashing as he spoke in a theatrical whisper: "I know. But I like you better."

"Huh. You'd *better* like me better."

Leaning closer, he gave her a saucy look. "We have to stop meeting like this. People might talk."

She wasn't in the mood to forgive him just yet. "Yeah, whatever. Check this out." She reached down into her sports bra and pulled out Salem's amulet, golden and shimmering. "You lose this somewhere?"

As she dangled it in front of him, his eyes went round, as if she'd just brought out a surprise birthday cake. "*What?* How did you . . . ?"

She smirked. "Because I'm a total badass."

He gave her a slow smile. "Yes, you are."

Slowly, she lowered the amulet over his head and hung it around his neck, enjoying the rare look of pure happiness on his face. Eyes half-lidded, he slid his arms around her and went in for a kiss.

That was when she saw the crystal sitting ominously on the shelf behind him. Blunt, unhealthy-looking, the color of rust, and the size of a loaded handgun.

"*Whoa!*" Rane jerked back out of his arms. "Heads up. What's with the crystal?" She pointed a warning finger.

With an exaggerated sigh, Salem twirled his wrist, as if presenting the crystal as a prize on a game show. "Yes, it's a crystal. They're everywhere. Someone has been extraordinarily busy placing crystals throughout the town, in little nooks and crannies like this. It's nothing to worry about."

"The hell it's not." Rane glared at the crystal, expecting it to start shooting out evil death beams at any moment. "We need Dru to identify this thing, stat."

Salem drummed his long fingers on the shelf, looking slightly uncomfortable. "She's been delayed. Won't be joining us. But"—he raised a finger to silence her as she drew in a breath to speak—"that's actually a good thing. She can stay safe and sound while you and I take care of business. Without having to worry about any danger from her hunka-hunka demon love."

Rane looked from Salem to the crystal and back. "Dude, you know this is bad news. Lucretia is a crystal sorceress."

Salem rolled his eyes. "She's only *one* sorceress." He led her away from the grimy windows toward the back of the store, past hanging pitchforks and hack saws. "We can handle her."

"Maybe. But she's also got her army of protean sorcerers, and those flea scratchers are running around looking for us right now."

Salem made a sharp clicking sound with the corner of his mouth and pointed at her. "And *that* is why Dru is not with us right now. This whole place was quiet as a tomb until she blundered in here and kicked the hornets' nest." He waved one hand at a shelf full of lampshades. "There's another crystal back here in the corner."

Rane stopped short, remembering something Dru had talked about several times before. Her stomach clenched up tight, the way it always did just before she got gut-punched. "Wait, hold up. How many crystals have you found so far?"

He shrugged. "I don't know. Dozens. Why?"

"*Dozens?* How many are here in this store?" Rane looked around, trying to picture the store the way Dru would. If Dru was super evil and monstrously powerful, why would she leave big crystals just lying around? She wouldn't, unless she had a plan. Lucretia had carefully placed these crystals for a reason. "Tell me something. The crystals are spread out along the walls, right? Around the perimeter of the store? Spaced out evenly?"

Salem turned around in place, silently poking a finger in different directions as he counted to himself. He nodded. "Now that you mention it, the spacing does seem a little obsessive-compulsive."

That clinched it. Rane made a fist around her titanium ring, feeling the rush as she transformed into solid metal. "Dude, this is a setup. They made you think this place wasn't being watched. But they're probably waiting outside for us right now." She jerked her thumb toward the watery light from the front windows. "Let's go. This place is a trap."

Clearly, Salem thought she was joking. "Not the scariest trap I've ever seen. Besides, no one knows we're here."

"It's a crystal grid, dumbass! She knows *exactly* where we are. She could have locked you out, but she didn't. If we got in here, it's because *she let us in*."

As realization dawned on Salem's face, the sound of a screaming engine reverberated through the hardware store. It wasn't Hellbringer's old-school throaty rumble. It was higher-pitched and tighter. Rane tensed for a fight, looking all around for the source of the noise as it rose until it was so loud it felt as if the car was right there in the room with them.

And then it was. The back wall exploded inward, and Soulbreaker's red front end punched through the wall, sending metal tools and clay pots flying in every direction. Bricks and debris tumbled and rolled across the floor. The entire building shook. Headlights burned through the clouds of dust.

Soulbreaker's engine roared as the demon car jerked back out again, withdrawing from the wall. Chunks of debris fell away, allowing sunlight to spill in. Outside, a horde of protean sorcerers, all in animal form, tried to crowd in through the breach. With a squeal of tires, Soulbreaker reversed, letting them in.

28

WHAT YOU KNOW IS TRUE

Dru was unsuccessfully trying to pick the lock on the door using bent paper clips when Ember reappeared in a swirl of black smoke. But she wasn't alone.

"What are you trying to do, kill me?" Opal shrieked, staggering away from Ember's open arms. "What kind of way to travel is that?"

Dru straightened up, jaw dropping open. "Opal? What're you doing here?"

"I could ask you the same question!"

"I told you to bring galena crystals," Dru said to Ember, who seemed eager to get away from Opal.

Opal held up a repurposed cardboard box from Costco. "You mean I could've just sent this along with her, stayed home, and avoided all this air sickness?"

Dru took the box from her. It was amazingly heavy and full of shiny galena crystals the color of mirrored sunglasses. Most of them were cubes with sharp or rough edges, although others had fractured into uneven chunks. But no matter which way galena broke, it always came away in right-angle pieces, due to its cubical molecular structure.

Dru hefted the box, satisfied with its weight. There was enough here to seriously damage Soulbreaker, if not destroy it completely. "Well, I mean, I'm really glad you're here."

Opal shot her a dirty look. "I'm a little bit less than thrilled about it, myself."

"Sorry."

"Where are we at, anyway?" Opal looked around. "Some kind of skanky back office on East Colfax?"

"Maybe a little farther away."

Ember impatiently jerked her chin at the box of galena crystals. "Now it's your turn to keep up your end of the bargain. How do I fight the speed demon with these?"

"Oh, it's a bargain, now, is it?" Opal turned the full force of her displeasure on Ember. "Honey, you can't just throw rocks at a demon and expect it to do a whole lot. Dru has to charge up the crystals first. That's going to take some time."

Ember looked decidedly displeased. "How long will it be?"

Opal blew out an exaggerated breath. "Oh, it could be a *while*. You really want to wait around here?"

Despite the time crunch, Dru lingered over the box of crystals. Realistically, she knew that she could charge up all of the crystals in under a minute, if she had to. But there was something in Opal's manner that suggested she should play along. "I don't know, exactly. I mean, every crystal is different, so there's really no way to tell. But we'll definitely need to get out of this room in the meantime, go get some fresh air. It's good for the magic. That's how it really works." Inwardly, she cringed. Even she could tell she was lying.

Ember was clearly unimpressed. "I will be right back." With a scowl, she twisted her coat and disappeared in a swirl of magic.

When she was gone, Opal let out a sigh and then chuckled, placing one hand on Dru's shoulder. "Sweetie, you do not need to be hanging out with people like that."

"I know. I'm sorry. I didn't mean to get you caught up in this." Dru set the heavy box down on top of a file cabinet. Quickly, she filled in Opal on recent events, leading up to the fact that as far as she knew, Greyson was still trapped on a rooftop somewhere in town, with the protean sorcerers closing in. "So we have to get out of here *now*."

"Should be a lot easier without teleporter girl breathing down our necks."

"Except that the door is locked." Dru picked up the bent paper clips and resumed stabbing them into the lock. As before, it did nothing at all, and Dru eventually gave up with an anguished groan. "Do you know how to do this?"

"Hold on a second." Opal went to the file cabinet closest to the door, opened the top drawer, and pushed the file folders back. Peering down, she fished something out of the bottom of the drawer. With a triumphant smile, she jangled a pair of brass keys from her fingertips.

Seeing that, Dru jumped up and down in excitement. "Yay!"

Beaming, Opal held out the keys. "Yeah, back when I had a government job, one time I accidentally locked myself in the file room. So I know where to look." When Dru reached for the keys, Opal held onto them a moment longer. "Now, you understand that's a statement about the inefficiency of the government, still having paper files. It doesn't say a thing about my age."

"I understand," Dru said somberly. "You don't look a day over—"

"Twenty-nine," Opal said quickly, "and holding."

"Twen . . . Really?"

"What?" Opal said with sharp indignation.

"Nothing." Dru cleared her throat. "Just, um, how long have you been holding, exactly?"

"Just open the damn door and let's get out of here."

As quietly as she could, Dru unlocked the door and peeked outside. A short hallway, nearly pitch-black, led past a tiny bathroom and ended in another door. The only illumination came from dying sunlight streaking beneath the floor, casting rough shadows across the surface of the carpet. Soon, it would be sundown. They were running out of time.

Dru put one finger to her lips, motioning for silence, and picked up the heavy box of crystals. As an afterthought, she grabbed one of the bigger galena cubes and held it in her fist. If Soulbreaker showed up unexpectedly, it would be in for a painful surprise.

She crept down the hall, Opal close behind her. At her motion, Opal reached out with her carefully manicured fingers and tried the next door. It wasn't locked.

The door swung open with a faint creak, letting in the odors of motor oil and exhaust. Beyond lay a huge garage with half a dozen truck-sized bays and equally tall garage doors. Truck tires were stacked high against one wall, next to giant metal drums of oil and coolant. Ruddy light streamed in through high windows, falling on five windowless white cargo vans, all parked with their noses facing the doors.

Strangely, they were all modern vehicles, not ones from the 1960s. Dru checked the month and year stickers on the license plates to be sure. One of them had expired a few months before, and the rest were current. The nearest van had a roof rack that jutted up in the front like devil horns. Dru tried its back door. It clicked, and she started to pull it open. Something inside it stunk to high heaven.

Opal was already heading for the exit door, heels clicking, when she saw what Dru was doing and hustled back. "Dru, have you lost your mind?" she whispered. "Come on!"

"I have to find out what this is all about," Dru whispered back, trying not to choke on the stench from inside the van. She handed over the box of galena crystals. "Why, in this old ghost town, are there suddenly five newer cargo vans?"

"I don't know. I don't care!" Opal struggled with the box until she could pinch her nostrils shut. "You want to do your car shopping? There's a used lot two blocks from the shop. Worry about it tomorrow. Something inside that thing smells *real* bad, and I've got no intention of looking in there to find out what it is. Some things can't ever be unseen."

"I know," Dru said. "That's why I'm going to have to ask you to take a good long step back." Drawing in a deep breath, Dru pulled the door all the way open. She expected to find a dead body, either a human being or some kind of horrendous creature. The blast of rotten-egg stink made her throat clench shut and her eyes tear up. Still, she stared in disbelief at the contents of the van.

The entire floor of the cargo area was piled knee-deep in sulfur crystals. It looked for all the world like the cleanup after an industrial lemon Jell-O accident. The sharp sickly sweet smell of it fouled the air, making Dru gag.

She shut the van door harder than she needed to. "Whew! What does Lucretia need with so much sulfur?"

"I dunno," Opal said, pinching her nose hard enough to make her voice go high and nasally. "Can we go now?"

"Hang on." Dru checked inside the other vehicles. She had to see what she was dealing with.

The next van was missing its front grill. It was loaded with jumbles of sharp-looking platelets the color of traffic cones. That was wulfenite, and although it didn't smell, it was toxic. Some sorcerers claimed that the poisonous crystal bridged the gap between light and darkness, but Dru had only ever seen it used for selfish purposes.

The van after that was knee-deep in cloudy pink-and-red vanadinite crystals. Short, stubby, and angular, vanadinite looked like chunks of raw meat. Dru had never been fond of it, and not just because it reminded her of the butcher shop. Vanadinite was used for focusing energy, and Dru had found that it often focused so tightly that it wiped away creativity and freedom of choice. Why would Lucretia need so much of it?

The fourth van was full of crystals that looked like arrowheads covered in shaggy black fur. Black kyanite was a powerful grounding stone, able to deliver energies directly into the earth. When used for good purposes, it could have a beneficial rejuvenating effect. But in the wrong hands, it could be used to do something terrible.

When Dru opened up the last van, she found it full of mottled blue crystals that looked exactly like wavy sunlight reflecting off the bottom of a swimming pool. Instantly, she recognized it as larimar. True to its summery appearance, most larimar came from the Bahamas, where it was also known as dolphin stone. But even though it looked like water, larimar was actually an earth crystal, and its energy was sometimes used to relieve geological stress. Unless it was reversed and used to cause harm. Seeing such a beautiful crystal ready to be twisted into evil nearly broke Dru's heart.

Each of the five vehicles easily carried half a ton of crystals. The quantity alone was mind-boggling, but what was even weirder was the fact that the crystals were completely separated by vehicle. But why?

Dru stepped back and pondered that. "Why load up a van with nothing but sulfur? Or any of these other crystals? Why not mix them together?"

Still holding onto her nose, Opal gave her a resigned shrug. "I dunno. To move them somewhere?"

"Well, yeah. But when we buy crystals for the shop, they all come boxed up together. We don't have a whole truck full of just *one* crystal." Dru looked up and down the row of vans, picturing them driving down the road in some kind of unmarked crystal caravan. "What's the advantage of keeping the crystals separated?"

Opal finally released her nostrils and took a breath, only to make a face. "I don't know, honey. Why does Lucretia move all these crystals around? Why does she want to blow up the world? Why does she do any of this? Because she's crazy, that's why. Can we go now?"

Dru latched onto something Opal said. "That's it! It's so she can move them around."

Opal's eyebrows went up. "You care to explain that?"

"She's going to make a crystal circle." Dru pantomimed setting out crystals around a circle. "She can drive these vans into position, arrange them to make a really, *really* big circle. With that amount of crystals . . ." Dru did the math in her head, at least the best she could based on a quick eyeball estimation of the crystals. "Maybe a thousand feet across. Holy cow! Did I do that right? The biggest circle I've ever calculated was thirty feet across." Certain that she must have misplaced a decimal point, she did the math again. "A half ton is about four hundred fifty kilograms. . . . Circumference is two pi R. . . . Five different crystals . . . Yeah, about twelve, thirteen hundred feet across. Wow. A quarter of a *mile*." The implications of that were hard to imagine. "Can anyone really power a circle that big? She would need an astronomic power source. Something like a hundred lightning strikes, or the surface of the sun, or a nuclear weapon."

"Maybe that's what the amulets are for," Opal said. "The Amulet of Decimus the Accursed, that might give her the kind of evil power she needs."

Astounded, Dru let out a low whistle. "This is it. This is her doomsday spell. Some assembly required." Suddenly, the row of windowless vans took on a much more sinister appearance. Alone, each of them was relatively harmless. But assembled in the proper sequence, they could form Lucretia's ultimate weapon of mass destruction.

Opal took her arm and tried to pull her toward the door, but Dru resisted.

"You know what we need to do?" Dru said quickly. "We need to steal these vans!"

Opal shook her head no. "Steal Lucretia's crystal vans? Are you crazy?"

"She needs all five of them to complete the circle, right? If even one of them goes missing, her spell won't work. Come on." Ignoring Opal's gasp of protest, Dru opened the driver's door of the larimar van and climbed in. But there were no keys in the ignition. She checked above the bare gray plastic sun visor and then peered into the empty glove compartment. Nothing.

Behind the seats, a metal partition separated the cab from the cargo area. Dru clicked open the cheap black plastic latch and opened the grated door, but there was nothing back there but ocean-blue larimar crystals.

Opal opened the other door and climbed into the passenger seat, struggling with the cardboard box of galena. "This is definitely a bad idea."

"It would be a lot less bad if I could find the keys." Dru felt deep in the seat cushion, finding only stale crumbs and wads of animal hair. "Ugh."

"If Greyson was here, I bet he could hotwire this thing. Where is he, anyway?" Opal said.

Dru tried not to think about that. Hopefully, he'd found a way down off that roof and was looking for her even now. She needed all the help she could get. But before she could answer, a metallic bang echoed through the garage. The exit door swung open, letting in a ray of blood-red sunlight. It was quickly blotted out by the silhouettes of five well-built young men filing in, like the start of some kind of low-rent all-male revue.

Opal's jaw dropped open. "Oh. My. Lord. They are *not* wearing any clothes. At *all*."

"Protean sorcerers." Dru ducked down to hide and tried to push Opal's head down to keep them from being spotted. "Get down!"

Opal resisted, peeking up over the dashboard. "They're all *naked*. Hallelujah, look at that. It's raining men."

Dru sighed in exasperation. "Yes, apparently, we're in the land of hot naked sorcerer guys."

Opal seized her wrist and gave her a deadly serious look. "Dru, this is the place I've always *dreamed* of."

"Well, that's great. Except that these sorcerers might actually kill us if they get the chance. Come on." Dru opened the little door in the metal partition behind the seats.

"No. I can't run in these heels," Opal whispered. "And I'm not leaving these shoes behind. That's a deal breaker."

"Well, we can't make it out through the garage without being seen. We'll have to hide back here. Come on." Ducking low, Dru slipped through the grated door into the back of the van. With some difficulty, Opal followed. They shut the door just as one of the men climbed into the van.

Hunched down on a rough pile of blue larimar crystals, Dru pressed her finger to her lips, signaling for silence. Although the metal partition hid them from the sorcerer's view, a single falling crystal could give them away.

Up front, metal keys jingled, and the van started. A second later, they jerked into motion.

Opal's eyes were wide in the shadowy van. She mouthed, *Where are we going?*

Dru shook her head. She had no idea where the vans were headed, but she had a bad feeling who would be waiting for them when they got there.

Lucretia.

29
RANE OF TERROR

R ane backed up fast as the giant animals—actually protean
sorcerers—poured in through the hole in the wall. She didn't recognize any of them from earlier fights. A spotted, hunchbacked hyena. A
squat, lumbering alligator. The rippling bulk of a bear. More crowded in
behind them.

"Somebody sure as hell let the zoo out." How could there be so many
of them? Where had they all come from? Pulse thudding in her ears,
Rane grabbed a sledgehammer off a nearby tool display. This was about
to get ugly.

Salem backed up in the opposite direction, flanked on either side by
the scaly alligator and a ragged-looking lion. He glanced back and forth
between the two of them, his fingers spread wide and crackling with
energy. She knew from experience that he was trying to decide which
one of the two was more dangerous. If he focused too much on one of his
opponents, he might leave an opening in his defenses. Whichever sorcerer he didn't take out first would probably hit him. That meant he had
to choose between getting bitten by the lion or the alligator. She wasn't
sure which option was worse.

Meanwhile, a snarling tiger and a burly green anaconda closed in
on Rane, followed by a bristly brown tarantula big enough to sink its
fangs into livestock. The hunchbacked hyena followed them, hanging
back with a savage grin.

In the shadows of the far corner, behind the hyena, a swirl of black
smoke coalesced into the form of Ember. Her thickly lined eyes went
wide as she took in the snarling proteans fanning out through the hardware store, preparing to attack. Rane fully expected Ember to do that

coat-swirling thing again and bail on them, leaving them to fend for themselves.

But to her surprise, Ember crouched into a fighting stance. The shining metal jewelry on her magic pokey finger glittered as she raised it behind the hyena's back. She made eye contact with Rane and nodded once.

Rane couldn't believe it. That girl was actually willing to stick around and fight alongside them. Could she be trusted?

Rane hefted the sledgehammer and eyed the tiger and its scaly green friend. Well, screw it. If Ember was still here in five minutes, that would mean something. But five minutes was a long time when you were staring down a radioactive hardware store full of mutant carnivores.

Rane shifted her stance, wondering which one of these ugly beasties would strike first. Because she could go either way. Her plan was to block their teeth with the sledgehammer, feint toward the other one, and knock their heads together. She'd see if that worked.

But Ember was a nagging problem. The proteans hadn't noticed her yet, so none of them had sunk their teeth into her. But that would change the moment she zapped the hyena with her pokey finger. And as much as Rane disliked the girl, she knew she would be dangerously out of her depth in a straight-up fight. The moment a couple of those proteans ganged up on her, they would eat her for lunch.

Possibly literally, as Dru would say.

A random thought popped into Rane's head. Something Dru had told her a long time ago, about using tactics to overwhelm the enemy. It went something like, "Blah-blah-blah, cause a distraction."

That gave her an idea. Maybe not a good idea but a noisy one, and that made it awesome.

She took a couple of forceful swings with the sledgehammer, making the heavy steel head *swoosh* back and forth through the air. It had the intended effect. Baring its teeth, the mangy tiger dodged back a step, golden eyes wide and wary. The army-green anaconda swung its big, hideous head in the opposite direction, trying to wriggle around behind her. She wasn't going to let that happen.

Instead, she climbed up on top of the nearest display rack, sending tools and buckets clattering to the floor. Standing astride the top of the metal shelf, she raised the sledgehammer overhead in both hands and shouted at the top of her lungs. *"Attention, Kmart shoppers!"*

Immediately, all eyes turned to her. A chorus of growls filled the hardware store. The only face that wasn't the least bit surprised was Salem's. He rolled his eyes in a way that suggested, *Really? You're actually doing this?*

Rane grinned, savoring the anticipation. The part of her that always wanted to start trouble, that constantly itched to fight, was about to have a field day. She had a sledgehammer in her hands, a body made out of solid metal, and an entire building full of sharp objects that were just built for collateral damage.

With relish, she smacked the long handle of the sledgehammer into her palm. She took another deep breath and shouted across the store. "Today, we have a special for you that's *really* kick-ass. Want some? *Come and get it!*"

With a collective roar, the protean sorcerers charged at her from all sides. The only one of them that went nowhere was the hyena, because Ember picked it off with a red spark from her zappy finger. It staggered and dropped to the floor, unconscious.

The chunky alligator, spotting Ember at last, twisted its long body and snapped its huge jaws at her. She disappeared in a churning cloud of smoke, only to reappear two aisles over beside the shaggy brown tarantula and its nightmarish tangle of striped legs. She let out a squeak of fear.

But Rane had troubles of her own. The thick green tail of the anaconda flailed at her, trying to coil around her legs. She nailed it with the sledgehammer and was rewarded with a pained hiss. But the tiger came right after it, and its slashing claws caught the hammer's handle, ripping it from her grasp.

Unarmed, she lashed out with a savage kick. The tiger twisted nimbly aside so that her steel foot only grazed its side. The blow knocked the tiger tumbling back for a moment. Still, it wasn't enough. Reinforcements filled the aisle below, crawling and leaping eagerly toward Rane.

In moments, they would be able to knock her down by sheer force of numbers.

She glanced around the store, looking for Salem, but didn't see him. That wasn't good. She needed help, and she needed it fast. "*Hey!*" she bellowed. "Cleanup, aisle three! *Right now!*"

Just when she was worried she was completely on her own, Salem strode around the endcap of the aisle. His black coat fluttered behind him as ripples of magic flowed off his body. It traveled down his arms in white flickers like lightning, nestling in electrified tangles around his fingertips. The proteans at the back of the horde turned around to face him, their teeth and claws flashing.

But Salem raised both arms, long fingers splayed out, and the aisle erupted into a blinding whirlwind of hurtling debris. All at once, every single object on the shelves became an airborne weapon. Rakes and garden shears flew like tree branches in a hurricane. Light bulbs hurtled through the air, flickering slightly in the maelstrom of magical energy before they shattered against tumbling animal bodies. Paint cans spun and broke open, disgorging their contents in colorful globs that stretched in every direction. The chaos was total and all-encompassing. It made Rane want to laugh out loud.

In the next aisle over, protected from the chaos, a massive white polar bear charged toward Rane. It lumbered on all four legs, closing the distance shockingly fast. As it reached her, it reared up to roar. Its purple-black lips split to reveal murderously sharp yellow teeth and a blast of fish-smelling breath that was nearly as deadly.

Rane bent and roared right back at it, feeling the tendons stand out on her neck. The bear came at her, all slashing claws and teeth and crushing bulk. Adrenaline rushed through Rane's muscles as she ducked and threw the hardest punch she could.

If the protean sorcerer driving the van had any idea that Dru and Opal were stowed away on the other side of the metal partition, he made no indication. Then again, she couldn't see him, since she was stuck in the back. All she could do was ride it out.

The drive was more or less a straight line with few turns, but they were going too fast to jump out the back door and make a run for it. After a few minutes, the ride turned bumpy and jarring, as if they had gone off the road. Blue larimar crystals shook and clattered around them, forcing Dru and Opal to brace themselves against the inside of the van or risk getting buried.

At one point, Opal tried her cell phone, but it was obvious she wasn't getting any reception. Clearly worried, she kept looking to Dru plaintively.

But the more Dru racked her brain trying to think of a way out, the more she felt hopelessly trapped. Unless she came up with a plan quickly, though, they would be delivered straight to Lucretia's feet. Or get cooked inside this van when Lucretia finally decided to energize these crystals.

But which spell would Lucretia cast? And was there any way Dru could cast a counterspell to negate it? It would depend on the exact order the crystals were positioned around the circle. If Dru could predict that, then she would have a chance. As she did the math, her heart sank. There were 120 different ways those five crystals could be arranged around the circle. And the number of possible combinations shot up if there were additional vans she didn't know about. Adding a sixth crystal to the mix would lead to 720 total combinations. If there were as many as nine crystals, it would result in more than sixty thousand possible combinations.

In other words, it was impossible to know what spell Lucretia was going to cast with these crystals.

Before Dru could come up with a plan, the van unexpectedly lurched to a halt. With a guttural groan, the protean sorcerer climbed out and slammed the door. In the sudden silence, Dru could hear the sound of her own rapid breathing, along with Opal's. The wind picked up, whispering across the van and pelting it with tiny grains of sand. In the distance, other van doors slammed shut. Just on the other side of the sheet metal, a slithering magical sound was instantly followed by the sound of soft footfalls as the protean sorcerer changed to animal form and bounded away.

From all appearances, they were alone. Heart pounding, Dru risked a peek through the grate in the metal partition. The van seats were indeed empty. Outside, a sandy hillside was covered with dry scrub brush that shuffled in the wind.

Larimar crystals clattered as Opal crouched next to her.

"What do you think?" Opal whispered.

"I can't see anything from here." Dru dug her spectrolite blade out of her purse and stuck it in her back pocket, where it was easily accessible. Then she got out her gold pyrite disk for protection. "I'm going to go outside and have a look."

Opal gripped her arm and started to voice an objection. Then she stopped and hugged Dru tight. "Be careful."

"I'll be right back." Dru pulled the plastic latch, slipped through the tiny door in the partition, and climbed out of the van.

There was no sign of the protean sorcerers, but all five vans were here. They were parked at the bottom of some kind of valley, on top of a thick cable, probably copper, that formed a vast circle. It looked like the diameter of the circle was slightly less than a quarter mile, but not by much. Unhealthy yellow grass carpeted the ground. Here and there, a few aspen groves struggled to survive, but the trees were stunted and twisted. On all sides, the walls of the valley sloped steeply upward, and the sickly grass dwindled into scattered patches. Above, the bare dirt rose into towering walls of brown-and-gray rock.

The wind carried the tang of trail dust and the cloying odor of decay. There was something else in the air she couldn't quite make out, something that reminded her of underground rocks and deep dirt. Every instinct told her to turn around and run. But she couldn't. They were almost out of time.

The sun had already fallen behind the rim of the rock walls above, plunging the valley floor into cool shadow. Fiery orange clouds swirled through the deepening blue sky. Night wasn't far off.

In the middle of the field sat a roughly pentagon-shaped concrete slab about the size of a large house. A square gray protrusion jutted up from it, looking like a pedestal. Or a gravestone. It appeared to have some kind of a metal plaque attached to it.

With a last wary look around, Dru hiked her purse up onto her shoulder and headed toward the concrete slab. The wind changed direction, plucking at her clothes. It shushed through the feeble trees and pallid bushes. The black-spotted blades of grass barely moved. She passed the sun-bleached skull of a deer on a bare patch of dirt, its antlers reaching skyward like clawed fingers.

Cautiously, she approached the concrete slab. It was cracked and pitted with age. Its edges were rounded off by the elements, surrounded by a halo of crumbled fragments. Dru tested the slab with her foot to make sure it was solid. The moment she stepped onto it, she felt a subtle shift in the air, as if she stood on the brink of another world. She had the unsettling feeling that something terrible had happened here, so dreadful it had warped the fabric of reality itself.

In the very center was the refrigerator-sized block of concrete she had noticed before, and to that was bolted the weathered metal plaque, long ago rusted dark brown by the elements. Cautiously, Dru approached it and wiped enough dirt off the plaque to read the engraved words:

PROJECT LUCRETIA
NUCLEAR EXPLOSIVE EMPLACEMENT WELL
No excavation, drilling, and/or removal of
subsurface materials is permitted.
U.S. Energy Research & Development Administration.
1963.

"Project Lucretia," Dru whispered to herself. What did that mean? Alarm bells went off in her head. This had to be the source of the radioactivity in the ghost town. But it couldn't possibly have been put there by the US government. Could it?

She barely had time to process that thought when an older woman's voice came from behind her. "I was twelve years old when the government men came. In their shiny black cars, their sweat-stained suits."

With a cold jolt of fear, Dru spun around to face Lucretia.

30

THIS DEMON GOES INTO A BAR

As the minutes ticked by and Greyson paced the roof alone, he became more and more convinced that Ember wasn't coming back. It was something about the way she had refused to meet his gaze when she took Rane. Something about the tension in Rane's body indicated that she knew it, too. But what choice did they have? The protean sorcerers, maybe dozens of them, howled and screeched through the streets, drawing closer.

With swift strides, he crossed the last few connected roofs to the far end, looking for another way down. The drop down to the street was too far to even consider jumping.

But there was a shorter addition tacked onto the back of the building across the alley. Its roof sloped down past a single window. If he took a running leap and was incredibly lucky, he could land on the addition, kick that window in, and get inside. If he did that, he could try to find another way out to the street.

But what then? Where was Hellbringer?

He reached out with his mind, searching for the speed demon that was so closely bound to him. He could feel the car's presence lurking out there, somewhere. He couldn't communicate with Hellbringer directly, yet the demon car lingered just beneath his thoughts, like an almost remembered nightmare.

Hellbringer wasn't human, but an immortal being. It thrived on speed and destruction, and it was happiest—if that could be the right way to describe it—when it was free to trample everything in its path. The only thing it hated more than rival speed demons was being trapped. And right now, Greyson got the distinct impression that Hellbringer was stuck somewhere nearby, unable to move. The speed demon's enraged frustration rang around the inside of his skull like a wordless shout, with no way to let it out.

Greyson leaned over the edge of the roof. As sunset crept in, the street below was swallowed by shadow. The blue-tinged darkness ate away at the fiery rays that still illuminated the lifeless buildings. The broken plate glass windows across the street gaped like an open mouth, and from within came the echoes of Hellbringer's revving engine, combined with the zipper-like sound of tires spinning just a hairsbreadth away from full contact with the ground. So Hellbringer was stuck in there somehow, unable to escape. If he wanted to get out of this town alive, he would have to get the demon car loose.

He crossed the roof again and peered down at the roof of the rickety-looking addition across the alley. If he misjudged the distance, or hit the sloping roof at the wrong angle and slid off, he could die. If it was rotted out and gave way beneath him, he could die. Or if he stayed here and let the protean sorcerers catch up to him, he could die that way, too.

At least he could narrow it down to two out of three. He wouldn't stay here and wait.

He gauged the jump as best as he could, then backed up, took a deep breath, and charged. As he raced toward the edge of the roof, he fought down the natural instinct to draw up short at the last second, knowing that it was too late to stop his momentum now. Instead, he pressed ahead, arms swinging, boots pounding the flat asphalt roof.

He reached the edge and leaped. Immediately, his stomach dropped out beneath him. The dirty alley below rushed up toward him. For a split second, he was sure he had made a terrible mistake.

Then he hit the sloping roof of the addition, hard enough that the toes of his boots punched through the sun-warped shingles. He started to slide and just barely caught himself on the edge of the window. With two swift kicks, he knocked in the metal screen and the dirty pane of glass.

Climbing inside, he found himself in darkness, but his demonic eyes allowed him to see. Giant rolls of dust-covered fabric, each the size of a person, hung suspended from the bare timbers of the ceiling. He ignored the itchy tickle in his nose and squeezed past them to reach a doorway, then crept through a larger room filled with furniture in all stages of disassembly and repair. Hand tools and rolls of fabric were set everywhere, as if all of the workers had gone on lunch break and never returned.

In the back of the room, a table was covered with maps and stacks of flyers, along with all of the materials for making protest signs: giant sheets of card stock, thin strips of lumber, hammers and nails, a mechanical staple gun, a few thin paintbrushes, and small cans of paint.

Hand-lettered signs leaned against the back wall, screaming with the echoes of long-dead outrage:

KILL NATURE for GA$ RICHE$?
No CONTAMINATION without REPRESENTATION
Soon YOU Will Radiate, Baby!
No NUKES! Radioactivity KILLS
Gov't "Plowshare": Planting the Seeds of DOOMSDAY

That last sign made Greyson stop in his tracks. He crossed over and picked up the dusty old sign. The wooden handle was dry and raw in his hand. The card stock rustled.

The word "Doomsday" was written in red paint, and the letters had dripped slightly, making them look like dried blood. Whatever these people had been protesting, they had a point. But they had failed. Some kind of catastrophe had irradiated this town, leaving it barren and empty.

As motes of dust drifted off the sign and swirled through the air, Greyson was acutely aware that everything in here was radioactive, even the dust. And he no longer had the protection of Dru's crystal.

Carefully, he set down the sign and wiped off his hands. Could this be where doomsday had actually begun? Could the disaster in this town have been the catalyst that led to everything that followed? The Harbingers, the group of evil sorcerers that created Hellbringer and broke the first seals on the apocalypse scroll, had originally been some kind of radical protest group. Dru had uncovered their manifesto at one point. Could the Harbingers have been formed here, in this nameless ghost town?

No matter what the truth was, he had to find Dru and the others, fast. He located a creaky wooden staircase and quickly descended to the ground floor. The hinges of the exterior door creaked as he eased it open. It let out into the alley he had just jumped across.

The teeth-aching whine of Soulbreaker's supercharged engine filled the street as the red demon car prowled past, hunting for him. Its headlights clicked on in the approaching dusk, bathing the street in twin cones of bluish light.

He could try to dominate Soulbreaker again, command it to back off. But when he had done that before, he had obviously caught the demon car off guard. He didn't know if the same trick would work twice, and he had no intention of finding out the hard way if it didn't.

Heart pounding, Greyson waited until Soulbreaker had turned the corner. Then, hoping he wouldn't be spotted, he sprinted across the street toward the broken shop windows. Even before he got there, he could see the red glow of Hellbringer's red taillights, pierced by the small white backup lights mounted beneath its rear bumper.

Inside the smashed plate glass windows was a small-town bar, which apparently Hellbringer had crashed into after losing the fight with Soulbreaker. The middle of the room was utterly destroyed, but the periphery was oddly untouched. Stacks of dusty glasses stood behind the bar, beneath cloudy stem glasses hanging upside down. A wide mirror covered the back wall, reflecting the angular shape of Hellbringer's long black body and tall tail wing. The nose of the car had stopped just a few feet short of demolishing the bar.

The remains of broken wooden tables and stools, splintered from the crash, lay crushed beneath Hellbringer's bulk, piled high enough to prop the car's back wheels a fraction of an inch above the floor. It wasn't much of a difference, but it was enough to immobilize the demon car, much to its obvious frustration.

Hellbringer revved its massive Hemi engine, making the rear tires spin just above the scratched wooden floorboards. The air was thick with the nostril-burning smell of smashed liquor bottles and exhaust fumes as Hellbringer struggled to free itself.

"Hitting the bar early, buddy?" Greyson said, rounding the car's pointed nose. "Need me to call you a cab?"

With a grinding clunk, Hellbringer's headlights slowly rose up from the sharp nose cone. They stared at him angrily, blinding in their brightness.

"Yeah, it's been a rough day all around," Greyson muttered. He bent down low and braced himself against the front of the car. "Ready?"

The engine revved again.

Greyson pushed. The car didn't budge. He let go and worked his shoulders, trying to loosen them up.

The engine barked at him, and the exhaust growled.

"Just hold your horses. We'll get this." Greyson planted his hands against the black metal, fingers spread wide, and pushed until it hurt. He strained until the muscles in his arms shook and his vision narrowed to pinpoints. It still wasn't enough. The car rocked slightly but didn't break loose.

With a gasp, he let go. He straightened up, breathing hard and sweating, and cast a speculative glance at the bar, wondering if there was still anything back there worth drinking. But there was no time for that. Dru was missing. Ember had taken her and Rane who knew where. Soulbreaker could circle back around any minute, and they were sitting ducks here.

"Tools." Greyson slapped Hellbringer's trunk. "Open up."

From the trunk, he got out the old-fashioned bumper jack. Less than a minute later, he had ratcheted the demon car up into the air, kicked the debris out from under it, and dropped it back to the ground.

Greyson got in, and the driver's seat fit him like a glove. He backed Hellbringer out of the bar and into the middle of the street, alert for the first sign of Soulbreaker, protean sorcerers, or any other dangers. Nothing moved.

He eased off the clutch and fed the gas pedal. With the Hemi roaring under the hood, they charged down the street.

Free once more, Hellbringer charges after his hated enemy. He recognizes the scent of the other speed demon, and the trail burns like fire in his mind. He stretches his spell-enhanced senses across this dead town, mapping the swiftest route.

His exhaust growls with menace. He will hunt down Soulbreaker and sate his bloodlust once and for all.

"Easy, buddy," his driver says. "Forget the other car. Where's Dru? We need to find her."

She is a pinpoint of pure sparkling energy at the edges of Hellbringer's vision, off on the horizon outside town. He ignores her. His thirst for vengeance narrows his senses to Soulbreaker, who is only a few blocks away and heading the other direction. It will be easy to come up behind and catch him unawares. . . .

"No." His driver interrupts his plans with a firm order: "FIND DRU."

Every bit of Hellbringer wants to resist, but he can't. With a growl, he obeys and heads toward the dirt road leading out of town.

At the next empty intersection, Hellbringer jerked the wheel from Greyson's grip and turned left. The engine throttled up, pushing Greyson back in the seat.

As they flew through the town at breakneck speed, he spotted debris lying in the street ahead, beneath a sign for a hardware and paint store. A hole gaped in the building's brick wall, making the place look like it had been bombed. Greyson slowed them down slightly, watching for danger.

Just then, Salem came hurtling out of the hole as if he'd been kicked. His black silk hat sailed off the top of his head from the force of the blow, and his long hair flew out around him. As he hit the ground, a giant brown-and-black tarantula charged out of the hole, thick fangs twitching as it pounced on him.

Greyson had only a fraction of a second to react. Eyeballing the distance to Salem's slim body, he swung the wheel and brought Hellbringer dangerously close. The passenger side would pass only inches away from the legs of the hideous tarantula pinning Salem down.

"DOOR!" Greyson commanded Hellbringer.

The speed demon obediently swung open its long black passenger door, letting in a blast of wind and the rush of road noise. The giant spider tensed, as if sensing their approach, but didn't get out of the way fast enough. The long door swatted it with a putrid crunching sound, not all that different from cracking into a large crab leg.

The impact slammed the door hard enough to make Greyson's eardrums pop. He worked the pedals and emergency brake as he spun the wheel, forcing Hellbringer into a gut-clenching turn. The rear tires howled in protest, spinning out clouds of white smoke as they slewed around to face the spider again.

Greyson was ready to run the thing down if need be, but it tumbled away across the road, its shaggy legs tucked tight around its body, and lay still. Greyson goosed the gas and rolled up next to Salem, cranking down his window as he approached.

Rane limped out through the hole in the brick wall, her body made of shimmering metal now gashed with scratches. Deep claw marks gouged one leg, and her face was twisted in pain. She carried Ember, who lay bloody and limp in her arms, black coat tattered and shredded. "Dude, Ember got her ass kicked. You get any spider drool on you?"

Salem sat up, dazed, and quickly patted down his chest as if looking for fang holes. He peered up at Greyson with sheer astonishment, which was quickly buried under a flicker of contempt, and then his expression transformed into quiet awe, as if he saw something in Greyson he couldn't even begin to fathom.

Greyson nodded. "Need a lift?"

31

THE NAME OF VENGEANCE

Lucretia was dressed just like the night before, when she'd broken into the Crystal Connection and blown open the safe. Knee-high black boots, tight black pants, black leather jacket. The wind blew her straight red hair back, making her thin face look even more gaunt as she mounted the concrete pad and strode closer. Her dark eyes bored into Dru's.

Swallowing down her fear, Dru squared her shoulders and faced her. There was no sense in trying to hide now. With far more confidence than she felt, Dru pointed to the Project Lucretia plaque behind her. "So. Lucretia isn't even your real name."

The older sorceress shook her head slightly. "In Latin, the name means 'profit.' As in money."

Dru mentally dug through her knowledge of Latin. "Okay, right, it comes from the same root as *filthy lucre*," Dru said. "I get that. What I don't get is why you would take on that name."

"For revenge."

"Revenge . . . for this?" Dru waved to encompass the concrete pentagon. "What is all this?"

"I thought you were supposed to be the smart one in the bunch, baby." Lucretia stopped a few paces away, her stance wide. Her hands hung loosely at her sides, empty but bristling with colorful crystal-encrusted rings. Dru was acutely aware that any of them could begin to glow the moment Lucretia decided to attack. Dru gripped her own iron pyrite disk tighter in her palm but kept it down by her side, ready to deflect the first thing Lucretia threw at her.

As they faced one another across the concrete, neither one of them moved. Neither blinked. The wind whistled between them.

Lucretia studied her with undisguised contempt. "You do know what's ultimately going to destroy the world? Or maybe you don't."

Dru ignored the jab and kept an eye on the rings adorning Lucretia's fingers, watchful for the first glow of magic. This could all be over in a heartbeat.

"I know what you're going to *try* to do," Dru said, doing her best to keep the fear out of her voice. "You're going to try to break the sixth seal of the apocalypse scroll and unleash the final earthquake. But I'm not going to let you do that."

Lucretia's eyes gleamed with amusement. "You're too literal, baby. No, what's going to destroy the world is *greed*."

Dru looked around, sure she was missing something. But nothing else moved in the valley. She faced Lucretia again, certain she had misheard.

"It's all because of greed. That's how this all started. Human beings killing each other to make a dime." Lucretia's red lips turned down at the corners. "You really don't know what I'm talking about. That's so disappointing. What do they teach you in school these days?"

Dru's gaze flicked to the vans in the distance, parked around the perimeter of the wide circle. Directly ahead was the van she and Opal had hidden in. To the right was a van with the roof rack that jutted up like horns. That was the van with the sulfur in it. To the left was the van missing its front grill so that it looked buck-toothed. That one was full of wulfenite.

She couldn't tell which of the remaining two vans behind either shoulder was which, but that narrowed down the order of crystals to only two possibilities. She thought back to everything she had read in Lucretia's spell book, trying to remember which spell this was. If she could remember it, maybe she could figure out how to counteract it.

"This all started before you were born," Lucretia said. "Back when someone discovered huge natural gas deposits right here in the shadow of the Rocky Mountains. Right beneath our feet. Natural gas deposits worth hundreds of millions of dollars. Actually, these days it would be hundreds of *billions*. Buried miles and miles deep. Too far down to drill. Can you guess what they used instead to unearth it?"

Dru glanced back at the plaque bolted into the concrete.

NUCLEAR EXPLOSIVE EMPLACEMENT WELL

"You don't believe me. I can see it in your face." Lucretia studied her closely. "But I was there. I listened to the government men talk. Great big dollar signs in their eyes." She spread her arms wide, as if to encompass the land around them. "They wanted it all. All the wealth they could shake out of this land, at any cost. So they drilled a hole halfway to hell . . . and then they dropped a nuclear bomb down into the heart of the earth."

Dru shook her head in disbelief. "No one in their right mind would drill using nuclear weapons."

"No? I watched them do it. They told us it was safe. I was a *child*." Lucretia paced around the perimeter of the five-sided concrete slab. Dru, with her back to the plaque, sidestepped to keep Lucretia in front of her.

"We had a station wagon, a brown Packard with tail fins," Lucretia said. "It was so hot that day, it was almost too hot to breathe. I was sitting in the wayback, on the tailgate. We were parked right up there, with all the lizards and bugs." She pointed to a rocky ridge that overlooked the valley. "Everything down here was all torn up. All bare dirt. The air smelled like broken rocks and diesel exhaust. I watched the men in hard hats pack up all of their drilling equipment and pull it back up onto the road. The things they left behind looked like they were launching a space rocket."

A shadow slowly crept over them, swallowing the valley as the sun fell behind the rocky ridge. The air grew chilly.

Sundown. Doomsday.

Lucretia's jaw set in a hard line. "They counted it down on a loud-speaker, just like a rocket launch. So exciting. I felt like we should've had popcorn, or noisemakers or something. Like it was some kind of celebration. Like the Fourth of July." Her face twisted with anger. "When they detonated the nuclear bomb, the entire *world* shook. I could feel it in every cell of my body. I can still feel it today." She inhaled deeply, nostrils flaring. "The ground moved in waves, out from this point, like ripples in a pond. Rocks broke off the cliffs all around and scattered across the road. Our station wagon bounced right up in the air. Tossed me out onto the ground. I couldn't have stood up even if I wanted to. But that wasn't the worst. The worst part was the *light* beaming up out of the hole." Her voice dropped to a hushed whisper. "There were colors I had never even seen before. Rippling up into the sky. Waves of light no human eyes should ever see."

Dru wanted to ask where this hole was, but she gradually realized they were standing right on top of it. The government had covered it up with concrete. The thought made her skin crawl.

"I knew then the human race had done something that could never be undone. We had committed an unspeakable trespass against the heart of the world. And I knew there was no coming back from it," Lucretia said. "Know what's ironic? It actually worked. They got all the natural gas they could ever want. More than they could *ever* use in their lifetimes. But there was one tiny little complication." She held up a single thin finger, waiting for Dru to respond.

"The gas was radioactive," Dru guessed. "The nuclear explosion contaminated the deposits, didn't it?"

Lucretia's hard eyes bored into hers. "Exactly. None of it could be used. *None* of it. Because it was poison." Her voice shook with barely suppressed rage. "They *destroyed* this place for all eternity. Just for a chance to feed their greedy hearts. And when they found out it was all for nothing, they simply plugged it up with concrete and told everyone to leave. After they had poisoned our land. Our bodies. Our *souls*."

The air caught in Dru's throat, as if she couldn't get enough oxygen. She tried to swallow, but her mouth had gone dry.

"I didn't start us on the path to doomsday, so you can wipe that judgmental look off your face," Lucretia said. "But I will finish what they started. I will put the entire *world* in that hole, and I will get my revenge. I'll make things *right*."

The venom in her voice made Dru's knees go rubbery. There was a lifetime of fury packed into those words. Defusing that wouldn't be easy, but she had to try. "Look. Lucretia, or whatever your name is. What they did was terrible, yes. But you can't destroy everything and kill everyone just because of one thing."

"*One thing?*" The cords stood out on Lucretia's neck, and Dru realized that maybe she had used exactly the wrong words. The rage radiating from Lucretia was almost palpable. "This was my *home*. Now it's nothing but a *tomb*."

Dru resisted the urge to back up a step. "I'm not trying to minimize what happened here. Okay? It was unequivocally terrible. But something like this would never happen today. You have to know that. We've changed. As a culture, as a society, we wouldn't let this happen again."

Lucretia's face contorted as she reined in her emotions. Once more, her expression became a cold mask. "So sad. I remember being like you, once. When I was a child. Before I watched my parents wither away. Consumed from within by an invisible evil no one could see. Until there was nothing left of them but skin and bones. And then nothing at all." She turned to look out across the toxic valley. "The world has not changed. The world will never change on its own. We must change it. We must remake it. We need to start over. Do it again, and do it right, so that kind of greed never returns. That's been our plan all along."

Dru cleared her throat. "So, when you say 'our,' you mean you and the other Harbingers? Where are they right now, exactly?"

"Waiting for me to finish my work. And when I'm done, we'll be together again to rule over a brand-new world. A paradise no one will *ever* spoil."

"Yeah, see, there's a little problem with that." Dru held up her empty hand. "If you go through with your doomsday plans, then that's it for everybody. Including you. Do you really want to die along with everyone else?"

Lucretia's smile showed unnaturally white teeth. "Oh, baby, I'm not going to *die* here. I'm not going to burn with the rest of the world. I'm going to come out the other side. My friends are already waiting for me there. They've been waiting there, all these years. And I miss them."

"Waiting on the other side. . . ." Dru immediately remembered a passage in Lucretia's book that talked about wandering the deserted cobblestone streets of some ancient nameless place. Actually, it did have a name, she remembered, and she struggled to pull it from the depths of her memory. "The Shining City."

"Yes." Lucretia's smile turned genuine, like a sudden beam of sunlight from a stormy sky. "You've seen it?"

"Seen it?" That was an odd choice of words. Nobody saw a city unless they went there. And how could someone go there without knowing where it was? Dru's thoughts raced, trying to put the pieces together. Lucretia spoke of the other Harbingers waiting for her on the other side . . . in the netherworld?

With a jolt, she remembered once seeing a city where it didn't belong. In the netherworld. What felt like so long ago, when Greyson had carried her across the length of the causeway bridge, above the endless flickering mists of the other side, she had glimpsed a dark city skyline in the distance. She had seen ancient towers glittering in the shifting lights of the fiery netherworld sky.

So that was the Shining City. Despite herself, Dru felt an overwhelming sense of awe. She had already uncovered so many mysteries, but there was still so much more for her to learn. "Yes, I've seen it. From the causeway."

Lucretia practically beamed at her. "I remember being where you are. With everything still ahead of you. So much to see, so much to discover for the first time. It's such a shame, it really is. The things I could teach you, if we only had the time."

Finally, Dru felt like she had an opening. She took a tentative step closer. "Why not teach me? You can do so much with crystals. Things I never thought were possible. I want to learn. And right now, there's no rush. We have plenty of time."

"Plenty of time. Ha." Lucretia gave her a sad smile. The corners of her mouth quivered, as if she was fighting off a frown, or perhaps even a sob of grief. "I've been telling myself that for fifty years, you know that? It's always *someday*. It's always *later*. It's always, '*We've got plenty of time.*' It's the same old story. Let somebody else handle it. And where has that gotten us?" Her gaze lost focus, as if adrift in memories. Her voice dropped to a self-mocking hush. "Plenty of time? That's such *bullshit.*"

"No, it's not." Dru swallowed down a sudden lump in her throat. "I'll be the first to admit, our planet may be messed up, but it isn't irredeemable. There may be plenty of things that are broken. But as sorceresses, our job is to *fix* those things. Make the world a better place. Not just destroy it all and start over."

Lucretia gave her a tired smile. "I wish that was true."

Dru took another step closer, reaching out her empty hand. "You don't have to do this. You can stop doomsday. Right now."

Tears shimmered at the corners of Lucretia's eyes. "You don't get it, do you? It's all a done deal. The bomb. The apocalypse scroll. Doomsday. I didn't start any of this. The only thing I *can* do is finish it." She reached inside her leather jacket and pulled out an ages-old roll of stained parchment the color of desert sand. Either end was crowned with an elaborate knob with twelve wicked-looking silver spikes. Seven red wax seals held the scroll shut, but five of them had jagged edges where they'd been broken. It took Dru a moment to fully realize what she was seeing. Lucretia held a scroll in her hand, but it wasn't just any scroll.

It was the apocalypse scroll.

Dru's jaw dropped open.

Lucretia's eyes darkened with rage. "This is it right here, baby. This is where it all ends."

32

WHERE IT ALL ENDS

*E*ngine roaring, Hellbringer rockets out of the old, dead town. His sharp black body pierces the encroaching night, tires flying over the rain-worn dirt road, carrying his driver and the other humans toward their fate.

From somewhere far ahead, he picks up the scent of ancient magic. The fabric of the world is weakening here. He recognizes the menace that hangs in the air, even if the humans can't feel it.

The dirt road ahead rises steeply. Hellbringer climbs it without any real effort. As they crest the top, a vast valley opens up far below. For a moment, Hellbringer wonders if they will keep going right over the edge of the rocky outcropping and out into the empty air.

He shivers with terrified excitement at the thought, the ultimate freedom of nothing but open air rushing past. But the crash at the end of such a flight would surely be fatal.

Hellbringer could recover from nearly anything. But not everything. Not that.

And more importantly, such a crash would smash to pieces the humans he carries. Right now, they are all filled with fear, though none of them admits it out loud. Hellbringer can smell it in their sweat. It brings out a fierce protective instinct in him. A sense of duty.

His driver steers away from the rocky ledge and finds a steep path, not even a real road, down into the valley. Sliding back and forth, they reach the valley floor. Hellbringer's tires hiss across the sickly grass. The blight of death permeates the ground here, seeping up from beneath the earth.

His driver steers him toward the sparkling silhouette of Dru, who stands in the center of the valley beside the burning red sorceress who created Hellbringer.

Seeing her, his engine falters and bogs in fear. But his driver hits the gas *pedal, so Hellbringer surges forward again. His duty is to obey, even if it means charging toward his own destruction.*

There are few things in this world he would run from, but she is one of them, the red sorceress who bound him here to this cold world with fire and torment so many decades ago.

His brakes itch with the desire to stop. To turn back. But his driver must have a plan. Hellbringer trusts him.

So intent is Hellbringer on this mission that he doesn't sense Soulbreaker closing in until it's too late.

"The first four seals were easy." Lucretia's voice crackled with cold anger, as if discussing a recent divorce instead of the apocalypse. Her long red hair flew in the wind, whipping back over her black leather jacket. "I used galena crystals to summon up the Four Horsemen. But you already knew that, didn't you? And I bound them into a Charger, a Mustang, a Bronco, and a Ferrari. Four horse-themed cars. That was my little signature thing."

Dru thought about that. "Technically, Hellbringer is a Dodge Charger, and a 'charger' originally meant a horse that a knight rides into battle. I get that. Mustangs and broncos are words for wild American horses. But a Ferrari?"

Beneath Lucretia's drawn cheeks, her blood-red lips twisted with annoyance. "There's a little black horse on the car. In the logo."

"Oh . . . yeah, I never got that," Dru said.

"Obviously," Lucretia snapped. "Well. The fifth seal, making the dead rise from the grave, that was a little trickier. That took montroseite, which was no picnic. But this sixth seal, this was the real killer. Took me years to figure out I could only break it with a painite crystal. Can you imagine how frustrating that is? Painite, the rarest crystal in the entire *world*. Luckily, you had one handy."

Lucretia dipped her free hand—the one that wasn't holding the apocalypse scroll—down into her shirt. She pulled out the chunky gold chain that held the Amulet of Decimus the Accursed.

Seeing it again sent a cold shudder running through Dru's core. All this time, Dru had been worried about the amulet itself. But it was actually the crystal at its heart that Lucretia wanted.

The faceted painite gem, glittering black in the twilight, seemed to stare out at Dru from a tangle of cast metal glyphs. A blood-red glow sparked to life in its depths, like dormant coals stirred by a gust of wind. A matching glow crawled across Lucretia's chest, pulsing through the veins beneath her skin as if her blood was on fire. Whatever dark power lay within the cursed amulet, it now flowed freely through Lucretia's body.

Dru tightened her grip on the golden pyrite disk that she held in one damp palm down at her side. This was about to get ugly. She had to get the apocalypse scroll away from Lucretia. She was afraid to even touch an artifact of such immense power, but she had no choice.

She went for it.

Lucretia reacted instantly. She extended her fingers, clawlike, at Dru. The crystal-adorned rings on her fingers burned with a dozen different colors, and a viselike force crushed the air around Dru.

But Dru was ready. Unlike the night before, when Lucretia had nearly choked Dru to death in the back room of the Crystal Connection, this time she had a crystal already in her hand. She brought the pyrite disk up in front of her chest, forcing her energy into it so that the disk flared with a golden glow.

The two spells clashed. A blinding flash of magical backlash hurled Dru backward into the air, as if she'd been yanked off the concrete platform by a giant invisible cane. She barely had time to gasp in surprise before she landed in the greasy dying grass and tumbled to a painful stop.

Her glasses flew off. She patted around blindly in the grass until she found them.

Engines sounded in the distance. A pair of headlights swooped down into the valley. Another pair, brighter and bluer, approached from the side. Could it be Hellbringer and Soulbreaker?

Far behind Lucretia, a sickly yellow light erupted from the sulfur van, shining out through its windshield and the gaps around its doors. A couple of hundred yards away, the vanadinite van erupted with an angry red glow. One by one, the vans around the perimeter of the circle became beacons of light as Lucretia's spell activated the crystals inside them.

Dru turned to the van Opal was hiding in, two hundred yards away. In seconds, it would light up with magic, too. And if Opal was still inside when that happened, she could be killed.

Could Opal hear her at this distance? Dru spit out blades of dead grass, put her fingers in her mouth, and let out a shrill whistle. *"Opal!"* she yelled at the top of her lungs, waving her arms overhead. *"Get out of the van!"*

Pinpoints of green, orange, and blue light leaped into the air over Lucretia and arced toward Dru like missiles, twining around each other as they homed in on her. They were crystals, sent flying through the air to stop or even kill her.

But Dru had lost her protective pyrite disk in the grass somewhere. She had nothing left to defend herself with except her spectrolite blade. And that was more of a soul-protective crystal than a real weapon.

She pulled it out of her back pocket and willed it to life. Its rainbow surface shimmered with colors. In soul-protective magic spells, spectrolite could serve as a kind of spiritual decoy, drawing away negative forces to keep the subject protected. Dru could only hope that it would work under these conditions, too. There was nothing in any of her books about how to defend against an evil sorceress's crystal missile weapons.

Dru stabbed the crystal point-first into the ground, then jumped back as Lucretia's crystals homed in on it. They exploded at her feet with an ear-ringing bang that pelted the grass with fragments of still-glowing spectrolite.

Dru didn't have time to mourn the destruction of her all-time favorite crystal. She was already running flat-out back toward the larimar van, fists pumping at her sides, breathing hard. Ahead of her, the van lit up with an eerie blue glow. Wide beams of shimmering blue light shone out through the windshield and open door, lighting up the nearby rock walls.

"Opal!" Dru yelled. *"Get out now!"*

But Opal was already out of the van, lying on the ground where she had jumped. Coughing, she picked herself up out of the dirt. "You don't have to tell me twice. I used to live on East Colfax. Things get wiggy, I'm out of there. But look what happened to my outfit!"

Dru barely slowed down her run before she collided with Opal and wrapped her in a tight hug, suddenly relieved. "Oh my God, I thought you were in trouble."

"We *are* in trouble." Opal released her and slammed the van door, cutting off the wave of oven-like heat that rolled out from the larimar crystals in the back. "What did you do out there, Dru? You were supposed to be stopping this!"

Dru cleared her throat. "Things didn't work out exactly as planned."

With an echoing sizzle, knife-sharp golden lines of energy shot across the uneven floor of the valley, connecting each van to the two across the circle. Moments later, the lines had drawn a glowing five-pointed star that was so large and bright that it was probably visible from space. At the exact center lay the five-sided concrete slab, now lit from all sides by the shimmering gold light.

"Well, *that* doesn't look good," Dru said.

In the center of the circle, Lucretia walked off the slab, turned around, and raised the scroll overhead in both hands. Cracks of white-hot light zig-zagged through the concrete. With a sound like distant thunder, the slab atomized and disappeared into a swirl of sparks, revealing a jagged pit in the ground. A ghostly light shone up, illuminating Lucretia from below.

"What's down there?" Opal said, craning her neck as if it would give her a better vantage point.

"Holy guacamole. She's going to use the power of the nuclear bomb to energize her spell." Dru wanted to smack herself on the forehead. "Of course. If the entire blast was contained underground, then the detonation could have fused the deeper rock into a sphere of radioactive trin-itite. Well, not *technically* trinitite, because it isn't from New Mexico, but essentially the same thing. We must be standing on millions of tons of it. The sheer power under this circle, if she can tap into those crystals . . ."

"Stop *analyzing* this." Opal, frowning deeply, took hold of both of Dru's shoulders and spoke slowly. "Honey. This is very important. *What* nuclear bomb?"

Before Dru could answer, bright headlights swept across them. She held up her hand to ward off the blinding light.

Soulbreaker charged at them, obviously intent on running them down. But Hellbringer swooped in from the side and struck the other speed demon. Metal bashed against metal as Hellbringer tried to turn Soulbreaker away from them.

Engines roared. Tires slashed the dirt and grass. The two speed demons were locked together side by side. Dru's heart leaped into her throat as the speed demons hurtled directly toward them. But in the end, Soulbreaker's slick drag racing tires lost their grip, and Hellbringer shouldered it toward the white van.

With a warning shout, she pushed Opal out of the way, tumbling to the ground on top of her. Hellbringer flew past, close enough for the wind to ruffle her clothes, and forced Soulbreaker nose-first into the back of the van. This close, the crash was like a thunderclap.

The impact tore the back of the white cargo van wide open, scattering a mixture of glowing blue and white crystals like a fountain of hot coals. Soulbreaker spun away, tires hissing across the grass, its blood-red body peppered with smoldering pinpoints of white light. Smoke gushed out of the small, square holes.

Dru suddenly remembered that they had left the tray of galena crystals in the back of the van, where they must have been charged up by Lucretia's energy until they glowed white-hot. Apparently, the force of the crash had sent that tray of crystals flying—right onto Soulbreaker.

Now, the red demon car zigzagged across the grass, as if trying to shake loose from the burning white galena crystals. But they were already melting their way through its steel, shooting smoke out of the holes they bored through its body.

The sight of it made Dru recoil in horror. She wouldn't wish that fate on anyone, not even an evil demon car that wanted nothing less than to kill her and her friends.

Hellbringer pulled up as Dru helped Opal to her feet, and the doors flew open. "Dru!" Greyson jumped out and swept her into his strong arms.

She had never been more glad to see him. But there was no time to embrace him. "Lucretia has the apocalypse scroll. We have to get it from her! Right now."

Greyson nodded grimly. "How?"

"How?" Salem repeated from the other side of the car. "God, I'm surrounded by amateurs." He helped Rane pull a bloodied and moaning Ember out of the back seat and then strode over to face Dru. His twitchy black-outlined eyes glinted in the glare from Hellbringer's headlights. "Do you mean to tell me that all this time, *Lucretia* had the apocalypse scroll?"

Dru followed his pointed finger to the center of the quarter-mile-wide glowing pentagram. The distant silhouette of Lucretia moved against the shimmering waves of ghostly energy rising from the hole in the earth.

"Well," Dru said, "apparently."

"And all this time, I thought it was your not-so-fresh boyfriend here who had it." Salem turned away and threw his arms wide. Sparks of energy danced across his skin, nestling in the spaces between his fingertips. Invisible waves of magic rippled up and down his black trench coat, fluttering his hair out beneath his top hat, splaying out the grass around his feet. An unearthly light fogged the air around him, making Dru's skin prickle. His long, spidery fingers kneaded the air.

Dru took a step back, motioning for Greyson to do the same. She opened her mouth to ask Salem what exactly he was trying to do, but a blur of movement made the words die on her lips. Something small and thin tumbled through the air toward them.

The apocalypse scroll.

Dru stared with disbelief as the ancient artifact cartwheeled through the darkening sky and smacked into Salem's outstretched palm. Its spiked silver tips shone in Hellbringer's headlights. Salem smiled with satisfaction as the glow of his magic faded around him.

"Holy cheese and crackers, that's amazing." Dru held her hand out for the scroll. "Thank you! Now I can—"

"Oh, no." Salem tucked the age-stained brown scroll into the inside pocket of his trench coat. "Don't start thinking you can tell me what to do."

Shocked, Dru stared at him. "That right there might be the most powerful artifact in the universe. You do understand that, right?"

"And now it's safe and sound." As he patted his pocket in satisfaction, the ground began to tremble under their feet. Salem looked around quickly, with a disapproving frown on his face, as if he had smelled something foul. "That's not supposed to happen. . . ." For once, he sounded unsure about himself.

Greyson put an arm around Dru, steadying her as the earthquake intensified, making it difficult to stand upright.

"Why is the spell not stopping?" Salem demanded, as if this was somehow all Dru's fault.

"If she already broke the sixth seal, then she doesn't need the scroll anymore." Dru raised her voice to be heard over the rumbling that shook the valley. "That's why she let you have it."

"*Let* me?"

Dru didn't have time to argue. The twilight sky above was only barely starting to sprinkle with glittering stars, but now it came alive with the glowing streaks of meteorites. Only here and there at first, but they quickly multiplied. Fiery lines of light plunged earthward, punching through the scattered clouds and rocking the rocky landscape around them with the distant thunder of impacts. Above, the clouds took on a ruddy glow as the moon turned blood red.

Dru looked around at the shocked faces all staring skyward. Salem. Greyson. Rane. Opal. Even Ember. Each of their expressions showed some combination of awe and fear, but they all silently said the same thing.

Doomsday.

33

START WITH
AN EARTHQUAKE

Within the vast burning circle, the five-pointed star lit the entire valley with an unearthly golden glow. At the center was a roiling pit of magic growing more powerful under Lucretia's control. Along the edge of the circle, at each point of the star, a van full of crystals glowed a different scintillating color, powering her spell.

The van near Dru had been half mashed by Soulbreaker's crash. The red demon car swerved erratically through the valley, still overwhelmed by the galena. Dru knew that wouldn't last forever, and sooner or later the demon car would recover and come back after them again. Next to her, the demolished van glowed with an uneven light, since half its crystals lay in the grass. On the ground nearby, the vast golden star sparkled.

Dru mentally flipped through the advanced magical combinations she had learned from Lucretia's spell book, trying to think of something that could help them. She had studied Lucretia's notes closely enough to give her at least a glimpse into how the masterful sorceress did her thing. But Dru still didn't know nearly enough to cast those kinds of spells without messing them up.

At that thought, she snapped her fingers. Right now, messing up a spell was *exactly* what she needed to do.

Squaring her shoulders, Dru turned to her friends. "Listen up, people. I know this looks bad. Really bad, actually. But we've been in tough spots before." *Maybe not this tough*, she silently added. "It doesn't matter how impossible things look. We are the only ones who can stop this. And we *can* stop it, if we all work together. If we all trust one another. I know among sorcerers, trust is an issue."

She nodded once to Salem, who had told her as much many times before. He inclined his head, studying her from under the brim of his top hat.

"But all of us know what we're doing," Dru continued. "And we are going to win. If you trust me."

All eyes were focused on her. She couldn't mess this up. Everything was riding on this. *Everything.*

Dru cleared her throat. "Ember, are you up to teleporting?"

Ember, bloody and bruised, barely had the strength to sit up. She looked down at her shredded coat, and when she met Dru's gaze again, the fear was plain in her eyes. Silently, she shook her head.

"Alligator." Rane's voice rang with grudging respect. "Real nasty one, too."

"That's okay. We can do this a different way," Dru said, mentally adjusting the plan that was only half formed in her head. "Opal, check over Ember, try to stop her bleeding. See if she can walk. Rane, can you run?"

Rane, still in metal form, flexed her right leg, which was deeply gouged with claw marks. She grimaced in pain. "If I have to."

"You may have to. Your job is simple. Get Opal and Ember as far away from the vans as possible. Carry them if you need to. A couple of minutes from now, when I get done with these vans, they will probably explode. Big boom. So everybody needs to get way back. Salem—"

He shot her a warning look.

She didn't care. "Reassemble this van behind me. Get all the blue larimar crystals up out of the grass and back inside, fast as you can."

He looked puzzled. "That will make Lucretia's spell stronger."

"Exactly. And then what you and I are going to do is reverse the order of these vans. Back and forth, across the circle, we're going to swap them left and right."

His eyebrows went up. "A counterspell?"

"Yeah. I need you to be ready to levitate this van the moment you see me coming back."

"Where do you think you're going?"

She pointed down the arc of the golden circle, toward the next van. "I'm going to go steal that van and bring it over here. When I do, I need you to levitate this van over into its place. The old switcheroo. Can you do that?"

He cracked his knuckles. "Don't be insulting. Of course I can."

"Good. Let's move, people! Go!" She turned to Greyson. "Give me a ride?"

He smiled wryly. "Thought you'd never ask." Just then, bright blue-white headlights washed over them. From a few hundred yards away, Soulbreaker charged at them, apparently recovered from the galena crystals. The speed demon closed in fast.

Greyson squeezed her hand. "I'll buy you some time."

As he started for Hellbringer, Dru caught him and planted a quick kiss on his lips. "Come back to me," she whispered.

His glowing red eyes looked deeply into hers, holding a promise. Then he slid into the driver's seat, slammed the door, and Hellbringer charged into battle.

Dru glanced over her shoulder to make sure everyone else was moving, and then she took off running in the opposite direction, toward the other van. The ground shook underfoot as another shock wave rolled out from the glowing pit at the center of the circle. Dru stumbled, found her footing, and kept running.

Behind her, tires clawed at the dirt and metal crushed against metal with a sickening *whump*. She glanced back long enough to see Hellbringer pushing Soulbreaker sideways. The red speed demon's engine bawled as it tried to wrench itself free.

Ahead of her, a few hundred yards away, the windshield of the next van glowed with bright yellow light. Just her luck, she had to pick the sulfur van. As bad as it would smell, the furnace of energy inside it would be even worse. She pulled the black tourmaline crystal out of her pocket and squeezed it in her palm, willing her magical energy to flow into it. It responded with a warm glow that seeped out between her fingers. Hopefully, its aura would be enough to protect her against the radiating magic of the charged sulfur crystals.

Another tremor hit, bouncing Dru off her feet. She fell face-first into dirt and half-dead grass. Spitting out the foul taste, she scrambled to her feet and kept running. She was almost there.

One big worry nagged at the back of Dru's mind. All of Lucretia's spells depended on layering multiple effects one on top of another. There was something about this massive spell that seemed incomplete, but she couldn't put her finger on what, exactly. What was she missing?

Breathing hard, she finally reached the van. This close, the glow from the crystals in the back shone out through every crack in the van as if a yellow floodlight had been turned on back there. The air stank like rotten eggs. She could feel the heat as soon as she touched the door handle. At least there was a metal partition behind the seats to help shield her from the crystals.

Sticking the tourmaline back in her pocket, she took a deep breath and yanked the door open. An oven-hot blast of foul air rolled over her as she climbed into the scorching vinyl seat and reached for the ignition keys.

They weren't there.

Fighting off panic, Dru looked behind the sun visor, in the cup holders, and in the glove box. Nothing. Finally, she had to admit there were no keys in the van.

"Oh, you have *got* to be kidding me!" She pounded her fists uselessly on the steering wheel.

Another tremor shook the earth, worse than the last. Outside, a jagged shelf of rock fractured and thrust upward, crashing up under the passenger side of the van. A moment of vertigo washed over Dru as the van tilted to the left, farther and farther.

"Oh, no, no, *no!*" Dru scrambled toward the rising passenger side, clinging to the seats as the van toppled onto its left side with a crunch of metal. The short door in the metal partition behind the seats clanged open. Fumes spewed from the hot, churning sulfur crystals, making her head spin. She blinked to clear her eyes, struggling to stay conscious.

As the earthquake continued, she fought to get the heavy passenger door open, opening it up over her head like a hatch. Gasping, she dragged herself out onto the warm, slick sheet metal of the van. Out here, at least, the air was cool and clear. But lying on its side like this, the van was clearly going nowhere.

Could Salem levitate it from this distance? She scanned the valley until she found him standing well clear of the circle, under the tallest rocky outcropping that loomed over the valley. "*Salem!*" she shouted, waving her arms overhead, but he didn't seem to notice her.

From this distance, she could clearly see the shock waves of the earthquake traveling outward like ripples on the surface of a pond. At the far end of the valley, Rane's body shimmered in the blood-red moonlight. She carried Ember toward the mouth of the valley and pulled Opal along, half dragging her as the ground shook beneath them.

With a deep, crackling roar that struck fear into Dru's heart, a rocky outcropping broke loose from the canyon wall above. It leaned outward, trailing dust and smaller fragments of rock behind it, then plummeted down the steep slope. It broke apart as it tumbled, gouging other rocks and dirt out of the valley wall, triggering a massive rockslide. Dru watched helplessly as the barrage of rocks and dust swept down at Salem.

A metallic warning shout rang out across the valley, and Rane sprinted toward him, legs pumping. The ground heaved and split beneath her feet. She vaulted over rocks and fissures, streaking toward Salem. But even from this distance, Dru could see she wouldn't reach him in time.

He had already turned to face the rockslide. With his hands shoved skyward, he parted the rockslide with a cone of invisible force. Spinning rocks bounced away from him, leaving comet-like trails of dirt flying behind them. For a moment, it looked like Salem would be able to turn the tide. But in the end, the rockslide was simply too vast.

Rane reached him, arms outstretched, just as the rocks thundered down around them, engulfing them in a cloud of dust.

Dru watched, frozen to the spot, hands covering her mouth, unable to breathe. Her heart thudded in her chest as she counted out the passing seconds. There was no sign of Rane or Salem.

Numb, Dru couldn't stop her hands from shaking. She could only stare, transfixed, as the dust settled around the fallen boulders and the last few rocks tumbled away.

There was no other movement.

They were gone.

Dru gasped, suddenly feeling as if she couldn't pull air into her lungs fast enough. She wanted to run to help, wanted to hide, but there was no way to do either. As another shock wave rattled the van, she crawled to the edge and dropped to the ground. Despite the heat from the van full of crystals, she felt cold to the core. The world started to spin around her.

Rane . . . Salem . . .

She forced thoughts of them aside. She had to focus on stopping Lucretia's spell. The sixth seal of the apocalypse scroll promised a globe-rending earthquake. It was only going to get worse from here. Every second counted.

On the ground near the van's upturned wheels lay the copper cable that circled the valley, forming the glowing circle that connected the crystals. Functionally, it wasn't all that different from the smaller circles Dru wove out of individual strands of copper wire. The difference was mainly one of scale.

At the center of it all, Lucretia stood silhouetted against the brilliant shimmers of light emanating from the hole in the earth. She raised her arms overhead, and the glow became brighter. She was trying to destroy the world, and she was succeeding.

Dru studied the glowing copper cable at her feet. If she could inject her own energy into the spell and disrupt Lucretia's efforts, her interference might be enough to distract the other sorceress and cause her spell to fail. It was a long shot, considering that Lucretia outclassed her by decades of experience. The chances of Dru knocking her that far off-balance were slim.

Worse, jumping into the middle of this spell would probably mean Dru's destruction. She just wasn't equipped to handle that kind of monstrously powerful magic.

But what choice did she have?

Blood-red moonlight spilled across the valley. The very earth moved, threatening to break apart soon. Stars fell all around, filling the air with deadly thunder. Headlights lashed across the dead grass as Soulbreaker bashed Hellbringer and Greyson, again and again. As for Rane and Salem . . . She couldn't bear to look at the still-settling rubble.

This was it. The only other plan she had was now blown to pieces. This was the only chance she had left. She had to make it count.

Dru knelt, squeezed her eyes shut, and grasped the cable with both hands. Instantly, the magic force of the circle roared through her. It felt like getting pounded by a hurricane of energy. The spell was hundreds of times more powerful than anything she had ever experienced, and it took all of her strength just to keep her thoughts from scattering in the currents of magic. The random chaos of the spell pulled her in every direction at once, threatening to rip her apart.

At first, Dru tried to force her own energy into the circle, in a desperate attempt to disrupt Lucretia's strength, but she could immediately tell it wouldn't work. Lucretia had been planning this spell for too long and had too much power racing through it already. Dru couldn't change the spell's course directly. But she did glimpse a way to dismantle it from the inside.

As she fought her way through the torrents of magic, Dru began to sense a pattern. It wasn't random chaos that assaulted her but magic of a more fractal nature. The complex spell was actually woven from deceptively simple concepts, the way a beautiful crystal was formed from a single chemical structure. The simplicity of it all was stunning. Despite everything, Dru couldn't help but be moved by the elegant symmetry of the heart of Lucretia's spell.

Once she saw the pattern at its center, Dru felt her consciousness soar freely through the spell. She was inside it now, and she could sense its complex invisible energies swirling around her. At its heart, Lucretia spun layers upon layers onto the spell, adding to its destructive force, making it grow ever greater.

To break the spell, Dru would have to physically move Lucretia away from the center so that she could no longer keep building the spell. If Dru could somehow get Lucretia outside the circle, perhaps with Hellbringer's help, the entire spell would fail. And the world would be saved.

But it wouldn't be easy. It would require an actual, physical, one-on-

one confrontation with Lucretia. Fighting wasn't Dru's strong point. But she would do whatever she had to, even if it meant dragging the woman outside the circle by her long red hair.

Dru gritted her teeth and forced her fingers to release the copper cable. Slowly, she opened her eyes and rose to her feet. The earth heaved in waves from the quake, but now that she was attuned to it, she knew how to move with it. The ground dropped away, and as she stepped forward, it rose to meet her again. She now knew the elaborate rhythms of the spell. She could see it all laid out in her mind's eye, chaotic on the outside, graceful on the inside.

Eyes locked on Lucretia, Dru strode toward her, ready to fight. She had seen this spell from the inside. She had seen the worst that Lucretia could do, and she had found a way to pierce through it. Now, it was time to take the fight to her. Dru would end this, here and now.

As if sensing her approach, Lucretia turned to face her. Even from this distance, Dru could see the pinpoints of bright light that were her eyes. The older sorceress held her hands clasped before her, seeming to study Dru.

With a simple motion, Lucretia opened her hands, palms up, to reveal the chunky green crystal she held. It glowed with a pale unearthly light, like sunshine through an antique green glass bottle.

Dru hesitated, trying to discern the exact kind of crystal Lucretia held. Crystals were sometimes difficult to identify even up close. But there was only one crystal that made that particular alien light.

Vivianite.

With that green crystal, Lucretia could open a portal to the netherworld. But why would she do that right now?

Lucretia's words came back to haunt her: *"Oh, baby, I'm not going to die here. I'm not going to burn with the rest of the world. I'm going to come out the other side."*

She was planning to escape into the netherworld. Lucretia intended to leave the world behind to crumble to dust while she alone survived.

And it looked like she could do it, too. Lucretia had built her earthquake spell to critical mass, and now she intended to let it continue on

without her, powered by the energy of millions of tons of radioactive trinitite beneath their feet. If she got away, there would be no way to stop the
spell from destroying the entire world.

All of the confidence Dru had felt a moment ago evaporated. She
threw caution aside and charged, fully aware that it could be a fatal
mistake. But she had no choice. She had to get that vivianite crystal out
of Lucretia's hands before the other sorceress escaped.

But before Dru got even halfway there, a burst of green glowing light
signaled that Lucretia was already casting the portal spell. The open pit
at her feet rippled, as if underwater. A high-pitched keening sound sliced
through the air, starting just outside the range of human hearing and
shuddering down to a bone-shaking low. With a flash of colorless energy
and a howling hot wind, the hole in the ground pierced the boundary
between worlds and opened itself to the netherworld. The light emanating up from the hole became a twisting whirlwind that reached high
into the sky, surrounded by spirals of ethereal energy.

"No!" Dru shouted, but it was already too late.

As if called, Soulbreaker streaked across the valley toward the blinding
white portal, door opening as it approached. With a triumphant glance
back at Dru, Lucretia slipped behind the wheel and slammed the door.
The red speed demon's back tires spewed dirt as it accelerated toward the
light.

Dru could only stare as Soulbreaker vanished into the light, carrying
Lucretia into the netherworld. All around, rocks, dirt, and sickly trees
broke loose, sucked into the vortex before it vanished, leaving behind the
crumbling pit at the center of the earthquake spell.

Dru staggered to a halt, stunned, as the edges of the hole collapsed
inward. The spell's insatiable hunger was eerily beautiful to watch, this
ultimate force of destruction that consumed everything around it. It grew
larger by the moment, devouring the valley floor.

The earth itself was beginning to disintegrate, and soon the entire
valley—and everyone in it—would be annihilated by the earthquake
spell. From there, the rate would only accelerate until the entire world
was broken into pieces. Dru's brain, on autopilot, did the math and

arrived at a figure of just under twenty-four hours until total worldwide destruction.

She sank to her knees on the shaking ground, all of her energy spent. Tears flowed freely down her face. Despite everything, she had failed. In the end, Lucretia had managed to cast the spell she had spent half a century preparing for, the spell to bring about doomsday at last. And there was nothing Dru could do to stop it now.

34

BURN WITH ME

Hellbringer pulled up in front of her, wheels locking up in the dirt. The passenger door swung open. "Get in!" Greyson shouted over the roar of the world coming apart.

Numbly, Dru forced herself to get to her feet and slide into Hellbringer's black seat. The demon car leaped into motion even before it slammed the door, shutting her inside.

"There has to be a way to stop this," Greyson said. "Lucretia's gone. How can her spell keep going without her?"

"She's powering the spell with radioactive trinitite. It has a half-life of centuries." Dru blinked the tears from her eyes, trying to focus on the facts.

"How do we get rid of it?"

"It's millions of tons of rocks at the bottom of that hole, created by the nuclear explosion. You'd have to dig it all out somehow. There's no time."

"Then we'll just have to get as far away as possible."

Dru knew that there was no escape. It didn't matter how far away they got, because the earthquake would reach them eventually. But in the meantime, she had to save anyone she could. As Hellbringer raced across the valley floor, Dru pointed toward the mass of boulders piled up against the rock face where they had fallen, still crowned with a cloud of floating dust. "That way! We have to help Rane and Salem!"

She could see in his face that he thought it was already too late. But still, he turned toward the fallen rock pile. As Hellbringer approached, one of the smaller rocks shook.

"Stop! Stop the car!" Dru shouted.

Immediately, Greyson slammed on the brakes. Dru threw the door open and jumped out, stumbling since the car was still in motion. Her heart in her throat, she scrambled up onto the sharp-edged rocks, barely daring to hope. "Rane! Can you hear me? *Rane!*"

A muffled curse answered her, ringing like metal.

Dru pulled at the rocks, not caring how they scraped and cut her fingers and palms. She pulled out every stone she could, using both hands. The earth shook beneath her feet, which made it that much harder. A bigger rock shifted and threatened to crush her legs, but Greyson pulled her out of the way in the nick of time. Then he was beside her, helping her dig.

Opal's voice carried through the valley. "Dru!" Opal hustled toward them, helping Ember limp along.

"Help us!" Dru called back.

With the deep scraping sound of stone against stone, a refrigerator-sized boulder tilted and fell over. Rane emerged from behind it, grimacing, her metal body covered in rock dust.

Dru let out a pent-up breath, feeling giddy at the sight of her. She wanted to climb up to her and hug her tightly. But then she saw Salem.

Limp and bloody, he hung listlessly from Rane's strong arms. She staggered over the rocks, past Dru, until she reached solid ground and laid him down. Panting and trembling with exhaustion, Rane collapsed beside him. Her metal skin flickered and turned human again in random patches, as if she had completely exhausted the last reserves of her energy.

Shaking, she propped herself up on her elbows and leaned over Salem's battered frame. Her blonde hair fell down around her face like a curtain, and her body was racked with sobs.

Dru clung tightly to Greyson, unsure what to do. Salem didn't deserve to die like this.

Opal reached them and knelt down next to Salem. Speaking softly to Rane, she felt Salem's wrist and his neck, then pushed her hair back and leaned her ear close to his lips. Her eyes lit up. "He's still breathing."

Dru's hands flew to her throat. Tangled emotions wrapped around her. There was still a chance Salem could be saved. But unless she found a way to break Lucretia's spell, they would all die here anyway.

Another tremor shook the valley. Each one was more violent than the last. She looked back to the center of the vast golden star, where the radioactive glow from the open pit grew wider as its edges crumbled in. Mentally, Dru cursed Lucretia for escaping through a portal and leaving the rest of the world to die.

Dru had her own vivianite crystal in her purse, she remembered, which was now sitting inside Hellbringer. She could have used that vivianite to open up her own portal to the netherworld. They could have all escaped that way, although that would have made them no better than Lucretia, because they would have left the world to die.

Greyson followed her gaze. "Lucretia. Did she . . . ?"

"She went into the netherworld. Whether she survived or not is anyone's guess. Too bad she didn't take that trinitite with her." Once Dru realized the implications of that thought, her heart lifted up on a bright ray of hope. "Wait, that could actually work! I brought vivianite, too. *I* could open a netherworld portal at the bottom of the pit. If I get it all the way down there, it could suck that trinitite right into oblivion. Get rid of the trinitite, and there's nothing left to power the spell!"

But as she stared out at the spreading hole in the center of the valley, she realized it would be impossible. There was no way for her to get a direct line of sight down to the bottom of the pit. The light of hope inside her was immediately snuffed out.

Greyson's red eyes burned with intensity. "Let's do it. I'll drive you over there right now."

"It's too late." She pointed toward the crumbling edges of the glowing pit. It was already five times as wide as it had been originally, and it was spreading fast. In minutes, the entire valley would be consumed. "To open the portal, I'd have to be right over the center of the pit so that the spell has a straight shot all the way down to the bottom. But now that the edges are collapsing, there's no way to get close enough. The angle is wrong. I'd have to get directly overhead somehow."

She glanced at Salem's unconscious form. If he had been up and about, he could have levitated her over the hole. But that wasn't going to happen.

She fought off an overwhelming wave of despair. There wasn't any other way to stop the spell. Her first plan had been to swap the order of the vans, but they were immobilized now. Then she had tried to disrupt Lucretia's spell, and that hadn't worked, either. Now, as long as it continued to be powered by that radioactive trinitite, it was unstoppable.

She squeezed her fists tight until her fingernails bit into her palms. There had to be another way. There *had* to.

Nearby, Hellbringer revved its engine. Its headlights blazed. The impatient speed demon hated to be kept idling. Its sleek black form looked ready to spring into motion.

A crazy plan began to form in her mind.

Another tremor shook the earth, making the jumble of boulders next to them knock together with menacing bangs and clatters. Dru pointed up to the top of the steep rock walls that overlooked the valley on both sides, and raised her voice to be heard over the rumble of the earthquake. "Can Hellbringer make that jump?"

All eyes were immediately focused on her. She knew how insane that question sounded, but right now her list of options was down to exactly one. And this was it.

Squinting, Greyson eyeballed the distance from one cliff face to the other. Solemnly, he shook his head. "Maybe a little over halfway, at best. And that's assuming there's enough traction at the top and a straight shot for making the final acceleration."

"Okay, halfway is fine. All I have to do is get right over the center of that pit. Then I can open a portal to the netherworld, get rid of that trinitite once and for all. And then *boom*, just like that, no more doomsday." Her spirits soared. She had a solution at last. There was a light at the end of the tunnel after all.

No one spoke for a moment. Greyson cleared his throat. "I don't think you understand. Jumping you over that pit is one thing. *Landing* is something else."

"What do you mean?"

"The canyon walls are maybe half a mile apart. Hellbringer is fast, but there's no way he can clear this entire valley and land safely on the far side. It's just too far. And that means, one way or another, the car will come down on the valley floor. That's probably a ten-story drop. No matter how it ends, it ends badly."

She swallowed down the hard lump in her throat. "Tell me."

He glanced at Opal, Rane, and Ember, who were all watching him intently, and then turned his attention back to Dru. He moved his hand in an arc, pantomiming the jump. "If we overshoot it, we'll hit the far wall of the canyon and probably die instantly." He clapped his hands together for emphasis, making Dru jump. Then he moved his hand in a shorter arc. "If we undershoot it, the weight of the engine and transmission will drag the nose down." He tilted his hand downward so that his fingers were pointed at the ground. "We'll hit the ground nose-first and cartwheel across the floor of the valley. If we aren't dead on impact, we will be by the time we roll into the rocks on the far side."

The silence was broken only by the deathly rumbling of the earthquake. Dru's stomach clenched into a knot as hard as stone. She locked gazes with him. "Not *we*," she said quietly. "Me."

He cocked his head as if he didn't understand her.

She didn't repeat herself. She simply held out her hand. "Give me the keys."

The muscles in his jaw clenched.

She steeled her resolve. "Greyson, if there was another way to do this, I would take it in a heartbeat. Believe me, I would. But I have exhausted *every* other option." Her voice cracked, and it took her a moment to get it back under control again. "Like it or not, that earthquake is coming. We have only minutes to sort this out. And this is the only way to stop it. If we stand around arguing about it, it'll be too late. I'm the only one here who can open the portal. I have to do this."

He straightened up, fixing her with a look that moved from hurt to determination. "You're not going to do it alone," he said flatly.

"I can't ask you to—"

"You don't have to ask," he said through gritted teeth. "I'm the driver. This is what I do."

"Look, I may not have a car, but I know how to drive," she insisted.

"Not like this, you don't." He stepped closer, so that their faces were only inches apart. "Listen. Back when I was turned into one of the Four Horsemen, I was supposed to destroy the world. And I would have, if you hadn't saved me."

She blinked back sudden tears. "Greyson, listen to me. You don't have to—"

"Yeah. I do." With his thumb, he wiped away a tear from the corner of her eye. "You said one time that you have a responsibility to save the world. But that doesn't mean you have to do it alone."

She could see in his face that he meant every word. What would he think of her if he knew that she was terrified out of her mind? There was only one thing that scared her more than doing this: the fact that if she didn't, the world was doomed.

"How much time do we have?" he asked in her ear.

She shook her head, ever so slightly, side to side. "We don't."

His glowing red gaze roamed over her face as if trying to memorize every detail of her features. He looked as if he wanted to say more, but instead he pulled her against him and gave her a kiss that made her heart race. When he released her, she was breathless.

"Let's go," he said softly.

Opal nearly sobbed when Dru hugged her and Rane, but she just barely managed to hold it together. She desperately wanted to talk Dru out of this, but she didn't have any other options. Rane, red-faced, shed a steady stream of tears as she hugged Dru tight.

Opal was still frantically trying to think of some other option as Greyson and Dru slammed the doors and disappeared up the slope of the valley in a cloud of dust. As Hellbringer's powerful engine droned into the distance, Opal watched Rane smooth Salem's long hair back from his face.

"Don't die on me, baby," Rane whispered to him, and then sobbed.

Ember looked close to tears, too. "We have to move him." When Rane ignored her, she turned to Opal, her eyes wide and frightened. "The rest of those rocks could come crashing down at any moment. We must move him!"

Opal considered the collapsing pit that was quickly consuming the valley. The shock waves were coming faster now, more intense. Before long, all of the canyon walls would come tumbling down. Did it really matter whether they moved Salem or not?

Now, it was all up to Dru and Greyson, and their suicidal last-ditch attempt at breaking Lucretia's spell. Opal needed to help them somehow, but she didn't know how.

Opal had never had magical powers like the rest of them. The people in her family were all sorcerers, so she had been surrounded by magic growing up. Part of her had always envied those who had powers. But in the end, it hadn't mattered, not having magic. She was still in the same boat with the rest of them. Staring down an epic evil magic spell that she couldn't do anything to stop. But there was one thing she *could* do.

She raised her palm and brought it down hard against Salem's cheek, slapping the unconscious sorcerer for all she was worth. Ignoring Rane's shocked expression, she lifted her hand and slapped him again.

"Wake up, Salem!" *Slap.* "Wake! Up!" *Slap.*

Rane seized her wrist. "Dude, are you *mental*? The hell do you think you're doing?"

"Honey. Let me go. I'm about to save everyone's butt."

Rane looked utterly confused, but before Opal could explain, the roar of Hellbringer's engine grew suddenly louder overhead. In a streak of motion, the black speed demon shot out over the edge of the cliff. Its wheels spun, glittering in the light of the shooting stars as it sailed across the ruddy clouds and the blood-red moon.

Dru had always thought that the moment before she died, her life would flash before her eyes. She figured that she would experience some sort of incredibly meaningful montage of her best memories. Collecting her first amethyst crystals as a kid. Awkward teenage years experimenting with magic. Starting her own business in her apartment. Trying to avoid getting asked out on dates by socially inept sorcerers.

And then, of course, the happy moments of her otherwise doomed relationship with normal-guy Nate, the dentist. Or the day she cut the red ribbon on the Crystal Connection, for which Rane had insisted she use an ancient samurai sword. That was immediately followed by a trip to the emergency room to get twelve stitches.

Then there were the epic all-night potion-brewing parties with her friends. Movie nights with Rane. Fashion nights with Opal. And her montage would all be capped off by that one sunny summer day Greyson had parked Hellbringer in front of her shop and pulled off his sunglasses to look at her with his deep blue eyes.

That was what she expected, anyway. But when they jumped off the cliff, none of that happened.

Instead of reminiscing, she was mostly screaming her head off.

Moments before, Greyson had driven up to the table-like rocks that formed the flat top of the valley. Dru had just enough time to dig through her purse and find the candy-bar-sized translucent green vivianite crystal, buried beneath an actual candy bar and an empty bottle of hand sanitizer. As she held the crystal in both hands, she took a deep breath and intended to ask Greyson if he was sure about this.

But she didn't get the chance. Greyson, grim-faced, nailed the gas. He gripped the steering wheel steady in one hand while using the other to slam the gear shift up and down.

The noise of the engine was like a thunderclap electrifying the entire car. The acceleration was like nothing Dru had experienced before. It crushed her back against the seat, making her insides feel like they'd been sat on by an elephant. She could practically feel her bones rearranging themselves into a configuration that was at least two dress sizes smaller.

In the blink of an eye, they reached the edge of the cliff and launched skyward. The rumbling and bumping of their launch instantly became a glass-smooth flight through the darkening sky. The dying rays of sunset still lingered on the highest clouds above them, rimming them with fire. The blood-red moon shone down on them, and shooting stars plummeted past them, all around. From this height, she could look out across the jagged black lines of the Rocky Mountains, each peak fainter and fainter in the distance, until they faded to nothing.

Greyson's fingers lifted off the gear shift and clasped her hand. His grip was warm and sure. She wanted to look into his eyes, but instead she focused on the vivianite crystal, watching intently. The instant they passed over the fiery pit of trinitite below, an invisible force pushed against the vivianite, jerking it in her hand. The crystal flickered with a pale green light. It had a direct line of sight to the bottom of the pit, miles beneath the earth.

She pushed everything she had into the crystal. Every bit of her magical energy and everything that flowed into her through Greyson's sure grip. Mentally, she formed the energy into the complex glyphs she had learned from Lucretia's spell book, casting the spell that could open or close a portal instantly. Lucretia had discovered a way to stack up magical effects so that they all activated simultaneously, which was a concept completely alien to Dru. But it worked.

In less than a second, Dru had emptied all of her magical energy into the vivianite crystal, making it flare and crackle in her hands, filled with a whirling green fire. With a soul-chilling jolt, she felt the netherworld portal flare to life far below her, opening a vortex deep inside the earth.

Her skin turned cold, as if a freezing wind blasted across her. Inside, she could feel the endless hunger of the netherworld pulling at her. And since it couldn't have her, instead it devoured the vast deposits of glowing trinitite around it. The earth itself jolted, not from the earthquake but from the sudden departure of everything in that deep pit, leaving a vacuum behind that the loose dirt rushed to fill.

Dru felt Lucretia's spell break like a whip cracked across her back. The golden pentagram flared and went dark. The dark valley below lit with bursts of differently colored lights as each van exploded in turn. With the spell gone, they burned themselves to slag, scorching the encroaching night.

It was over.

Dru held tightly to Greyson's hand as they plummeted earthward. The analytical part of her brain noted that Hellbringer's nose dipped down as they fell, just as Greyson had predicted. They hurtled head-first toward the hard ground, like a dropped bomb. She couldn't bear to watch.

She looked at him instead, wanting to tell him how much she loved him. But a paralyzing fear overwhelmed her, choking her throat so that she couldn't speak. And it didn't help that Greyson was grinning like a madman, showing all his teeth.

"Look!" He pointed out her window.

Dru's head snapped around to follow his finger. Twenty feet below them stood Rane and Opal, propping up Salem between them. Though bloodied and bruised, he was standing more or less upright, with both of his arms outstretched toward them. Sparks of white lightning crackled between his fingers.

It took Dru a moment to realize they had stopped falling.

Instead, Salem's magic gently lowered Hellbringer to the ground until the tires touched down and the demon car's suspension creaked in protest. As Hellbringer's weight settled, Salem sagged, completely spent. Rane, grinning widely, scooped him up in both arms and kissed him. Opal, laughing, laid her hand on his head. She turned to Dru and waved to her through the car window.

Dru waved back, overwhelmed with giddiness. Unable to find words for what she was feeling, she turned to Greyson. But she never had a chance to speak, because he was already kissing her.

35

EVERY DAY IS DOOMSDAY

The evening was pleasantly warm when Greyson picked up Dru at her place and took her for a leisurely ride in Hellbringer, though he wouldn't tell her where they were going. He wore a brand-new leather biker jacket, rather than the designer jacket he'd worn the last time they'd tried to go out on a date. He seemed so at ease as they drove, smiling, sunglasses flashing in the sun, that at first she didn't notice what was hanging down from Hellbringer's rearview mirror.

"Fuzzy dice?" she asked, giving them an experimental twirl with her finger.

Greyson shrugged. "That's as dressed up as Hellbringer gets. But *you* look fantastic."

"Thank you." Heat rose to her cheeks. Opal had spent the entire afternoon making Dru try on one outfit after another until they had finally arrived back pretty much where they had started: a fifties-style red dress with a knee-length full skirt, belted waist, and black fitted top. She felt as if she had stepped back in time, and she was glad Greyson had noticed.

On the radio, somebody started singing ardently about waxing up his car, getting his girl, and heading out to Drag City to burn up the quarter-mile strip.

Greyson reached forward and patted the dashboard. "Take it easy, buddy. We're not going racing. We're just going out to dinner."

A sharp squeal came out of the radio, along with a burst of static. The song instantly switched to Dick Dale and His Del-Tones belting out their now familiar song, "426 Super Stock."

"Oh, a song about your engine. Very subtle," he said, turning down the volume. To Dru, he said, "Sorry. This car has a one-track mind. Generally a racetrack."

"So if we're not going racing, where are we going?"

"Just dinner," he said with exaggerated innocence, making her more than a little suspicious.

A few minutes later, they arrived at an old fifties-style diner. The long building was adorned with glass block windows and long strips of neon. A black-and-white checkerboard pattern embellished the edges of the polished aluminum entry doors. Above them hung a painted sign on the wall: BURGERS . . . MALTS . . . FRINGS.

Dru wasn't sure what a *fring* was, but she had the feeling it would be the least-threatening mystery she had investigated lately.

The parking lot was packed with old cars of all kinds, in every color of the rainbow, but mostly red. Loud stripes and painted flames were everywhere. The low-hanging sun shone off headlights, chrome bumpers, grilles, and five-spoke wheels. Crowds of people in shorts and T-shirts strolled through the parking lot, peeking in through rolled-down windows and gawking at chrome-adorned engines displayed under open hoods. The air was thick with the smells of exhaust fumes, cleaning solvents, and french fries.

"Well, look at that," Greyson said with feigned surprise as they rolled past. "It just happens to be cruise night."

"Uh-huh." Dru adjusted her glasses and looked across at Greyson. "You take me out for our first official date, and we happen to be surrounded by old cars. What a coincidence."

"Well. Since it's how we met . . ."

"I thought we met because you walked into my shop worried you were possessed by a demon."

He frowned. "Well, really, it was because Opal had a flat tire."

Dru thought back. He was right. "Huh. And you changed her tire for her. You're so sweet."

"You know, she gave me her phone number that day? I still have it around here somewhere."

"Uh-huh. Well, you better not be taking *her* to any cruise nights at the diner."

Greyson grinned. "Actually, Ruiz might bring her. He likes the burgers here."

So *that's* how Opal knew what kind of dress she'd need. "But I thought Ruiz's van got destroyed."

"Salem fixed it for him." Seeing her surprised look, he shrugged. "I think Rane talked him into it. Guess she felt guilty about getting it totaled in the first place."

"I'm just glad Salem is recovering so quickly. Probably because Rane is playing nursemaid."

Greyson looked amused. "I'll bet she's thrilled about that."

"Yeah, not exactly. Nurturing is not her thing. I think Salem is driving her crazy." Dru elected not to share the last message Rane had texted her: *Worst part? This nurse costume doesn't even fit.*

Stifling a laugh, Dru had texted back, *Too much information.*

As Hellbringer circled the parking lot, Dru glanced at the chrome radio. "Don't you think you-know-who might get a little jealous here, with all these other muscle cars around?"

Greyson looked a little guilty. "I may have hinted we would head up to the speedway later."

"Oh, really?"

"It's a thought."

He parked Hellbringer at the end of the lot, far away from the other cars, drawing more than a few admiring looks from the crowd. After he shut off the engine, the sudden quiet reminded Dru of the ghost town, bringing on more than a few dark thoughts.

His leather jacket creaked as he shifted in his seat. "What's wrong?"

"Nothing. It's just . . . We finally have the apocalypse scroll. Which is astonishing. We've been looking for it for so long, and now we have it. It just doesn't feel real. It feels . . . dangerous."

He shook his head. "There's nothing to worry about. We saved the world. You realize that?"

"I do, yes. But . . ."

"But nothing." He took her hand in his. "You did great. We all did."

She nodded, struggling to put her fears into words. "It's just . . . When I started up the Crystal Connection, it was because I wanted to help people. And I guess deep down, I never really believed that *I* could be a sorceress myself. So I just wanted to be around all the magic, you know? I just wanted to do my part. I never thought—I never dreamed—that we would get this far, any of us. I never thought I'd have these powers and have to be responsible for an artifact as powerful as the apocalypse scroll."

His forehead creased with worry. "You'll find a way to keep it safe."

"I hope so. But I'm starting to realize that the very same people who have the power to save the world also have the power to destroy it. I don't know how anyone crosses that line. But as weird as it sounds, it feels like it's a very thin line. Lucretia and I, there's not that much difference between us, except that she's so much more powerful. And I guess when you amass that much power, maybe you start to feel like you can shape the world the way you think it should be, rather than the way it is." Dru shivered at the thought. "I just never want to end up thinking like that. I never want to be the one who other people have to risk their lives to stop."

He didn't speak for a long moment as he considered her words. "You think Lucretia is still alive?"

"In the netherworld?" Dru shook her head. "I don't know. Maybe. In her journal, she kept talking about going to someplace called the Shining City. And she told me that the other Harbingers were waiting for her there. I don't know what that means, exactly. Could the rest of the Harbingers still be alive? And what will they do when they find out we have the apocalypse scroll?"

"Listen. She's gone. If she did survive, she's trapped in the netherworld. Long as she stays there, you have nothing to worry about. Because we have the scroll, and the Harbingers don't. No one will ever use it again."

She clutched his hand tighter, hoping he was right. "There's one seal left. If that seal gets broken . . ."

He took off his sunglasses. His eyes were now piercing blue instead of glowing red. That meant they were out of danger, and that was relief enough, but she could never get over the effect his gaze had on her.

When he stared deeply into her eyes like that, she felt as if she were floating. She felt a lightness in her heart that she never wanted to let go of.

Softly, he said, "I know you. You're never going to destroy the world. I promise."

She swallowed, trying not to think about the fact that he'd once been a Horseman of the Apocalypse.

"But you're worried about me," he said, as if he could guess her thoughts. "Because Salem is convinced that someday I'm going to transform back into a creature and destroy the world."

She hesitated, unwilling to face this side of him. But she had no choice. "Do you think you will?"

He stared off into the distance. She found herself holding her breath, waiting for his answer.

"No," he said finally, meeting her gaze again. "If there really was something evil inside me, it would have shown itself in that valley. It would have made me help destroy the world, instead of help save it."

That was the answer she expected, but she still felt a startling release of tension inside her. It left her feeling shaky. "I used to think I had a duty to break your curse. And if I looked long enough, I bet I could find the cure somewhere in my books."

He nodded once. "I'm sure you could."

"But I won't."

Greyson tilted his head to the side but didn't ask any questions.

She struggled to find a way to explain. "Before you met me, you never used to believe in magic, or monsters. You thought the world was totally rational, totally logical. Instead, it turned out to be a crazy supernatural mess. It can't be easy to get a grip on that for the first time. Now I kind of know how you feel. Before I met you, I never believed a demon would help save the world."

He looked away. His lips pressed together in a slight grimace.

"But you changed my mind about that. And so did Hellbringer." She took her glasses off and leaned closer to him. "You told me one time that the world needs me, and my friends, and our powers," she said softly. "But the world also needs you."

The sudden intensity of his gaze left her feeling breathless.

"And I need you, too," she whispered.

His forehead wrinkled. "I know we don't have much in common."

"Well, that's what it looks like, on the surface. You like cars, I like crystals. You're more of a lone wolf, and I have to have my friends around me." She shrugged. "There's so much I don't know about you. Like why, for instance, you refuse to have a cell phone."

One of his eyebrows tilted up. He drew in a breath to speak, but she held out her hand to forestall him. She had to get this out before the words failed her.

"The truth is, none of that matters," she said. "Because when I'm near you, I feel like I can be more than I could ever be on my own. The two of us together . . ."

"We make a good team," he said simply.

He was right. That was the truest way to put it.

A hard lump formed in her throat. "Greyson, I can't save the world without you."

His leather jacket creaked again as he shifted in the seat, leaning closer to her. "I bet you could." Gently, he brushed the hair back from her face. "But you don't have to do it alone."

The events of the last forty-eight hours threatened to overwhelm her, and it took an effort for her to push them out of her mind. "Sometimes, it feels like every day is doomsday."

He gave her a wry smile. "Not today."

For the first time in so long, she felt as if the heavy burden of the world had been lifted off her shoulders. He was about to say something else, but she didn't give him the chance. Instead, she wrapped her arms around his neck and kissed him.

ACKNOWLEDGMENTS

First, my heartfelt gratitude goes out to all of the fine readers like you who make Dru's amazing journey possible. Thank you for reading!

My deepest thanks go to my literary agent, the intrepid Kristin Nelson, for her boundless vision and wisdom.

As always, thanks to the whole team at Nelson Literary Agency for helping make miracles happen.

Special thanks to my editor, Rene Sears, for elevating me from a halfway decent writer to at least a three-quarter-way decent writer.

Many thanks to artist Liz Mills for the spectacular cover art.

Thanks to my publicist, Lisa Michalski, for spreading the word.

Thanks also to everyone else at Pyr for making this book a reality.

Above all, words cannot express my gratitude to my lovely wife, Cyndi, for being my first and constant reader, my cherished listener, and my ceaseless inspiration.